In the Shadow of a Tainted Crown

In memory of my parents, whose motto was
Love is all and death is naught, which I
thought most appropriate for this book.

In the Shadow of a Tainted Crown

FRAN NORTON

Fran Norton

Ellingham Press

Copyright © Fran Norton 2010

British Library Cataloguing in Publication Data

A catalogue record for this book is available from the British Library

ISBN 978-0-9563079-2-7

Published by Ellingham Press

www.ellinghampress.co.uk

Ellingham Press, 43 High Street, Much Wenlock, Shropshire TF13 6AD

Cover design by Gooseygraphics www.gooseygraphics.co.uk

Typeset by ISB Typesetting, Sheffield, UK

Printed in the UK by Lightning Source

CONTENTS

ACKNOWLEDGEMENTS

I owe a debt of gratitude to the staff at the following institutions for their invaluable help in researching this intriguing period of history: Leominster Library Archives, Shrewsbury Library Archives and Tenby Library Archives.

Special thanks go to John Norton, former curator of Ludlow's old museum, where we discussed Ludlow in medieval times at great length.

And a big thank you to Adrian Williams who at the time of my research was at Newport library and enabled me to study Dugdale's Baronage and other documents used in his own university studies of the period. Adrian is now at Ludlow library.

I am also grateful to Barbara Warner, who constantly urged me to publish my efforts; to Liz Phillips, whose invaluable help and humour kept me sane during the final stages before publication; to Alice Gardiner (the Goosey Graphics Company) for her stunning visual art work; to Gareth Thomas for his amazing Ludlow cover photographs (© Gareth B Thomas FRPS); also to Ian Mortimer, an honorary president of the Mortimer History Society, for his kind assistance with the Mortimer family tree and the debate on the place of Edmund's death; and of course to Ina and Colin Taylor for making it all possible.

A final thanks to my husband Tony, who has assisted me in numerous ways.

DRAMATIS PERSONAE

Edward I, ageing Plantagenet king, father of Edward II
Margaret of France, second wife of Edward I
Edward II, son of Edward I and father of Edward III
Isabella, Princess of France, Edward II's queen
Edward III, son of Edward II and Isabella
Robert the Bruce, Earl of Carrick and King of Scotland
Edmund Mortimer, 7th Baron of Wigmore, father of Roger
    Mortimer[1]
Margaret Fiennes, wife of Edmund Mortimer
Roger Mortimer[1], 8th Baron of Wigmore, later 1st Earl of March
Joan de Geneville, wife of Roger Mortimer[1]
Edmund, Margaret, Maud, Roger, Geoffrey, John, Joan,
    Isabel, Katherine, Agnes, Beatrice and **Blanche**, children of
    Roger Mortimer and Joan de Geneville
John Mortimer, brother of Roger Mortimer[1]
Maud Mortimer, sister of Roger and John Mortimer, later
    married to Theobold de Verdun
Hugh, **Walter** and **Edmund Mortimer**, other brothers of Roger
    Mortimer[1] and sons of Edmund Mortimer and Margaret
    Fiennes
Roger Mortimer[2], the Lord of Chirk, uncle of Roger
    Mortimer[1] and brother of Edmund, 7th Baron of Wigmore
Lucy le Waffre, the Lord of Chirk's wife
John de Warenne[1], last Earl of Surrey, heir to John de Warenne[2]
Jeanne de Bar, granddaughter of Edward I, wife of John de
    Warenne[1]
Olympia, daughter of Laurence of Ludlow

Maud de Nereford, John de Warenne[1]'s mistress

John de Warenne[2], Earl of Surrey, grandfather of John de Warenne[1]

Adela de Giffard, wife of John de Giffard

Vincent Botelier, brother of Adela

Piers Gaveston, later Earl of Cornwall, boyhood friend of Edward II and later the first of his favourites

Hugh Despencer the elder, nobleman and father of Hugh Despencer, Edward II's favourite

Hugh Despencer the younger, acquisitive favourite of Edward II

Gilbert de Clare, Earl of Gloucester

Humphrey de Bohum, Earl of Hereford

Henry de Bohum, nephew to the Earl of Hereford

Sir Gryffiths, a Welsh knight

Brother Matthew, Augustinian monk

Meyrick, servant to Roger Mortimer[1]

Hamo, groom to Roger Mortimer[1]

Raoul, squire to Roger Mortimer[1] in France

Seth, groom to John de Warenne[1]

Will, page to John de Warenne[1]

EXPLANATORY NOTES

À l'outrance: to the bitter end
Annwyl: Welsh term of endearment
Arglwyddes: Welsh for lady
Ashlar: masonry made from square-cut stones
Azure and or: blue and gold heraldry colours
Barbary: North African
Barbette: medieval headdress
Caparison: richly decorated covering on a horse usually
    emblazoned with the rider's heraldic device
Cariad: Welsh term of endearment
Carl: lower order of servant
Checky: check heraldic design
Cote-hardie: over-garment
Destrier: strong agile horse used in tournaments
Gambeson: leather cloth coat
Garderobe: medieval lavatory
Gonfalon: standard
Great Seal: king's seal of state
Gwladus Ddu: Welsh for Gladys the Dark
Huckster: hawker, seller of wares
Jongleur: medieval entertainer
Justiciar: a supreme judge
Liripipe: an exaggeration to the original peak of a hood
Prydferth: Welsh for beautiful or handsome
Quintain: a tilt post used by knights and squires for practising
    with the lance

Rounsey: horse mainly used by squires

Saddle bow: pommel

Surcoat: over-garment usually worn over armour and bearing owner's heraldic device

Tiring-woman: a lady's maid

PREFACE

In the mid thirteenth century the ineffective reign of Henry III resulted in open conflict with many of the powerful nobles and magnates of the age. The leader of the opposition was Simon de Montfort, Earl of Leicester. The bitter dispute culminated in the Battle of Lewes.

Henry and his young son, the Lord Edward, were defeated and taken captive along with many loyal nobles of England and Scotland. De Montford, being aware of the threat along the Welsh borders, allowed some of Marcher barons to return home under oath. Roger Mortimer, Baron of Wigmore, was one such powerful lord. However, on his release Mortimer and his wife Maud,[*] together with the Earl of Gloucester, devised a plan which enabled the Lord Edward to escape from his prison at Hereford. He took refuge at Wigmore from whence swift-riding messengers were sent to rally those still loyal to the crown.

The confrontation at Evesham resulted in de Montfort's death and Henry's return to the throne. Mortimer's part in events was never forgotten by Edward and the Mortimer star began its ascendancy.

On the death of Henry III in 1272 the nation looked towards the new reign with optimism and confidence, hailing it as the Age of Chivalry and Honour, under the rule of a strong, handsome king and his gentle Queen Eleanor. The optimism quickly faded as Edward plunged England into numerous wars in France, depleting the exchequer. Heavy taxes and levies were imposed on Edward's already impoverished subjects, causing much dissension and dissatisfaction.

Towards the end of the thirteenth century the Welsh rose against

---

[*] Maud de Braose is credited with the plan. The king sent Maud the head of Simon de Montfort as a prize.

Edward's brutal rule, but with the aid of Mortimer and other Marcher barons Edward crushed the Welsh into his iron grip.

The deaths of his last Welsh opponents Prince Llywelyn[**] and his brother David enabled Edward to build a string of castles across Wales like a stone yoke, holding the Welsh fast in an uneasy peace. Mortimer featured in the capture of Llywelyn, thus endorsing his place in Edward's esteem. The defeat of the Welsh left Edward free to turn his attention yet again across the Channel, this time to Flanders.

Meantime, Scotland was also poised on the brink of civil war following the untimely death of King Alexander. His only heir, Margaret, Maid of Norway, drowned before she reached Scottish shores. The vacant Scottish throne led to fierce disputes amongst the nobility as to the rightful successor. This situation only served to fuel Edward's voracious ambitions and he quickly established himself as 'Lord Protector of Scotland'.

The scholastic nobleman John Baliol was eventually crowned as the Scottish king and for a few years ruled under Edward's heavy hand, but not even Baliol could countenance Edward's style of domination and openly rose up against the Plantagenet king.

These are the events festering in England in 1296, a poverty-stricken realm in turmoil, a cauldron bubbling with unrest and dissatisfaction waiting to boil over and throw the beleaguered nation once more into uncertainty and confusion.

By this time Edward's old adherent, Roger Mortimer, was long since dead, succeeded by his son Edmund. Against this turbulent backdrop my tale begins.

[**] Welsh spelling.

FOREWORD

Although my story has its feet planted firmly in fact, I would like to point out that the following characters are from the pages of my imagination:

> Monique Benoir, Olympia, Adela de Giffard, Meyrick, Hamo and other servants.

Maud de Nereford was in fact married to Sir Diniloa when she went to live with John de Warenne, Earl of Surrey, and I hope Laurence of Ludlow will forgive me for casting him as the father of Olympia for the period of my tale.

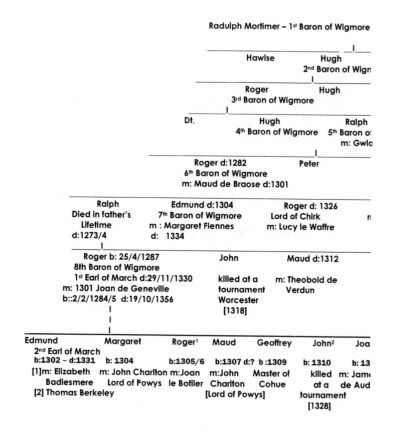

Radulph Mortimer – 1st Baron of Wigmore

Hawise	Hugh
	2nd Baron of Wign

Roger	Hugh
3rd Baron of Wigmore	

Dt.	Hugh	Ralph
	4th Baron of Wigmore	5th Baron of
		m: Gwlc

Roger d:1282	Peter
6th Baron of Wigmore	
m: Maud de Braose d:1301	

Ralph	Edmund d:1304	Roger d: 1326	
Died in father's	7th Baron of Wigmore	Lord of Chirk	n
Lifetime	m : Margaret Fiennes	m: Lucy le Waffre	
d:1273/4	d: 1334		

Roger b: 25/4/1287	John	Maud d:1312
8th Baron of Wigmore		
1st Earl of March d:29/11/1330	killed at a	m: Theobold de
m: 1301 Joan de Geneville	tournament	Verdun
b::2/2/1284/5 d:19/10/1356	Worcester	
	[1318]	

Edmund	Margaret	Roger[1]	Maud	Geoffrey	John[2]	Joa
2nd Earl of March						
b:1302 – d:1331	b: 1304	b:1305/6	b:1307 d:?	b :1309	b: 1310	b: 13
[1]m: Elizabeth	m: John Charlton	m:Joan	m:John	Master of	killed	m: Jam
Badlesmere	Lord of Powys	le Botiler	Charlton	Cohue	at a	de Aud
[2] Thomas Berkeley			[Lord of Powys]		tournament	
					[1328]	

1.Roger [son] m: [2] Dowager Countess of Pembroke, Marie de St Pol but died before 132
who was slain at a tournament at Shrewsbury 1328

[Came over with William the Conqueror]

William	Robert
nore	

Ralph	William

d: 1246	Robert	Philip
f Wigmore		
adus Ddu d:1251		

John	Hugh of Chelmarsh	Isabella

Isabella n:John [1] FitzAlan	William Canon of Wigmore	Geoffrey Knight d: in father's lifetime	Margaret m: Robert de Vere [Earl of Oxford]

Joan	Hugh	Walter	Edmund
Nun	Rector of Radnor	Rector of Kingsland	Rector of Hodnet

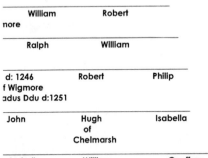

n	Isabel	Katherine	Agnes	Beatrice	Blanche
:12	b: 1313:	b:1314 –	b :1317	b:1319	b:1321 d:1347
es:	d: In a	m: Thomas	m: Laurence	m: [1] Edmund	m: Peter Grandison
lley	nunnery	Beauchamp	de Hastings	Earl of	
	[1327]	[Earl of Warwick]	later	Norfolk	
			[Earl of Pembroke]		

28 as his Irish Estates went to his brother John

BOOK ONE

THE FALL OF THE HAMMER

CHAPTER I

Wigmore
May 1296

The boy lay in the rich spring grass and watched the kestrel hovering high above. The scent of the crushed grass filled his nostrils and he sighed contentedly. His hands were laced behind his head to act as a pillow and to shield the dark curls from the damp turf. His golden eyes flickered as the bird finally swooped onto its unfortunate prey. A blackbird belled a warning and the sound split the soft May morning. A bee hurried about its own trade and landed near the boy's hand onto a cowslip, and promptly disappeared into the yellow centre. The boy remained motionless, savouring his stolen solitude, for it was no easy matter to accomplish, being as he was the heir to the mighty marcher Lord Mortimer of Wigmore.

He heard the sound of horses and knew that his moment was dashed. The kestrel screeched and carried off its prize to higher ground and the blackbird bustled into some distant trees. Only the bee seemed oblivious to the new arrivals. The boy rose silently to his feet and surefootedly leapt across the marshy ground to the firmer track, ducking around some scrubby bushes and emerging on the riders from their rear.

He stood legs apart, arms akimbo, laughing roguishly at the panting riders.

'Why, I've been to Ludlow and back,' he teased. The ageing groom edged his sweating beast closer to the speaker.

'T'was a fool thing to do, m'lord, for sure. There are plenty of cut-throats and brigands abroad would as leif slit thy throat as look at ye, for all you be the son of yon baron, and where have ye left thy rounsey?'

'He's safe, Hamo. I tied him over yonder. He's well screened and will come to no hurt.' The groom muttered and made to where the boy had indicated.

Roger, meantime, turned and winked wickedly at his brother John, who sat his own mount with the natural ease of a born horseman.

He too was dark of hair but lacked the curls and the strange golden eyes of his brother. His grey eyes looked down into the laughing depths of those unusual golden ones.

'Roger, it was a foolhardy jape and Hamo is right. There are still many deserters and robbers at large and...'

'They would not have taken this Mortimer so lightly.' The older boy interrupted boastfully, brandishing a narrow deadly-looking blade. His eyes flashed as bright as the dagger in the midday sun.

'An arrow would lay ye dead before ye were ever aware 'ont,' growled Hamo, leading the dark-bay steed of his young lord.

'Now let us be for Wigmore or thy father will lay my hide raw if aught befalls his babes.'

Roger leapt onto the gleaming bay and snorted his disgust at the comment. He no longer thought of himself as a boy but the heir of Wigmore. He turned and shouted a challenge to John to race for home, and the two boys galloped off, leaving the still grumbling Hamo to bring the two younger boys, Hugh and Walter, who could only giggle and nudge their ponies to follow on at a more sedate gait.

The two brothers raced onwards and, at the sight of Wigmore Castle, did nothing to check their steeds as neck and neck they galloped. Roger grinned and crouched lower over the bay's sweating neck and whispered softly as he lightly squeezed his mount for an extra burst of speed. The rippling muscles of the animal gathered, and stride by stride went away from the chestnut. Roger whooped in triumph as he swept into the outer bailey a full length in the lead.

A groom ran forward and quickly took the bridle from the elated rider, who had pulled up in a cloud of dust.

'Give him extra oats and a good rub down for he's lacking nothing in heart.' Roger patted the sweat-streaked neck as he spoke.

John, peeved at being beaten, rode his horse directly at Roger and had to rein back so sharply that the poor beast reared to avoid trampling the victor. John leapt from his saddle and toppled his brother into the dust of the outer bailey where they proceeded to wrestle. The two rolled over and over, arms and legs flailing, punching, biting, kneading each other, much to the amusement of the quickly gathering crowd, all too eager to watch the free sport.

Wagers were quickly placed amongst the contingent of soldiers who were at the castle, glad of the diversion caused by the two boys. By now there were shouts of encouragement as the punches flew and dust filled the throats of the onlookers. No one heard the approach of Edmund Mortimer until he pushed aside the spectators to see the scuffle. When he realised that the fighters were his own sons he stepped forward and caught each of them by the scruff of the neck and shook them like disobedient curs.

'Enough! If fight you must, then do it in private and not for the sport of these jackals. Now get you from me and I will learn more of this when you have removed the dirt from yourselves.' He turned and spoke curtly to the remaining crowd.

'I suggest you quickly find some occupation for yourselves or there will be too few hours in the day to accomplish all I shall set for you all.' Without further ado he spun on his heel and strode back towards the inner bailey. The crowd melted away like morning mist and the two grubby boys now looked at each other in dismay. Blood trickled from Roger's nose and a dark bruise was already making itself known on John's cheekbone.

'Oh, sakes and saints preserve us! For if I know aught of our sire he will mete out greater punishment than any fisticuffs could afford,' moaned John.

'I'll wager neither of us will be able to sit a horse for a week after our next interview with our sire,' grinned Roger wryly, wiping his bloody nose with the back of a grimy hand. They could hear the brisk commands of Edmund as they resounded round the grey walls of the inner courtyard.

The two begrimed boys entered into the cool walls of their ancestral home. A tall handsome woman came towards them, her dark kirtle brushing the flagstones of the floor as she walked.

The girdle about her waist was of plaited leather and the snowy wimple fluttered in the draught as the great door swung closed to enfold the brothers.

'Sweet Jesu!' she cried. 'Have you fallen from your horses?'

In unison they both answered 'No.'

'Then pray, what manner of fashion is this?' She indicated their filthy apparel. A pregnant silence hung in the air as she awaited a response.

At last Roger spoke. 'We were fighting, mam,' he said flatly.

'Fighting! Whom were you fighting?'

John now joined in sheepishly. 'Each other!'

She looked at the battered faces before speaking again. 'Think you not there is a surfeit of fighting in the land that you needs must bring it within the walls of your home? You will have your bellies filled with fighting afore too long, I dare swear. What, pray, was this fight about?' Her eyes were intent on the dishevelled pair.

'We raced…' Roger began slowly when John burst in, 'and he won and I'm heartily sick of being beaten, after all I'm the taller and but a year his junior…'

She held up her hands to silence them both.

'Now listen to me, and listen well. Mortimer shall not fight Mortimer. Not over a race, gold, land, nor, when you are older, a woman, or anything else that you can lay name to! Soon, Roger, you will go to be a squire at the court of the king and learn its ways and the art of knighthood. John will also follow that path, though in a different household, and you will both countenance many trials, jealousies and envy. There will be those who would delight in setting brother against brother, simply because you are who and what you are: Mortimers, sons to the Baron of Wigmore who holds the trust and esteem of Edward the king. I entreat you both, never betray a kinsman. A true ally is more precious than a priceless jewel. Cleave always to each other and, when the time comes, to your younger brothers and sisters. Promise me here and now that you will always remain true to your blood. Should you ever have cause to doubt the love or loyalty of one another, then do not take arms before you have faced each other with the grievance and had proper discourse 'ont. You will have your differences, God knows, all do, but do not let them become insurmountable. Now go; and never forget what I have just imparted to you.'

She held out her hands and the two chastened fighters bent in turn and kissed her cool fingers.

'Mam, I truly love my brother and would beg his pardon in

your hearing.' John blurted out the statement in a rush of pink embarrassment.

Roger's battered face split into a grin and the handsome woman nodded her satisfaction.

Margaret Fiennes had lived in the shadow of war for most of her life. She had married Edmund Mortimer when little more than a girl, then flung into the turbulent affairs of the Welsh Marches, which had soon taught her the value of loyalty and friendship.

These were not her people, for in fact she was kinswoman to Eleanor of Castile, and her upbringing had been in a gentler frame of learning and culture, shielded from the starker realities of warfare; that is, until her marriage at fifteen.

The king had held the Mortimers in high regard ever since his youth and had been delighted when Edmund, son of his old adherent, had applied for a licence to marry the dark-eyed Margaret, bringing the relationship to a closer plain, a trait that Edward would follow throughout his reign, binding by marriage the powerful families of the realm to his own family, whenever possible.

It scarcely seemed fourteen years since Edmund had brought her here after their marriage. Within these walls she had borne all of her seven children, the last one barely three months before. She sighed. Edmund had been a dutiful and considerate husband, at least when he had time. For the king kept him busy and even more so during the years of the Welsh uprising. Wigmore was the centre of much activity, ever pressed to send trained men into the king's service.

Margaret had been left on many occasions to see to the needs of the mundane private grievances of tenants and farmers on her husband's estates. It had been the mark of Edmund's respect for his wife that he had heaped her with so much responsibility and she had not failed him, or caused him to rue his decision. Only in a single instance had she referred a matter back to her husband and that was because it had concerned one of his own squires.

She had proved herself more than equal to the task of Marcher wife and was a devoted mother, admired and respected both at court and in the shires. Her quiet charm and determination had created a haven at Wigmore for Edmund and their children during these difficult and troublous times.

John was very much like his mother, both in looks and temperament and she recalled herself as a girl, and smiled as she remembered her own mother chastising her for being too quick to take offence and too slow with forgiveness. John would learn. However, Roger was another matter. He was fierce in his loyalties and for the few who won his regard or approval he could be all too generous. Nothing seemed to overturn his self-confidence and at such a tender age it could be a little disconcerting. He had never shown the slightest signs of fear, not even as a tiny child, and possessed a magnetic appeal for animals. The most vicious hound would fawn and follow him, the most mettlesome horse, calm under his touch, and in the training of the hawks it was nothing short of uncanny, but there was another side to Roger that she knew no one touched, neither man nor beast.

It was as if an unearthly spirit lurked within him and at the thought Margaret shuddered involuntarily. She prayed that her son would not grow into another such a one as her brother-in-law, Roger Mortimer, Lord of Chirk. He was as ruthless and violent as her own dear husband was just and loving.

She shook herself mentally; maybe her fears were unfounded and the boy merely inherited the mystical qualities of his great-granddam, Gwladus Ddu, daughter of the now legendary Llywelyn the Great.

Balladeers still sang of her beauty: hair as black as jet and eyes like golden wheat. Gwladus had broken the hearts of many men, or so the songs proclaimed. This was a strange land. It boasted the fiercest fighters, the sweetest singers, and women with the power to lure men, whatever rank they held.

Margaret offered up a silent prayer. Let not her son grow towards wickedness but, with the grace of God, become a true and honourable knight. Her mind moved to her other children and she gave thanks. For all the unrest in the world she had much to be thankful for. The boys were strong and clear-witted and her daughters already had the promise of loveliness about them.

Whilst Margaret was busy with her reveries the brothers were standing before their sire.

Edmund Mortimer was a tall, slightly greying man with a strong weather-beaten face and piercing grey eyes, the same colour as John's, but his were of a softer nature.

Edmund studied the pair before him and was inwardly filled with pride. His gaze rested on Roger, his first born. There was a strength in the boy that shone through even at this age. Those golden eyes did not lower or flinch under his father's inspection. He stood, feet slightly apart, chin thrust forward, his hands twisted behind his back.

John, two inches taller, had the distinct look of his mother, and although he showed no outward sign of fear he did not stand quite as defiantly as did the older boy.

Edmund was secretly pleased with his sons. However, it did not alter the fact that their conduct was unbecoming and they needs must learn that lesson before the day went apace.

'Well, I am more than a little displeasured at the performance in the outer bailey this morning. Not for the fact that you fought, it is natural in brothers, but that you fought like felons in the dirt before all the militia and household carls of the castle. You lack nothing in spirit, nor do I doubt either's courage, but you must learn respect: for your opponent; your name, and most of all, for yourselves. Never lower your standards to such a degree again. Roger, fetch me that birch cane.' Obediently he did as his father bade him.

'John, the trestle.' John reluctantly dragged the wooden bench to the spot indicated by his sire.

'You will receive as many strokes as you have years.'

Roger made no sound as the sharp cane cut into his back and buttocks. The nine strokes were watched by John who held his breath in anticipation for the eight which he would have to endure.

Afterwards Edmund looked at the pair, hiding his true feelings behind a stern expression.

'Now tell me why you have just been beaten.'

John stood biting his lips, tears escaping down his swollen cheeks. Roger's face was bereft of tears but he had grown paler and chewed at his lower lip somewhat savagely. He answered thickly.

'So that we never resort to brawling in public and bring the name of Mortimer into disrepute.'

Edmund nodded and signed for them to leave, for he knew John's self-control was on the verge of collapse and he did not wish the boy to suffer pangs of shame, not at least for crying.

As the door closed behind his sons, Edmund moved to the desk where a letter lay half-finished. He reread the contents. It was to the king, reminding him that his eldest son Roger was now of age to be summoned as squire to the royal household. Edmund felt a pang of regret. He loved his sons dearly and Roger held a unique place in his heart, though he never consciously showed any especial favour towards him.

The times together had been all too few. There had been so much warfaring during these latter years on his beloved Marches and now the threat from Scotland loomed large to join with the storms that beset poor England.

Edmund walked to the window and gazed down over the gentle landscape that had nurtured his family for more than two centuries. No matter how far the call of duty had taken him, it was this pleasant scene that never failed to ease his soul, and woo his senses. The vivid freshness of the long, green grass would soon fall before the reapers' long scythes for the fodder that was vital during the long winter months.

Wigmore and Margaret were Edmund's sanctuary and through all the trials and tribulations they teamed to bring sanity into his rigorous and uncertain life-style. The crown was the brood of lusty young children that God had seen fit to bless their union with and now, as was the custom, Roger must go from his own family and learn the craft of knighthood. The boy would be a man all too quickly. Edmund sighed; that was the way of life and he could not change the order of it even though at this moment he was surely tempted to try.

Sometimes he longed for a quieter existence where books and solitude could reign rather than chaos and bloodshed. He smiled wistfully; it was the onset of middle age or maybe being born a second son. He could sympathise with John, always in the shadow of an older brother. Fate had taken a hand in promoting Edmund to heir of Wigmore, when his brother Ralph had died prematurely.

The sun passed behind a cloud, casting a running shadow over the scene and Edmund knew that his musings were at an end. He was a seasoned soldier, who, like any old warhorse, would answer the bugles of battle with blood pounding and nerves tingling, ready once more for the fray.

He had hoped for peace so that his family could grow into maturity without threat or fear of war, but he realised that would never be as long as Edward remained alive, for age had not dimmed the ambitions of England's monarch. One could only pray for strength and guidance in such hazardous times.

That evening Edmund and Margaret sat together before a crackling fire whose flickering flames replaced the warmth of the sun, for the evening had brought with it a mist and a drastic drop in temperature. The bright glow cheered the somewhat gloomy mood their conversation had left them in.

Margaret threaded her needle and deftly worked the colourful skein into her intricate pattern that edged a cote-hardie. The plain green now started to advertise the scarlet and silver of the lady's own motif. Earlier she had visited the chamber shared by the two older boys. They had both been quiet and subdued, scarcely answering her inquiries. She had left a jar of soothing unction for their sore places but had refrained from offering her administrations as she understood their boyish independence.

Edmund had been eager for news of their wellbeing and she had been able to allay his doubts regarding the harshness of his punishment.

'John will miss his brother, I fear!' Margaret ceased her stitching and leaned across to touch the sleeve of her husband. How close they had become through the years, welded together by adversity and strife.

She recalled one of her kinswomen proclaiming her theory on the lot of women in marriage.

'A woman's duty can be a heavy mantle to wear.'

As Margaret studied her husband's piercing grey eyes and stern face, she noted a tender smile soften the firm mouth. Oh, how wrong those cynical words of warning now sounded. She had been in awe of her husband in the beginning, but that had been replaced by a deep feeling of security and affection. His words broke in on her thoughts.

'Time to the young seems eternal, but how quickly do those precious years melt into adulthood and then fly like a deer before the hounds.'

They fell into a long silence broken only by the logs dropping, splashing sparks high into the darkness of the vast chimney. At last Margaret spoke:

'When do you think he will be summoned?' Her voice was low but clear.

'Who can tell nowadays? Methinks the mighty Edward himself is not entirely his own master. The Plantagenet demon is taking a stronger hold on him daily.'

'And what of his son, the Prince Edward?' Margaret asked, putting her needlework into a fine wicker basket that lay at her feet as she spoke.

'Oh, he is healthy, learned, pleasing to the eye and soft-spoken. Likeable enough but...' he hesitated, a frown playing across his strong features, 'but I fear there is not the steel in his make-up strong enough to forge a king to hold this tormented nation in check. He lacks resolution, and much as I hate to say this, steps in his grandsire's path and not that of his sire's.'

Margaret could see how disturbed Edmund was by his utterances and she said softly, 'Maybe your fears are unfounded, my dear, and the young Edward will meet the challenge of kingship with more merit than you give him credit.'

'You are probably right, sweeting. Our fate lies in the hands of the Almighty and, as for our son Roger, I think we have little enough to fear on that score.'

She rose, indicating for her servant to remove the basket.

'Come, my lord, I grow weary and would seek the comfort of my bed.'

He stood and took her hand.

'If you are not too tired I would share your night.' She caught his look and smiled into his face.

'Then I will bid you adieu and not godnight. Do not linger too long with your potent thoughts, my dear. They will not disappear, and the more you dwell on them the more malignant they will seem.'

'Mm, you have the right of it as always. Then let us retire as a pair and trust in God for our wellbeing. Remind me to give especial thanks for giving me such an understanding wife.'

She kissed his cheek and led him unprotestingly to bed.

CHAPTER II

During that same soft month of May, another man gazed across the folding hills and vales of Shropshire.

The man was in his late middle years with a generous waistline and his hair, though still thick, was now pure silver. His face was deeply lined around the mouth but he had a youthful and jovial expression, for he had much to be proud and happy about.

Laurence of Ludlow stared out from his window at Stokesay and contentedly watched the scene below. A herd of plump cattle were being driven up to higher pasture and a flock of sheep cropped in the meadow, whilst a shepherd busily counted the new season's lambs.

Workmen could still be heard hammering and sawing as they put the final touches to their handiwork. A lilting tune drifted upwards and mingled with occasional shouts, noises that filtered through the open window of his private solar. Above the sound of industry, his ear caught the note of a child's bubbling laughter and he moved across the room to look onto the inner courtyard.

A little girl, with hair as pale as moonbeams, tottered after a bead ball which was being tossed by a petite young woman, whose face was wreathed in smiles at the antics of the child. Her clear voice stumbled on some of her words as she endeavoured to use the tongue of her husband.

'Come, sweeting! You will never catch the ball if you do not watch its flight from my hands. See!' She tossed the bright sphere high over her head and deftly caught it in her own dainty hands, to the obvious delight of the little maid.

'Now let me see how clever you are, *ma chérie!*'

The face of the child became serious in its concentration, and that look enchanted the watcher. It was a moment to treasure.

When most men were facing the uncertain prospect of old age,

Laurence had met and married Monique Benoir. His former wife Emilia had died years before and he had never thought to wed again until chance had brought him into the company of a sweet-faced young Frenchwoman on his last visit to France.

Monique had breathed fresh life into Stokesay, adding comfort and colour into the light and spacious chambers.

The tiny castle nestled in the arms of the rolling Shropshire hills. Surrounded by a sparkling moat, the soft grey walls exuded charm and prosperity. Even the servants had an air of wellbeing as they went about their duties, donned in fine neat liveries.

Laurence had purchased Stokesay a number of years before and he and Emilia had planned to spend their declining years within its pleasant walls. They had been granted a licence by Edward to improve and embellish the castle and Laurence had set about the task with great enthusiasm. However, after Emilia's death, it was left to Laurence to continue with their schemes alone.

He had never thought he could be so happy. Monique had given him the child Emilia could not, and with each passing day Laurence counted himself the most fortunate of men.

They called the babe Olympia and she was the jewel of their lives, a constant source of joy and amusement to them both. In fact, the young damsel charmed all who met her. She had a way of turning a pair of huge green eyes upon a stranger which left them in no doubt whether they pleased or offended her tiny importance.

It had become the custom during the long winter evenings, for minstrels, storytellers, mummers and jongleurs to visit the great hall and entertain, bringing with them news of events occurring throughout the land.

Suddenly, Laurence's attention was caught by a company of riders as they approached the manor. The bright livery of Mortimer of Wigmore blazed its unmistakeable colours of azure and or. As one of the riders broke away and crossed into the courtyard, Monique beckoned the child to her and gathered her up in her arms as the messenger dismounted. He bowed to the woman and gave a broad wink to the tiny girl before being directed to Laurence.

Beads of sweat trickled down the brow of the open-faced young man as he stood admiring the vivid tapestries which hung about the walls. Cushions of all shades were scattered around and thick leather ones padded the stone window seats.

Laurence sat in a heavily carved wooden chair and pointed to a stool for his visitor. He took the proffered scroll and the merchant broke the Mortimer seal and read:

'To the most venerable and esteemed merchant, Laurence of Ludlow. Greetings!

'I, Edmund Mortimer, Baron of Wigmore, have presently to send my eldest son and heir into the service of his most sovereign lord and king Edward.

'It is therefore expedient that he should be attired in the finest garments that your trade can provide, not mistaking this request for gaudy fripperies but materials of the highest quality.

'I am aware that you are no longer actively engaged in your former trade, but feel sure that in this instance you would not be unwilling to be of service to my son, and so doing be of service to me.

'My messenger is entrusted with a note of hand for your reimbursement.'

It was signed by Edmund Mortimer's personal seal.

Laurence let out a long sigh. This was unusual to say the least, but he was not a man to have succeeded in business for so many years without recognising a God-sent opportunity when it presented itself.

Without further ado, he directed his servant to send for his steward and to see that Mortimer's courier received refreshment.

Together, he and Owen his steward made their way to the cool interior of the storeroom. As, one by one, the flickering torches took a firmer grip on the flames in the sconces dotted around the thick dark walls, the piles of tightly wrapped bales of cloth and fleece became visible. They pulled back the dust sheets and oiled wrappers, which kept the precious materials from the damp and vermin.

Almost gleefully, Laurence sorted through his most prized wares, still feeling a thrill at the sight of the heavy folds and delicate textures of the yarns.

Carefully he selected his choicest goods and as he did so the germ of an idea became a firm design in his mind. He was not hailed as the most astute merchant and trader throughout the length and breadth of England for nothing. Even Edward the king turned to Laurence on matters concerning the wool trade.

At last, satisfied with his selection, he called some of his house carls to load the bales and parcels onto the waiting pack animals. As the messenger handed the banker's draft Laurence waved it aside.

'I would commission you to do a task for me.'

'If it is within my power, sir, I shall be glad to be of service.'

'I will draw up a letter, which I charge you to deliver into the hands of your master Edmund Mortimer and no other. If all comes to a happy conclusion, then you shall receive a cloak with the longest liripipe in the shire.'

The young man grinned.

And as soon as Laurence had completed the missive and handed it to the waiting squire, the party clattered out under the new archway, over the narrow wooden drawbridge, to join the men-at-arms who sat waiting patiently in the warm sunlight. The young messenger turned to the sergeant.

'I think our best course is to avoid Ludlow, for we do not seek trouble and at this pace we are fair game for the bolder members of yon town.'

There had been bad blood between Ludlow and Wigmore from a time dating back to when one Hugh Mortimer had been taken captive by the owner of Ludlow and held to ransom. The antagonism born then had descended down through the ages, although the origins had been long forgotten.

The sergeant-at-arms grinned, showing a mouthful of yellow and broken teeth.

'Aye, and I've no wish to be flayed for failing to obey the baron's commands.'

So the little party struck off the main highway and followed the narrower paths of drovers and shepherds back to Wigmore.

CHAPTER III

Edmund watched the shining face of his wife as she looked through the luxurious fabrics sent by Laurence.

'Oh Edmund, there is far too much here for the boy. Did you make it clear that it was only one son we send to court and not a whole regiment of Mortimers!'

'Our merchant is a shrewd trader and no mistake. He will accept no gold for these goods.'

'Why so, my lord?'

'It would seem that the good Laurence has sired a daughter in his old age, and our clever trader has requested that she be attached to your household when she is of age.'

'The daughter of a merchant?' Margaret exclaimed in astonishment. 'His request is naught if not bold, even for all this finery.'

Just at that moment Margaret had unwrapped a bale of pure silk. The pale-rose material slid through her white fingers like liquid.

'Edmund!' she gasped and then smiled knowingly.

'This was never meant for the boy, I'll be bound. A tempter for a poor vain woman, I dare swear. Have you ever seen such fine quality? Or such an exquisite shade?'

He stood looking down at her. The years had dropped away from the handsome face like a veil and he could see again the girl he had brought to Wigmore. The memory held him captive to the sweetness of that time long ago. He said, 'Lady, for this pretty bribe, I think we can forget the child's parentage, don't you?'

So the plans of the wily Laurence had succeeded and a young squire in the Mortimer household would be able to boast a brand-new cloak ere long.

The news, however, did not please Monique. She had many misgivings when acquainted with the prospect of her child's future. Men would indeed be attracted to a pretty face, but nobility married within its own ranks. Daughters of merchants could look for nothing more than a position of mistress or courtesan, learning and wealth notwithstanding. That was not the future envisaged for her babe.

Due to the opposing opinions on this one subject, a shadow came between the relationship of Laurence and Monique. Silence on the topic served only to drive the rift deeper. She would often slip away from her busy household into the tiny chapel, which stood beside the handsome castle. There within the cool silent walls she would pray most ardently for reconciliation between herself and her husband.

The breach was healed but not in the desired manner.

Laurence, who had been sent to Flanders on the king's business, perished when his ship foundered and sank in heavy storms. His death was a severe blow to both Monique and England's sovereign.

Monique was bereft. They had had such a short time together. For the most part it had been an ideal marriage, filled with true happiness and contentment. On hearing of her husband's death Monique bowed to his wishes regarding her little daughter's future, bitterly regretting that single disagreement.

After the service of remembrance, Monique made plans to enter a nunnery. She sent word to Wigmore acquainting the baron of Laurence's death and requesting that Olympia join the Mortimer household as soon as it was convenient.

With tears streaming down her gentle face, Monique parted from her small daughter. Her own life was now so empty. She had lost the two people that meant everything in the world to her, one to the sea and the other to a nobler but uncertain future. There was nothing left but to place her trust in God and hope that they would all be reunited in death.

Through that autumn and onset of winter, Margaret Mortimer was kept busy preparing for her son's imminent departure. She stitched the devices of Mortimer and Plantagenet onto the fine new garments which now lay in neat piles around the chamber. She ticked the items off her list one by one.

Six shirts of cambric; six of fine lawn; six pairs of hose in various shades; two pairs of riding boots, one of soft kid; two pairs of leather shoes; one pair of felt; two tunics of leather; two of fine wool; a variety of caps, gloves, belts and a handsome cloak lined with squirrel skin.

To this she added two surcoats she had sewn with her own hand. She surveyed her handiwork with satisfaction. The details could have been left to Meyrick, but she had chosen to supervise the inventory of her son's wardrobe to see that naught was amiss.

'Meyrick, place lavender bags in the linen and herbs with the tunics.'

The sombre-faced man moved to follow his lady's bidding. He had been selected to accompany the young lord to court, for he was a reliable, honest and diligent servant.

Margaret pulled from her pocket a soft leather purse filled with newly minted coins. She tucked these into the toe of one of the riding boots.

'See that he spends the silver wisely, Meyrick. I shall instruct him to pay close heed to your advice on such matters.' The man nodded.

'He will take some of his own favourite things, of course, and the undergarments, which were too big last year, will do nicely now, methinks.'

Meyrick moved to the heavy oak door and opened it for her to pass through. He bowed respectfully, and she turned and said softly,

'Serve my son well, Meyrick, and I shall see that you are well rewarded.'

'Have no fear, my lady, I will look to the young lord's interests with all the wit I possess and guard his life with mine own.' With that she left him to finish his work and made her way back to her own bower. She was anxious to inspect the parting gift she had commissioned for Roger's leave-taking.

The clasp of silver shone and glistened. The chips of amethyst, opals and aquamarines had been delicately worked into the form of a peacock's tail. She studied the fine workmanship and felt well pleased with her choice.

'Yes, I think it will suit my young knight-errant admirably.' She spoke to herself, turning and twisting the clasp into a variety of angles so that each gem caught the light.

At that precise moment Edmund was also looking at a gift for his son, a fine harness. The scent of the new leather filled his solar and the silver buckles and embellishments winked and glittered in the pale sunlight that filtered through the high windows of the chamber.

Tomorrow would see his son on the way to a new life, bright-faced and eager for unknown adventures. The sadness at leaving all the familiar faces and places would be felt later.

Edmund sighed; he remembered his own departure from Wigmore and knew that Roger's childhood was rapidly drawing to a close, as he stepped ever closer to manhood.

Hereafter he would meet his son as man to man and not sire to son as before. He hoped that through these former years he had instilled the right values in the boy and, when presented with the vanities and trivia at court, he would not succumb to its shallowness, but follow only the steps to true and noble knighthood.

Roger's courage Edmund never for an instant doubted; it was his impetuosity that was the trouble, and reports regarding the Prince of Wales's conduct with the Gascon, Piers Gaveston, did nothing to alleviate Edmund's fears. Roger would have to judge that situation for himself. He had the intelligence and lacked nothing in sharp wits. Edmund could only offer a prayer and mourn his son's departure in silence.

CHAPTER IV

Dunbar Castle
May 1296

The Earl of Surrey stood scratching his chin thoughtfully, his mind filled with doubts. The sallow face was deeply lined and the hair thin and sparse. Blue veins stood out on the thin claw-like hands. A deep scar ran between the finger and thumb of his right hand from some old encounter with a blade.

The map of his thoughts only served to deepen his mood of gloom. The uncomfortable foreboding he felt within persisted in its intensity.

Edward was adamant, the Scots must be brought under his sovereignty or feel the hand of a hard master. The earl shook his grey head slowly from side to side. The Scots would never willingly submit to any English king, even the mighty Edward Plantagenet.

As yet there was dissension within the ranks of the Scottish nobility and Dunbar had fallen easily enough to the English forces, but that did not signify that all would fall in like manner.

Scouts and messengers were constantly riding into the castle bringing fresh tidings of events in Scotland and at the court. There was a hum of activity everywhere. Sounds reverberated: troops marched in and out of the courtyard; the clash of steel on steel from a company of knights practising their skills; iron-clad hooves clattered on the cobbled stones beneath the high-vaulted window where the earl stood.

He was too old now to look forward to war with anything other than personal irritation, though much of his long life had been spent in the service of the Crown. Battlefields and fighting were as natural to him as breathing, but the fervour and relish of victory no longer afforded him any delights.

Cold and discomfort gave as many barbs nowadays as the enemy's steel. Hours in the saddle succeeded only in bringing old wounds to life although the sinewy arms could still wield a sword with accuracy and dash – alas, for no great spate of time. Stamina was deserting him, but his almighty willpower did not diminish, nor his stubborn, unbending determination.

During the many seasons of campaigning, the earl had held fast to the belief that Edward worked towards a peaceful and prosperous era. Now he knew this to be otherwise.

Where had all those fine and noble ideals fled to? That band of knights, led by a king, all fired with the true traditions of the legendary Arthur. Gone! Edward's vision had been blurred by the lust for power and wealth. He had constantly led his country into wars, both at home and abroad. With the passing of the years Edward's appetite for land and possessions had increased and England was spared nothing in their pursuit.

The earl mused over the most important thing in his life, his grandson. By God's will this new venture would be concluded before the boy reached the age of manhood.

He had poured all his vast knowledge of life and battle strategy into those eager young ears, but hoped with all his heart that he would be spared a while longer to ensure that all went well for his heir in these tender years.

His own son William had been slain in a tournament a few months after the boy's birth. Feeling the loss so acutely, John de Warenne, Earl of Surrey, had taken his namesake into his own household and from that time forward had been both guardian and mentor.

The boy was now almost ten years of age, a sturdy, swarthy-faced lad with a pair of deep-blue eyes fringed by long lashes, which served to relieve the somewhat heavy features and jaw-line. He had thick, straight, black hair and strong white teeth, albeit a little crooked.

The young Warenne took no pleasure in his scholastic studies. However, Latin and Greek were learned as easily as the Norman French he spoke. He excelled in all things physical, riding, running, wrestling, and even now was quite an expert at the quintain, which held far more satisfaction for him than books.

His personal appearance left much to be desired and the old earl could not suppress a smile as he thought of how often his grandson had had to be forced, or unceremoniously dumped, into a bath tub and cajoled into fresh linen. There was no vanity in the boy's make-up, only a burning pride.

He followed his grandsire round like a devoted hound. His most prized treasures were the broadsword and shield scaled down to his own proportions, exact in every detail to those used by the earl.

Already the young heir of Surrey could use them with a natural inborn skill and dexterity. He had even trained his rounsey to wheel and turn like the mighty destriers in the tournaments. Many hours he spent in practice, tucking a long wooden staff into his shoulder and charging at the quintain when it was not being used by the older men. There was no more enthusiastic squire in the whole of the kingdom.

Of matters masculine the young Warenne had a thorough knowledge. Of matters feminine he was as ignorant as a boy could be, his mother and granddam both long since dead. He had, therefore, grown up entirely in the world of men.

Soldiers in his grandsire's service would joke and make lewd remarks whenever a wench entered the yard, but the more noble ranks of knights and squires acted with respect and reverence towards any visiting ladies. The contradiction served to make the boy avoid any unnecessary speech with women. However, on the rare occasions when this was not possible, he answered briefly or merely nodded, quite content to remain silent in their company.

Once he had overheard one such matron chide his grandsire on the deficiency in the boy's upbringing.

'Of course, my dear earl, your heir will grow up a complete barbarian. How will he fare in the presence of any gentle-born maid?'

The old man's reply had brought a smile to the lips of the boy.

'Why, my dear lady, the lad will come to the ways of women at his own speed, I dare swear! There will be plenty eager enough to take on the task when he comes of age. Of one thing I am certain, no female wiles will impress that one, I'll warrant.'

So the matter had closed to the complete satisfaction of the eavesdropper and he never gave it another thought. Life was much too busy to worry one's head over women.

War was the all-important factor and there was now a name which was fast becoming familiar to all those garrisoned along the

Scottish borders, that of William Wallace. It would seem that this one man had taken up the challenge of Edward Plantagenet on Scotland's behalf.

Though only a lowly Cumbrian-born squire, he was fast proving to be a vicious thorn in the side of the English forces. With a handful of followers he harassed, ambushed and burned his way across Scotland, causing Edward's obsession with crushing the rebellion and bringing Wallace to a terrible reckoning, as he had Llywelyn in Wales.

CHAPTER V

Berwick
Spring 1297

Towards the end of 1296, the Earl of Surrey had been appointed Viceroy and Warden of Scotland and in his new capacity had moved his headquarters back to Berwick where he spent the autumn, winter and spring of 1297, directing the English forces against the constant harassment of the accursed Wallace. This base-born knave adopted tactics beyond contempt. He never came openly into battle, but used guerilla tactics to great effect, allowing the English neither respite nor forage. He made the land his greatest ally. He would attack quite without warning, then vanish back into the hills and forests, only to rise and strike again, many miles away.

Edward had become increasingly incensed at the failure to bring the Scots to heel and decided to relieve the ageing earl of his wardenship.

By August, however, much to the chagrin of the old earl, he had been reinstated. Throughout this period Warenne acted as his grandsire's squire and quietly served his venerated guardian. Theirs was not an effusive relationship. Nevertheless, there was a deep bond between them and each drew great comfort from the other's presence.

One evening they sat together and the old man said slowly as he gazed into the dying embers of the brazier,

'I fear that Scotland will be a tougher nut to open than Edward has anticipated. Should its nobility take arms and join this Wallace, then blood would run as freely over the land as the mountain streams. Come, boy, let us retire; my aching bones are in need of much ease these days and your young ones will benefit, methinks.'

A private moment shared thus was indeed a rare occasion, and the boy was loath to let it pass so easily.

'You do not think we shall overcome these Scottish hordes ere long then, my lord?'

The still keen eyes of the old man looked at the precious sprig of his noble lineage.

'As you know, my daughter's husband, John Baliol, played the puppet king to little effect and even that mild-mannered man rose against the Plantagenet's insults. However, when he did raise an army it was of little consequence and he did well to escape Edward's wrath with his life.

'To you I speak with all honesty, knowing that my words will go no further than this chamber. I have an uneasy feeling about this Scottish venture and my fears grow apace daily. Should a leader arise capable of uniting all the clans and noble houses, then I think our adversary would be an awesome opponent. We must thank God that John Baliol was not of that calibre. It could have proved a ticklish division of loyalties for us, lad.'

He placed his arm around the boy's shoulders.

'This latest obsession of our sovereign king will, I fear, be the downfall of many. We must trust in our strong arm and steady nerve to carry us through this unhappy period and pray for better times in your future.'

The boy smiled at the speaker and his whole face lit up.

'Methinks your fears are groundless and the might of the English chivalry will trounce the upstart Wallace, and the Scots. We will triumph as we did in Wales and bring this nation under the king's rule.'

'Then let us hope you have the right of it and we shall forget an old man's morbid ruminations.' He bent and kissed the dark head of the boy in an unguarded moment of sentiment. The sudden gesture brought a flood of colour to the boy's cheeks which reached far below the surface.

In the weeks that followed that intimate encounter, Warenne and the earl were kept uncommonly busy. A flurry of messengers came constantly from Flanders, where once again Edward was making his presence felt.

It now appeared he wished to split the command in Scotland between Surrey and Cressingham, and this new move did nothing to endear him to either commander.

Cressingham already had the reputation of being hated by the Scots for his frequent acts of unprovoked brutality.

This current situation led to uncertainty and confusion amongst the ranks of the English. That problem was still unresolved when, in September of 1297, the two disgruntled commanders found themselves confronted at Stirling Bridge by none other than Wallace himself.

The English drew up their forces under the standards of Surrey and Cressingham. Gonfalons and banners flew aloft over the proud chivalry, and it was plain for all to see the superiority of the English host.

However, William Wallace, a master of guerilla warfare, had chosen his position wisely. It profited the English nothing that they outnumbered the Scots. Only a few at any one time could cross the mile-long narrow causeway that straddled the River Forth.

The young Warenne looked on the scene before him with an odd mixture of excitement and anticipation. This was his first encounter with a battle proper. He stood quietly at his grandsire's stirrup.

The thin notes of a bugle sounded and the first wave of knights and foot-soldiers charged across the deadly strip which spanned the swirling waters. Warenne felt the muscles in his stomach tighten. There was a mighty crash of steel and many fell victim to the shrieking tartan-clad Scots.

Some had cunningly placed themselves under the bridge and, with long spikes, halberds and pole-axes, pierced the bellies of the English horses before their riders had perceived the danger. Wave after wave of knights and men-at-arms were cut down ignominiously on that causeway.

The screams of men and horses as they fell into the now bloody waters made a terrible noise in the ears of the onlookers. Some had been pitched from their mounts unscathed but were held fast in the river by the weight of their armour until they too died. The stench and sounds of battle were beyond comprehension. There were men running, crawling or limping away from the fearsome Scottish horde but these were all too few. Most would never rise again from that horrendous encounter.

Warenne heard his grandsire grunt.

'Look you, boy, are those not the colours of Moray? See yonder.' He pointed, the boy following the direction of the steel-clad hand.

'So…' hissed the earl, 'the man Wallace has recruited one of the noblest families to his cause. Pray God others will not follow his lead, for I swear England would rue that day.'

As the boy turned back towards the thick of the battle he saw a horse, a once proud and beautiful creature, careering away from the mêlée on three legs, the fourth having been hacked off. His eyes had followed the poor demented beast's final efforts before it crashed dead.

Just then a gurgled cry to his right brought his gaze back to see a squire fall with an arrow through his throat.

Where was the glory in this massacre? He looked up to see the flinty eyes of his grandsire through the visor of his burnished helm. Suddenly the old man raised his arm, the signal to strike his standard. Without further ado he wheeled his mighty courser round and indicated the herald to sound the retreat.

Before he could argue, Warenne felt a strong pair of arms pick him up and thrust him into his saddle to be led off that disastrous battlefield, numb with shame and horror.

They made their way quickly back to Berwick. A sweat-streaked messenger overtook them, bringing tidings of Cressingham's horrendous death, his skin cut into strips by Wallace who then distributed them to his followers.

The mood was grim throughout the stronghold of Berwick when the news of the defeat at the hands of Wallace was heard. Furtive glances that were cast towards Warenne and his grandsire did nothing to ease the boy's black humour.

The earl, too busy to take time out to speak with his grandson, was, however, well aware of the effect the defeat had had on the boy. When he ordered Warenne to return to England with a party of wounded he was not surprised at the boy's acquiescence.

On the slow journey back through the Scottish Marches, Warenne travelled in silence. His was not a physical wound, but he was sore of spirit, and the sights he had witnessed at Stirling would remain with him for many months.

It transpired that among the party of wounded was a number of archers, some of them from Wigmore and Ludlow, and Warenne somehow became separated from the main group and found himself and his servants heading towards Shropshire.

At last they came in sight of the grey ashlar walls of Wigmore castle and heard the shouts and cheers of the families of those who returned, if not entirely unscathed, then at least with their badges of scarlet courage, worn proudly for all to see.

Warenne had entered with the rest of the company and would not have made his true identity known if Margaret, Countess of Wigmore, had not quizzed him about the welfare of the Earl of Surrey, having noted the azure and or checky emblazoned on his tunic.

'My grandsire was hail and well when I last saw him.' Warenne was somewhat abashed in the presence of a woman.

'Then you must be his heir and namesake.' She smiled and proffered her hand. Instead of kissing it, he shook it vigorously. Margaret was amused and some at the table chuckled at his actions.

'Pray come, sirrah!' she said. 'This humble greeting will be put aright and you shall be made as welcome as your station commends.'

He tried to dissuade her but she would brook no refusal. So he rose and followed her sheepishly to the guffaws and quips of those still seated.

Finally they arrived into the private chambers of the Mortimer family and there seated before a great roaring fire were Roger, Maud, Hugh and Walter. The latter pair were idly throwing dice. The dark-haired girl was busy stitching a sampler. Roger lay sprawled half in, half out of a leather chair, fondling the ears of a hound. John was reading.

'Look who we have here!' exclaimed Margaret.

'It's John de Warenne, heir to the earldom of Surrey, no less.'

The boy felt embarrassed, being as he was the centre of attraction. He nodded towards the boys and affected an awkward bow at the girl.

'Ah, good, now we shall know first hand what truly happened at Stirling Bridge,' Roger said, cocking a knowing look towards the newcomer.

'Roger, remember the first lesson in hospitality. I'm sure our guest is fatigued from his long journey and will answer any questions on the morrow.'

Warenne shot a grateful look at his benefactress. Margaret made the introduction to her family as briefly as possible, then without further ado guided him to the baron's own chamber.

'I'm afraid my husband is from home at present but avail yourself of anything you may need to make your stay as comfortable as possible.'

He thanked her and assured her that a good night's rest was

his only true need. Seeing the weariness etched on his young face, Margaret quickly left him and the boy threw himself onto the large bed. Tired as he was, sleep would not come and he tossed and turned trying to sort out his troubled thoughts, feeling for the first time in his short life totally unsure of himself.

He could not staunch that terrible nagging feeling that his grandsire had in some way let him down. On reflection, what other course had lain open? The odds had been too great; any other action would have been foolhardy, surely.

With the tattoo of his thoughts beating through his head like some demented drummer he finally fell into deep dream-filled slumber, until he was awakened by a vigorous shaking.

'Are we under attack?' His voice was thick and his speech slow, still only half conscious. A merry laugh greeted his question.

'The only attack you're under, my fine fellow, is from a Mortimer no less.'

'Have a care, Mam will be angry if we do aught to upset our visitor.' The gentler tones of John only succeeded in making Roger laugh the louder.

'I seek only to hear about the battle. Is it true that after the Scots had slain the fat Cressingham, they skinned his body and sent strips of it throughout Scotland?' The golden eyes were alight with curiosity.

'Aye, 'tis true.' The deep-blue eyes of Warenne looked defiantly back into the lighter ones. Before he could say anything further, John spoke.

'What was it really like? Were you actually in the fighting? How many were killed? Did you see the man Wallace? Is he as tall as they say?' His questions gushed like a fountain.

'Yes,' piped up Roger, 'did you lay eyes on him? Some say he's seven feet tall and is truly the devil incarnate.'

Warenne studied the two bright-faced questioners. They had jumped onto the bed either side of him.

'Wallace is no devil,' he answered slowly, watching the reaction of his audience, 'though he is uncommon tall, but I think not fully seven feet. He was lucky in this ambush.'

Roger spoke again. 'Some say that the English were ill-led and such a travesty should not have occurred. Indeed, that some of the leaders fled the field almost at once.'

The air became pregnant as the sentence hung like a great thick curtain between them. John stammered, 'I think my brother spoke without thinking.'

Warenne interjected, 'But I do not. Your brother knew full well what he implied and I'll brook no insolence from such as you, Master Mortimer.'

Without further ado his fist shot out and landed squarely on the point of Roger's chin. The golden eyes opened wide with amazement.

'I think we will finish this interview tonight behind the stables at midnight.'

So saying, Roger leapt from the bed and walked swiftly from the chamber. John followed close on his heels. He turned at the door and made an apologetic gesture, then ran after his brother.

Warenne lay there for a while. Maybe he would feel better now that his own doubts had been aired by another, but this Mortimer would find out to insult the name of Warenne was no light matter.

After rising, he breakfasted alone, then wandered around until he came to a tiny orchard set at the side of the castle walls. In its midst, on a green sward, sat his hostess nursing a baby in her lap. At her feet Hugh and Walter played with a set of bells.

He drew back into the cover of the branches. At that moment a fair-haired girl ran towards him. He suddenly became aware of his own sorry state. His tunic was still stained from the dust and mire of the long miles of his journey. The fresh linen had been ignored and his hose sported holes. His hair also had been completely forgotten that day.

The child called back to the two boys. 'Oh, do let's go and see the horses. Please Hugh, Walter, you can play with the bells later.'

Warenne thought she looked and sounded like a nymph. She was so full of light and grace. The little maid stopped in her tracks. Her huge green eyes widened as she caught sight of him hiding in the depths of the lower boughs.

'Oh!' she exclaimed. 'A tree spirit.' She came closer. Her curiosity outweighed her fear. Obviously no one had heard her for they were not joined by any of the others. Cautiously she came closer to where he stood.

'Are you a good spirit or a demon?' She giggled a little nervously. 'You must be an earth goblin, for you are all dirty.'

He coloured at her words. 'I am John de Warenne, heir to the Earl of Surrey.'

She chuckled softly at his reply and he thought how like the bells it sounded.

'And who, may I ask, are you?' he said gruffly.

'Oh, I am Olympia.'

'Are you daughter to the Mortimers?' he asked stiffly.

Again her merry laugh.

'No, I'm just me. When my father died it was his wish that I be placed in the household of the Mortimers. My mother retired to a nunnery and so I came to Wigmore.'

For the first time in his life John de Warenne was won over by a dainty girl.

'Do you still want to go and see the horses?' He no longer felt ill at ease.

'Mm, yes please.' She ducked down and came amongst the leafy foliage. The autumn tints were already starting to show their bright hues, but on that warm October morning they did not outshine the face of young Warenne as Olympia took his hand and together they went to the stables.

He found her a knowledgeable companion for all her lack of years. They made an incongruous couple, the swarthy thick-set boy and the diminutive fair-haired girl. That fact was completely lost on them for they had found a topic which engrossed them both: horses.

They walked along the rows of tethered animals and he pointed out to her the difference between destriers, used for tournaments, and coursers or warhorses.

Warenne now found himself in the role of teacher with Olympia his willing pupil.

'I know that the palfreys and rounseys are used for hunting,' she said. They continued together; she made him chuckle at some of her childish observations, but in the main he thought her advanced in intelligence for her six years.

After they had exhausted themselves with the horses she, in turn, guided him around the castle bailey and keep, waving greetings to various servants as they passed.

That evening, Olympia had been allowed to remain with her companion in the Great Hall for the meal and had proudly shared her trencher with her new friend. Warenne was all too conscious of Roger's watchful gaze.

Margaret looked across at the ill-matched pair as they sat side by side. Olympia was chatting to Warenne quite easily and Margaret was pleased to see that the boy looked more relaxed. His air of aloofness had slipped from him under the spell of the little girl's special magic; a pity that he would be gone in a few days, back into his almost friendless existence.

As soon as the victuals were finished Margaret insisted that Olympia should retire. Warenne suffered the childish kiss meekly as she wished him godnight, and the sniggers of the Mortimer boys did not quench the warm feeling that the girl had aroused in him. With a promise of further adventures on the morrow Olympia went to her own chamber happier than she had been for a long while. This dark boy, although a little unkempt in appearance, did not treat her like a girlish nuisance, as did Roger on occasions.

Long after most had sought the comforts of their beds, Warenne slipped out into the chilly autumn night. A bright moon cast its unearthly light over all. He skirted around the main walks, seeking the deepest shadows to hide his progress. A dog barked, and he froze in his tracks, but when all went silent again he continued towards his assignation at the stables.

As he turned the corner he heard a noise, which warned him of his rival's presence. Roger stepped out from his hiding place. Neither spoke. Warenne nodded curtly and without further preamble they stood squaring up to each other.

At first they circled around warily, then both tried a quick lunge and feint without landing a blow. Suddenly the younger boy flung himself forward low at Warenne's knees and the fight began in earnest.

This was no ordinary boyish fight. The hurt of the insult goaded Warenne into giving no quarter. His powerful young shoulders went behind each blow and he aimed many at the head and body of the Mortimer heir.

Roger fought back as best as he could, but found his opponent was an elusive adversary. His efforts became more laboured and he grunted and gasped as he tried to avoid the onslaught. Nothing he did seemed to make any impression on Warenne. Truth was, he was almost spent but was loath to be laid in the dirt by the older boy.

A sudden rain of hard, well-timed punches finally felled the young Mortimer. He lay there, his body home to a thousand aches and bruises all clamouring for recognition. His hands and face were a mass of cuts and gashes. Winded, and hurting desperately, he still strove to rise. The only other sound in the icy air was the deep breathing of the victor, who stood poised ready to rejoin the contest.

A horse nickered close at hand. Roger tried times aplenty to gain his feet but his trembling legs and winded body would not obey his will and he kept falling back to the damp earth. A strangled moan escaped from his split lips as he finally conceded his defeat, and lay still, face down at the feet of his conqueror.

Warenne watched the boy's inert figure and then all the pain and anguish that had racked him since Stirling deserted him. His opponent was soundly beaten, lying prone, bloodied and bruised but there was no shame in the defeat.

He had fought with all his strength and courage, and Warenne felt no elation at his victory. He moved to where Mortimer still lay and grasped him by the arm.

'You lack nothing in courage, young Mortimer,' he panted, 'but needs let your body take the punishment truly deserved by your tongue.'

Roger did not, could not answer. His world had taken on an unnatural aspect. His vision was blurred, his head swam and the gruff voice of Warenne sounded a thousand leagues away.

The older boy aided his battered rival back to his own quarters and the concerned ministrations of Meyrick. He then wearily retraced his steps back to his chamber and called for his body servant to fetch hot water and towels.

The following day many gaped at the bruised and cut faces of Roger and Warenne, but by the warning looks pursued the enquiries no further. Even Olympia was quick to note the look which passed between the two boys and did not ask any pertinent questions on the subject.

From that somewhat doubtful start a grudging friendship was born between the houses of Warenne and Mortimer, and Roger was thankful that his leave from court would be long enough for his wounds to heal.

CHAPTER VI

Canterbury
September 1299

The castle was abuzz with activity in readiness for the marriage of Edward I to Margaret of France. The last-minute preparations were at their zenith. Visitors poured into the castle bringing their own retinues and each demanded to be housed instantly.

The team of cooks bemoaned the fact they would never be able to feed all the extra guests. Grooms had to be inventive regarding stabling the multitudes of horses, which all had to be fed. Servants of the many households found themselves thrust, somewhat unwillingly, into each other's company.

It was also the time for reunions. New friendships blossomed, whilst some old ones were broken.

Roger Mortimer had embraced his family with his usual exuberance and all were astounded at his extra inches. John could no longer claim to be the taller, for in the last two years Roger had shot up like a weed. He brought tears of joy and pride to Margaret and a lump of gladness into Edmund's throat. It had been many months since they had all been together.

During their first breathless meeting Roger had tried to impart so much information to his weary family that Margaret had become quite dazed. His manners and turn of speech had taken on the style of the court, and she noted the boy's own awareness of himself. She inwardly mourned the passing of the childish innocence, but marvelled at his maturity.

After they had been safely housed, and Meyrick's account of the intervening time truthfully retold, Roger insisted that he should be their guide around the castle. As they went along, the dark, curly head would turn and indicate to this personage or that, giving a pocket history of each. It made Margaret and Edmund smile, for they were well acquainted with most but it did their hearts good to see the esteem in which their son was held.

John had been assigned to the Earl of Hereford's household and, though reports were naught but praise, they were concerned at his new reserve, almost as if there were an invisible shield around him. He noted all that went on, but remained silent, even at Roger's playful banter.

Roger took John aside and introduced him to the squires on duty, teasing and cajoling him, but the old camaraderie was lost and Roger mourned its going more than a little, for he had looked forward to showing off to his younger brother.

However, Hugh and Walter were still impressionable enough to be totally won over by their brother's new status, and the girls were busily getting acquainted with daughters of other houses. Only Olympia was missing. Her mother had been taken seriously ill and had called for her presence.

When Roger had enquired more deeply about Olympia's welfare, he noted a look pass across John's features, and couldn't quite make out if it were of pleasure or pain, for a steel mask had fallen shut like the slamming of a new visor.

'Come, let us walk a while, for there is much I would know of you since last we met.' Roger linked his arm through his brother's and guided him out of the throb of activity and away to the quieter walks of the palace gardens.

'Now, tell me how are things with you.'

'Well enough,' John answered, and then again fell back into silence.

'By all the saints, John, have you taken a vow of silence? Or are you so overwhelmed at this spectacle it has driven all natural speech from your comprehension?' Roger quipped lightly, trying to draw some response from the younger boy.

'I care naught for this frippery.' John shrugged off Roger's arm.

'Would you have secrets from me?' Roger's face had become serious. He liked not the change that had taken place in John, the familiar voice which now struck so discordant a note on his ear.

John shot him a quick look and the grey eyes searched the golden depths for an instant.

'There has been…' He hesitated. Roger waited. He began again,

'Is it true? What has been said of the prince and Gaveston?' The words had come in a rush.

Roger guided his brother to an arbour seat, turned his head and his strange eyes watched a group of riders wending their way on some distant track. He sat motionless, unspeaking. The birds continued their song. Insects hummed amongst the flowers and herbs of the well-tended gardens.

At last he spoke, 'And exactly what is it you have heard, brother mine?' He did not move.

'I overheard that, for certain favours of the bedchamber, Gaveston...well...that Edward and he are...well...lovers, and that all who serve in their household are tainted.'

Before John could utter another word Roger jumped to his feet, eyes blazing like burning torches.

'So...' he hissed. 'Now we have the demon by the tail, have we not? Do you think that your own brother indulges in these... these unnatural practices?' He glared at the younger boy. 'I tell you true. I have never seen aught with my own eyes other than they are always in each other's company; I have never heard of any other squires being invited into the private chambers in anything other than in a normal capacity. I should thrash you soundly for even thinking that I would indulge in...in...so godless an act as you have implied.'

John was convinced by his brother's outburst and that he need worry no further on his behalf. It was a relief to have spoken of the topic, which was gossiped of around the shires.

'Have you discussed this matter with anyone else?' enquired Roger.

'Only to my father confessor. It was he who advised me to bring this to your attention in private, and to warn you against such devilish practices. Should you rise in the prince's favour, then the finger of suspicion would point at our family...' His speech was halted as Roger held up his hand.

'You need have no fear; if this Mortimer rises to higher things, it will not be through a man's bedchamber, I swear.' He suddenly flashed a smile at John.

'Now, if it were through a woman's...' He grinned mischievously and the dark mood vanished.

John rose and punched him playfully on the shoulder and as

they walked back towards the palace their conversation was of horses, tournaments and the like.

The baroness never found out what Roger had said to John that had removed the sullen cloud from his shoulders, but rejoiced as the inseparable pair laughed and gamed together as they had done at Wigmore.

Her own days were full of meeting with womenfolk from far and near and she indulged herself listening to all the latest gossip from around the court.

There were banquets most evenings and tumblers and troubadours from both England and France vied with each other to gain the greatest applause from their audience.

One evening the Earl of Surrey entered with his grandson; at thirteen, the boy was fast becoming a man. He stood patiently at the old man's side, the deep-blue eyes missing nothing as his restless gaze swept up and down the lines of lords and ladies, until at last he espied the Mortimer family towards the rear of the hall.

He studied each of them in turn, but the face he sought was not among them, and he felt a sharp pang of disappointment run through him. He had really made a special effort for this occasion. His hair was neat and shining, as was his whole appearance. Time had mended many of his former lax habits, but he had on this visit been almost fastidious in choosing and purchasing new garments.

The excuse made was of the importance of the event, but deep down it was to impress a pair of pale-green eyes that went with the elfin face of Olympia. Now to his chagrin she was not there to witness his transformation. A sudden panic gripped him; maybe she were dead or married. Although she was so young it was the custom for a child bride to be brought up in the house of her husband until she was of an age to become a wife in the full sense.

He would find out the truth before the evening travelled much further apace, but until the feasting was over he had to remain where he was. As the night progressed the company became rowdier, wine flowed in great quantities and the laughter shook the rafters at some of the antics of the entertainers. Edward himself was not present for this particular gathering but the young Prince of Wales and his inseparable companion Gaveston, whose dark, fine, good looks contrasted with the fairness of the Plantagenet heir, were to the forefront of the merriment.

Roger caught himself studying the two as he had never done before. The golden eyes watched intently and he knew from now on he would be wary of all personal contact with the handsome duo, for he was determined to find out the truth of the accusations cast on them ere long.

He suddenly espied Warenne and waved cheerily across the Great Hall and grinned, all animosity from their previous encounter long forgotten. Warenne came over to where they were seated and politely enquired of each in turn, being introduced to another member of the family – Roger Mortimer, Lord of Chirk, brother of Edmund.

After the formalities were observed, Warenne learned of the reason for Olympia's absence and although moved by the child's misfortune was somehow gladdened by the information. He could now relax and enjoy the merry surroundings with only a hint of regret at his fair damosel's absence.

CHAPTER VII

Lewes
October 1304

Warenne checked his horse as he came in sight of Lewes. The castle and old Cluniac priory lay in a gap of the South Downs where the valley of the Ouse broadened out into low marshy ground. To the north-west rose the High Downs.

His emotions vied with each other at the sight, but the sense of belonging did not alter, even at this sad time. It had been his main home through the years of his childhood. His father lay buried there, together with many of his ancestors, and now his grandsire would join them in his final resting place. He was the only person who had ever really loved him.

With a heavy heart he wended his way homeward. At just eighteen he was not afraid of the new responsibilities, for the old man had tutored him well. Only the thought of life without the stern, outspoken mentor weighed him down with grief.

The days that ensued after his return were hectic and filled with many visitors demanding his attention. For the diversion from his gnawing sense of loss he was more than grateful. Thoughts of times spent hunting together with hawks and hounds across the Downs kept stealing into his mind. He had only ever felt truly at ease with the old man and a pale-haired, green-eyed child. She had come unbidden to his memory and acted like a soothing balm to ease his turbulent sorrow.

He was no longer the ill-kempt boy, but a man. His powerful frame had fulfilled the promise of boyhood and long hours in the saddle with sword and lance had hardened him into a warrior knight.

In the darkness of night when sleep eluded him, another woman stole across his thoughts and even in the dark his cheeks flamed with guilty shame.

It had been almost two years ago when Edward Plantagenet had gone to visit his daughter Mary at the nunnery of Amesbury. Warenne had been one of the squires in attendance and when he had been presented to the Princess Mary had been made acutely conscious of her attraction.

Those days and nights were to haunt him. The nun's habit and life of piety could not hide the Plantagenet passion which burned within her, and she had quickly seduced the young squire, introducing him to the fierce pleasures of the flesh. She had been four-and-twenty at their first encounter and he just sixteen, but beneath his stoic exterior was as lusty a nature as her own.

The hours they had spent together had been furtive and guilt-ridden, but he could not break the hold she had on him and he would sneak away from his duties whenever possible to spend a few moments of physical delight.

How many days of penance he had been given upon confessing his fall from grace, but now he was determined that with his new role as Earl of Surrey he would no longer seek that royal lady's favours.

He knew if Edward heard of the association, then his life could well be forfeit and excommunication certain for both transgressors.

All that must be put in the past. Now he was no longer a callow youth to be swayed by the call of the flesh; besides, it would seem that the king had another member of the Plantagenet family in mind for his wife: Jeanne de Bar.

Only eight years of age, she was the granddaughter of Edward and had been made his ward at the death of her parents. Warenne was not insensible to the honour bestowed on him by the betrothal, nor was he blind to the policy pursued by the king to bind all the mighty houses of the realm to the Crown by marriage wherever possible.

As the new Earl of Surrey, Warenne had attended his grandsire's funeral, placing on the lead-lined coffin the tattered and faded gonfalon and spurs, symbols of the seasoned warrior who had succumbed to death from old age, not by the hand of his enemies. Warenne's strong, dark features had shown nothing of the inner feelings of grief during the ceremony.

On his return to court he met, quite by chance, Roger Mortimer, who was now Baron of Wigmore since his father's death at Stirling during the summer. They had greeted each other with commiserations on their dual loss.

When Roger invited Warenne to spend Yuletide at Wigmore, he had accepted with gratitude, not wanting to spend the festivities at court, or for that matter in lonely splendour at any of his castles.

The icy December winds tugged mercilessly at their thick cloaks as they rode along the muddy roads towards Wigmore. Roger had appeared ill at ease for much of the journey. Suddenly he turned to his companion.

'Did you know that I have been placed in the guardianship of Piers Gaveston?' He waited for Warenne's answer but the stoic young earl rode on in silence. Roger continued, 'It had been my father's wish that when I married the Lady Joan de Geneville, we should make our home at Ludlow. The marriage served to bind our two families and as our lands lie side by side it was a convenient match. I feel with the responsibilities of both Wigmore and Ludlow I do not wish to be under the Gascon's control. I have many plans for the castle's improvement, especially now Joan has already proved a fruitful wife and we already have two children.' They rode on for a while in silence.

'I seek your advice in this matter. What would you do in my predicament? I know under that dark brow lives a quick wit; that is, when it chooses to function.'

Warenne laughed at the dubious compliment. It was a rare and warming sight. His white, somewhat crooked teeth split the swarthy face and the eyes seemed to lighten with inner mirth.

'Then my simple advice, for what it's worth, is to buy yourself free from the Gascon. I do not think that if you pay a high enough sum he will refuse you. On the contrary, he will fill his own coffers and relinquish any responsibility to your family.'

Roger let out a long sigh. 'I knew you could be relied upon to come up with some good idea. I will speak of this matter with my lady mother and feel sure she will agree with your good sense.'

'What does your wife make of this union?' Warenne's question was almost lost on the wind.

'Joan prefers marriage to life in a nunnery. Her sisters had no choice, her grandfather made certain there would be no future dissent on his decisions.'

'And how does marriage sit with you and your wife?'

'It lies most easily.' Roger grinned. 'My father chose not only a wealthy heiress but someone possessed of a most pleasing nature.'

'Unlike the bride they have appointed for me!' exclaimed Warenne, and the wryness of his words was torn from his lips as the storm increased in its intensity. The rest of the journey continued in forced silence as they needed all their horsemanship and concentration to restrain their nervous horses.

As the lights of Wigmore came into view the first drops of rain splashed onto their faces. They spurred forward, covering the last mile at a gallop. Neither saw the pale figure of a girl watching their approach from a window high up in the castle keep.

CHAPTER VIII

Wigmore
1304

It was the first time that Warenne and Olympia had met since their childhood and the child had grown into a tall, slender maid of thirteen. At the sight of her Warenne's usual self-control almost deserted him. Her long, pale hair laced with black, silk ribbons hung about her shoulders like a shining mantle. The eyes had a look of haunting sadness about them, but it could not disguise their beauty. Her oval face, and skin as soft as candle glow with the upward curving mouth, sent his emotions reeling.

Warenne was stunned by his own feelings. Not even at the height of any passionate encounter with the voluptuous Lady Mary had he felt so utterly aroused. It was like being unhorsed by a well-couched lance and it disturbed him not a little.

During the first few days, propriety dictated that he should not speak alone with Olympia, and they were only able to converse in the presence of the Mortimer family.

However, after a day hunting he and Roger spied Olympia carrying the weeping figure of Edmund, Roger's first-born child. Both men spurred their horses to where the little group of Maud, Olympia and Edmund had stopped to await their arrival.

Roger leapt from his horse full of concern for his little boy.

'Whatever have you done, child?' But Edmund could not speak; he just continued to sob, so it fell to Olympia to tell the tale.

'He tripped whilst playing and has grazed his knee.' Warenne's pulses raced at Olympia's clear, warm voice.

Roger knelt and gathered his son in his arms as he murmured, 'There, there! 'Tis but a scratch, little man.'

'Roger, you ride ahead with Edmund and I will escort the

damsels back to the castle.' Warenne had taken charge without thinking.

Roger nodded and leapt lightly onto his horse, then Warenne's strong arms lifted the child up to him and Roger made his way carefully back towards Wigmore.

Warenne then turned to where Maud was standing silently by and picked her up and placed her on his saddle. He indicated for Olympia to follow suit but she shook her head.

'I'll walk beside you, my lord earl?' she murmured.

'So formal, Olympia?'

'We are children no longer and you are now one of the most notable lords of England and I...' the words hung in the air... 'merely the daughter of a merchant,' she said softly.

'To me you are as gently born as any I have met.' She smiled at his words.

'Have you, like Roger, been versed in court gallantry? Or maybe by a woman?' She looked under her lashes at him as she spoke and noted the deepening of his colour.

'You give yourself away,' she chided him gently.

'What is it you have heard?' He was not proud of his liaison with the Lady Mary, but became a little alarmed at his companion's words. Maybe his erstwhile affair was no longer a secret.

'Oh...' she hesitated, not quite sure whether this mature Warenne was as approachable as the boy. 'Nothing of substance.' Her green eyes held an unreadable look.

'And you listen to idle gossip?' he said flatly.

'Of course, it is meat and drink to us who have to stay in our own castles during long winter evenings. Any news is pounced upon like a hound with a bone and gnawed on for hours. Our needs are served by such discourse and adds to our entertainment. Can you honestly say you do not indulge in this ancient pastime?'

'I have better things to do with my time than prate on like a broody hen.'

They had fallen into their childish banter, although the theme was of a more mature nature.

'It is good to talk of less serious subjects than of late,' she said. 'I greatly feared for my lady's sanity when the news first came of the baron's death.' She reached across and lightly touched his sleeve.

'I have prayed for you on your bereavement also, but mayhap you have more interesting comfort than I can extend you?'

He turned and a pair of dark-blue eyes locked, for an instant, with the pale-green ones, before they walked silently on again. The look had stirred deep feelings in both of them. They had almost forgotten Maud and their surroundings in this new intimacy, but she sat humming a tune from the back of Warenne's mighty horse. She was too lost in her own girlish world to pay any heed to the conversation of her escorts.

After a few moments Warenne spoke again. 'As you like to keep abreast of local gossip, tell me what are your own views on the marriage of Mortimer and Joan de Geneville?'

'I think it to be a most felicitous match, and the Lady Joan happier than most in her husband. Their union is already twice blessed.'

He cocked a black brow at her words. 'Do you envy the young baroness?'

'Nay, I did not say that, but Joan was a somewhat lonely damsel. Her two sisters have long since been immured in nunneries and her grandsire is almost a recluse. I think she enjoys her married state, especially to someone like Roger. He has brought life and love into her life and besides…she dotes on her husband and babies.'

'And how do you get along with the new mistress of Wigmore?'

Olympia smiled. 'I believe Joan feels that Wigmore is the dowager's home more than hers. She and Roger are to make Ludlow their family home. As to how I fare with Roger's wife, I think she is a sweet lady. However, you must judge for yourself on our return for the lady in question will have returned from her visit to her kinsmen. But I fear she is not to your taste, I'll warrant.' She twinkled up at him.

'And you are conversant with my tastes? I swear you are a minx, and truly pity the man whose lot it falls to wed you.' He teased her with words he did not wholly agree with.

Suddenly Olympia's face became serious again. 'I shall never marry.'

'Come, mistress, do you think you will be allowed to escape from inflicting your sorcery on men?' There was a chuckle in the statement.

Her voice took on a sharper note. 'I tell you no man shall I marry.'

'So vehement, then are you to follow the pious path into the cloisters?'

'No! I have spoken truth; mark me well. You will not draw me further on the topic.'

He turned to look and noted the defiant tilt of her head. 'Does marriage so offend you? Why should one so young shy so violently from the very thought, as do you, Olympia.' He studied her set profile and was caught again by the delicacy of her beauty.

'Maybe I shall love, maybe not, but it will be a man of my own choosing, for I swear I will not go through with any mockery or arranged match.'

'Mm, you speak thus now, but the female mind is like quicksilver and about as constant. You will change your tune when some sweet-faced youth pays pretty compliments and woos you with soft words.'

'Well, there speaks the voice of certain experience, I'll warrant. Do you understand the whims of women through aught else but your own experience, my lord earl?' She uttered the speech in a lighter tone.

'Pah! Witch!' he scoffed.

'Did you not sweep your paramour off her feet through words or silent signs and sighs?' she quipped.

'It was not through worthless flattery, that's for sure.'

'Then you do have a lover.' She pounced triumphantly on his sentence.

'I'll say neither yea nor nay on that matter, and think you are too young to speak to me so, damsel.'

'Oh! We resort to dismissing me as a child still! Well, that I cannot deny totally, for I am not yet come to full womanhood, but I am not thick of wits. True, I have no right to play the tease and hope that it will not offend your manhood.'

'You do nothing to offend me, Olympia, of that be assured. Our friendship will, I hope, withstand more than a few jibes. I pray you, do not become a primping, vain creature as do so many women of the court. Stay as guileless and honest as you are this day.' He took her slender white hand as he spoke and raised it to his lips.

'Beware, my lord earl, remember your quotation regarding us poor females.' She laughed softly at him. 'But I thank you for your concern and think that we shall remain friends. Turning from trivia, methinks I remember Roger speaking of a marriage contract for you!' She tried hard to hide the urgency of her question.

His face became sombre and a frown played across his dark brow.

'They have seen fit to choose a child for my bride. Jeanne de Bar, granddaughter to the king, no less. And you claim immunity through age. Sweet Jesu, she is only eight years of age.'

She looked at the hardness of his expression, and for all his height and outward maturity she heard the uncertainty and distaste echoed in his voice.

'But they cannot...she will not be your wife...yet. Will she?'

'No. Thank God!' His answer came out in a soft groan.

'My poor friend, but it is not so hard for a man. He can take his pleasures elsewhere after marriage, although we are taught by Mother Church that it is sinful. A woman on the other hand must be faithful to whome'er it falls her lot in a husband.'

Warenne spoke slowly. 'How little you know of Edward Plantagenet and his accursed family. They look with the eye of a blind man towards their own family indiscretions, not so for those allied to them. Besides she is a peevish, spoiled, mischievous brat!'

'Mercy!' Olympia did not have chance to say aught else for the familiar walls of Wigmore came into sight and their private moments were ended.

That night was chill, and the wind moaned round the walls and through the passageways of the castle. Torches and candles dipped and danced before the draughts and even some of the heavy tapestry hangings swayed at the mercy of the icy blasts.

A vast fire crackled and smoked in the huge fireplace. The soft strumming of a single minstrel served to underline the sorrow that pervaded the company. Even the Yuletide feast seemed to tempt but few of the Mortimer family and talk was very low key. Their loss at this normally festive season touched one and all, but especially Margaret Fiennes. It took all of her considerable willpower to hold on to her tears.

Roger suddenly dismissed all but the serving carls and signalled for the theme to be of a livelier nature. He coaxed John and Maud to sing a carol. His mother looked across at his handsome face with a thankful nod. She did not underrate his own feelings of grief at this time, but fatherhood had made him more aware of the emotions of others.

'Come! The wind, it seems, would shame us all into singing the louder to drown its dismal descant.' He clapped his hands in time to the new rhythm and indicated for his brothers and sisters to follow his lead. His young wife Joan joined in the merriment conscious of her role as the new Baroness Mortimer of Wigmore.

They all sang as loudly and discordantly as possible to banish their inner gloom. Warenne's dark-blue eyes studied each of the group as they chanted bravely, his eyes lingering on the form of Olympia. Her pale-moon hair framed her lovely face and the huge green eyes held an impenetrable look. On her lap sat a red-bound book, her dress of dark purple hugged her slender young body. He shuddered. She seemed almost unreal in the candlelight. She must have noted his shiver, for she came over and sat at his feet still clasping her precious book.

'Are you cold, my lord earl?'

'No, 'twas naught! A goose on my grave, that is all. Your book holds you faithful.' He bent forward and the soft fragrance from her hair drifted up, and he wanted to protect her from the harshness of the world. She could evoke such powerful emotions in him and yet she was scarce come from childhood.

She smiled up at him, a lip-curving smile that was echoed from the green depths of her eyes.

'A book of poems, some tales and verses of the legendary Arthur, and of lovers. You would find naught to catch your attention.'

'You appear to know my mind, as you so often like to tell me what is and isn't to my liking. Methinks you are a witch and cast your spell over all who dare cross you.' His eyes filled with a rare tenderness as he reached to brush a tendril of hair from her face. She had unwittingly charmed away the sadness the festive season always aroused in him.

'If you are very good I will copy a verse of a battle and its noble victory. I think you would not feel it too offensive.'

'Nay, I have no time for such nonsense and, besides, it is for dreamers and young maids who would have their heroes snow white, untouched by human faults.'

'You think thus? That I would have such a one as my hero?

Forsooth you know me not at all.' Young Maud came over at that and without ceremony fell on a cushion beside Olympia.

'What are you two whispering about?' she hissed.

'I think Mistress Olympia would make a poet of me!' exclaimed Warenne at the bright, dark girl.

'Then from your derision I say that our Olympia has failed.' She laughed roguishly at them both, and with that went off to tease and torment her younger brothers.

The earlier melancholic mood was beginning to lift and, as is the way with young people, they found a joy and pleasure simply being in each other's company.

The dowager Lady Mortimer sighed deeply. She was still wrapped in a cloak of personal grief but she felt glad her family could enjoy the evening. Edmund would have approved of their son's attempt to allay their sorrows.

Long after the fire had guttered and died in the Great Hall and the last of the servants had crept into their beds, when all lay at rest except the wayward wind, Warenne lay on his bed still wide-awake. He felt a yearning so intense that it was almost tangible. He rose and poured himself a goblet of rich red wine and moved to where the fire still glowed. He sat lost in thought, his strong brown fingers clasped around the shiny vessel.

So enmeshed was he in his own thoughts that he did not hear the door open. Only when the torch, in its sconce, flickered in the draught did he become aware that he was longer alone.

He rose quickly and after replacing the goblet drew a wicked-looking blade from his discarded belt, which hung close at hand.

Olympia stood in the pitching light, which traced eery shadows on the grey-stone walls.

'You felt it too!' She didn't explain further but edged closer to the fire. 'I have learned you have been called away urgently and will be leaving on the morrow,' she said softly.

'Yes...' His voice sounded unnatural and husky. 'You must not stay here, Olympia.'

'Nor will I go, my lord earl, for this night I will obey my own instincts. We may never be able to speak alone again and I did not wish you to leave without...without...' She came to a halt. She tried again. 'I fear our paths will lead us apart and I would not be at ease with myself if I did not...' Again she faltered.

He could not move for he felt suddenly bemused, like a knight facing a mighty foe, bereft of horses and armour.

She drew from behind her back a tightly clenched fist and held it out towards him. Very slowly he took the proffered object, putting aside his dagger as he did so.

The cloak clasp flashed in the light of the fire. The rubies and diamonds, so exquisitely worked, lay in his palm. She said almost breathlessly,

'It is thought to have magical qualities. My father received it for some kindness to an old man who claimed to be a wizard.' She hesitated for a moment, then continued, 'I know what it is like to be alone and...and...'

She did not finish her speech. He had gathered her up in his powerful arms and held her so gently she could scarce credit the tenderness with which he held her.

'I will not break,' she murmured in his neck.

'You must not stay, Olympia. God's wounds! I am but human. Nor can I accept your expensive gift.' She wriggled free from his grasp, a look of disbelief in the green eyes.

'I place no obligations on my gift, nor would I usurp any mistress you may or may not have.' Her tone was chill and wounded. The child in her spoke out.

'Olympia, you misunderstand! I am a blunt, ill-mannered soldier, whose knowledge of women is purely...carnal. You... you are deserving of someone who can fill your life with love and understanding.'

'I am not offering my body, but a trinket, a...a...keepsake, you dolt! You are the only friend outside of the Mortimer family I have. Is it so wrong to give a present to...a...friend?' Tears hung in the corners of her eyes and he could feel his body's ache.

'Go, little friend, you know not what torment you inflict on me by staying.'

Suddenly her anger dropped and she came very close to him.

'I will go if you promise me you will wear it, Warenne, for friendship's sake if naught else, to please a childish maid!'

He nodded. He did not wish to hurt her feelings and spoke gruffly to hide the ferment in which her closeness placed him.

'In friendship will I in honour wear it, but if you do not quickly go from this chamber then you will be a maid no longer, and of that sin I have no wish to be branded.'

She suddenly laughed up into his swarthy face.

'Oh, my great bear of an earl, I shall keep you in my prayers for you truly need someone to look to your spiritual wellbeing, for I fear you do not.'

He pulled her roughly against him and stroked her soft pale hair.

'And if you go into men's bedchambers with scarce naught but a thin shift to cover your girlish form, a virgin you certainly will not remain o'er long.'

She kissed him straight on the mouth and the kiss was answered by his own. Her lips parted as she felt his tongue touch her lips but he drew away and patted her on her little rump and propelled her firmly to the door.

'For your keepsake I thank you! For your prayers again I thank you! But stay longer at your peril. Now godnight, child, and God keep you.' So saying he closed the heavy door and left her in the chilly passageway.

She hurried back to the warmth of her bed, glad she had not woken Maud, well content with her visit. Whilst he wore the clasp, nothing ill could befall him, nor would he be ensnared in any other woman's trap.

As she lay in the darkness, his kiss still warm on her mouth, she was aware of vague longings and her young body throbbed as never before. She little realised in what a dilemma she left poor Warenne.

With the dawn she rose, bathed and dressed. The winds of the previous day had dropped and grey skies threatened rain. She hastily pulled on her woollen kirtle and russet cote-hardie. Maud still slept, but Olympia was determined to see Warenne's departure alone.

She spied him down at the stables and hurried to the spot she knew they must pass. At last she stopped, her breath wreathing like a dragon's breath in the cold morning air.

Presently she heard the sound of hooves and the company rode into view headed by Warenne. He sat his fine, tall horse which pranced and sidled, anxious to make better speed. She drew back into the dark shadows of the bushes until he almost drew abreast of where she stood, then stepped out onto the path to salute his departure. Warenne drew rein and edged his restless mount to where she stood.

'You'll take a chill in this raw dawn, damsel.' But his voice was filled with the warmth of the pleasure he felt at seeing her again.

'Would you leave without courteous partings?' she challenged.

'I thought to serve all with leaving thus, no formalities. My lady hostess will understand my actions, of that I'm sure.'

'And what of the rest of us?' She was not to be placated so easily.

'I thought to leave you still wrapped up in girlish dreams.'

'Then I wish you God speed and safe journeying…' Her voice no longer flippant, she moved to his stirrup so her words were heard by no other.

Suddenly he stooped and swung her up onto his saddle and kissed her soundly on the lips. Her arms folded about his neck and the kiss grew into a more significant one than that of parting friendship could afford.

He put her down swiftly and waved his company forward. When he turned to raise his hand in salute, he saw the tears gleaming in her green eyes and his heart felt a pain so physical in its intensity that he winced. Urgently he spurred his mount forward, his swarthy features hiding the inner turmoil. The dark-blue eyes held an unfathomable look as he rode away.

When he turned again to where she had stood, he caught the glimpse of a fleeing figure, head bent, and he knew she wept as she ran back towards the keep.

CHAPTER IX

London
1306

That Whitsun of 1306 all roads led to London. The highways were thronged with nobles and tradesmen alike, everyone wishing to share in the festivities. The streets were packed and the liveries of almost all the notable dignitaries of the age were there represented.

The cries of pedlars, piemen and traders rang through the narrow streets and filled the air with raucous discordant rhymes. Folk of every rank and style were jostled indiscriminately in the crush.

Roger Mortimer sat watching the hustle and bustle of the scene below his window, the golden eyes searching the crowds for the retinues from Wigmore and Ludlow. He turned to look back into the chamber.

'One can almost taste the excitement of the city. Edward Plantagenet will be pleased at the spectacle he has created, I'll be bound.' John came to join him at his vantage point. Pungent aromas rose from the cobbled streets and the younger Mortimer wrinkled his nose.

'Lord, London has the most odious odours that could ever insult a man's senses. I for one shall be glad to be away from here and that is no idle statement.'

The next few days would mark a notable change in Roger's existence for he was among the three hundred or so chosen to be knighted.

His gaze suddenly alighted on the familiar form of John de Warenne, the famous checky and or heraldry emblazoned on his surcoat. Roger swiftly vacated his seat and, calling to his brother to follow, hastened down to join with his erstwhile friend, the Earl of Surrey.

It was two years since Warenne had ridden away from Wigmore, and in that span of time he had thickened and grown taller. His face now wore a moustache and beard, which hugged the strong jawline and served only to make him swarthier in appearance.

Roger had also grown apace, but although dark-complexioned, there the resemblance betwixt the two young men ended, for Mortimer was undoubtedly handsome. His golden eyes and thick, curling hair added to the noble features and air of graceful strength which served only to denote how the two had grown apart in looks.

However, their friendship could now be renewed. It was at Warenne's suggestion that Roger had gained his freedom from Gaveston's wardship by offering a substantial sum of gold. Warenne's brusque, outspoken manner did nothing to endear him to his fellow lords, whereas Mortimer's company was much sought after, not least of all by the female members of the court.

Warenne's previous liaison with the Lady Mary had long since gone the way of all ardent love affairs, burnt out by its own intensity, and his name had not been linked with any other since that time.

Mortimer's, on the other hand, was coupled with many, but he only smiled when challenged with the truth ('You forget, I am both married and a father'), and the golden eyes and pleasant voice held fast to their own counsel.

The two now stood together amongst the vast, milling crowds awaiting the arrival of the Mortimer family. Roger kept scanning the thronging courtyards and gateways, pointing to various groups of new arrivals, until at last he grabbed the thick muscular arm of Warenne.

'Look, look you! Over there, I swear it was old Hamo. Meyrick, go and see.' The sober figure of Meyrick emerged from the shadow of his young master and made quickly to where Roger had indicated.

As soon as it was established that the golden eyes had not been deceived, Margaret and company came stumbling through the masses, and she and Roger fell on each other's necks and wept tears of pure happiness in their reunion.

Warenne moved to where Olympia still sat her palfrey.

'May I offer my services, damsel?' She slid into his strong arms, the green eyes noting the changes from their last meeting. He held her for an instant and she brushed his cheek with her lips.

'Warenne, I swear you get broader each time I see you, and the beard and moustache...' She had spoken quickly to hide the feelings that the sight and touch of him had caused within her.

As he turned his head to salute the Lady Margaret, Olympia saw the end of a scar that obviously ran away down into the depths of the moustache. When he turned back to her again he did not miss her discovery and said simply, 'It serves to hide the signature of a blade.' He could scarce contain the happiness and yet utter misery she brought to him. They were quickly drawn apart by other greetings and moved out of each other's sphere for the rest of the day.

Olympia stood brushing the grey-flecked hair of Lady Mortimer; she deftly dressed the thick strands and wound it neatly over the ears, pinning it to the *barbette*. She added the fillet and stepped back to admire her handiwork. The older woman nodded her satisfaction. Olympia moved to put the finishing touches to Maud's dark hair, finally placing a narrow gold circlet over the shining tresses. She looked at her own reflection and brushed the pale locks until they shone like moonlight. Expertly she plaited two thin strands down each side of her face and joined them at the nape of her long neck. Into these plaits she threaded tiny pearls and amethysts which matched the girdle that hugged her tiny waist. Her dress was of palest lavender and its rich folds enhanced the fragile form beneath. She was thankful that her skin was clear and unblemished. Her eyes appeared large and luminous in the steel mirror.

At last they heard the voice of Roger as he came to escort his family to the feasting. His wife had sent word that she would be joining them within the hour and his eyes were alight with merriment. The forthcoming ceremony held nothing but a furtherance of his own ambitions. He was now master of the much coveted Ludlow and already had plans for its embellishment and improvement, but first things first. Tonight they would all be joyous.

Roger noted the change in Olympia almost for the first time. She was indeed one of the fairest young maidens he had encountered heretofore. There would be many at court who would pay dear for a look from those green orbs. He took the arm of his mother and sister as out of the shadows Warenne moved to take his place beside Olympia. He could find no speech to tell her how beautiful she looked, so let his eyes convey all that was in his heart.

'Alas, I am unable to spend the rest of the evening in your company. As you must know, the Lady Jeanne has arrived and I must attend her. Forgive me! I hope you will understand the position in which I am presently placed.'

Olympia nodded, unable to answer. How could she, he looked so distinguished and austere, gone the unkempt boy. Was this stoic young earl still her true friend? She had pondered on that when travelling from Shropshire to London, but at their meeting had noted that he wore the diamond-and-ruby cloak clasp and her fears had been allayed a little.

He walked at her side without further conversation and saw her seated in the Great Hall before leaving to take his place amongst the foremost magnates and earls of the land at the king's table.

That night, there was feasting and merriment that would be recounted in halls and around firesides throughout the coming years by many who attended the colourful banquet dubbed the Feast of the Swans.

Gaveston, as usual, was so richly clad that any not knowing would take the tall, elegant figure of the Gascon as the heir to the throne and not the fair, more casually attired Prince of Wales.

The tables groaned with savouries of every description. Swans, their feathers replaced and silver bells garlanding their long necks, appeared to glide down the tables. Sucking pigs, with huge apples neatly placed in yawning mouths, joined with saddles of lamb and beef, haunches of venison, and such a variety of pies that it put a heavy strain on the choice of all who dined thereof. Dainty sweetmeats, nuts and raisin, figs and dates aplenty, all arranged and decorated with great skill and artistry. Wine and ale flowed in copious measures and ladies offered their companions choice pieces from their own trenchers.

Olympia looked on in awe at the quantities of food and drink that were consumed during the evening. The newly arrived Joan de Geneville had joined them at their table and the golden eyes of Roger rested lovingly on his wife. She sat now at his right hand and her dark, sloe-coloured eyes glowed with pleasure in the occasion. Her visit to London was much to her taste, judging by the rapt expression that filled her face each time that Roger spoke.

His mother sat on his left and looked far happier than Olympia had seen her for many long months. John was laughing at some court fool who had singled him out for his lewd attentions. How good it was to witness the ofttimes serious expression slip from that gentle face. Her gaze moved along and rested on the Lord of Chirk, Roger Mortimer, brother to the deceased Edmund and uncle to his namesake, Roger Mortimer, now Baron of Wigmore. She could not suppress the shudder that ran through her frame.

The dark, saturnine features and black glittering eyes were studying a comely young woman on a nearby table, and Olympia felt sorry for that unsuspecting female, for he had a reputation for taking what he had a mind to whether it be freely given or no. At his side sat his pale-faced wife, Lucy le Waffre. She alone seemed ill at ease in the midst of all the feasting. She fingered her knife nervously and took many sips from her goblet, as if to aid the food down which threatened to choke her.

Suddenly, at the top table King Edward banged his golden cup onto the trestle before him and cried, 'By God and these swans, I swear to avenge the death of Red Comyn and bring Scotland into a true repentance under my rule. Death to the usurper Bruce.' He raised his cup and the whole assembled company rose as in a body and cheered his words.

The once handsome face now showed the evidence of fierce living. His one eyelid drooped, almost closing the eye altogether, and Olympia could see by the spittle that flew from his flaccid lips that the wine was beginning to affect his speech.

Further along the top table she could see the dark features of Warenne, his expression closed and stone-like. The girl seated on his right was obviously Jeanne de Bar, and on that figure Olympia's green eyes lingered in an intent study.

There was no denying her ancestry: she was a true Plantagenet. The thick, red-gold hair and pale-blue eyes contrasted with the fresh complexion that oozed health and vitality. Her lips were wide and she now appeared to be pouting, her obvious attempts to entice her companion into conversation seeming doomed to continual failure.

Olympia watched as the girl offered choice pieces from her trencher to the swarthy earl, but she could see by the vigorous shaking of his head that this was doomed to failure as well. On the

other hand, the Prince of Wales and Piers Gaveston were enjoying
the evening's revelries with their usual gusto. The minstrels at
last struck up a rhythmic tune quickly followed by shouts for the
dancing to commence.

Servants rushed forward at a signal from the king and went into
action like a well-trained regiment. The tables at one end of the
large hall were left to carry what remained of the feast, and the
others were swung back against the walls, leaving the grey-flagged
floor clear after a team of sweepers brushed away all traces of bones
and morsels that had been cast aside during the meal.

Gaveston, so elegantly and richly attired, led the dancers to
whistles and cheers of encouragement. He was as graceful as a girl
as he moved around the vast expanse. For a moment, Olympia's
gaze alighted on her dear friend who was being led protesting onto
the floor with a look of absolute horror etched across his face.

Rich notes of drums, tambourines, flutes and harps rang to the
rafters which caught the tune and chased it back to the company
beneath. Joan de Geneville skipped lightly alongside Roger, and
Olympia thought how well suited they were, embracing their
marriage with such obvious enthusiasm. Although only tiny, Joan
held herself very straight, which made her appear taller, and it was
only when she came up against her husband did one see just how
diminutive she actually was.

Olympia's green eyes moved to the couple who followed on in
the intricate figure of the dance. Hugh Despencer and Eleanor
de Clare made such a contrasting couple; they had neither grace
nor style about them, and Eleanor was having more than a little
difficulty keeping in step, being either one move ahead or one
behind her partner. Hugh's foxy face flushed with his exertions, a
band of sweat causing his thin hair to part and stick in clumps to
his brow. Their efforts had been seen by Gaveston who did nothing
to hide his mirth at the couple's inelegant antics. It seemed almost
impossible to believe that Eleanor was also a granddaughter to the
king.

The shadow of John Mortimer fell across Olympia for an instant
as he stood before her.

'Pia, will you venture into this throng of prancers?' He smiled
down at her unable to hide his deep affection.

'Indeed, kind sir, I thought I found favour with none here

present tonight.' She took his hand and they bowed towards the royal dais, then proceeded to step lithely in time with the music, watched by the two older Lady Mortimers, who sat beside each other taking particular note of that couple who danced with such grace and ease. John's dark good looks complemented the fair delicacy of Olympia's.

'The child's a beauty and no mistake, though she's a mite on the narrow side for childbearing, methinks!' Lucy le Waffre, Baroness of Chirk, spoke in her rather timid manner. 'She will not be short of admirers, I'll warrant. Why, even John cannot take his eyes off her! Mark my words, you will have your son seeking a match.'

'I think John is already enamoured of her, and I will not try to dissuade him at this juncture, it would only harden his resolve,' Margaret said softly.

'Surely you would not countenance a match with a *merchant's* daughter?' Lucy looked askance at her sister-in-law.

'You must realise, dear Lucy, that Roger's marriage has cost us dear. The Gascon demanded 2,500 marks before he would release my son from his guardianship. Besides, Olympia is as fair in temperament as she is to look upon, and for all her lowly birth she is an heiress of considerable wealth.' She smiled wistfully. 'And I think it would be a happy marriage.'

'It is not to be countenanced, a Mortimer and a mere merchant's offspring, even if there is great wealth...' Further speech was cut short by the untimely return of the Lord of Chirk, and Lucy hastily returned to her former seat.

As the pace of the music slowed, replaced by a soft, lilting refrain which echoed to the high, vaulted roof, John whispered to his partner.

'Pia, you are by far the loveliest damsel at court and I have thought of you so often.' Olympia sensed that he was about to speak on a matter she was unwilling to hear, and returned his compliment in a flirtatious and light-hearted way.

'Faith, you must have the dust of the road still in your eyes if you see me thus. I can count at least a dozen much prettier than I, and I will not have you cozen me so.' She did not wish him to become serious, for she guessed what was on his mind and she was no longer free to consider a match with anyone. How could she speak of love and marriage, when her own heart was breaking and it wasn't a handsome face that disturbed her dreams, but that of the dark, swarthy Earl of Surrey, John de Warenne.

It had been on that final morning at Wigmore, when he had picked her up and kissed her farewell that Olympia had realised how deeply she loved the burly young Earl of Surrey. From that day, she had kept him in her heart and prayers and every waking thought during the long months of their separation. Weeks before this great event she had lain awake tossing and turning in anticipation of seeing him once again. She even pushed from her mind the thought of his forthcoming marriage.

She had managed to follow something of his career from snippets of information gleaned from letters received from Roger and John. Warenne was fast gaining a reputation as a champion in the lists. His successes at the tournaments caused her both elation and abject misery, for she lived in fear of his safety.

Roger too was proving to be no mean warrior at the contests he managed to attend, but as luck would have it had never come up against Warenne in the tourneys. However, it was not of such contests that Olympia found herself worrying about but the one that was brewing up betwixt her adored Warenne and Piers Gaveston.

Gaveston's sleek, resplendent figure now stood alongside Warenne, and Olympia could tell by the tone of their voices that all was not well between them. Just then Gaveston's voice rose above the clamour.

'Your brawn is sometimes in your head, Surrey. I suggest you leave it where it serves best – in your sword-arm.'

Warenne, who had been walking towards the Mortimer family, half leading, half towing the Lady Jeanne de Bar, now almost knocked Olympia over in his haste to move away from the Gascon's taunts. He was afraid that if the conversation continued along the same course, he would lose control of his temper and cause a breach of the peace before the king, and that was tantamount to treason. Only his quick reflexes saved Olympia from falling. She could sense his dilemma.

'Smile, my lord! Let not that popinjay see you are put about by his childish quips.' She spoke in a whisper, the music drowning her words to all but her saviour.

He slowly raised her back steadily onto her feet and murmured.

'You have his measure, my sweet Olympia,' and with all the guile
he could muster smiled woodenly between gritted teeth.

'Why, if such encounters with the Gascon brought your
sweetness into my embrace, I would cross his path right willingly.'
Then, before introducing the totally bemused Jeanne, he whisked
Olympia off amongst the whirling throng, leaving John agape in
the presence of the royal maid, who were now left standing facing
each other. However, John's quick wits quickly saved what could
have been a rather embarrassing situation. He introduced himself
and his mother, then engaged Jeanne in pleasant conversation as
he watched the couple dance away towards the far end of the hall.

'Oh, my dear Warenne, now you *have* caused a stir,' murmured
Olympia. 'Just see how the heads are turning.' She was peeping
from the security of his broad shoulder and could not resist a little
giggle at the expressions she spied from that safe spot.

'I would as lief cut that coxcomb's throat. He walks too
proud and casts too long a shadow for my liking. Mincing dandy!'
he growled, spinning her round at a rapid speed. Only his powerful
grip on her waist saved her from falling into the crowd.

'My lord earl! Have a mercy, my ribs ache from your grasp and
I swear I shall fly through yon window should you loose me.' She
was gasping and laughing all at once and felt her laughter would
become out of hand if she did not steer their course to calmer
measures.

At last they came to a halt. She guided him to the far end of the
hall where the crowd thinned somewhat.

'I swear I have never been danced off my feet before, but then,
methinks my lord earl never does things by half.' She could see
that his rage had subsided and he laughed down at her, his crooked
teeth gleaming in a gleeful grin. He looked almost boyish and she
longed to take his face in her hands and kiss it but instead just
wagged a finger at him.

'Warenne, you are in truth a "Great Dancing Bear" and I needs
must put a chain around your neck and lead you from this august
gathering before you cause further chaos.'

The grin slipped from his face and he suddenly became serious.

'Damsel, lead on. I would follow gladly where'er your chain
directed.'

He caught her hand and pulled her through the door close by

into the cooler shadowy passageway. He took her roughly into his arms and kissed her hard. At first she pushed against him with all her might, but the intoxication of his nearness melted any resistance and she slowly yielded to his embrace. After some moments he released her.

'I want you, Olympia! More than I have ever wanted anything in my life. Even knowing I have neither the right nor the freedom to speak thus, yet I can no longer contain all that I feel for you.'

They stood close, all mirth gone from their faces.

She stood in the reflection from an overhead torch and was unaware how pale and ethereal she looked.

'Oh, my lord, all of my heart is yours, and my love you had unbidden. God knows, I've tried to drive you from my mind and heart but it was like trying to stop time. Now it has run beyond my control and I am resigned to my fate.

His fingers caught a tendril of her pale hair and wound it gently round his hand, making a silken chain of it.

'See how your golden hair holds the "Dancing Bear".'

He bent and kissed her and the kiss grew and flamed and the yearning in her slender body caused her to tremble at its intensity. His hands moved slowly over her breasts and down to her tiny waist. Her own arms encircled his neck and she ran her lips along the edge of his beard. He lifted her off the ground and murmured, 'Maid, you fill me with such an aching desire! I fear my passions would destroy your sweet body leaving all knightly vows as dust.'

He gently placed her back on her feet again and they stood looking deep into each other's eyes, shaken by the burning longing their encounter had aroused in them.

Footsteps broke into their new-found intimacy. He pulled her deep into the shadows and folded her into his arms. She pressed deeper in his embrace. The footsteps came nearer, then carried on up the passageway and out through a door beyond.

'Tomorrow night I must stand vigil in the New Temple before taking the vows of knighthood, but tonight my senses reel at your potency and I would renounce all if you would be mine.'

She knew he did not speak lightly for he was not a man of shallow intent.

In answer to his confession, her own pent-up emotions broke free and she kissed him in such a long and sensual manner it caused her to moan under his mouth. From somewhere deep within her, however, voices of conscience filtered into her blissfulness and she reluctantly pulled away.

'Forgive me, my love, but I fear if I stay long, you will think me too free. Already I know I have offended God by loving you.' Almost desperately she gasped, 'Now, maybe you understand why I said I would never marry. Your course has been laid out and I have no legitimate part in your future, nothing can change that now. But – oh joy, I think you feel as deeply as do I...' She did not manage to say more as he had swept her up into his powerful arms and kissed any further speech from her lips. When at last they drew apart she whispered,

'Warenne, I will love you always, but am torn betwixt desire and conscience. Do not think ill of me! I am truly tormented by the thought of you marrying someone else; my mind is in a turmoil ...' With that she tore herself away from his grasp and ran back into the hot, noisy hall to rejoin her companions.

The tears that threatened were held in tight check and she tried to ease her inward ache with a goodly draught of strong wine. She spied John still with the Lady Jeanne de Bar. He had obviously made a good impression on that young lady, judging by the smug expression on his face.

The music that had earlier delighted Olympia now palled, and she felt the tune beat in her brain like a tattoo. She wanted to run and hide from this illustrious crowd but was held fast by etiquette.

She saw Warenne return and for a moment thought he was coming across to where she stood, but his progress was checked by Thomas, Earl of Lancaster, whose haughty face was stained red from the heat and the quantity of wine he had obviously consumed during the course of the evening. He looked unusually animated in his discourse with Warenne and she could tell by the darkening expression on his face that he would get no further in his quest to join her again. Lancaster had taken his arm and was guiding him back towards the royal dais and she knew that he was helpless to break free from England's premier earl.

Somehow, Olympia endured the rest of the evening's revelries but she felt bereft of any hope for her future. Happiness for her was gone, and only the knowledge that Warenne suffered the same pangs of heartache kept her from weeping and running away, for she knew he would follow her and bring the royal wrath upon his head.

Wearily she sought refuge at last in her own bed and the tears so bravely kept at bay now spilled out in bitter grief and frustration. For what seemed like an age she tossed and turned. Her weeping had caused her throat to ache and the only effect the wine had had was to create a raging thirst. She rose quietly to look for a pitcher of water but to her dismay found it empty. Her need was so great that she knew it could not be ignored.

Silently, she pushed her feet into the soft felt slippers and shrugged on a dark-grey mantle, then went in search of a page, carrying the empty pitcher in her hand. She wandered aimlessly along the cold, stone passageways, but all remained still. She crept past sleeping servants, some propped up in doorwells or slumped in heaps on the floor, but none, it would seem, able to be of service to her. She was continuing her quest when a door to her right suddenly swung open. Breathlessly she jumped into the shadows, not wishing to be discovered. The voice sounded gruffer than normal, but she recognised it as Warenne's. Her heart hammered within her at the sound.

'Bring me a pail of heated water and quickly.' The door closed and she heard the disappearing footsteps of the hurrying servant as they echoed down the corridor.

She stood for some minutes torn between running back to the safety of her own chamber or remaining close to the door which guarded the one she most wished to fill her sight. Whether her nearness had somehow transmitted itself to his own longings she never knew but the door reopened and he stood peering out towards the darkness that concealed her.

'Who stands there shielded by shadows? Speak or I will call the guards.' She saw him take his dagger from his belt and come towards her as lightly as a cat. It was only when she jumped into the pool of light that he recognised her.

'By God's wounds, Olympia! What brings you abroad at this hour? Come in quickly before you catch your death of cold.'

She could tell by the tremor in his voice that he had come very close to attacking her. He drew her into the chamber which was bathed in soft, mellow candlelight. She still held the empty pitcher in her trembling hands. Gently, he extricated it from her grasp and placed it on a table nearby.

She was so parched and frightened that when she tried to speak only a croak emitted from her throat.

'It is not safe to wander abroad at this unearthly hour.' But his tone was softer now and he poured a goblet of wine and water and proffered it to the still trembling figure of the girl. Her hand shook so that she could not take the drink he held. Her eyes were red-rimmed from her weeping and he could see that she had been sorely distressed. He lifted the drink to her lips and held it whilst she sipped thirstily.

At last she shook her head. He placed the vessel back onto the table beside the pitcher.

'Whatever brought you to my door this night, I for one shall be ever grateful, for any time spent in thy company is precious to me!' He stepped towards her and took her in his arms, kissing her soft hair. She leant against him, all her anguish and sadness melting away at his touch.

'Warenne!' Her voice was husky with emotion. 'Do not send me away, I know now that my love for you is deeper and stronger than my conscience. Tonight you are not bound by any vows, either to God or…or…and I would hear you say just once…that…that you love me!'

He bent and kissed her long and tenderly on the mouth and the kiss ignited the sweet flame of passion which met and enfolded the two lovers. Gently he unfastened her mantle and it fell to the floor at her feet. Her arms crept up around his neck and she could feel the heat of his flesh through her flimsy shift. His strong hands ran over her frame and she yielded to his caress.

Deftly he untied the lace at her throat and the shift slipped like a whisper to the ground beside the grey cloak.

His dark-blue eyes drank in the soft, pale loveliness of her nubile young body and he groaned at its beauty.

He picked her up and carried her to the fur-draped bed and laid her down amongst its soft depths. Her green eyes were luminous in the yellow glow from the candles as he kissed her throat.

A knock at the door made them both start, but Warenne quickly leapt to answer. He took the steaming pail and dismissed his body servant for the night. Olympia had pulled the soft coverlet around her nudity and watched Warenne from beneath her long lashes. The sight of his powerful form stirred so much tenderness within her she could scarcely breathe.

The aura from the candles played over his dark hair, which shone like polished jet and painted his skin to an even darker hue. He gazed at her and his look quickened her pulses. He moved back to the side of the bed and pulled off his wide-sleeved shirt and hose and stood naked before her. For all his bulk there was not an ounce of fat on that hardened torso. He was almost square of build, lacking the tapering waistline of the Mortimer menfolk.

However, she did not have long for her study as he came and lay beside her, very aware of her innocence, so gently did he stroke her skin.

'You are so soft and fragile!' he whispered. 'I have no way of bringing you to womanhood without hurting you. Try not to hate me, my love.' She quivered at his touch and was deeply moved by his endearment and concern.

'Foolish man, I will never hate you.' She leaned over and kissed his doubt-filled face. 'I'm not completely ignorant, you know! Surely all maidenheads must be broken on a marriage bed,' then very softly she whispered, 'and this...is...my marriage bed.' Her green eyes were wide and tender as she spoke.

'But you are so slender...' She bent forward and kissed his fears into silence. He could no longer hold onto his iron self-control and his muscular arms came round and crushed her hungrily to him.

In the dark hours of night Olympia surrendered her virginity to Warenne and cried out in an ecstasy of love which she knew must live and die in those few stolen hours, and each was so aware of the coming dawn, it only served to make their coupling more urgent and complete.

The pink fingers of daylight stretched across the grey sky and Olympia clung to her lover with all the strength she possessed in a final embrace. No words could either speak, for they were too full of the bitterness of parting. At last, she tore herself from his arms and donned the discarded shift, picked up the heavy cloak and swung it around her slim shoulders. He drew her back to him in a last tormented kiss and they clung to each other's lips. With a groan that came from the depths of her soul, she broke away and ran blindly to the door and out into the silent passage, hurrying

lest her new-found courage should desert her and she might run
back and fling herself once more into his arms.

Warenne stood and looked at the closed door, his eyes filled with
abject misery and longing. There had been no guilt, lust or shame
between them, only love and sweet passion. Now he was powerless
to stop her. She had spoken truth when she said their paths ran
on different courses, but there, with the light of the coming day
strengthening, Warenne, Earl of Surrey, vowed that somehow he
would bring about their reunion and then he would never let her go
again.

The rest of the day was a round of duties that Olympia performed
in a state of dumb grief. Margaret Mortimer had looked at the pale
face and dark-rimmed eyes and had put it down to the previous
night's merrymaking. She was too engrossed in her own happiness
to dwell for long on her protégée's downcast countenance.

Only John really noticed the drastic change in Olympia, but
when he pressed her as to the reason he found her distant and
unforthcoming in her replies.

'What ails you, Pia? I thought that life at court was to your
taste, now it seems to pall.'

She shook her head and would not be drawn as to the cause of
her distress. Seeing that he was not about to win her from this dark
humour, he shrugged and went in search of his brother, thinking
it was probably some female malady that had brought about the
alteration.

Still feeling a little peeved at his rejection, his annoyance was
quickly forgotten in the company of Roger and his wife, Joan de
Geneville, who chattered and laughed up into his brother's golden
eyes with undisguised admiration. Their company was a sure
antidote for any melancholy.

Roger was finding no difficulty in impressing his wife. True,
she was no startling beauty, lacking both height and any striking
features, but she had glorious, long black hair that shone like
lovingly polished ebony. Her face was round and she had deep-set,
sloe-coloured eyes and a neat straight nose, a prim rosebud mouth,
and a dimple in her cheek. She was comely enough and carried
herself with grace, which added inches to her diminutive stature.

The match was auspicious, for Joan was the de Lacy heiress and brought great wealth and lands to her husband both in England and Ireland. John sighed; he wished that Olympia would look at him with such devotion. He would marry her on the morrow, but he did not deceive himself, he had yet to win his sweet lady and the thought brought a blush to his gentle face.

Warenne had also been kept busy that day. He had sought to have his forthcoming marriage contract cancelled and in so doing had incurred the wrath of Edward Plantagenet. The clash of their verbal exchange had been heard ringing down the corridors outside the royal apartments, causing looks of consternation to all those who had heard the outburst.

The king had brought the interview to an abrupt end, threatening Warenne that if he should fail to appear at the wedding, his head would adorn London Bridge. So events moved towards their fateful conclusion, and for certain members of that great assembly the seeds were sown that would set the pattern of their lives entwining and interlacing, one with the other.

The day after, Edward Plantagenet, recently named 'Hammer of the Scots', once styled the greatest knight in Christendom, dubbed his son and heir, Edward, Prince of Wales, in a private chapel within the Abbey of Westminster.

Age now dictated the king's need to save his waning energies and it had been decided that the newly knighted prince would then continue to dub the rest of the company of young nobles in the formal ceremony.

The Abbey was filled to overflowing. People craned their necks to catch a glimpse of the colourful spectacle, as each of the richly dressed young men moved forward in solemn pomp to kneel before the pleasant-faced young prince at the high altar. The great nave spilled over with three hundred knights errant and their families anxious not to miss a second of the pageant.

Olympia, whose slender young body still ached from the attentions of Warenne, could feel her heart thunder within her as she watched his dark head bow in homage and the great sword 'Curtana' flashed as it touched his broad shoulders. He moved back into the throng and she waited for the turn of the Mortimers.

The closeness of the congregation threatened to stifle Olympia and she kept clenching her nails into the palms of her hands to stop from fainting. A gasp from Margaret Mortimer and Joan de

Geneville brought her back to reality and she forced her concentration back on the long ceremony.

Roger and John knelt beside each other as the great sword of state dubbed them knights of the realm. Olympia could feel Joan's excitement. She did not have to look at the dark, shining eyes, or see the tears of their mother, to understand what that moment meant to them both. Indeed, she felt ashamed at allowing her own self-pity to overshadow their day.

Besides, Warenne had worn the clasp she had given him all those months before, and she knew that it was a sign of his feelings and regard for her on that momentous day.

At last it was over, and Olympia was pushed forward in a surge of people, now all trying to leave the abbey en masse. She no longer cared what became of her and she did nothing to save herself from being swept away from the company she had been standing with. She was pressed and jostled, elbowed and bruised without mercy. All wanted to escape at the same instant.

Suddenly she felt herself in a strong grasp and was lifted out of the crowd. Warenne had seen her plight and unceremoniously forced his way to her assistance.

'Olympia, are you all right?' His face filled with concern.

'I'm thankful that you have rescued me from that crush. I swear they have all gone mad.' She smiled wanly. 'Your first chivalrous deed as a knight, to save a merchant's daughter.'

'To save,' his voice dropped to a whisper, 'my love.'

She longed to throw herself in his arms and tell him of the tormented hours she had spent since their last meeting, but she knew she had not suffered alone, for his dark-blue eyes were as pained as her own.

Out of the colourful throng stepped John Mortimer.

'Ah, my lord earl, it would seem you have our sweet maid in your care. My mother saw her in distress and sent me to her aid, but I see she is in good hands.'

Olympia moved towards John with stiff resignation, managing to cast a loving glance at Warenne. She followed the younger Mortimer obediently back to the Wigmore contingent, hanging onto his arm as she did so.

John led her out of the abbey and back to the palace into the Great Hall. When they eventually reached their appointed table, Joan de Geneville was bubbling over with joy at her newly knighted lord and chattered merrily up at him, pouring a torrent of questions over him until he raised his hands in mock surrender.

Margaret Mortimer had a look of contented maternity on her face and John just grinned at the rest of the party. There was a wealth of happiness radiating around the famous hall of Westminster that night. The festivities took on an even greater note of intensity, and Gaveston and the Prince of Wales were as usual to the fore of the fun and games.

Edward the king, tired but well contented, gazed out over the vast assembly. Although he was ailing, with age fast becoming the most insistent enemy, he could not help but congratulate himself, for only a few weeks since, his young French wife Margaret had given birth to their third child, a daughter Eleanor. Aye, old he might be but still a lusty man for all that. The thought comforted him not a little. His bleary gaze rested on his tall son and the smile faded. How by all that was holy had he and his first wife, Eleanor of Castile, sired such a one? He was more disappointed each day with that young man who was at that moment prancing and laughing with the Gascon.

Edward was determined to watch their relationship which had caused him much concern of late. He turned his attention to his granddaughter, Jeanne de Bar, and read the discontent etched across those proud Plantagenet features. Beside her sat the future bridegroom and his swarthy face looked as though it was carved out of granite.

Edward shrugged; many marriages started thus and had been turned to a sweeter vein after the wench became old enough to bed, and that young earl looked well able to satisfy any woman, even a Plantagenet appetite. The idea amused the old man, for he sat chuckling to himself for some time. If he could only bring Scotland to his will, but the very notion of that running sore was enough to put a scowl where a smile had so lately sat.

Warenne and Joan, completely unaware that they had been the subject of a detailed scrutiny by their monarch, sat in uncomfortable silence until at last the girl could stand the strain no longer.

'You wear your displeasure like a mask, my lord earl. I can only think that my company is not to your liking.' Her pale-blue eyes held a warning challenge.

'I assure you the fault is not yours, damsel.' He had not turned his head to look at her as he spoke.

'I have heard that this marriage is not of your choosing.' She cocked an enquiring eyebrow at him. 'However, we are both bound by duty and obedience to our lord and king, and must follow his dictates.' He nodded.

'Your displeasure I can countenance, understand even, but your lack of courtesy I will not suffer.'

At her words he turned and looked hard at the proud, flushed face.

'You must come to terms with my deficiencies, lady. I'm afraid courtly grace and idle gossip are not amongst the attributes of the man to whom you find yourself bound. However, if you have felt slighted, then for that I do most sincerely apologise. For the rest...' He shrugged and would have relapsed into silence but for the girl's persistence.

'Our vows of marriage will be but an empty mockery, I fear. Remember, I too am used as a pawn in my grandsire's game and am no better pleased with this match than are you.'

'I am not insensible of the honour in this arrangement, but will keep as far out of your presence as possible. On that count, have no fears,' Warenne muttered.

For all her lack of years, Jeanne de Bar heard the vehemence in that sentence with something bordering on disbelief. It was customary for a child bride to go and live in the house of their husband until they were old enough to become a wife in truth, but by the sound of it in her own case it was not to be so.

The sour looks and harsh tones between the man and girl had not gone unnoticed by the sharp-eyed Gaveston, who eagerly pounced on the couple's obvious disenchantment.

'I do believe that dear Surrey is mightily peeved at having to wait for the years to pass before he can savour the delights of connubial bliss.' The pearly teeth flashed in the darkly handsome face of the Gascon as he spoke.

The exchange had drawn attention from the masque to the two so different young nobles. Olympia tensed as Warenne remained seated and mute. She could see by the set of Warenne's jaw that he was close to breaking point and she clutched the folds of her skirt in anticipation. The music ceased as he rose slowly to his feet and advanced on the tall, lithe figure of Gaveston. He caught the silken surcoat and thundered,

'Have a care, Gascon, you will not always be protected by royal protocol and then Surrey will make you eat English dirt. This I promise you, I shall be avenged for this insult.' So violently had he laid hold of the fine tunic that it ripped as the Gascon tried to free himself from the iron grip.

The expression on Gaveston's face was a sarcastic sneer as he retorted tartly, 'We shall continue this amusement the next time we meet in the lists, Surrey.'

The prince stepped between the two glowering adversaries.

'Gentlemen, methinks the war in Scotland will cool both your hot appetites for fighting. Let us direct your spleen in that direction and, I have no doubt, Bruce will be defeated within the season.'

There were murmurs of assent at his words and a quick-witted mummer started to ape a Scottish jig.

So in a somewhat tenser atmosphere the evening progressed. Olympia sensed the chagrin Warenne felt at being the centre of attention and noted also the ashen cheeks of Jeanne de Bar.

Roger leant across and caught Olympia's hand. So deep in his own happiness had he been until that moment that all else was lost to his comprehension. But the sad, haunted face of the pale, lovely maid had struck a chord of compassion within his breast.

'Do not let this evening's antics upset you, sweeting,' he said. 'Warenne and the Gascon are well able to stand toe to toe in any competition, be it on the field or verbally. Piers is well known for the sharpness of his tongue, ask any. Why, even the revered Earl of Pembroke has been dubbed "Joseph the Jew" and Warwick "The Black Dog of Arden". He enjoys provoking and feeds on the notoriety it causes.'

Olympia smiled back into the golden eyes.

'Pray do not concern yourself on my account; I think there has been too much festivity for my humble palate. I beg your leave,' and she hurriedly left the table, her anguish threatening to engulf her; on reaching the cool corridor she leant against a cold stone pillar and wept uncontrollably. The flood, once released, washed over her in bitter relief. The force of it racked her slender frame.

Finally the storm subsided and she made her way noiselessly back to her own chamber, glad to have been unobserved. Upon reaching the door, a page dressed in the livery of azure-and-or checky stepped forward and placed a small scroll in her hand, then bowed and hurried away. Eagerly she broke the seal.

> I have tried, unsuccessfully, to put the marriage contract from me, but alas to no avail!
>
> You have the courage of heart to endure what is to come. Trust me, for I swear I will find a way to bring us together one day. This I promise you by all that I hold sacred.
>
> I love you,
>
> W.

She read and reread the words, then committed the missive to the flames. She would keep nothing that could incriminate her lover, should it fall into the wrong hands. His words 'you have the courage of heart to endure what is to come' rang through her brain and she ran blindly out into the cold night.

The dew soaked her felt slippers with its sweet dampness but she neither noticed nor cared. The ache she felt was of the soul as well as the body, and she must meet the challenge in her own manner, for she knew if she did not contain this grief it would consume and destroy her. This she must not allow to happen; had he not promised to find a way? And beyond all else she loved and trusted him with her very life.

As she walked along the neat paths of the palace gardens towards the dark shadow of the abbey, which only a few hours ago had been filled with the greatest families of the age, the heady scent of gilly flowers, violets and herbs hung in the spring night air like a perfumed mantle.

At the abbey door, Olympia stopped for a moment, then entered the dim interior. The sweet perfume was replaced by a musty odour of incense and cold dampness, which caused her to shiver involuntarily. The eternal flame shone above the great altar and all was bathed in an unearthly hush, causing her to hold her breath for an instant.

It was some moments before Olympia realised she was not alone. A solitary figure knelt before a magnificent statue of the Virgin and Child. Curiosity penetrated through her shroud of misery and she moved closer to the bowed form. The hooded figure turned as she became aware of Olympia's presence, and there, in the eery light from the guttering candles and the eternal flame, Olympia met the Lady Adela de Giffard.

For more than an hour they remained in companionable, silent prayer, until a group of monks entered chanting the Kyrie.

At the intrusion, the Lady Adela rose, crossed herself, genuflected and made towards the side door through which she had come earlier that evening. Olympia silently followed, not wanting to lose this new-found ally.

The stars hung like diamonds against the blue-blackness of the night sky and the air was crystal-clear. The lady breathed deeply and with the loveliest voice Olympia had ever heard said,

'The hallowed home of God is a sure sanctuary against sorrow, I find.' She turned and held out her hands. 'My name is Adela de Giffard, wife to Sir John de Giffard of Brimpsfield.'

Olympia took the extended hands and grasped them warmly.

Olympia gave her name and style as they walked slowly back towards the palace.

'Pray, what brings one as pretty as you to seek solace in the dead of night?' The voice ran through Olympia like a pleasant chord.

'Forgive me if I do not...cannot...' Adela raised her hand.

'Hush, child, say no more, I did not wish to pry. Indeed we will become friends in silence, for I would find it more than a little difficult to explain my own conduct.' With that she leant forward and kissed Olympia's cheek.

'I think we shall become good friends, dear Olympia...a friend-ship so founded and in such a holy place...yes...until tomorrow then.'

Olympia nodded. She liked Adela de Giffard instinctively and drew some comfort from the knowledge that they would meet again. Olympia felt that she would be in sore need of a friendly face during the coming ordeal.

'Now we must part or have the guard asking unwanted questions. Godnight, pretty one, and may the daylight bring a lessening of your sorrow.' Without further ado Adela turned and made her way back to her own apartments.

That night Olympia slept fitfully and wept bitter tears. Her body ached with longing for Warenne's touch, and a deeper desire so newly awakened was making itself plain in its demands, demands with no way of being assuaged.

In her agony she prayed for strength to meet the coming day. The very thought of Warenne being wed to another struck at Olympia's heart like a hammer blow but, come what may, she must carry her sorrow in secret silence.

CHAPTER X

The day had dawned bright and clear and now the sunlight streamed in through the stained glass windows of the abbey. The high altar was a mass of white flowers and the choir chanted in perfect harmony, the clear notes resounding around the richly decorated roof.

Beneath, all the nobles and magnates, magnificently dressed for the occasion, jostled their neighbour for a better view. Adela de Giffard had somehow managed to find her friend in the crush and at the sight of the pale, drawn face with the dark circles etched around those magnificent eyes she almost cried out in alarm.

She caught Olympia's icy hand.

'Have courage, your hurt will pass in time, believe me. You will be the stronger for the wounding.'

Olympia could not reply but clung gratefully onto Adela's comforting hand.

Just then a fanfare rang out and the procession began to wend its way towards the altar. Edward headed the ranks, his huge frame robed in the royal purple. Next followed his son, the Prince of Wales, walking beside the ever-constant Gaveston, who was even more outrageously dressed than usual. His long-toed shoes were decorated with silver bells which tinkled as he walked and the crimson and yellow parti-coloured costume dazzled the onlookers. By comparison the bishops and prelates appeared almost dowdy in their rich vestments. Finally came the servers carrying large candles and swinging the incense, which filled the abbey with its pungent aroma.

The slow file of the bridegrooms then followed and Olympia could hardly bear to watch, so intense was her misery. Adela's hand tightened around hers and Olympia clung to the comforting grasp with all her might.

Warenne headed the ranks, being the highest order of nobility, and at his appearance many gasped, for he was clothed all in deepest black.

'Lord a'mercy!' whispered one lady. 'He looks like the devil,' and she hastily crossed herself as he passed.

Olympia wanted to cry out his face was so gaunt and haggard. For one brief instant their eyes met and Adela felt the tremor that ran through Olympia. Comprehension as to the cause of her friend's dilemma now dawned on Adela and by the look on Surrey's swarthy face he felt as unhappy as the girl.

Tears welled up in Olympia's eyes and trickled slowly down her pale cheeks. Adela felt helpless; she wanted to hug her sad friend and wipe away this day's torment. Instead she continued to hold on tightly to the slender hand.

'Look, doesn't the Baron of Wigmore look simply splendid!'

Olympia blinked the tears from her eyes and focused on the slow-moving line. Her aching heart leapt with pride as she watched the tall handsome figure decked in amber which made his eyes look like burning topaz. He nodded and smiled, obviously enjoying every minute of the pageant in his role as robe-bearer to the prince.

At Roger's heels, Hugh Despencer, though lacking nothing in the quality and cut of his garb, did not impress a single onlooker with his costume of grey edged in sable which served only to make him look somehow lifeless.

Next came the turn of the brides. At their head was Jeanne de Bar. She was in blue and silver, and on her red-gold hair a diadem of sapphires and diamonds winked and sparkled as she walked. Her handmaidens scattered petals as they went. A little way behind came Eleanor de Clare, and although she was also a granddaughter to Edward, there was nothing in either her appearance or carriage which advertised the fact. She had chosen to wear purest white for her gown, which failed to flatter her somewhat sallow complexion. However, that certainly could not be said for the petite Joan de Geneville. Her gown was of pale-blue silk, cut quite plainly, and she wore only fresh spring flowers in her long, black hair. The jewels were the lights that shone from her dark eyes, matching her husband in her role of flower maiden to the brides.

'Our little Joan is the epitome of happiness, methinks!' whispered

Adela. 'She looks lovelier than many of the brides.' All the while she spoke she continued to hold Olympia's hand.

'At least some will remember this day as a joyous occasion.' Olympia tried to sound unenvious, but... Adela heard the catch in her voice.

Olympia never knew where she drew the strength to endure that day's nuptial service and could find no words to thank Adela enough for being such a staunch ally.

At the evening feast Adela again kept close to Olympia's side, introducing her first to her husband, John de Giffard, and then to her brother, Vincent Botelier. Olympia studied them both in fine detail. John de Giffard was a hard-faced man of early middle years. He was not over-tall but with his well-lined, weather-beaten face looked like a seasoned soldier. He did not fill the title of stylish courtier but somehow Olympia felt that he would be a valuable ally in times of crisis. She judged him for no ladies' man and his stiff formal bow underlined her suspicions.

By his side stood his complete contradiction. Vincent Botelier was both handsome and courteous. He had the same dark-chestnut hair of his sister and his eyes were of darkest brown. The rest of his features were fine and almost delicate for a man, but there was a strength about the mouth and chin. His gaze was all admiration for his sister's new-found friend and he took no pains to hide his feelings.

He took Olympia's long, pale fingers in his own and lingered rather too long in holding them to his lips in salutation.

'Oh, Vin,' exclaimed Adela, 'do not overwhelm poor Olympia already. She is unused to the ways of the court and your honeyed tongue will turn her head, I swear.'

'I think not,' added Olympia quietly, 'but I will meet an honest phrase with honesty, and flattery treat in the manner fitting.'

Vincent laughed. 'Ah, I see she is as witty as she is beautiful; how clever of you, Adela, to make such an entrancing friend.'

It was good to be surrounded by such people at a time like this and for a while Olympia focused on the light-hearted banter. Soon the two groups of Mortimers and Giffards merged as the evening grew apace.

Across the Great Hall, Warenne had noted the handsome affable young man who appeared to be dominating Olympia's company. He felt an emotion hitherto unknown to him, that of pure jealousy and he wished to kill the man who smiled so meaningfully at his Olympia; the phrase almost caused him to choke on his wine, when only hours before he had taken Jeanne de Bar to wife, but had he spoken those words to a thousand women, it was to Olympia alone they were truly meant. His helplessness in this situation caused him to seek refuge in the wine and he offered up his goblet frequently for replenishment, ignoring the food almost completely.

Olympia took care not to look towards the top table too often as it might draw some attention. She listened to the happy discourse of Roger and his wife, and did not miss the wistfulness in Joan's comments regarding the brevity of this time together.

'On our return to Ludlow my lord and husband,' Joan said the last words blushing prettily before carrying on, 'is to muster five hundred men for the Scottish wars.'

So the cloud of war finally penetrated the festivities and many began making plans for the coming confrontation. Even Prince Edward had taken an oath to go immediately from this court to fight in Scotland.

The horrendous death of William Wallace in the previous year had been hoped by all to signal the end to Scottish resistance. This had not been so, and now Robert Bruce, Earl of Carrick, lately crowned at Scone, looked certain to pick up the gauntlet of resistance dropped by Wallace at his death.

Edward's wrath at this knowledge was now well known and the title of 'Hammer of the Scots' was proving well founded. So once more England stood on the brink of bloody conflict, and nobles and commoners alike groaned at the prospect. More taxes, more levies, more requisitioned stores, more horses and men called to pay the price of the king's bottomless quest for power. He would never be content with the titular title of 'Lord Paramount of Scotland'.

'I think the season of merrymaking is over,' Adela said to Olympia. 'The theme of war is more to my husband's liking as he finds the company of soldiers far more enjoyable than that of courtiers.' The younger girl nodded; she could not tell her friend how mismatched she thought John and Adela Giffard. She would bite out her tongue rather than give offence to one so kind and considerate. She for one would be glad to flee from London back to the haven of Wigmore, though she would not see her beloved Warenne. It was proving almost too much anguish to see him fettered like some bear, ready to be baited by the royal family. Plantagenets never forgot an insult, and Warenne's request to stop his marriage would not be forgiven lightly either by the king or his granddaughter.

CHAPTER XI

Ludlow
July 1306

Joan de Geneville stretched lazily and looked down at the still-sleeping figure of her husband. The dark, curly head lay in the crook of his arm, his breath coming soft and rhythmically in sleep. She bent and kissed his cheek, rose and went to the window.

Already there were people about their everyday routine. Servants and grooms, soldiers and laundresses, scullery carls scuttled about busily bringing in the wood and kindling to light the evening fires of the day, for even on a hot day the castle became chill at sundown.

The outer bailey would soon be filled with men training for their service to the Crown: butts bristling with arrows, the clash of steel as the high-ranking men practised their sword drill, knights at the quintain, wheeling and charging their mounts in readiness for the real confrontation soon to be met.

Joan had been in a world of idyllic love. Roger Mortimer was all she had hoped for in a husband. He was attentive, witty and obviously ambitious, for no sooner had they reached Ludlow than he had sent messengers to his various demesnes to call to arms all those eligible to fight. Stores had been gathered, sheep and cattle herded onto the lush meadows flanking the Teme. He had also been in deep discussion with builders and planners for the alterations he wanted carried out on the castle itself, as soon as the required licence had been obtained from the king.

It was the evenings she enjoyed the most as he devoted them entirely to her own amusements: dancing, music, reading and listening to the sweet voices of the Welsh bards, enjoyed amongst the company of some intimate friends. The nights had been filled with love-making that brought blushes even now to her cheeks and she turned and looked at the slumbering form who, hours earlier, had filled her with such ecstasy that she felt it must be sinful. Such inner feelings she did not dare to confess to her chaplain.

She went and lay down beside her young lord, touching his naked shoulders and running a dainty finger down the muscular arm, weaving her fingers through his. She thought she would burst with love for him. How lucky she was, and only the dread of his departure to Scotland marred her horizon of happiness.

The thick eyelashes fluttered and he looked at her with those strange golden eyes which always caused her heart to miss a beat.

'My little love, how long have you been awake?' His voice was still thick with sleep.

'Just now,' she said snuggling towards him.

'Come, hussy, I have much to attend to and little time to see to all.' He leapt out of bed and called to Meyrick to come and attend to his bodily needs. His clothes had been neatly laid out in the next chamber and she could hear him humming a little melody as he bathed and dressed. There was no need for her to rise so early and she nestled back into the warmth of the hollow he had so recently occupied and fell back to sleep with a little smile curving her mouth.

Roger breakfasted, attended his scribe with the clerical matters which had arisen since yesterday, then emerged into the July morning to inspect the men-at-arms and to see how his plans progressed for his coveted castle.

The young Baron of Wigmore was well pleased with his lot. Joan was, if not the most beauteous of women, a delightful companion whose only aim appeared to be finding ways to please him. She had brought him many lands, both here and in Ireland, and was connected by birth to the de Lacy and Lusignan family tree; indeed for a man in his formative years he had advanced the house of Mortimer greatly in this marriage.

There was just one cloud on his skyline: Scotland; in the next few days he had to leave for those uncertain parts and was loath to part with all that pleased him here. He felt part of these Welsh Marches and hated any time spent away from his homelands. However, when one's king ordered, subjects high- and low-born obeyed with alacrity, or suffered the consequences.

His thoughts were interrupted by the Lord of Chirk who came striding purposefully towards him.

'Ah, so you have managed to leave your love nest? I must say, nephew, you have much to bring a smile to your lips, I'll warrant. Tell me, is she…?' Roger cut him short.

'Come now, uncle, I'll not divulge my marriage-bed secrets to you or anyone. Suffice it to say she pleases me well.'

However, the older man continued. 'Ah, with two babes already you do not neglect your marital duties for certain.'

They walked towards the armoury together. The younger Roger had commissioned a new coat of mail and some plate-armour in the style he had seen worn by members of Edward's court.

All should be made to know that Roger Mortimer, Baron of Wigmore, was a force to be reckoned with amongst the Marcher lords for all his lack of years. His intention was to continue as his ancestors had done before him as a loyal follower of the Crown. It had been thus since the first Mortimer had set foot on English soil in the pay of William the Conqueror.

The Lord of Chirk's glittering black eyes admired the handsome new harness. He liked his brother's son better than any other human being since his own father. There was an adventurous spirit in the youth, coupled with an air of confidence and bravado which would carry him in good stead with the fighting men of Wales and the Marches.

'Good uncle, did you see the new charger my wife has purchased for my Scottish venture?' He was almost childlike in his pleasure at showing the beast to his kinsman. The two spent the rest of the day reviewing men-at-arms and watching the archers' skill and speed in practice. Men were still coming to Ludlow for their military duty, and the outer bailey was a continual hub of activity.

Horses were being shod, the blacksmiths pressed hard to attend to all the new mounts. Fletchers were busily reflighting quivers of arrows, wheelwrights, saddlers, all were aware of the impending departure. Grooms with fodder and water were kept busy along the line of stables. Some great horses were being groomed and stood dozing as their coats were tended as well as any maiden's hair.

The Lord of Chirk murmured, 'You appear to have all well in hand, nephew. Edmund taught his son well, methinks.'

Roger's face grew serious for a moment.

'It is my great sorrow that my father did not see all that we talked of now starting to take shape. Some of these men served with him in Wales and have done much in training the newcomers.'

'Not long to the testing time, but I think you have little to fear, nephew, from all I have seen today.'

Roger did not let his uncle see the light of satisfaction shine from his golden eyes at his words.

High up from her bower Joan watched the two Mortimer menfolk and could not help but feel glad that it was to the younger she was married and not the somewhat satanic Lord of Chirk. She had dressed carefully, patted her dark hair, then went down to the Great Hall to see all would be ready for the midday meal. How she enjoyed this role of mistress of a busy household. She called to one house carl to remove some soiled rushes and scolded him for his omission.

'Clean daily, how many times must I tell you?' she snapped, her dark eyes missing nothing. She was determined that all should be as perfect as she could make it for her lord. She turned as the two men entered, followed by members of their retinues.

'Ah, I see you are being a solicitous hostess, my sweet.' Roger came forward and took her hands, kissing them whilst looking deep into her eyes. She blushed under that intimate gaze.

'Come, all is ready, my lord. I pray you, do not embarrass me in front of our guests.'

Roger's white teeth gleamed in a radiant smile and he linked his arm around her waist and pulled her between his uncle and himself to go and eat in an atmosphere that was tinged with a little sadness at the thought of the imminent departure.

Roger was all too aware of his wife's concern and did his best to turn her mind from gloomier avenues which, after some effort, he successfully managed to achieve.

On the morrow Joan's dark eyes were filled with tears and she was unable to speak. She had tried to tell him a dozen times that she thought she was again with child, but somehow neither the moment nor the correct mood had lent itself to her purpose. Now she must watch as he made ready for his departure and who could say when he would again ride back through the gates of Ludlow and into her safe-keeping.

At her side stood her brother-in-law, John Mortimer. It would now fall to him to oversee the Mortimer estates of Wigmore and Ludlow and also those of his uncle at Chirk. It said much for the serious-faced young man, who at seventeen would have charge of such vast domains, but for all that he wished that he too was for Scotland with his kinsmen and not left with the responsibilities of the Welsh Marches.

Joan held his arm tightly.

'Do you think this venture will be of any duration?' She looked pleadingly into the grey eyes of her companion.

'It should not, for Edward's army is superior in all categories, but...' he hesitated.

'But what?' she asked anxiously.

'A nation that fights for its very existence has naught to lose and now with Bruce at the head I think it will be a knottier problem than many think.' He was looking out at the splendid spectacle that was forming in the outer bailey of the castle.

He could see his brother mounted on the magnificent courser Zeus, whose coat gleamed and whose mane and tail danced with every stride it took.

The Mortimer standard with the arms of de Geneville recently impaled onto their armorial was carried at the fore of the procession. Following the standard were Roger and his uncle, the Lord of Chirk, mounted on a great black charger heading a company of knights, the pennons flying proudly in the summer breeze which blew up from the swift-flowing waters of the Teme. Bowmen in their green leather tunics were in strict ranks with a mounted commander at their head. Pack-horses carrying food, armour and all the necessary trappings of war made a less orderly line in the rear, together with blacksmiths, wheelwrights, carpenters, cooks and all manner of people that accompanied a body of fighting men.

Roger, the young Baron of Wigmore, stood tall in his stirrups and raised his gauntleted hand in a final salutation to his brother and wife as they stood on the drawbridge of the inner bailey.

John and Joan waved back, each filled with such different emotions at this parting.

'Do not let him see you weep, dearest Joan, let him carry a prettier memory.'

She pulled herself up to her full height and took a deep breath, a watery smile playing bravely around her trembling lips. She would not let her lord go thinking her lacking in courage.

With a shout of command the company moved forward. Some horses, keen to be off, sidled and pranced towards the drawbridge. The chink and rattle of accoutrements, bits and spurs echoed behind the clatter of hooves and the sound rang round the walls of Ludlow for some minutes until the last horse had finally exited on the long journey. The tears now flowed unchecked down the round cheeks of Joan, and John, ever courteous, guided her back into the hall and called for refreshments to soothe the lady's distress, but she waved him away.

'Please! I must watch until they are out of sight.' She hurried to the steep, narrow stairwell of the tower and, panting, emerged to see the colourful column as it moved along the dusty road. Peasants in the fields stood and watched as they stole a moment from their tasks. Children ran forward to touch the garments of the knights and to seek blessings from the holy men that rode with the party.

For nigh on an hour Joan stood until her eyes grew sore and she could no longer distinguish the blue and gold surcoat of her husband. She descended to where John awaited her. He came forward with a goblet of wine.

'Come, little sister, we will aid each other in the days to come and see that all will be as our dear Roger would have it in his absence.'

She nodded dumbly, knowing that in the form of this young brother-in-law she had a true and loyal ally.

So the days ran together filled with all her motherly duties, but when alone her longings and prayers for her husband caused many sleepless nights and private tears. As the summer ripened into autumn so did Joan, for she was indeed with child and the experience both delighted her and filled her with dread. Child-bearing was still a mystery and she suddenly found herself alone without any intimate company. Her mother no longer resided in England, her sisters, Matilda and Beatrice, were both in nunneries and she was loath to seek solace from servants, however loyal and long-serving, so she held her fears and doubts to herself and sought spiritual comfort in the chapel she visited daily, praying that this child would be a healthy son.

CHAPTER XII

Berwick
October 1306

A company of men straddled the windy plain at Berwick. Before them their commander paced restlessly to and fro, whilst they sat awaiting his orders. By the frown that played across his handsome features the thoughts that passed through his mind at that time did not lie easily upon him. Inwardly he fumed at the work that had been undertaken by him and his company of late. His knightly vows were still crystal-clear in his memory and yet here they were following the orders of the Prince of Wales in a path of pillage, rape and utter destruction, murdering all who came in their way – old men, women and children – and slaughtering beasts and burning buildings across the length and breadth of the Lowlands of Scotland.

An inner anger blazed in the golden eyes and he slapped his thigh in his agitation. Not for activities such as these had he trained his men at Ludlow, nor seduced the seasoned campaigners from their retirement. What had taken place over the last few weeks in the name of war had offended the young knight's honour and he had witnessed a growing bloodlust among some of his men that bordered on barbarity.

It was as though the same terrible affliction that had infected the king now corrupted the son, and nothing but the complete annihilation of this land could appease either. What in pity's name were they doing using the cream of English chivalry and the famed skill of the Welsh bowmen to slay women and children? It would do nothing for the morale of the troops, nor would it sway any of the Scottish people to the English cause.

He shuddered; not even the thickly padded tunic and shirt of mail could combat the cold wind which blew off the North Sea across this bleak plain, and mingled with his chilly humour he felt something snap within himself. How could all this useless destruction aid Edward? Surely it would only serve to unite the people who would rise up and fight the English oppressor. Bruce would be quick to take advantage of an angered populace and win them to his own cause.

Winter would be upon them soon and there was no sign of a confrontation with 'the Bruce' himself. The weather would lock them in fast and all would be hard-pressed to find fodder and shelter in that harsh climate and scarred landscape. The more he turned the thoughts over in his head, the more determined Roger Mortimer became in his resolve.

He could achieve nothing further here and the letter from Joan burnt holes in his pocket at her news. Upon reading her missive he had felt the double-edged blade of fear and pride. Joan was carrying a child, but not easily it would seem, and he was all too aware of how many women died in childbed, and the thought perturbed him more than a little.

The Lord of Chirk rode in on his musings.

'I think this is a cursed, cold country, nephew!' he remarked as he dismounted wearily from his spume-flecked mount. 'Where are the others?' The black eyes studied the scene around him and duly noted that only his nephew's contingent had arrived as yet.

'I know nor care not!' hissed the younger Mortimer. 'This is not meat for knights nor true soldiery, methinks! Winter will soon lock us all fast in this godforsaken country and I for one am for home.'

The older man looked askance at his nephew's words.

'God's blood, Roger! You cannot leave without the king's signed warrant.'

'I tell you, warrant or no, I'm for Ludlow. Joan is ill and I feel my duty lies in that direction and not here.' He indicated to Meyrick as he spoke.

'Bah, you'd have a wench lead you by the nose just because she feels sickly. Childbearing, that's all women are good for and they can do that quite well without any further help from you. You did your part, now let the wench alone to do hers!'

'Hold your wind, I'll brook no interference from you or any.'

'Think you she will thank you for being dubbed a traitor and slain for your folly?' But his words were lost on the wind for the younger man had turned on his heel with Meyrick at his side.

Within two days of his conversation with his uncle, Roger Mortimer had made good his words and with a small, well-armed group had headed south for Ludlow.

The weather had turned to icy rain which drove into their faces as they rode, adding its own miserable tenor to their journey. They rode fast across the northern Marches and into the gentler countryside of England, but did not check their speed.

At last he saw the bountiful, low hills which flanked Ludlow and he urged his weary horse to a final effort to reach his stronghold before dark. It was old Hamo who came forward in the deepening twilight to take charge of the tired animal.

'Lord be praised, m'lord, mebbe you'll cheer the young lady's ills away for she's bin held fast to her bed these weeks past.'

Roger nodded and quickly made his way to his wife's bedside, still wearing the dust and grime of his journey so anxious was he to see for himself what ailed his wife.

An elderly waiting woman stood at the door of Joan's chamber and motioned him to be quiet.

'My lord baron, I fear the child lies awkwardly within the womb. The lady has been feverish, and so sick she's scarce kept aught down for the last week.'

'Have you sent for a physician?' His golden eyes looked wild and unreal in the light of the torch.

'Aye, three days since, but she cannot keep his potions down.'

'Send for my mother at Wigmore, she will know what to do. Hurry!'

The woman curtseyed hastily and almost ran to do his bidding. She would not bring down the anger of this young man on her head, for by the expression in his eyes he was capable of anything in his anxiety.

Softly he entered the musty, humid chamber of his wife. He could scarce credit the change wrought in her in so short a time. Is this what childbearing could do to women? But he pushed these doubts from his mind and went and held her tiny hand.

'Lady, my little sweeting, I see that all is not well with you, but have no fear, I have sent to Wigmore for aid. How long have you been so indisposed?'

The very sight of him had done more for Joan than anything during the last weeks.

'Oh, you will think me foolish, but I thank God you are home.' She broke down and wept uncontrollably. He bent forward and gathered her up in his arms.

'Come now, you will be well directly. I cannot have my wife mewed up thus because she is with child.' He crooned and rocked her gently as if she were a babe herself, and presently the weeping ceased and she lay quietly in his embrace.

'I have been so afraid!' she whispered.

'And have no need to fear further.' He spoke with more confidence than he felt for she was so pale and thin. But he seemed the certain cure for her condition, for in his presence she took heart and no longer felt alone and afraid.

'You must think me foolish, and I've tried so hard to be brave… but…' The sentence melted into tears.

'Now, you must not weep so! To be sure, you will drown the babe, I swear.' And from amidst her tears she found a wan smile.

'Oh, how I have missed you, my husband,' she whispered shyly, clinging to him, all her apprehension falling from her at the strength of his body, and the sweet concern in his wonderful eyes. He seemed to surround her with his own special aura, and she felt safe at last.

The next morning John and Olympia rode into Ludlow. Roger ran out to greet them, embracing his brother unashamedly and kissing Olympia swiftly on the cheek.

'How's this, Roger, that you are so soon back from the Scottish venture?' John's dark eyebrows rose in question.

'They achieve naught but scorched feet and hoarse throats for all that I saw. Besides, my little Joan was in sore need of my comfort. She is not carrying this child with ease and is full of demon doubts, I fear.' The golden eyes were fixed on Olympia's lovely face as he spoke.

With a little grimace she said, 'I swear if babes were born by men, the population would soon be brought to a standstill.' They all laughed and made to join Joan in her chamber.

The colour had returned faintly to the young baroness's face and she no longer felt the terror she had experienced of late. She was glad that it had been Olympia who had come with John, and not her mother-in-law. For all that stately lady's charm, Joan sometimes felt a little ill at ease in her company.

It was agreed that Olympia should stay until Joan's lying-in, which was thought to be March. Olympia had quickly got in touch with a woman famed for her skill with difficult pregnancies. The woman quizzed Joan, asking many intimate questions, but in a way that caused no offence to the shy young mother-to-be. In fact, she was so relieved to be surrounded by sound good sense and affection combined with the wise woman's ministrations that the sickness and low spirits she had previously been afflicted with were fast becoming a bad memory. Her young body was now blossoming with new life and she felt sure it would be another son.

However, the words of the Lord of Chirk were now coming true. Roger knew his sudden departure from Scotland would be made known to the king and that Plantagenet retribution would follow swiftly on his heels. He felt little surprise when the royal messenger arrived at Ludlow, flanked by sheriffs from a number of neighbouring counties, with orders to seize the lands of the Baron of Wigmore in the name of the king.

The following day Roger had ridden off to seek an audience with the king, but, finding his request unheeded, had turned to the serene and gentle Margaret of France for support. He explained most eloquently his reasons for his abrupt withdrawal from Berwick and emphasised his love and loyalty to the king, but felt sure that in like circumstances he could not have acted otherwise.

Margaret had listened closely to the young baron's plea for her intercession and was moved by his obvious sincerity. She had lightly touched the dark, curling hair as he knelt before her, and promised to do all in her power to bring the king to a proper understanding of his situation. She thought him so young to be unfairly punished.

Roger had sworn his allegiance to this charming French queen and felt sure that if anyone could aid him at this time, it could only be Margaret. He had returned to Ludlow with a lighter heart than of late, and celebrated the Yuletide feasting with Joan, John, his mother, sister Maud and Olympia. Even the commissioners were cordially invited to share in the Mortimer hospitality.

The castle rang with laughter and gaiety, for youth will frequently find the happier side of life, and these young people enjoyed the time of festivities together.

Fires blazed and candles burned brightly throughout that merry festival. Food was enjoyed by one and all, and even Joan's fluctuating fancies were well pleased. Olympia too gained comfort from the happy atmosphere and kept her constant thoughts of Warenne locked within herself. He was ever in the forefront of her mind and heart and always in her prayers.

It was on Twelfth Night that a mud-spattered rider was allowed into the presence of this family circle and announced that Edward the king had recalled his commissioners, and Mortimer was forgiven his transgressions through the mediation of the queen.

The joyous young baron made so much of that bewildered messenger that it took him some hours to take in all that had been bestowed upon him in the way of gifts. The hall rang with extra merriment that night and the toast on everyone's lips was, of course, the generous and bountiful Queen Margaret, their patron.

However, the king had made it quite clear that Roger would be expected to serve when the next move was made against the Scots, which was planned for the coming summer, and the Lord of Wigmore sent assurances that when he was called he would be amongst the front ranks of the king's army.

It was almost by chance that Olympia had word from Warenne. The castle was always busy with messengers and holy men, travelling to and fro from one great house to another. When one liveried page singled her out with the utmost guile to impart a private letter for her eyes only, she was at odds to hide her excitement and could hardly wait to find some quiet corner so that she could read his words in private.

The letter seemed as though it lived as she felt its crispness crushed against her skin. At last she managed to steal away unnoticed and broke the heavy Surrey seal. The words danced up at her:

> I have achieved naught in my quest for freedom and ask your forgiveness at my singular lack of success. Know it is not from a lack of diligence in this matter. I seek your patience and trust, for without you I am destroyed. My heart I send with this plain missive and all my love and loyalty are yours.
>
> W.

She kissed each word and pressed the whole letter to her breast. 'Oh, inanimate letter, what was he like when these words he did place on your surface? Did he smile or frown? Was he happy or sad? Speak, speak. If only you could…'

She shook her head at her madness but could not bear to destroy his words, not yet at least, for they were like a light in the darkness, a light to give her hope and strength to live until the day when they would be together.

Subtly Olympia's mood changed, there was a softer light in her eyes, and John noted that sometimes a gentle smile would linger on the corners of her curved lips at some inner happiness.

As the weeks passed Joan's body became more swollen and ungainly, and often she would grip Olympia's hand when climbing or descending the steep, narrow stairwells of the castle, fearing her lack of balance would upend her, and in so doing she would lose the precious child.

All the arrangements had been made for the lying-in. The woman who would attend the young baroness had been fetched to stay at the castle until the appropriate time, and all was now in readiness.

CHAPTER XIII

There was new life at Ludlow, a baby girl who was both hail and healthy. Roger was relieved that all had gone well and was truly delighted with his tiny daughter, but nothing seemed to please the child's mother, who did nothing but weep at the sight of the infant, even after many assurances by her husband.

So it fell to Olympia to take charge of the daily routine of the babe and it was a duty most willingly and happily fulfilled. She found an inner contentment in nursing the tiny mite and prayed that one day she would hold a child of her own, born out of her love for Warenne.

Roger spent hours comforting his wife. They were both young and strong and she must not feel so downcast. He was assured such moods sometimes affected women after childbirth.

Slowly the little baroness recovered and started to take a keener interest in the welfare of her daughter. Olympia was somewhat loath to relinquish her pleasurable duty, but understood the importance of handing over the child to her mother.

The winter slackened its grip, and with the lengthening days and spring's promise Roger once more made ready to leave for Scotland. This campaign would be undertaken with a better heart than heretofore. He was beginning to feel restless in the domestic world of women, not a state he endured willingly.

A messenger came from the Earl of Surrey to inform Roger that he would be passing through Ludlow on his way to recruit men from his estates at Bromfield and Yale. When Olympia heard the tidings her happiness threatened to overwhelm her.

In the days following, she tried to hide herself in some trivial task so that her state of excitement would go unnoticed. At night she lay awake in a torment of anticipation. Whenever possible she would make her way to the tower and climb the steps to watch for any signs of the azure-and-or checky standard of Surrey.

'Olympia, I swear you are on strings. How many times have you climbed that tower today?' Joan was at her most important self and now fully recovered. Motherhood had done much for that young woman's self-esteem, and she chided Olympia right soundly.

'We do not know the numbers in the earl's retinue and the sooner I gain that intelligence the quicker I can convey the knowledge to your kitchens and therefore bring neither waste nor want to your table, lady.'

Joan flushed. It was not often she found fault with Olympia, and, being fair-minded, saw the logic in the statement, but she would not admit the fact, and so turned on her heel and stalked away.

Late one afternoon, as the thin, watery sunlight started to fade into pale twilight, Olympia spied the longed-for sight. A large company displaying the colours of her lover came into view. Her large eyes filled with lights more brilliant than any gem, and her normally pale cheeks glowed. It was many months since she and Warenne had parted, and these last few moments seemed like an eternity.

Quickly she informed a page to alert the kitchens and then made her way to her own bower to bathe and dress. She donned a dark-green kirtle and cote-hardie. Her hands trembled so violently as she tried to arrange her long, pale hair that she had to leave it free.

She forced herself to take some deep breaths to regain her self-control, then after a few moments walked calmly down into the Great Hall. Already many of the earl's party had started to filter in. She stood, her hand seeking support from the heavy trestle, which was fast being filled with dishes of bread, fish and fruit. This was Lent, a time of fasting, and therefore no meat could be offered or eaten by any.

Just then Roger came in chatting amicably with Warenne. At his side Joan walked sedately, her hand on her husband's arm. Olympia could hear Roger extolling the virtues of Ludlow and outlining some of his plans for the castle's alteration. Neither noticed the look which flashed between Warenne and Olympia.

Olympia felt her limbs turn to water, they no longer obeyed her and her heart threatened to leap from her breast. She stood rooted to the spot, leaning on the trestle.

Roger called across: 'Come, Olympia, greet our noble guest.' He was always at his best when entertaining.

Somehow she managed to make the distance between them and extended her hand. Just the touch of him sent the blood pounding through her veins. She did not dare to look into his face, for all would recognise her true feelings. He bowed low and kissed the captive fingers in all civility.

'Lady!' His voice was low; fortunately his host and hostess had turned their attention to the fare that was before them.

'My lord earl, you are most welcome!' Then she raised her eyes and looked into the dark-blue depths where she read the message of his love and longing. The moment passed, and Olympia managed to go through the motions of propriety.

After what seemed like a lifetime Warenne excused himself and sought the privacy of his own apartment. Within minutes Olympia slipped into the chamber and flew into the arms for which she had ached for so long.

'My love, my love,' she gasped as he swept her off her feet in a delirious reunion. His lips sought hers in a passionate kiss, so rich in love and desire. Presently he held her away from him for an instant.

'The girl has become a woman without my permission.'

'Time does not obey any, even the dearest earl in all Christendom.' As she spoke she searched his swarthy face and traced the dark, swarthy contours that were etched in her memory.

He could stay his desire no longer, and carried her to his bed where they answered the ardent demands of their love. Some time after their first passionate encounter, they lay bathed in that soft world of contented happiness and satisfaction. The urgent needs of their bodies had been assuaged for the present.

'How is the Countess of Surrey?' Olympia tried to keep any bitterness from her query.

'She was hail and hearty when last I saw her.' He grinned, his crooked white teeth gleaming in the moonlight.

'Beast!' Olympia punched him playfully. The tension was now released and they fell into their old bantering habit. 'You know I'm eaten up with curiosity at what has befallen you since last we talked, and yet you play the mute bear with me.' Her green eyes shone from the soft folds of his warm, fur-covered bed.

'It has been a time to live through. The king's obsession with Scotland has premier consideration; that, and keeping his son and the Gascon from too many indiscretions.

'As for my own house, the Lady Jeanne has been ensconced at Reigate and I visit that establishment only when I am forced to do so. Enough of my events, tell me what you have been up to, minx?' He kissed her tenderly, his hand stroking her pearly, satin-soft skin as he spoke.

'Except for the Lady Joan's confinement and being entrusted with the babe's first few weeks of life, nothing untoward. Only my longing for you.' She nestled closer to him as she spoke. 'I would like to give you a child.' She looked deep into his eyes to see the effect of her words.

His expression was almost unfathomable under the black lashes, but he murmured, 'First things first, damsel. I have made enquiries in the church as to my position in this marriage and though their methods are exceedingly slow, I have been given some hope. Fear not, if necessary I shall seek the aid of Rome. We will be together as soon as it is humanly possible, believe me. My life is empty without your sweetness to fill the hours.'

'And what of other wenches at the court? Do you tell me that since our last meeting you have been faithful…to me?' Olympia teased him, satisfied that he was doing everything to break free from his vows of marriage.

He grinned at her question. 'Did not my body tell you of my constancy? Or must I show you again how you ensnare this poor "bear" in your cage?'

Her mouth curved in a smile. 'Then I pray my cage is strong enough to hold you for as long as I live.'

The touch of his flesh lit her passion and she murmured, 'Oh Warenne, I adore you.' The flame of the flesh ignited in them, and he possessed her once more. They surrendered completely to the demands of their love. Only the waters of the Teme played minstrel to the sounds of their love-making.

Roger lay on his back looking at the vaulted ceiling of the chamber he shared with his wife Joan. She lay sleeping and he was totally unaware of her presence, so lost in his own thoughts. The first flush of marital bliss was now over for him. The last pregnancy had somehow changed Joan and she was no longer the same young woman of a year ago. He loved her dearly and delighted in their family life together, but it was not thoughts of his wife and family which troubled him now. It was not Scotland which worried him unduly; that war would rumble on for some time yet. But the recent news from Ireland, there had been a ring of urgency about that situation, and he wanted to go there and judge matters for himself. There was also Ludlow to be considered. Since receiving the licence for the improvements to the castle, workmen had already started to create two completely separate apartments for himself and Joan, an arrangement he had seen at court which he now wished to feature in his own domicile. With that, and the new fortifications, he was pleased with the work in hand. Ever conscious that the lands at Wigmore and Ludlow were vulnerable to a Welsh attack, the young baron was determined to make everything as secure as possible, should such an occasion arise. Joan moaned in her sleep and he looked down at her fondly. He was beginning to realise the responsibilities that his position as Baron of Wigmore and husband and father now entailed.

He stretched his arms above his head and laced his fingers to make a pillow for his dark, curly head, a habit he had retained from boyhood. He wondered what the wheel of fate would spin into his life during the coming months. Edward's health was failing fast by all accounts, but that indomitable spirit was as keen and sharp as ever. No wonder the name of 'Hammer of the Scots' seemed so appropriate. And what would happen when the Prince of Wales became king? Would he, Roger Mortimer, be able to step higher on the ladder of ambition under the new rule? But whatever was at the forefront of his own wishes it was the events in Scotland which now dominated everyone's lives. It would never be an easy problem to resolve, that was for sure. For one thing, the lines of stores and fodder would be far harder to maintain than they had been in the Welsh conflict, and the land was continually devastated by both the English and Scots alike.

Roger had no fear of fighting; it was the way of life for a Marcher lord. He had been brought up during the Welsh unrest, and a sword lay as easy in his hand as a quill, but he felt a dark foreboding within his heart about the Scottish situation. Long discussions on the matter with Warenne had shown that, in this,

they were of like opinion. But Edward was their sovereign lord and
king, and if in his dotage he sought the annihilation of the Scots,
then they must obey his commands or suffer the royal wrath.

He turned his mind from thoughts of war back to Ludlow itself.
It was a thriving township and he wished to foster the trades, for
prosperity went hand in hand with industry and he was all for
progress.

The notions tumbled through his head in an unending variety
until sleep finally banished any further plans to another time.

The days drew closer to their departure, and this time the lady
of Ludlow did not feel so desolate at their parting. She now felt
capable of dealing with almost any situation that would present
itself in the absence of her husband.

However, this was not the case for Olympia. She felt devastated.
She had known a brief span of the sublime happiness that only
love can bring. Now she was forced to stand mute and watch as
her lover made a show of a casual farewell. There was no knowing
when they would meet again, either by accident or design.

Warenne looked even grimmer than at their last parting, and
he was firm in his resolve to send directly to the Pope for an
annulment of his marriage. Somehow he must free himself so that
he and Olympia could be together.

The day dawned blustery and the clouds hung over Ludlow like
great curtains, shrouding the surrounding hills in invisibility.

The two young women stood side by side, one a tall, slender
wisp of womanhood, with tears lurking in the vivid green eyes, and
the petite figure of Joan de Geneville, already showing the signs
of plumpness, waving confidently to her departing husband. She
was accepting the fact that there would be many farewells in her
married life. She was also aware that she had stepped from girlhood
to womanhood and motherhood which had given her a maturity.
Joan's love for Roger had moved to a quieter, more seemly plane
and sat more lightly on her conscience. Her role in life was clear,
and she knew it was a part she could play with confidence.

Nothing of the younger girl's sadness penetrated Joan's awareness, and she prattled on cheerily of time passing quickly and how
soon they would all be reunited.

However, Olympia was numb. A terrible coldness gripped her

heart. When, if ever, would she see that adored earl ride back into her life? She stood long after the last man and horse had left the scene, and it was only when the first drops of heavy rain splashed onto her hands and face that she became aware of her surroundings again. She ran back to her own bower and wept, her sobs racking the slim shoulders. For the rest of the day she remained alone.

On the journey north Roger tried in vain to draw his companion into conversation, but Warenne remained aloof. In fact, for almost the entire ride into the borders of Scotland, Warenne only barked the occasional curt orders to his troop, or answered briefly when spoken to, and seemed lost within himself.

Roger put Warenne's mood down to the futility of the impending confrontation.

CHAPTER XIV

February 1307

Edward Plantagenet sat impatiently awaiting the arrival of his son. His thick, gnarled fingers drummed an impatient tattoo on the polished trestle table before him and the servants moved uneasily in attendance, conscious of the brewing storm. Of late the once great king had lost much of his self-control, especially where his son was concerned.

At their last encounter Edward had pulled his son to his knees by the hair, saying, 'Whoreson! Misbegotten boy! Wilt thou give away lands who has never gained any? As God liveth, if it were not for fear of breaking this realm asunder, thou should'st never enjoy thy birthright.'

The outburst had been brought about when Edward had learned of his son's wishes to bestow the lands in Poitou on his favourite Gaveston. Edward had made them both swear, under pain of severe punishment, neither to give nor receive lands from each other.

Why oh why was he, Edward of England, so beleaguered by such a wastrel son and heir? Had he not quelled the rebellious Welsh, added lands in France and Normandy to England's domains? Now, when he most needed a strong son to continue his campaign in Scotland, the foolish youth was not only aiding his enemy Bruce to unite against England by laying waste lands which would provide precious forage for the English forces when they launched a full-scale invasion.

Eventually the almost indolent figure of his heir slowly entered. His clothes, although of the finest quality, sat carelessly on the tall frame of the young Plantagenet. Even the sight of him now offended Edward. The old man noted the weakness about the mouth and chin, the indifferent stare, and he felt a red rage rise up in his breast.

'So…how does the blood of undefended peasants lie on those lily-white hands?' The sentence was shouted at the younger man. The prince noted the slight impediment in his father's speech which was becoming more apparent with every word, noted too the flaming colour that flooded the once handsome face.

'I merely carried out your orders…' Before he could continue, Edward had risen, slamming his fist on the trestle as he did so.

'Liar! Would I send mine own son to aid the devil in his work, think you? I sent you to catch Bruce and his leaders, not kill the innocent. We would have had their aid, but now, due to your total lack of restraint and murdering forays, they will flock to Bruce's banner for revenge. I swear that some day I will strike you from your life if you continue to gainsay me.' Then in lower tones he hissed, 'I pray God will watch over this kingdom when I am worm bait, for I swear my son will bring it to its knees. Now get thee from my sight, the look of ye offends mine eyes.' He turned his back on the prince who merely shrugged and left the still fuming figure of his sire.

The ageing king stood for some time, still at the mercy of his rage, but as it slowly receded he thought of the French marriage he had recently negotiated with Philip of France. There lay the hope of England in the form of Isabella. The women of France were noted for their wit, charm and fruitfulness. Indeed, she would bring his son to a man's appetites and push the Gascon from his position. With these positive thoughts rising through the disappointment, Edward turned his attention to other pressing matters of state.

Some weeks later Edward was again thrown into a mean mood. Bruce had emerged from hiding and, with a handful of men, had won a decided victory over Aymer de Valence at Loundoun Hill, quickly followed by an even greater conquest of Ralph de Monthermer, Earl of Gloucester, at Ayr.

Two of Edward's most experienced commanders had been beaten by a small band of men led by his bitter enemy Robert Bruce, erstwhile Earl of Carrick. Somewhere deep in Edward beat a white-hot rage against his one-time friend and protégé Bruce. So the flame of freedom still burned in Scotland, but the 'Hammer of the Scots' was determined to quench that flame e'er long.

Already many of the great families of Scotland had fallen to the English executioner or been butchered in horrendous fashion:

Fraser, Wallace, James Douglas the elder, the Earl of Atholl and Bruce's own brothers, all dead. Even Bruce's wife and daughter were Edward's prisoners, together with his sisters and the proud Countess of Buchan, who even now hung in a cage outside the castle of Berwick. But nothing, it seemed, would bring the Bruce to heel.

As England's king brooded on recent events and made his plans for the imminent invasion of Scotland, Mortimer and Warenne made their way slowly to the royal standard at Carlisle. Information about the interview between Edward and his son came to the ears of the young lords, and they had exchanged knowing glances at its import. Roger felt sure that his action in leaving the field in the autumn must now be clear to his sovereign.

Warenne's old adversary Gaveston had been sent from court and there was hope that the impending marriage of the Prince of Wales would make the break a permanent one.

News of Edward's slow progress reached their camp. The health of the monarch was now causing serious concern. He was forced to make the journey on a litter, and this information alone told them more than words how low their sovereign's health had sunk.

'Nothing short of impending death would keep Edward from his saddle, I swear,' said Warenne quietly. ''Tis only his ire against Bruce coupled with his willpower that has kept death at bay for this span of months. God's teeth, with all his failings, I shudder to think what will become of England once the prince is king.'

Mortimer looked hard at Warenne. The thought had never been aired in public before, and the two fell into a deep and sombre silence. The weather was humid, and thunder rumbled round the tents where the men of Surrey and Mortimer were camped. Many sat dicing or cleaning their weapons. The sound of a flute soared skyward to mingle with the oncoming storm.

Tethered horses sidled and nickered nervously in their lines. Pages and squires sat burnishing armour; there was an air of expectation about them, accentuated by the storm. The raucous voices of the men-at-arms, laughing and shouting lewd stories and jokes to one another, joined with the noise from the blacksmith's forge, and the rhythmic beating of the hammer. The smell of cooking, sweat, and leather hung in the afternoon heat, like a pungent curtain.

Suddenly a shout from one of the scouts rang out above the din of the campsite.

'A rider, a rider comes.'

Warenne strode forward and waited the arrival of the messenger. Minutes later the sweat-soaked rider slid to a halt and slithered from the saddle to fall at his feet. He handed a crumpled scroll to the earl.

Warenne turned and entered his tent away from the prying eyes of his men. He quickly broke the seal and read its contents. A loud hiss escaped his lips as he let the missive fall to the ground. He rubbed his chin thoughtfully before bending to retrieve the historic message, then without further ado sent his page to summon all the commanders to his presence.

When all were assembled, Warenne looked across at the group of now familiar faces and raised his hands for silence.

'Gentlemen, the news I have to convey to you is of the utmost importance.' He paused awaiting their full attention before continuing. 'I'm afraid that our lord and king Edward Plantagenet is dead.' For an instant there was stony silence. The news had stunned young and old alike.

Some of the older knights who had served with Edward on many of his campaigns fell to their knees and prayed, shedding unashamed tears of grief. From those still standing, a murmur ran through the company like a ripple, echoed by a clap of thunder from the storm outside.

The news ran through the camp like the summer lightning that now flickered across the lowering heavens. Mortimer came and stood by Warenne.

'What of this campaign now? Do you think the son will continue on the same route as the sire?' Their eyes locked for an instant.

'For the time being at least, he must in all honour continue, but I do not think it will be to the young Edward's taste. If, with all these forces, he cannot bring about the defeat of the Scots, then in my estimation Bruce will have time to grow strong enough to prolong this war. Now that the 'Hammer of the Scots' has fallen, Bruce will see this as a chance he could not have expected. He has providence to thank for this day's news, seeing as he is now excommunicated.' Warenne's eyes flickered as he spoke.

Almost the first act of Edward II as king was to recall Gaveston and bestow the title of Earl of Cornwall on his favourite. He removed Aymer de Valence as commander-in-chief in Scotland and replaced him with his uncle, the Earl of Richmond.

The vow that Edward I had sought from his son, to carry his bones into battle against Bruce, was to be ignored, and almost from the first it became obvious that Edward II would withdraw his army and there would be no confrontation with the Scots at this time.

As the solemn procession bearing the body of the late king made its way to Waltham Abbey, Roger Mortimer moved to the side of Warenne.

'What do you think of this turn of events?' Roger kept his voice low, not wanting anyone else to overhear their conversation.

'Carrick will have cause for celebration, I'll be bound,' muttered Warenne. 'He would almost certainly have been crushed by the old king's forces, but now...who knows when, if ever, such a host will be brought across the borders again.'

Mortimer nodded and still even more quietly said, 'I think this move to disperse our army will prove an obstacle, by which this king will forever find himself stumbling over.'

'Mm, but we can only wait and see, at least for the time being.' Warenne's dark-blue eyes did not disclose any of the thoughts that whirled in his head. Maybe now he would gain his freedom. Whereas the older king would never budge on the subject there was just a chance that the son would be more amenable to the annulment.

Mortimer carried on in a lighter vein. 'Well, after the season of mourning we shall see a coronation and a wedding, I'll warrant. More to my taste than funerals.'

Warenne grinned wryly. 'First we must bury the old Plantagenet, and bury him deep, for I have a curious feeling that his son will do many deeds that not even death will chill his rage.'

BOOK TWO

CONFLICTS

CHAPTER XV

Wallingford
December 1307

The day was cold and a north wind whipped the flaps of the pavilions and tugged at the brightly coloured pennants unmercifully. However, the inclement weather had not deterred the crowds from venturing forth to watch the tournament at Wallingford that December of 1307.

It had been broadcast that Piers Gaveston, the newly created Earl of Cornwall, had thrown down a challenge to any Anglo-Norman knights to come and face a contingent of Gascons in the lists. It was a challenge that no true English knight could refuse.

The first to pick up the gauntlet was none other than John de Warenne, Earl of Surrey. He and a number of Anglo-Norman nobles had been quick to accept. They were all eager to rub the noses of the proud Gascons in the dirt.

After the first day of the contest the Gascons had been ahead on points. Twelve of their company had bested their opponents on the field, leaving only eight victorious Anglo-Normans. But the battle which was causing the most excitement was that between Gaveston and Warenne.

Both had won the heats and their first encounter with each other had ended in a draw. Now the tension mounted as the contestants made ready for the second day's event, the mêlée.

Warenne sat grim-faced, the breeze blowing in through the tent as his squire strapped on his armour. The great helm advertised a brilliant blue plume, the only adornment to his plain harness.

Gaveston, however, had a spectacular coat of armour, embellished with gold leaf. The decorations on his helm were in the shape of a prancing horse with semi-precious stones for the eyes and hooves. He looked magnificent, as he sat his chestnut destrier in the parade towards the platform, where Edward II sat amongst his courtiers.

The intimate smile which passed between Gaveston and Edward denoted the confidence they felt in the outcome of the day's competition. No one in the crowd seemed to notice the cold, for as the minutes passed the tension became more acute. It was no secret that there was bad blood between Warenne and Gaveston; on the field their actions would be allowed to speak stronger than words.

At last the fanfare rang out; the single note brought all the combatants to horse and the richly caparisoned procession paid formal tribute to the king. The Gascon contingent waved and smiled at the crowd, bowing to any pretty maiden who caught their eye, aware of their reputation in the lists.

The Anglo-Norman knights were less ostentatious in their apparel, and did not court the crowd's favour as did the foreigners. Headed by Warenne, they rode to the dais where Edward sat swathed in an enormous fur cloak. He nodded to the herald to start the day's entertainment. Again the fanfare blared out, causing some of the great destriers to prance and squeal in anticipation, for they knew the signal as well as any human contestant.

The mêlée was in fact a simulation of a battle. The two sides drew up opposite each other and, at a given command from the herald, charged towards each other with couched lances. Should a contestant quickly defeat his quarry he was then free to take the horse and, in some cases, the armour from his vanquished foe. When this had been noted, he would look for another adversary. There was much to be won at a tournament: honour, prestige, to say nothing of monetary prizes and of course a young damsel's favour.

None of these things were uppermost in the mind of John de Warenne that day, only the burning desire to oust Gaveston from his pedestal and make him eat English dirt, as he had once promised. To see the proud Gascon on his knees would be more than enough reward, especially before Edward and this critical crowd.

Warenne took his place at the fore of the English line. He turned his destrier round to face the hated enemy, picking out the figure of Gaveston before he snapped shut his visor, for he would devote his whole attention to this popinjay's downfall in the coming battle.

Across the bleak sward a single blast from the herald brought the whole mass of mounted knights into action. The earth shuddered under the hooves of the mighty horses. The crowds leaned forward pressing each other for a better view. Even Edward held the arms of his gilt chair so tightly that his knuckles showed white. Jousting was as dangerous as it was exciting; many had fallen in the lists never to rise again, or had been carried off with such terrible wounds that they were never able to fight another battle.

The crash of the impact rang out over the noise of the crowd. Above the howl of the wind, horses squealed and men shrieked out as well-aimed lances found their mark and felled them like wheat before the scythe.

Warenne had spotted his prey and had ridden straight and hard at the figure of Gaveston. He gripped his lance and held it steady with all his powerful strength. He urged his fine destrier to an even faster pace. The Gascon had been well aware of Warenne's intention and he held his horse steady until the instant before impact, then hauled on the reins to try to avoid Warenne's deadly lance. But Warenne was quick and accurate, and he had developed an uncanny knack of being able to anticipate his opponent's next move. As Gaveston feinted to the left, but spurred his horse hard to the right, Warenne slightly altered his angle of approach, and his mount, obedient to the touch of his spur, moved instantly to his rider's bidding. The crash, as Gaveston failed to achieve his manoeuvre, even brought a grunt from Warenne's lips. The Gascon could not withstand the force of Warenne's thrust and he fell heavily to the ground.

There was a gasp from the crowd for Gaveston was no mean fighter. Warenne wheeled his great steed round, dropped his lance and drew his mighty broadsword. Then as the Gascon rose slowly to his knees, another unhorsed Gascon, seeing the plight of his patron, ran forward with his own horse and with amazing speed aided Gaveston back into the saddle.

Although the horse was strange to him it had been well schooled in the art of jousting and quickly gathered its powerful muscles to adhere to its new rider's will. There had only been enough time to mount and catch the reins before Gaveston saw the mighty frame of Warenne bearing down on him. With all his inherent agility, Gaveston managed to draw his sword just as Warenne's flashing blade crashed down in a slicing movement. Gaveston could only brace himself against the blow, which jarred him until his teeth rattled within his helm, but somehow he withstood the onslaught as Warenne thundered past.

Warenne's destrier was nothing if not supple and within a short space had slid to an abrupt halt and, in a remarkable movement, reared up and swung round on its haunches. The crowd was by now in uproar and cheered and hooted in their appreciation of the exploits of the contestants, especially at the duel going on between Warenne and Gaveston.

But although Warenne knew he had the upper hand, he would not let over-confidence be his master or ruin his revenge. By the time they came at each other again, Gaveston had collected himself and his wits in readiness against the burly Englishman's onslaught. However, Warenne was not to be so easily thwarted. He stood up as high in his stirrups as he could and smashed his blade down at the vulnerable part, the point where the armour and the helm joined. The Gascon was nothing if not nimble, even in his heavy armour, but still not quite quick enough to avoid the deadly blow. It failed to strike exactly the right spot but caught Gaveston a stunning blow at the side of his head. No one could have withstood that savage attack, and the Gascon toppled from his borrowed horse like a lifeless puppet.

The crowd rose to its feet. A moan escaped from Edward's lips and his face turned deathly pale. Warenne knew that Gaveston would not rise to face him again that day and he wheeled his sweating mount round and flung himself into the thick of the gritty competition once more.

He felt so elated at his victory, invincible in fact. But by now the action had slowed down considerably. Many horses ran about loose and Gascon and Anglo-Norman alike were being helped from the field. For of that doughty group that still stood toe-to-toe battling it out with all their skill and courage, only two remained mounted; the rest, dog-weary, fought with flagging strength and ebbing stamina.

Warenne had seen the only remaining Gascon still horsed and urged his labouring mount towards his foreign counterpart. The knight was galloping towards him swinging a mace in a figure of eight motion. Warenne gripped his shield and at the last instant hauled his mount right across the path of the oncoming Gascon, thrusting his shield hard into the face of his opponent. The mace glanced off the shield, and the Gascon's mount, not wanting to crash full tilt into Warenne's horse, squealed its protest and reared violently trying to avoid the other animal. Warenne's steed neatly dodged the flying hooves and remained unscathed, thanks to its agility, but the two consecutive moves were the undoing of the ill-fated Gascon, who tipped backwards from his horse and lay motionless on the ground.

Warenne could feel the sweat running down his body, his hands wet inside the steel gauntlets and his muscles screaming for rest, as he urged his weary beast to seek another foe, but by this time the contest was ended. He alone remained unscathed, the undisputed victor of the mêlée.

He was thankful as he made his way triumphantly back to the royal rostrum, patting his sweat-streaked steed, which had proved such a worthy partner that day. The herald announced the results in clear tones, but the uproar of the crowd threatened to drown all in their clamour for the hero of the field. Patiently the herald waited until some semblance of order had returned and continued undaunted.

'The winner of the mêlée for the Anglo-Norman contingent is Sir John de Warenne, Earl of Surrey. The score at the end of the second day's competition: the Gascons lead by three clear strikes.' There was some hissing from the crowd mingled with cheers. The herald continued, 'I charge you all to meet here at noon tomorrow for the final event of the meeting.'

Almost before the words had died Edward made a hasty departure to learn how his friend fared after his fall. Even that slight could not diminish Warenne's sense of wellbeing.

Just then a bright-eyed girl ran out of the throng and caught at his bridle. In her hand she clutched a bright-blue kerchief.

'My lord earl, I beg your indulgence, pray wear this favour for the morrow's contest.'

He sat looking down at the dark, round eyes and bright, coppery-red hair. She was like a flame in the dark winter's afternoon. He judged her to be no more than ten years of age.

'Pray give me one good reason why I should obey such a forward young maid?' He could not resist teasing the child. She looked all eyes and hair.

'The truth is I had a wager with my brother that you would wear my favour.' Her face had suddenly become serious, but there was still the eagerness in the brown eyes.

'And pray, what did you wager?' He was caught by her complete lack of self-consciousness and guile.

'His pony! It's faster and bolder than the one I've been given. Almost as brave as the one you rode here today. Will you? Please! Please! It means so much to me.' Her face was alight with her earnest pleas.

'Indeed!' He could no longer keep the smile from his lips and he bent down and caught her little kerchief.

'Then you can tell your brother you have won your wager. Now, tell me, what is your name? For if I win the tournament you shall be queen of the festivities.'

Her eyes sparkled like autumn pools as she answered gaily. 'Maud de Nereford, my lord. I am from Norfolk.'

'Then Maud of Nereford, wear your prettiest dress tomorrow for I have it in my heart to win this contest.'

There was a commotion amongst the tightly packed throng, as a well-dressed man of early middle years pushed through and caught Maud by the hand. He turned to Warenne, bowed, and said apologetically, 'My lord earl, I humbly beg your pardon for my daughter's pertness. She shall be punished for this act of impropriety.' Warenne held up his hand.

'Nay, I implore you, do nothing so harsh. She shall be my lucky talismaid. What more fitting than a damsel from Norfolk?' He looked at the girl again.

'We are more than a match for these Gascons, eh lass?'

She smiled and nodded vigorously, but did not speak in front of her father, for it was obvious that he was still displeased at her act.

Warenne moved on, a smile flickering around his mouth. He wished with all his heart that Olympia had shared this day with him and seen the child with the flaming hair. She would have admired the innocent, daring spirit. He came to his tent and dismounted wearily. The groom rushed forward and took charge of his steed whilst he was aided out of his coat of mail. He then let his body take its well-earned reward in a hot tub.

At the evening's celebrations many of the ladies cast admiring glances at the Earl of Surrey, and he found the new experience quite amusing. He had never considered himself a ladies' man, but there was no denying that during that evening he was well favoured by women young and old alike. Olympia would have had the right phrase for the occasion, he did not doubt, and would have pricked his air of self-satisfaction before it took too great a hold on him.

However, most of the men did not endorse the women in their choice for admiration, for it was now blatantly obvious that Piers Gaveston's peevish frame of mind was reflected in the king's attitude towards the Anglo-Norman knights.

Warenne was moved neither by the inviting glances from the women nor the dark glowering looks of the Gascon.

His dark-blue eyes held a light of triumph that reached far deeper than any of the superficiality which surrounded him, and he joked and drank with circumspection. Already he was thinking of the morrow's contest and he would not overindulge his appetites that night, like the hounds before the hunt. He glanced towards his quarry who was now sharing a trencher with Edward. They were so engrossed in each other that it almost turned Warenne off his meal. Maybe the arrival of the French Princess Isabella would put a stop to this unhealthy relationship.

Warenne slipped away from the company as soon as he judged his absence would cause little comment. Those who did spy his departure merely smiled and nudged each other, thinking some lady waited for his attentions. It would have been a correct assumption had Olympia been present. However, no one waited on his company.

Warenne strolled towards the place where he knew his pages and squires would be spending their evening. He decided to make a diversion and went to stroke the soft muzzle of his great bay destrier Pellinore.

'Have plenty of rest, we have much to do on the morrow and I shall need all of your courage and skill, my friend.' The animal nickered at his soft tones. He pulled its ears gently and patted the hard muscles on the gleaming neck. He turned as he heard soft footsteps approaching.

'Oh, it's you, my lord! I thought someone might be attempting to misuse Pell.' The bow-legged little groom emerged from the shadows. Warenne grinned.

'I'm glad to see you have your eyes and ears open, Seth, you should never underestimate the cunning of the Gascons.' The craggy face of the groom cracked into a toothless smile.

'I reckon your lordship and Pell will show them foreigners just who's master, eh! eh!' He chortled.

Warenne nodded. 'That's certainly my intention. Now I bid you godnight, Seth. Stay close to Pell.'

'Aye, m'lord, I will that, have no fear.'

Warenne walked away, confident that all was well with his stallion as there was no better groom in Christendom than Seth. He moved softly amongst the shadows of the tents as he made his way to his own. The voices of the various nationalities echoed on the frosty night air. There was a special atmosphere surrounding a tournament, not the same as war but no less exciting, and he felt a tingle run through his body. Everything seemed sharper, clearer somehow: sounds more concise; aromas more piquant; friendship more acute. It was as though the sense heightened in expectation.

Warenne entered his tent and smiled at the fresh faces of his squires that gazed back at him with undisguised hero-worship. They had won their wagers with the Gascon squires and, although they knew all rested on the morrow's outcome, were confident in the prowess of their lord to win the victor's crown of laurels.

'Off with you, we have a busy day ahead of us and a good night's rest will not come amiss.' Warenne watched as they all bid him godnight and then threw himself onto his couch. He lay thinking about Olympia and racked his brain for some excuse to visit Ludlow. He had not yet approached Edward about his divorce, and knew it would be foolish to make any attempt at this time. He had, however, sent emissaries to Rome, but it would take time before they returned with any answer. Nothing could dull the ache he had for the pale, willowy merchant's daughter.

He wished that his grandsire still lived. The old man had been a stickler for convention in matters feminine and he was sure that he would not have approved of his grandson's relationship. But that did not alter the fact that he would have liked him to have met Olympia for all that.

Finally, weariness won its battle and he fell into a dreamless sleep.

Next day he woke refreshed just as dawn's wan light began to paint the winter sky. There had been a severe frost during the night and everywhere was covered in a mantle of white hoar. He rose and went to where his stallion was tethered, and after a few brief words with his groom mounted and rode away from the village of canvas across the frozen landscape. He kept Pell to a steady, rhythmic trot at first.

The wind had dropped; it looked set fair for the final day of the contest. Warenne felt good; he had waited a long time to meet Gaveston on a field of combat and bring to fruition the promise he had made at the Feast of the Swans. Now the time was almost here, he felt confident he could bring the proud Gascon to his knees.

The sound of hooves and chink of bit and spur mingled with a robin's solitary morning song. In the distance a dog fox barked and from somewhere nearby cattle were lowing. A distant cock heralded the new day.

Warenne urged his great steed into a canter and as the stallion plunged forward he felt such exhilaration he wanted to shout aloud. If only Olympia were here to witness today's event... As he reached a rise, he reined back and stopped to survey the surrounding countryside. The mettlesome horse was restless. The stallion just wanted to be off again and Warenne knew that he must keep the powerful beast from becoming too excited or he would be too unsettled for the coming joust.

Soon Pell relaxed under Warenne's steadying hands, content to jog back towards the awakening campsite. Seth ran forward to take the bridle as Warenne dismounted and patted the bay's shining neck. It was too soon to don the heavy armour for the tournament, so Warenne wandered round the camp exchanging a word here and there with the members of the Anglo-Norman knighthood who would also be in the day's contest. An armourer, long known to Warenne, laughed at an apprentice's antics. The boy was trying to beat out a piece of dented plate from yesterday's mêlée and seemed so ham-fisted that even the most serious of watchers could not help but be moved to a burst of merriment.

As Warenne continued his walk he met one of the Hospitaller Knights, there to tend the wounded, and as they fell into step he made some wry comment about hoping that would be the last time he would see him that day.

At the edge of the encampment he decided to continue towards the gaggle of hucksters and traders, pedlars and dealers, who always attended a tournament trying to sell their wares. There he spotted the bright, flaming hair of Maud de Nereford bobbing about among the growing throng. She had stopped before a pedlar selling ribbons and stood thoughtfully choosing from the streams of coloured silks hanging from a large wooden tray.

Warenne moved to her side and waited until she became aware of his presence. He noted that her pale face was sprinkled with freckles. She wrinkled her nose, then said to him without any preamble, 'Which shade do you think I should choose, my lord earl?' She held up half a dozen bright ribbons in her hand for his inspection.

'Choosing maiden's fineries is not one of my talents, I fear, damsel,' he said mockingly.

Her dark, round eyes studied him for a moment, then she said, 'Well, tell me your favourite colour and I shall buy that one.'

'Child, I like many shades – green, crimson, purple, blue…'

She interrupted, 'I scarce think red with my colouring. Blue I have in abundance and green; so I think I shall pick a silver one. How think you of that choice?'

He smiled, delighted by her bright, cheerful personality and complete lack of self-consciousness. 'Yes, I think you have chosen well.'

She paid the pedlar and carefully folded her precious ribbon away, then, quite without thought, tucked her hand through Warenne's arm and walked beside him through the ranks of men and women who were busily inspecting and buying the wares on show.

'Are you not married, my lord earl?' She spoke in a soft, lilting accent.

'Aye, to a royal maid not much older than yourself.'

'Then why is she not here to watch you vanquish the Gascons?'

The question was completely artless and he paused before he answered. 'She has only recently gone to my castle in Sandal, and I thought the weather too cold for her to travel such a long way for a mere tournament. Besides, she is at present making ready for the Yuletide season, I believe.'

Maud frowned. 'I would not let a little cold put me off seeing my husband at a tournament.'

'Ah, but you are of a stronger stock than the royal bud, Mistress Maud.'

'Rubbish!' she said vehemently. 'Well, if she be a Plantagenet, they are renowned for their strength and longevity. I think there must be some other reason why you are unwilling to impart your reasons to an inquisitive maid, my lord.'

He rubbed his beard at her words. 'I think you are too sharp by half, Maud de Nereford, and if my blade has but half the edge of your tongue, then my task will be easy this afternoon.'

She shrugged. 'But surely the contest is not *à l'outrance*. Mm. So…you also think I am too outspoken?' She did not wait for his reply. 'My father scolds me constantly and says it is a bad fault and I must curb my speech. But I charge you, how can I change what I am? If I say other than I feel, would I then not be dubbed hypocrite? Or remained silent – then surely a dullard would be my title.' She sighed deeply. 'It would seem nothing I do will please. My father says the sooner he can wed me to some unsuspecting man the better, and then my shortcomings will be the problem of my spouse. But I do not wish to leave my home, at least, not yet. Nor do I wish to be constantly curbed and chastised.' She pulled at Warenne's sleeve so that he stopped and looked down at her anxious face. 'Do you beat your wife?'

'Heaven preserve us, child, I scarce see the maid, and when I am in her company it usually is on formal occasions and certainly not a place for beating her.'

Maud seemed satisfied, for she continued again in step with her champion.

'I hope when they do find a husband for me he will cast a similar shadow as the Earl of Surrey, and be not afraid to fight.'

'That was prettily said and I thank you for your compliment. I know you speak honestly. For your sake, Maud, I hope they find you a man worthy of your spirit and forthrightness, but think we would make a mismatched pair and no denying. Now I must take my leave of you and make ready to bring the Gascon to earth. Remember, wear your prettiest apparel. Adieu!'

He bent and kissed her hand solemnly, then turned on his heel and left her watching his retreating figure with a look of undisguised sadness on her face. She was loath to lose his company. To her, he seemed the only person who did not find fault or rebuke her fast-running tongue.

The sun grew stronger as the morning progressed and the frost melted into tiny vapour spirals which wreathed up from the earth like miniature Medusas. On his return to the lines of tethered horses Warenne saw Pell's caparison and accoutrements all neatly polished and hung up in readiness. Seth was busily grooming the stallion's shining coat.

The big horse stood restlessly stamping its hooves, impatient for action.

'He senses this is an important day,' Warenne said to Seth, running a knowledgeable hand over the well-muscled frame of his mount as he spoke.

'Aye, my lord, but he'll not let you down.'

'I only hope I can do the same for him, Seth.'

They looked at each other for a moment both reading the other's thoughts on the matter. It was not uncommon for a horse to be mortally wounded in a tournament and that very idea tormented the tiny, bow-legged man, who had seen the bay colt born and been instrumental in his schooling.

However, there was always so much to be done on the day that there was scant time to dwell on any misgivings. Seth had a habit of pinning a medal of the Blessed Virgin to Pell's bridle for protection and today would be no exception.

Maud de Nereford forced her way towards the front of the platform. A large, florid-faced man angrily abused her for her impertinence.

'But the Earl of Surrey is to wear my favour,' she returned in her defence.

''Pon my soul, what next? Such nonsense! Do you think me addled in the head, wench? The Earl of Surrey would not lower himself to such a degree as to be associated with a carrot-topped jade.' His small, piggy eyes scanned the child's defiant stare.

'Oaf!' She kicked his thick shin with her tiny foot. 'Take that for your pains, numbskull. I do not speak untruths.' By now the crowd were becoming involved in the altercation and smirks and nudges were exchanged.

The man was known to most of the locals as a former sheriff of Wallingford, a man much in love with his own person and blown up with self-importance. To be attacked so forcefully by a maid was causing much amusement amongst the onlookers.

Thick veins stood out on the man's bull-like neck, and he was just about to strike Maud when a commanding voice rang out above the clamour.

'Who dares to raise a hand against so fair a maid? I think the match unfair. The maid would win on words alone and no mistake but if that contest is too tame for your taste, then I shall be at your service presently to test your skill in arms.' A ripple of mirth ran round the platform.

Maud, wide-eyed, smiled down at her benefactor, grateful for his timely intervention. Warenne looked magnificent in the brave wintery sunlight. Gone was the dowdy garb of yesterday. His armour gleamed and his surcoat of azure-and-or checky was of the finest silk; on the one shoulder, a clasp of diamonds and rubies glistened with such intensity it almost seemed alive. The gems dazzled the eyes of the beholder.

By this time the crowd had turned its attention from the main parade to the scene between the resplendent earl, the one-time sheriff, and a pert, flame-haired girl. Warenne's voice rang out again.

'Come, sirrah! I would learn the name of the bully who harries the damsel whose favour I carry this day. On this you can rely, you shall carry home a remembrance of *my* displeasure.'

At these words Maud blushed to the roots of her flaming red hair. She looked quite striking in her cloak of rich-brown velvet trimmed with squirrel fur. Beneath was a gown of palest blue and her dark-brown eyes shone with pride and excitement.

'May God go with you, my lord, and give you this day.'

'My thanks, Mistress Maud.' He bowed deeply to her, then rode on again to regain his place in the parade. Her tiring-woman was just in time to witness the last exchange and was still gasping from her efforts to keep pace with her energetic young mistress.

Some people had moved aside to give Maud a seat and a better view. It was not every day that one of England's premier earls played a gallant to such as Maud de Nereford, and the crowd had taken her to their hearts, for the English are renowned for their love of the underdog.

No doubt she would be severely punished when her father was told of the day's events, but she did not care what she must suffer in the future; today was hers. She scarce heard the words of the roll-call or the order of the fray, and only when Warenne's name was mentioned did she take heed. It would seem that Gaveston and Warenne were to be the final bout of the day.

The first two rounds were, to say the least, lacking in entertainment; the Gascons won both rounds with little effort. However, the next contest was a complete turnabout. The Anglo-Norman knight, one John de Leyburne, had used his lance to such devastating effect that, even though blunted, it had run clean through his opponent's shield, causing a nasty fall. His adversary, saved only by the thick armour-plate from receiving a serious wound, and although he had tried to continue the fight, it was clear that the doughty Anglo-Norman was more than a match for the Gascon. The crowd cheered their approval as the herald announced the victory.

There were now only another three bouts before Warenne's and Maud could scarce contain her excitement. Another Anglo-Norman won, but the next two rounds were Gascon victories, and one of the Norman knights had been sorely hurt into the bargain.

As the final contestants rode into the lists the crowd was abuzz with anticipation; all knew by now of the feud between the two earls and after the wounding of the Norman, feelings were also running high.

Maud rose to her feet and cheered her champion's name at the top of her voice. Only the firm grip of her tiring-woman reminded her that she was a young lady and not a member of the common rabble. It was a hard task for the somewhat plain, unimaginative woman, who found her charge more than a handful.

A hush fell over the colourful crowd; all felt that the moment of truth was at hand. Victory would be fought for with no quarter given or requested, with only the skill of the contestants to aid them, the vain Gascon and the proud Anglo-Norman, both premier earls of the realm.

Maud plucked anxiously at the fur on her cloak in her nervousness as Warenne and Gaveston rode before the dais whereon Edward the king sat flanked by his courtiers and minions. Thunderous applause broke out as the two rode forward, both sitting tall and straight in their saddles, each filled with a hard resolve to vanquish the other.

Gaveston smiled broadly towards his monarch and friend, his high-cheekboned face almost feminine in its beauty, with large, limpid eyes and full-lipped mouth.

Warenne in contrast had nothing feminine about his countenance. He was broad and powerful, oozed masculine prowess,
and in Maud's eyes was by far the more handsome of the pair. She
dismissed Gaveston in her childlike loyalty towards her champion
which blinded her to the charms of the other man.

She could not hear what was being said by the king and the earls,
but knew some manner of discourse was passing between them
for she could see the movement of their mouths. Then Edward
signalled for the fanfare to be sounded and the scene was set for
the final, and most vital, bout at that tournament of Wallingford.

The two adversaries rode towards their respective pavilions
where the standards of Surrey and Cornwall stood boldly at each
end of the arena, bathed in bright sunlight. They took the heavily
plumed helms from their saddle bows and donned them as the
crowd buzzed with growing excitement.

Then, almost in unison, they went to collect the blunted lances,
the tension of the moment communicating itself to their highly
bred mounts, which danced and capered to the allotted places
at each end of the wattle hurdles which marked the line of the
charge.

A signal from the herald and the two mighty destriers plunged
forward as the two knights levelled their lances. With visors shut
tight, two pairs of eyes gleamed from the dark depths, judging,
gauging, marking the other's position and finally narrowing as the
moment of impact became imminent.

The crowd gasped and rose to its feet as Warenne's lance snapped
on impact with Gaveston's shield.

To Maud it was a terrible moment; all could end with this first
blow. But without being shifted from his saddle Warenne quickly
rode to gather another lance from his end of the arena. It gave the
Gascon the advantage in the next charge for he was able to gain
maximum momentum, whereas Warenne was still urging Pell to a
gallop when the next strike took place.

A loud ooh! aah! from the crowd as neither scored, the gleaming
lances glancing harmlessly off the shields. Pell was by now at full
gallop and Warenne checked the bay hard, causing him to rear
round in an almost impossible turn, gaining precious seconds in
so doing.

The next strike again both took on their shields with no points awarded. Maud felt her chest contract; she was quite sure she had not taken a breath since the contest started.

On the third missed strike the herald sounded for lances to be discarded and field weapons to be used. Gaveston had chosen to use the ball and mace, more commonly known as the 'morning star', Warenne the more usual battle-axe.

Surrey knew that he must keep a steady nerve and cool head against the Gascon's deadly weapon. Even though the spikes on the steel ball had been blunted it could still split a steel helm or armour-plate and shatter mail as easily as a maid pushes a pin into a cushion, but it could also be as lethal to the user if not correctly controlled.

Gaveston was counting on his extra height to gain an advantage for even he knew Surrey was the stronger of the two, but fast reflexes and cruel cunning had won Gaveston a reputation as a champion of the joust.

By now the two destriers were breathing heavily and plumes of steam were hitting the cold afternoon air, causing the two bedecked beasts to look like fiery dragons. The earth shook under the thundering hooves as each man prepared for another strike.

Warenne could see the deadly ball begin to swing in the Gascon's grasp. There would be no second chance; he must not fail to judge the exact rhythm of that fearful spherical object, or he would not see the morrow. He saw Gaveston bring back his shoulders and stand high in his stirrups ready to smash the spiked orb onto his head, but Warenne's accurate timing and cool nerve did not fail him for, just as the chain holding the ball snaked upwards, he hauled hard on Pell's bridle causing the stallion to swing violently away from the line of the wattle hurdles and out of reach of the deadly weapon. But, in missing the man it crashed down onto Pell's flank and not even the heavily padded caparison could save the stallion from a searing wound.

It screamed in agony and tried to run from the scalding pain. Only the expert horsemanship of Warenne saved them from a disastrous exit. Somehow, he steadied the wounded steed as he leapt off. Seth ran forward leading a second mount and took charge of the bleeding Pell.

Warenne quickly mounted his new destrier, leaving the stricken animal in the care of his groom. There was no time to think, only to act, to bring to bear all the years of practice for just such a moment as this. Rage now burned through Warenne. Nothing would stop him bringing about the Gascon's downfall before his own castle of Wallingford.

Whilst Warenne was busily exchanging horses, Gaveston was having his own moments of anxiety for, when the swinging sphere had found nothing but thin air to beat against, it had swung out of control. At full gallop Gaveston found trying to avoid his own weapon no easy matter. Moreover, his mount had been unnerved by the screams of the other stallion's agony. The incident had caused groans from the crowd, but had also given the Earl of Surrey the precious moments needed to rejoin the fray.

Warenne gritted his teeth beneath the burnished helm with its bright plumes tossing and dancing in the afternoon sunlight. Again the two men charged at each other; Warenne held himself like a coiled spring, sitting almost motionless in his saddle; he was on a fresher mount and must keep the animal's stride even for his deadly purpose. About a dozen strides from impact he swung his axe just once knowing the action would catch the Gascon's eye. In that split second Gaveston misjudged his own timing and as the 'morning star' came whistling through the air, Warenne brought his shield arm up sharply, and the polished metal catching the rays of the sun caused Gaveston to close his eyes for just an instant. It was enough; Warenne's shield had become entangled with the chain and, knowing his opponent's dilemma, he used all his strength to snatch the wicked ball and mace from Gaveston's hand and swiftly brought his own axe down accurately upon the Gascon's head.

The clash of steel resounded in the still afternoon air, echoing and re-echoing back from the walls of the castle. Maud could scarcely breathe, her stomach tied into a thousand knots. She had known real fear during the last encounter, only daring to breathe when she saw that fearful spiked ball snatched so neatly from the grasp of the Gascon. In her unrestrained joy Maud emitted a resounding whoop.

Meanwhile, Gaveston lay panting on the ground; he was barely aware of horses' hooves near his face and made no effort to save himself, as yet unable to move. Through the haze of his semi-conscious state he heard the deep tones of Warenne:

'Now taste the earth of England, Gascon, 'tis the only part you truly deserve.'

Without further ado Warenne spurred away from his victim to the shouts and hollers of the spectators gone wild with his success.

He turned to where Maud sat and bowed deeply towards her, then with great dignity rode towards the king's rostrum to receive his accolade. If only Olympia had been here to witness this moment of victory, his triumph would have been complete.

The king's herald announced Warenne's name and titles as the swarthy knight removed his helm; sweat streaked his face and hair as he bowed towards Edward. Triumph blazed from his dark-blue eyes. This was the sweetest victory he had ever tasted.

The king whispered something to the herald, who, just for an instant, looked in blank amazement at his monarch, but quickly regained his composure as he nervously cleared his throat.

In clear ringing tones he announced: 'My most sovereign lord and king, Edward II of England...wishes to thank all here present this day for giving such excellent sport in this contest of arms between the factions from Gascony and England...' He paused, glancing at the powerful figure of Warenne, then continued, 'and awards the wreath of honour to...to...the Earl of Cornwall, Sir Piers Gaveston...' The rest of the speech was drowned thereafter as the crowds set up such a clamour the very walls of Wallingford shook.

Just for a second Warenne sat thunderstruck, not believing what was taking place around him; certainly the Gascons had won on a majority but it had always been the custom that the winner of the final bout of a tourney was awarded the crown of honour and his chosen lady would be announced as the queen of the tournament.

Without a word Warenne swung his mount around and rode along the lines of cheering spectators, his gauntleted hand raised high above his head in a clenched fist. He stopped before Maud de Nereford who sat speechless for once. Fetching the little blue kerchief from his belt he handed it to her. 'It would seem, Mistress Maud, that we are both to be thwarted of our prize this day.'

'Oh, the prize matters not one whit to me, my lord, but all here are witness to your victory and therein lies my own joy and pride.' Her voice trembled as she spoke and he could see the tears of the child hidden in the dark, round eyes, and he felt his chagrin the more for those unspilt girlish tears than for his own injured honour.

'Do you dare to ride before your monarch, damsel?'

She understood his intent immediately and without hesitation nodded her assent. He leapt over and caught her deftly around the waist and lifted her onto his richly caparisoned steed.

When the masses realised what was afoot they went wild and clapped at the incongruous pair. Maud's pale cheeks alternated between pallor and puce and she clung to the pommel of the saddle with one hand whilst she waved back to the cheering mob. The rest of the Anglo-Norman party joined in their wake and the reception left no one on the royal dais in any doubt where the loyalty of the crowd lay, and Edward and Gaveston were left helpless at the spectacle.

Warenne did not attend the feast that night; he had already ridden away from Wallingford to his own estates in Surrey. However, there was one erstwhile sheriff who had been given a painful lesson in chivalry: Robert Hereward was never quite the same again after the Earl of Surrey had delivered the promised punishment for bullying a Norfolk maid. As for Maud de Nereford, she recounted that day's events on many occasions throughout that Yuletide. During the winter months, Seth nursed the wounded Pell back to health. The mighty stallion would never again serve in tournaments, but instead enjoyed life at stud.

CHAPTER XVI

Wigmore
December 1307

John Mortimer sat before a glowing fire recounting the events at Wallingford to an attentive audience. The hall at Wigmore was festooned with evergreens in readiness for the Yuletide season. Sweet-smelling rushes were scattered thickly over the freshly scrubbed floors; no effort was spared for the comfort and wellbeing of the occupants of Wigmore Castle.

Roger, his elder brother, Baron of Wigmore, lay sprawled out on some heavily embroidered cushions, idly watching his guests through half-closed eyes, the reflection from the flames making the golden depths burn red like glowing embers under the thick-fringed lashes.

He cast a glance towards his wife, Joan de Geneville, who sat nursing a child on her lap, again heavily pregnant. The golden eyes flickered for an instant, then passed to where his mother Margaret Fiennes sat. She was still a handsome woman, but since the death of her husband Edmund, deep lines were etched around the mouth and eyes which had not been there before. Straight-backed and intent, her needlework ignored, her whole attention was on her younger son's narrative. She had always thought of Warenne as a lonely boy.

A movement to her left drew the watcher's gaze to a slender figure, whose pale, moon-silver hair, shone under the pools of rushlights, her green eyes hidden in shadow.

The watcher could not read Olympia's thoughts as she listened to Warenne's exploits. Her long fingers stroked the head of a brindled hound lying dozing at her feet.

Theobold de Verdun scraped his chair as he moved back from the heat. The golden eyes shifted to the new subject. Theobold had married Roger's sister Maud almost a year before, and, though yet too young to be anything but wife in name only, she had gone to live in de Verdun's household, but had prevailed on this gruff, stocky magnate to spend the festive season with her family.

The union had been greeted with enthusiasm by everyone but Maud, who dreaded the day when she would be of an age to perform all her wifely duties to this stern, taciturn man. De Verdun had made it quite plain from the outset that he would be obeyed in all things and Maud's proud spirit had railed against the invisible bondage. In the shadows her dark eyes blazed with resentment and she failed to notice her brother's intent stare as she looked towards her husband.

The golden eyes narrowed. A tiny nerve twitched at the corner of his mouth; he must make it his business to look deeper into that relationship before too long. Maud's expression had spoken more than a volume on the subject and he would not see his sister unhappy if he could do aught to alter the situation.

Joan, Roger's youngest sister, wore the plain coarse habit of a novice nun with the same grace as if it were made of silk and satin. Her gentle face held such a tranquil expression that Roger was sure she had a true vocation and was more than content to enter the life of the cloisters.

Two of his younger brothers were absent, both at the Abbey of Hereford where they continued with their education. Roger could not refrain from an inner smile; he hoped they now had the ear of the Almighty and that they prayed for the Mortimer cause.

John continued his narration, describing the scene where the red-haired maid was borne, in defiance, on Warenne's saddle before the throng at Wallingford. Roger noticed Olympia's face tighten. It was almost imperceptible. A pulse beat in her throat, which he had not noticed previously. So…she was more moved by the tale than she would willingly have anyone know.

Roger had guessed at Olympia's secret some time since and still found it hard to believe that such a delicate, ethereal creature could be captivated by the rugged, soldierly knight John de Warenne, Earl of Surrey. No one in all honesty would ever hail him as a ladies' man, but…love…the golden eyes closed for an instant and turned back to look once more into the flames, love was the unfathomable mystery.

Margaret Fiennes broke into the narrative. 'Who was this maid?'

John halted his story, then continued disinterestedly. 'Some nonentity! A little Norfolk maid, by all accounts. But she certainly caught the imagination of that crowd and Warenne was the hero of the hour.'

From the gloom came Maud's question. 'And what became of the Norfolk girl? Did Warenne take her home with him?'

'Good heavens, no. Warenne left Wallingford within the hour and the child returned to her family.'

Olympia sighed with inner relief, but the sound was inaudible to the rest of the company. It failed to quell the sudden fear awakened within her for the safety of her lover. Gaveston, renowned for his spiteful tongue and vengeful nature would never allow Warenne's actions to go unavenged.

The hound rose and started to scratch itself. Olympia rose gracefully to her feet.

'Well, like the Earl of Surrey I think I shall leave the scene and seek my bed. I bid you all godnight.' She went and kissed Margaret Fiennes lightly on the cheek and left the hall in a fragrant cloud of rosemary and lavender, her long kirtle whispering at her feet and the felt slippers crushing the rushes as she went. Roger's golden gaze noted how John's eyes followed as she left.

CHAPTER XVII

February 1308

The bells of London boomed and chimed in mellifluous confusion on that February morn of 1308. People flocked to Westminster, ignoring the chill of the winter air in their eagerness not to miss the spectacle of the coronation.

Gone were the weeds of mourning, forgotten everyday cares! Now the only urgency was to watch the spectacular pageantry surrounding England's young French queen. But not everyone shared the enthusiasm for the occasion.

As Warenne sat pulling the leg off a roasted capon, his twelve-year-old wife, Jeanne de Bar, stood watching him in disgust.

'How can you be so boorish?' Her pointed chin was thrust out in anger, the pale-blue eyes blazing with temper. Somehow, every time they came in contact with each other, he had the same devastating effect on her. He always managed to shatter her self-confidence into a million fragments.

The swarthy earl ignored his child-wife and continued with his repast. It would be a long day in the Abbey and he was not going to fast simply to get his wife there for a better seat. They were assured of a place; was she not the king's niece? He could not understand the wench, truth was he did not wish to understand her or, for that matter, have anything to do with her at all.

A tall, thin page stood with a flagon of wine ready to fill the silver cup at his master's elbow. But his wife would not be denied.

'Mercy, sirrah! I swear if you do not attend me instantly I shall...I shall...' She stamped her foot, words unable to express the deep annoyance she felt.

'I shall be ready anon, fear not, we have time aplenty.' He indicated for the boy to fill his cup.

'Oh, and have you forgotten? You have still to dress! Remember the streets will be crammed with sightseers and it will take time to reach the Abbey. Oh, hurry!' Her voice rose in agitation.

'I have already bathed and have only to change into my ceremonial robes. The coachman has his orders and will be below when I am finished. Do not get yourself into such a lather, girl, you will be swooning afore the day is out, I'll be bound, and all due to your plaguey Plantagenet impatience.'

The girl walked up behind him and punched him hard on the shoulder. 'I wish you in hell. I cannot think what I have done to deserve your constant displeasure! You send me to Yorkshire to spend a lonely, cold winter there, then, when you do send for me, it is to…to…'

Warenne turned and caught at the hands of his outraged wife.

'Be assured, Mistress Plantagenet, as soon as it is earthly possible I shall sever the loathed knot which binds us and we shall both be the happier, I'll warrant.'

She shook free from his grasp; her wrists advertised the imprint of his fingers on her white skin which left a crimson brand.

Her breast heaved with her childish indignity. 'I swear I will not make matters easy for you. I shall cling closer to this marriage than a limpet to its rock. For all time you will be bound to this Plantagenet, on that, sir, you have my oath.' With that she stormed from the chamber.

Warenne cocked a knowing look at his embarrassed page.

'Take care when choosing a bride, my lad. Seek only a maid with a gentle disposition and a willingness to do your bidding. These ladies of the royal blood are a prickly, passionate breed and that's no lie.' He wiped his mouth and then rose to go and change for the day's events.

In another part of the city Roger Mortimer and his brother John also prepared themselves. For Roger it was a great occasion; he was to be one of the robe-bearers, an honour indeed, but the Mortimers had long been at the forefront of the monarch's esteem.

Joan his wife would not be able to attend. She had suffered a slight fever and remained at Ludlow, leaving Margaret Fiennes to take care of matters at Wigmore.

'Do you like the cut of this surcoat?' Roger's eyes glowed like flaming torches as he studied his elegant figure in the steel mirror.

'God's blood, Roger, you have stood a full hour preening and surveying your image in that reflector. If you do not tear yourself away I shall proclaim you have a Narcissus complex and beg you to be excused from your royal duties.'

Roger turned and cuffed his brother lightly across the ears, his white teeth flashing in a devilish grin.

'Well, you must admit I am uncommon handsome.' John, unable to stand any more of his brother's vanity, reached over and ruffled the curling locks of Wigmore's baron.

A discreet cough brought the two brothers back to sobriety as the king's messenger stood in the doorway.

'His Most Royal Highness awaits his robe-bearer.' And with that, hastily running his fingers through his hair, Roger followed the serious youth, throwing a backward grimace at his brother.

John watched the little party leave the inn and make their way through the archway into the main thoroughfare. He smiled; Roger would be sure to make the most of this day's pageant, that was certain. Then he looked into the reflector and was passing pleased with what he saw. His features were undoubtedly Mortimer, but his was a gentler face than his brother's. The grey eyes did not burn with ambitious fires. His was a more studious nature, but it did not signify that he was any less passionate or courageous. Whenever he thought of Olympia, the grey eyes held a fathomless look and only he knew how deeply he was enamoured of that fair damsel.

When Roger Mortimer rode through the gates of the palace he was totally unaware that a pair of crystal-blue eyes followed his progress, noting his flashing smile, shining, curly hair and handsome features.

Isabella, Princess of France and Queen of England, stood patiently whilst her maid brushed her thick, curling, brown hair. The merry little company she had been watching chatted and laughed as they dismounted and entered into the cool, grey shadows which formed the labyrinth of corridors and passageways.

Her eyes missed nothing, and she was determined to look her very best for this most important occasion.

Her aunt, Margaret of France, widow to Edward I, had prepared her for this day and she remembered again the words of her beauteous kinswoman,

'Gain the love of your subjects, it is worth more than any crown that will be placed upon your head. Never abuse that love, it is a powerful weapon for a foreign queen to own.'

Isabella was nothing if not shrewd for all her lack of years, and she had grown up in a court of culture, learning and excellence in all things, both spiritual and temporal, and when she had first met Edward had thought herself the luckiest of princesses to have such a tall, fair husband-to-be. Edward had been an amusing companion, well-versed and literate, a dancer of some skill. In the hunting field he cut a fine figure on horseback and did not lack charm or wit. Yes, she had been well satisfied and he would make her a queen; she did not forget that important fact. Isabella was truly a daughter of France.

She let them drape the heavy coronation garments around her comely young body and pulled herself up to her full height. She would make her husband proud of her for she was older and wiser than her twelve years.

The way was lined with cheering crowds all craning forward to catch a glimpse of England's new queen. A shout rang out, 'Isabella, Isabella the Fair', and the crystal-blue eyes followed the origins of this cry and nodded and smiled graciously towards the caller.

The cry was taken up along the route, 'La Belle Fair, La Belle Fair', for no one could deny Isabella was fair, her skin so delicately clear, her thick, brown hair shining and cascading down her back, her neat, straight features softened by a generous mouth. Edward was well satisfied with his bride. She appeared to please his subjects, a double bonus as she had brought treasures in abundance with her dowry.

At the feasting afterwards, Isabella, still with the oil of her coronation on her brow, tried to remember the names of all who were presented to her, but it had been a tiring day and she was preoccupied with a matter which was to become a bone of contention between the English and French for many a long season.

On her arrival in England, Isabella had noted a number of the jewels and gifts bestowed on Edward by her father 'Philip the Fair' now adorning the brilliant Gascon, the Earl of Cornwall, Piers Gaveston. Pressing Edward further on the matter Isabella received naught but offhand remarks and assurances. However, Edward was to learn that Isabella was as determined as she was lovely and his feeble excuses did not allay her anger nor placate her feelings of outrage at the affront to the honour of her family. Letters and messengers were sent to the court in France and all Isabella's pent-up bitterness had been poured out to her beloved father.

She had been brought up in an atmosphere of family love and security as her father's pet, the jewel of her mother's heart and adored by her three brothers Louis, Philip and Charles. But even in this haven she had been aware of the supreme power with which her father ruled his kingdom, and what influence he had throughout the Catholic world, and it was this knowledge which prompted her to seek her father's advice in this crisis in her life.

During that first year, Isabella was to learn many hard and unpleasant facts regarding the 'special' friendship which existed between Edward and Gaveston. Outwardly she showed nothing of the shock and disgust she felt, which said much for her character and personal self-possession.

But not all was anger and humiliation. During those first uneasy months Isabella and Jeanne de Bar had met and, on Isabella's instigation, Jeanne had become one of her ladies-in-waiting. Much of an age, the two girls found great pleasure in each other's company and a friendship blossomed between them which would endure the trials and tribulations of a lifetime.

There was much to keep Isabella busy, for she was eager to learn all she could of English customs and her duties as queen. She quickly earned the respect of many at court. Amongst their number were the Bishop of Winchelsea, the Earls of Lancaster and Warwick and the elder statesman Henry de Lacy, Earl of Lincoln.

Whilst Isabella applied herself to learning the craft of queenship it was becoming daily more apparent that Edward was failing to devote himself to his role as king. He had inherited nothing of his father's strength of character and art of manipulation. Magnates and peers pressed for more personal powers and urged that the Scottish issue be resolved once and for all. Gaveston's position was also causing a bitter rift betwixt the king and his nobles.

Though not immune from court intrigues, Warenne managed to keep his animosity for the Gascon on a more personal level and, along with many, hoped that when Isabella became of an age to be a wife in the true sense of the word, Edward would be weaned from his unhealthy influence.

Roger Mortimer was also careful not to be drawn into any open conflict and listened and watched the unfolding events around him. His ambitious gaze was set on advancement. He had managed to return to Ludlow frequently throughout that year, especially when he learned that Joan was once again pregnant.

Olympia had stayed at Ludlow to be both companion and helpmate to Joan. It was a warm and vibrant place and she loved both the castle and its beautiful countryside. But she felt a deeper love – a love that burned so hot it sometimes threatened to overwhelm her. At such times she would seek an excuse to ride out through the portcullis and gallop towards her one-time home of Stokesay. Often, by the time she reached the little church the fierce longing would be again contained and she would tether her horse and enter the cool, grey walls to seek refuge from her own passions. She would quietly pray for Warenne and for forgiveness for their forbidden love.

The world beyond Ludlow and Wigmore seemed far off and a little unreal to her; she knew only that out there Warenne lived, and her spirit, like a caged bird, longed to be free to go and seek him out just to look on that dear face and hear his voice whispering against her hair. Such thoughts roused her pent-up desires and she felt restless and lonely.

Was this love? Did it have to tear and wound so? How many times had she tried to lose herself in some task or other, but all to no avail. He was as much a part of her as her hand. Gallantly she strove to live at peace within herself and often sought solace in prayer and fasting and good deeds.

It was a blessed relief when Joan gave birth to her fifth child. There was much to be attended to at that time, and with Roger at home and many visitors bringing gifts and good wishes Olympia found her days filled to overflowing.

As soon as Joan was well enough to be abroad again, Roger arranged for a great feast, a celebration not only for a third son safely delivered, but because Joan's grandsire had given his lands in Ireland to Roger as a gesture of approval. The old man had been pleased with the reports he had received and felt perfectly justified in his actions. As soon as possible he wished to retreat from the world into a friary and end his days in prayer and meditation, assured that his granddaughter was well cared-for by her young husband.

Olympia hoped against hope that Warenne would come for the celebrations, and when a messenger wearing his livery arrived at Ludlow she thought she would go mad at being kept so long in suspense. There had been a twinkle in Roger's eye when he had finally told her that the Earl of Surrey would be making a short stay at Ludlow on his way to his estates in Bromfield and Yale. Adela de Giffard and her husband John would also be amongst the guests. Olympia felt herself doubly happy at the prospect of the reunion.

It was in fact John and Adela de Giffard who arrived first and the reunion between the two young women was a truly joyous occasion. They chatted and laughed, teased and gossiped, and Olympia was agog with all the news of the court which Adela was only too pleased to relate in detail.

'Is she beautiful, our new queen?' Olympia plied so many questions at her friend that Adela just laughed.

'Steady, I will try and bring you as much information about events of the past months as I may.' She seated herself on a window seat. The early April sun turned her chestnut hair to copper. Olympia tried to remain calm.

'Is she? Oh, I've heard they are already calling her "La Belle Fair".'

'Yes, my dear Olympia, she is lovely, though still little more than a girl. I think there is a great deal of growing for our young queen, and methinks she will be a beauty when nature has finished with Isabella.'

Olympia was still not satisfied. 'Is she tall, dark, fair, redhead? Her eyes, what colour are her eyes?'

'Oh Olympia, if you will let me tell my tale in my own good time I shall reveal all, I promise. Now, she is of a good height. Her hair is light-golden brown, thick and curling, not blonde you understand. The eyes, ah! They are as blue as harebells but as cool as a mountain stream. She has skin as delicate as...as...gossamer.'

Olympia laughed. 'She sounds wonderful.'

'Yes indeed, England has itself a fair queen, of that there is no doubt. I only hope that all she has to face will not change her in any way. She is so young to contend with...with the likes of that knave Gaveston.'

'Maybe Edward will fall in love with her when she comes of age.' The words were said a little wistfully by Olympia and the two young women looked at each other.

'I fear you are a romantic, my dear Olympia. I think Isabella has been lucky enough to have been born with good wits and a shrewd brain. I pray to God she has, for the hounds are already baying round the throne of her husband. They sense the old rule is dead and in the new leader there,' she paused, 'there seems a lack of purpose. I fear a weakness in this second Edward.' Adela caught Olympia's hand. 'Enough of court gossip, tell me how you have been faring?'

'As you see, I am well, have been uncommon busy what with the banquet and Joan filling the Mortimer nursery.' They laughed. Olympia cocked an impish look at her friend. 'Is there no sign of a Giffard heir hiding under that riding habit of yours?'

Adela, with still the remains of a smile playing around her cupid-like mouth, shook her head. 'I fear not. It would seem that we do not mix well, the doughty Baron John and myself, we cannot seem to make a child, though he does his duty by me,' the last sentence said with a wicked gleam in her eye. 'Ah, but surely you should be doing something on those lines, young woman. At least I have a husband.' As soon as the words were out, Adela knew she had spoken without thinking. The pain that filled Olympia's pale-green eyes caught at Adela's heart-strings, for she was not renowned for over-softheartedness.

'Forgive me, child! I am a stupid, unfeeling female who deserves a trouncing. Can you forgive me?'

She slipped on her knees before Olympia and caught at the long, slim figure. For a moment the solar was silent. Adela could sense the younger girl's struggle with her emotions. Olympia slowly replied,

'Of course I forgive you, it's…it's…just that…'

'I know, child, you are in an impossible position.' Adela rose and turned towards the window. 'For what it's worth, he has been in good health, though disgruntled and on occasions positively morose, but he has not sought another woman's favours, of that you can be assured.' She turned back and clapped her hands together. 'And he is coming here, is he not?'

Olympia looked hard at her friend. 'Yes. Oh yes, he is and I'm delirious with the very thought of seeing him again. I think I would die for one night in his arms.' She blushed, she had not meant to speak thus, not even to Adela.

The older woman looked at the tenderness in the girl's expression. 'So in love, are you, so in love?'

'Yes, yes, a thousand times a thousand. I hear his name and I go weak inside. Oh Adela, tell me I'm foolish and wicked, that I should do a year's penance on my knees. Tell me I shall be damned in hell for all eternity. That I shall never know the meaning of peace of mind…'

'Hush, now! I shall do no such thing. True love is a rare thing, it comes unbidden and for those lucky enough to find love, why, in my humble opinion that is the greatest reward this life can offer. So suffer the minor inconveniences with a good heart. Thank God, you have been one of the chosen. I can hardly wonder at the meaning, let alone feel that such an emotion could ever be mine. The very notion frightens me, to be so vulnerable…'

They stood facing each other and Olympia suddenly caught her friend and hugged her hard. 'Thank you, dearest Adela. Now we must make ready for the evening's entertainments and I shall do my best to make this visit a truly happy experience.'

The next few days were filled with hawking, hunting and merrymaking and Olympia found a degree of contentment in the company of Adela de Giffard. One afternoon as they rode back towards Ludlow and looked out over Whitcliff, Olympia drew rein and sat looking across the river at the castle. The late April sun had sunk and a mist now rose off the river, giving the dark walls a mystery all of their own.

'I think it is one of the best places on earth, this Ludlow.' Olympia sighed and then urged her palfrey on again. 'That view never ceases to please my senses. I feel…' Her sentence was left in the air as she spied a group of riders approaching the castle.

Adela saw Olympia's hand fly to her breast, heard the sharp intake of breath. The clear green eyes filled with stars and she whispered, 'He's here. Oh Adela, at last he has come.' With all the calmness she could lay claim to, Olympia rode on and only Adela could guess at what that sedate pace must have cost her friend.

How Olympia got through the formalities she never knew. Her heart was leaping erratically within her breast and her thoughts ran riot with joy. The very sound of his voice, the brief touch of his hand were all that they could exchange in that moment. But just for a brief instant their eyes met and the months of parting were forgotten in that one look.

Roger quickly took charge and greeted the swarthy Earl of Surrey with a flourish, then swept on up to the castle in his usual flamboyant manner. He left John de Giffard to escort his wife and her friend and thank the falconers for a good day's sport. The sound of the bells on the birds' jesses tinkled as they returned to the mews.

As Olympia dressed her pale hair, she could not fail to see how her happiness shone back from the mirror. She had taken every care to look her very best. Adela knocked at the chamber door, stood for a moment, then said softly, 'I hope your earl knows the worth of your love, my dear. I have never seen such a fair or more beauteous creature.'

Olympia smiled graciously. 'I can hardly wait until I can speak with him alone. Do you think anyone suspects? I do try hard not to betray my feelings but each time it gets more difficult, and I do not wish to be the one to place him in the king's disfavour.'

'I will watch and listen this night and see if there is any idle chatter or ribald remarks. Words ofttimes said in jest carry more weight than a judge's sentence. Be of good cheer, I shall be your friend in this. Now let us go and dazzle the poor male populace with your presence, and I shall bathe in your reflected glory.'

Olympia rose and joined her friend and the butterflies which circled and danced within her stomach became busier than ever. When Olympia realised where she was placed at the table, the feeling in her stomach became a hundred times worse. Roger Mortimer sat at the head, on his right was Warenne and then to the earl's right the place had been allotted to her. On Roger's left sat Joan his wife, to her left John de Giffard and then Adela, who, on noting the arrangements, tipped a broad wink towards Olympia when she felt that no one was watching.

'Lady, it looks as though it falls to you to be seated next to an unworthy companion such as myself.' Warenne's dark eyes twinkled under the thick straight brows.

'Hardly unworthy, my lord,' she murmured, but Olympia felt glad he had made things easy by his teasing manner

'Aye, you know the answer to that question. I shall not be the brunt of your witchery tonight.' His words were too low for anyone else to catch.

'Then my Lord Mortimer has failed in placing me at your side, for I'm sure he thought that I could win you from your usual reserve.' She felt his hand catch at hers under the table, their fingers locked and entwined, his very touch seemed to burn into her flesh.

'In words I would always fail, but I think not in my actions. Hold fast, lady, and I will make plain to you what a poor soldier is capable of.'

'Then I shall look forward to that meeting, sir.' Their hands drew apart and there was no more time for private discourse between them, for their host and hostess had gone to great lengths to make the evening's entertainments memorable.

There were jugglers, fools, fire-eaters and of course the inevitable minstrels. It was a boisterous night and no one enjoyed it more than the host, Roger Mortimer.

Long after viols and lutes were lain aside, when only the hounds lay before the dying embers of the fire in the Great Hall, when Roger and his lady had retired contentedly to their beds, and pages and squires curled up wherever they could, a shift whispered across the stone flags, and bare feet sped noiselessly over the icy floor. A door opened and two lovers were reunited in a long, breathless embrace.

Tears of unashamed joy coursed down Olympia's face and the earl's swarthy features were lost in the sea of pale, scented hair. It was many minutes before either had enough control over their emotions to speak. At last Warenne managed a gruff, 'Your loveliness never fails to conquer me, mistress.'

She laughed up at him amid her tears. 'Then all is well in my world, and you, my love, are my entire world: heaven, hell, limbo and purgatory.'

He kissed her throat and hair, then pulled her round so that his mouth could seek her lips, and there they stood locked in each other's arms and lost in a long sensual kiss. Outside, the waters of the river babbled along, and to Olympia it was the sweetest sound in the world.

The night passed all too quickly for those who had been parted by circumstances. Olympia found a new scar on Warenne's shoulder but he would not divulge how he had come by it, not even when she was at her most appealing.

'Don't you know that I wish to share everything in your life, good, bad or indifferent. Do you speak untruth to me then when you said you belong to me?' The green eyes were opened wide and her curving lips slightly apart as she looked down at him. Her long hair fell across his dark, broad chest. He lay looking up at her drinking in her ethereal delicacy, his hand slowly caressing her naked arm and along her shoulder. Then, quite suddenly he caught her and kissed her hard, passionately. The move was so sudden and fierce that all the girl's breath was forced from her at the sudden contact with Warenne's hard body. She struggled for a while to try and free herself from this hard, raw grasp. Without warning, he released her just as suddenly. For an instant she lay across him gasping, trying to read the dark-blue gaze which burned from his face. Just as suddenly the expression softened and he whispered, 'Forgive me. I sometimes want to crush your sweetness into my flesh so your imprint is branded on my body forever.' She touched his face.

'As you are so much a part of me, so am I a part of you and nothing can change that.'

They looked deep into each other's eyes. Then Warenne, stroking the long silken tresses, said softly, 'I am no closer to ending my marriage.' Then after a long pause he whispered, 'Would you defy convention and come and live with me? I vow to move heaven and earth to make you my wife in the eyes of the world. But it will take all your courage, so do not answer lightly. Believe me, it will be far from easy, you will be branded a whore.'

Her heart bounded within her. 'Need you ask? I would follow you to hell and back.' Olympia clung to him with all her strength.

'Be very sure, Olympia,' he said gruffly, not wanting the girl to know how close he had come to tears. 'Edward Plantagenet, though not the force or the personality of his sire, is of that blood and will not suffer a slight to his family without revenge, be assured of that.'

The green-eyed girl looked at her lover, fires burning in the green depths. 'Do you think me so lily-hearted that I should falter at the first hint of royal displeasure? The Mortimers too will not be over-pleased, methinks, but I would renounce the world to live with you for just a day.'

The time for words was over except for endearments and they renewed their vows in the way lovers have from time immemorial.

In another chamber in the castle of Ludlow, as Adela de Giffard lay beside her sleeping husband, her thoughts touched upon the affair of her friend, and she caught herself wondering at the delights that were being enjoyed by Olympia and Warenne.

Adela looked at her slumbering spouse and smiled in the darkness. They had never been lovers, dutiful wife and husband yes, but when their coupling was over Adela felt a deep void. John de Giffard was not a demonstrative man, but neither was he a mean one, for never had he complained of her barrenness. He was generous in his fashion and treated her with a diffident courtesy. There was much to thank God for. Adela shook herself mentally. It was foolish to go wishing for the moon, she must be thankful for this modest mating. Maybe she ought to be relieved that she had never been moved by passion.

She leaned over and dropped a kiss onto her sleeping partner's brow. 'War is your mistress and I would not have it otherwise,' she whispered, then turned over and fell into a dreamless sleep.

CHAPTER XVIII

June 1309

Some eight weeks after the festivities at Ludlow in honour of the baron's third son, Roger Mortimer was summoned for military service against the Scots. Commissioned to raise 500 foot-soldiers in Wales and the Marches, he had little time to listen to the outraged voices of his mother and wife who, on learning of Olympia's sudden departure with the Earl of Surrey, tried to bring as much pressure to bear upon Roger to intervene and demand Olympia's immediate return. Thankful that he had a legitimate excuse, and inwardly amused at the outcome of that liaison, Roger neatly ducked behind his royal duty to evade the issue.

However, when the two women entreated John Mortimer to act for them, they were surprised at his terse refusal. How could either of them know what anguish John suffered at Olympia's departure? He recalled the day when Olympia had come and told him of her decision and begged for his silence.

He would live and relive that moment a thousand times, each detail as clear in his mind as on the day it had happened. The pain that the girl's secret had caused him grew deeper as the days passed and, with Roger away and no one to share his torment, he grew more withdrawn than ever.

After the banquet for his new nephew, many of the guests had ridden away. Only John de Giffard and Adela had remained for Giffard was to send for his men and leave for Scotland with Roger. The Earl of Surrey had gone to his lands in Bromfield and Yale to call men to arms, but would also be returning to Ludlow within a few days.

John relived the afternoon. As he had watched a young merlin being trained, he became aware of Olympia's light footsteps and his heart quickened. She looked radiant in the sunshine. A breeze played with the tendrils of her hair. She stood beside him for a while unspeaking, her green eyes intent on the antics of the hawk.

Then she spoke, still without dropping her gaze from the bird, 'Is he yours, John? Methinks he will give you good sport, see how quickly he swoops on his lure!'

John's soft, grey eyes turned on the speaker. 'I had thought of giving him to you, Pia.'

'Oh John, you are so good to me and I really do not warrant your generosity. Besides…' she hesitated and he could see a look of uncertainty in her eyes, then she squared her shoulders and said very solemnly, 'I am going away quite soon…'

Before he could question her, she placed her long fingers across his lips.

'Let me explain, but first I must have your promise that you will speak of this to no other, promise, please promise!'

He felt the dreadful apprehension and the gnawing at his stomach, sensing that what she was about to tell him would throw him into a pit of despair with no hope of escape or reprieve. Flatly he promised to stay dumb and listened to her soft voice as she told him that as soon as Warenne returned she would go away with him and live openly as his wife.

John could still feel those words ring round his head beating into his brain. Why did the poets write of breaking hearts? It was not his heart that felt the sensation but deep in his guts. From somewhere far off he had heard himself say, 'Are you sure that the earl is not amusing himself?' There had been a long pause at his statement, then Olympia had come and stood directly in front of him her, green eyes serious, her chin thrust out a little.

'You think I take this step lightly, John? I have loved Warenne from the day I first saw him among the branches of an apple tree in the orchard at Wigmore. True, I did not recognise it, for we were both children, though he was closer to manhood than I to womanhood, but the seed had been sown. It is not easy for me to confess my feelings or intentions to you, for I think you are a little in love with me yourself, and of all the people in the world I wish only good things for you.'

She had caught hold of his hand as she spoke. He tried hard not to show his emotions but knew that she had felt the tremor that had run through him at her words. He could not answer, did not dare to trust his voice. The phrase 'a little in love' kept running over and over in his head. He wanted to cry out 'not a little but totally, all-consumingly, completely, in love with you'. Her touch almost unmanned him, but he held fast his self-control.

'Oh John,' she whispered, 'forgive me, forgive me. You are as in love with me as I am with Warenne.' Tears welled up in the green eyes as her grip tightened on his hand. 'We must endure our fate with courage, dearest John. Pray do not grieve, you will find a love that is free. You deserve someone to love you, sweet John, for you are a very special man. Please give me your blessing. I could not bear to leave without your forgiveness.'

'Is there nothing I can say to change your mind?'

'Nothing.'

'Then whether I bless or curse you, you will leave. Be dubbed a harlot and incur the wrath of the Church.'

'There is no other way, I fear. All the things you have said are true, God help me. But it is your displeasure I fear most. Through the long years of our childhood we have been true companions, do not let love be the word which turns all of that into dust.'

The two stood facing each other, both torn with anguish. They were oblivious to the screech of the merlin, the scent of lavender wafting on the summer air, the warmth of the sun on their bodies. Only the searing, heart-wrenching torment stood stark and terrible between them.

John caught her to him, unashamed tears in his eyes. 'How could I ever curse the sweetest damsel that ever breathed? I wish you joy, Pia, and should Warenne ever prove untrue, then know I shall be here waiting, living in hope that one day you may return.'

She clung to him and through her tears whispered, 'Most steadfast and loyal of hearts it is you I shall miss more than any other. I do love you, dear John, but not in the way that…' She did not get any further, for John in a rare moment had lost his normal reserve and kissed her long and desperately on the lips, then turned and walked quickly away, his head slightly bent so that the tears in his eyes would not be witnessed by any he should chance to encounter.

For a long while Olympia remained rooted to the spot. The realisation of the depths of John's feelings wounded her deeply. 'May God forgive me!'

No longer able to hide her feelings she ran weeping out through a postern gate down the steep descent to the river where she flung herself on a grassy bank and cried bitter tears of grief.

As soon as Warenne had returned to Ludlow, Olympia made ready as discreetly as she could, packing only the most treasured possessions and her very best apparel. Seeking a moment when she knew John would be alone at his devotions, she crept softly into the chapel, clutching a leather-bound Bible in the folds of her cloak. His dark head was bent on his hands and he did not move as she knelt beside him. She gently touched his arm, then slipped the holy book into his hands and as quietly as she had come left without a word.

In the light of the flickering candles John opened the Bible and on the first page the familiar hand of Olympia danced up at him.

'On each page there is comfort if you will seek it! From Pia to her steadfast friend.'

The dark head dropped back onto the hands which held fast the parting gift.

Warenne never asked Olympia why she rode so tight-lipped away from Ludlow that June evening of 1309. But he did not doubt for a moment that she was regretting her action. It was only normal that, after almost thirteen years living with the Mortimer family, she did not feel remorse at leaving their household forever. Only as they turned to ride towards Hereford did Olympia turn and look back at Ludlow Castle, but her look was unfathomable as she tugged at her palfrey's bridle and spurred on into the thickening gloom.

CHAPTER XIX

13 November 1312

Isabella lay back and looked down at the pink face of her new-born son. He would never know the humiliation his conception had caused his mother, or the racking pain she had suffered to bring him into the world. All now forgotten, and only a feeling of her triumph remained.

Outside the wind soughed and whispered around the grey walls of the castle. Here in her own chamber all was light and warmth. Edward king of England gazed down at his tiny son with a look of pure joy and fatherly pride.

The last four years had been full of bitter intrigues, jealousies and unrest. Isabella had been forced to face her husband's weaknesses. She looked across at his tall frame. The vaguely handsome face, stamped with the tell-tale features of the Plantagenet about the hair and eyes. England's king cooed as he held the tiny infant destined to become a king one day.

Isabella sighed. Maybe this tiny scrap of humanity would be the bond that would heal the breach between them. The years since her coronation in 1308 had been filled with disappointment and resentment.

Gaveston was, after all, dead. The thought made her shudder. How she had longed for his dismissal or banishment but never his death. She tried hard to thrust the bitter memory from her, but even here in the safety of her own chamber, his spectre was ever present like some ghostly guest.

In Edward's grief Isabella had hoped for a way to win his affection and sway him from his unhealthy trait. She acknowledged to herself this was the true cause of Gaveston's savage death. Now there was a royal son and heir for England. What more could she do to wipe that terrible event from her husband's memory?

It had, however, served to bring two of the most respected earls back into the king's circle, Aymer de Valence, Earl of Pembroke, and John de Warenne, Earl of Surrey. These two lords had been so outraged by the ignoble way in which the Gascon had been butchered that they had turned their backs on Lancaster and Warwick, the chief perpetrators in that foul act. Their actions now caused a break from the Barons' Party, which had been formed in 1310 to oppose King Edward's ineffectual rule.

Lying back on the thick cushions, Isabella mused over her memories of the past four years. Crowned queen of England at twelve, she had been ill prepared for the rivalry for her husband's affections. The shadow of Piers Gaveston, that ill-fated knight, had been the cause of so many sleepless nights. Nights filled with frustration and abject misery. No one would ever know exactly what pain that 'friendship' had caused her. But it had served to teach her self-control, and she displayed to the world the appearance of equanimity. It had gained her respect amongst many nobles and in particular from the clergy, who had been quick to recognise the shrewd intelligence of their French queen.

However, Isabella had vented her fury in letters to her father, Philip the Fair, regarding her dowry jewels, which Edward had seen fit to present to Gaveston. That insult could not, or would not, go in silence. How naïve she had been to think Edward would put aside Gaveston once she became his wife in more than name. The realisation that she was unable to satisfy her husband's physical appetites had been a blow to her self-esteem. Even in this hour of triumph she could still taste the bitterness that had tinged those former years.

In a few weeks she would be up and about again, her body free once more, and there were the Yuletide celebrations to look forward to. Isabella knew she would continue in her efforts to gain her rightful place in her husband's affections, after all it was her solemn duty. She saw her role clearly for the first time since arriving in England. Her plan was to fill Edward's life with so much happiness he would soon lose his mantle of grief. She would bury the memory of Edward and Gaveston making love. Bury her humiliation and step into the future with hope of a new beginning.

During those four years there had also been many changes in the lives of the Mortimer family. Roger had served for a short time in Scotland. On his return he had taken his wife and children to Ireland where he had fought and won back lands from the usurping de Lacys. In that time two more children had joined the ever-growing brood, John and now baby Joan. It had also been a time of deep concern for Roger and his wife. Their oldest son Edmund was often sick, and Joan frequently expressed her concern for the child's welfare. He was so unlike their other lusty children.

Roger had grown to manhood in those intervening years and had proved his worth both as soldier and statesman. He was undoubtedly a force to be reckoned with. The Irish, a nation of quixotic personalities and fickle loyalties, had come to respect the young Anglo-Norman lord, who had quelled the once mighty de Lacy family into submission. So soundly had they been beaten they had fled Ireland and now sought succour in Scotland.

Roger had received the news of Gaveston's death in a letter from his mother. He had experienced a mixture of emotions at the news. There was no denying the Gascon had possessed a wicked wit, had been both flamboyant and outrageous, but he felt that England's court would be a far duller place with the passing of such a colourful character. Perhaps now the queen would replace Gaveston in her husband's affections.

Memories of events which led to that brutal finale now flooded back to him. On his return to England he had been kept busy raising troops for the never-ending Scottish wars. It was the time when Lancaster and Warwick had approached him over their concerns at the influence Gaveston had over the king, an influence so resented by the barons and magnates it threatened to provoke a civil war. It resulted in Gaveston being sent to Ireland where he had been governor, a position he had filled with ease, bringing a special vitality to the Irish court.

However, Edward had fretted at the separation and even with the threat of excommunication over the Gascon's head had managed to bring his beloved Piers back to court.

In 1310 Roger Mortimer had been made Constable of Builth and Brecknockshire, proud of his continued rise in status. In that same year he had once more been sent to Scotland against the persistent

Bruce and his hardy band of warriors. However, after a short period, he returned to Ludlow, only to be sent once again back to Ireland. Turbulent times meant ever-changing events prompting ever-changing action.

Joan and their children had accompanied Roger to Ireland. They were both glad to escape the looming troubles at court. Here in their Irish lands life was never dull. Roger spent many hours in the saddle, both as a soldier and huntsman, for the sport was uncommonly good. Joan enjoyed the more relaxed life and enjoyed the months in Ireland.

There had, however, been one sad occurrence in 1312: the death of the once lively, vivacious Maud Mortimer, who had died in childbirth. It had stirred a distant memory for Roger of a look Maud had given her husband, Theobold de Verdun, that Yuletide so many years before. He felt a deep sadness that Maud, his sister, would never again be part of any family celebrations. This news added to concerns for another family member, John. It seemed he had retreated deep within himself, a state, Roger could only guess, brought about by Olympia's absence.

As to Olympia herself, there was no happier or more contented woman in the whole of England. Warenne had bestowed on her a manor house once belonging to his mother, and Olympia had refurbished the whole place to her satisfaction. The feeling of having a home of her very own pleased the pale-haired, green-eyed lady beyond measure.

As expected, Warenne had earned Edward's displeasure by taking Olympia as his mistress. He had been ordered *not* to seek adventures in England either in the field of battle or at the tourney. The ban meant that Warenne spent most of the year 1309 in his lady's company and it was a time that he would remember for the rest of his life as the happiest he had ever known.

In the following year Edward had grudgingly ordered Warenne's presence in Scotland. Under his command the English had overrun Selkirk in 1311. The king had been so pleased with Warenne's success that he granted him for life the farm and castle of High Peak in Derbyshire, and the hunting in the surrounding forest.

It had been the period when the growing unrest was surfacing amongst the Barons' Party who now were ranging themselves against the king and his favourite. Warenne was all too aware that Edward was seeking to win him from their swelling numbers.

It had not been the 'bribe' that had brought Warenne back to the royalist ranks, but the manner of Gaveston's shameful death. Both he and Aymer de Valence, the Earl of Pembroke, had been duped by Lancaster and Warwick, who had carried out the kidnap of Gaveston and executed him before anyone was aware of their intent. The two earls, Surrey and Pembroke, were so outraged at this dishonourable act that they both went over to Edward's side.

CHAPTER XX

March 1313

Roger sat before a great roaring fire in his own apartment at Ludlow. A letter from Edward charging him to present himself at court with all speed lay on his oak desk. It would seem the Crown had urgent business abroad and needed a trusted and discreet messenger for the task, and Mortimer had been chosen.

The March winds howled and tore at the stout walls of his beloved castle, as the waters of the Teme rushed and plunged along, foam-flecked spray covering the banks in the headlong race to the sea. Debris could be seen floating on the tempestuous river. Trees and branches, even new-born lambs, had been snatched by the frenzied torrents, all victims of the river's rage. But the stormy scene outside was lost to the man within.

Roger's golden eyes glowed with the fires of ambition. At last Edward had need of him; maybe if he succeeded on this mission it would pave the way to his further advancement.

Within a few days the young lord of Wigmore left Ludlow to ride hard to answer the royal summons. On his arrival he was quickly ushered into the king's presence. Edward lounged, rather than sat, behind a great table. At his side, bending unhealthily close, was the thin, shifty figure of Hugh Despencer the younger.

Mortimer noted the furtive look in the beady, deep-set eyes. To Edward's left sat Isabella and, at the sight of England's queen, the unusual golden eyes of Mortimer opened wider.

At their last encounter, she had been a girl still, but here on this spring day, with the feeble, fretful sun playing hide-and-seek through the long windows, sat a truly beautiful woman. Her figure had blossomed to ripe maturity, the once childish features would now defy any artist's brush to catch their true quality. Her skin glowed like pearls, her mouth well-defined and inviting. The crystal-blue eyes gazed back into his with complete detachment. He looked across at Edward and sensed that all Isabella's charms were lost on that man.

A quiver ran through Mortimer's body. Here was a woman to drive a man wild with desire, a woman whose beauty could set a poet's pen on fire with sonnets of love and desire. Yet here she sat, tied by bonds of duty to this…this half-man. Instinctively he felt Isabella's unhappiness locked behind the steady, unfaltering gaze, sensed her unsatisfied longings behind her calm, icy exterior, and his desires flamed.

At least Gaveston had possessed wit and a brittle charm; with this wily fox now vying for position of favourite, Isabella could look for no humour or hollow gallantry. The 'Black Dog of Arden', Warwick, had silenced his tormentor, but who would hunt this brace of 'foxes'? Both the Despencers, father and son, were self-seeking opportunists, cunningly avaricious, a deadly mix.

Mortimer's sympathies were immediately aroused on Isabella's behalf. England's queen sat in a den of vipers, and he was helpless to do aught about it. First Gaveston, and now, it appeared, his position filled by the hateful father and son. The look in Edward's eyes as he spoke to the younger Despencer was enough to turn Roger's stomach. In that instant he realised he must dance to the devil's tune. If in so doing he might advance the House of Mortimer, and subsequently come to be of assistance to Isabella. She little guessed at the Marcher baron's thoughts as she nodded towards him, missing nothing of his virile strength and handsome countenance. The chamber had appeared to fill with a breath of invigorating air at his entrance. He oozed life and vitality, a quality sadly lacking in the other male occupants.

Although not quite as tall as Edward, Mortimer held himself proudly with a rugged grace and style all of his own. His face was clean-shaven with good, strong features and Isabella's crystal eyes rested on his lips, and for an instant she caught herself wondering what it would be like to be kissed by such a man. Those eyes too were unforgettable, with laughing lights lurking in their golden depths. He aroused an emotion within her that she had never felt before. Even his voice she found pleasing, with its melodic lilt. Yes, here was a man any woman would be proud to win. Hurriedly she pushed the unbidden thoughts away. She was England's queen, not some simpering wench, moon-struck and lovelorn.

None of her inner feelings were betrayed in her composed expression, but Mortimer sensed she was aware of him. Edward indicated for him to approach as he outlined the details of the mission. Gascony was the destination, but even though Isabella strained her ears to catch any further clues as to Mortimer's journey, the voices of the three men had dropped to the merest whisper.

At least in Gaveston's time she had been privy to private matters of state, now, thanks to this insipid fellow Despencer, she had been edged out of her husband's confidence once again. However, as mother of their son and heir, she would now have a strong hold on Edward's family loyalty.

When the interview was at end, Mortimer turned and came to stand before her. He dropped elegantly to one knee and she suddenly extended her white scented fingers for his kiss. At the contact she felt a flame run through her hand and the look in the golden eyes made her heart beat unsteadily. 'We wish you a safe journey and God speed, my Lord Mortimer.' The words were quietly but concisely spoken, and her voice was as cool as her appearance.

'I thank my queen, Ma Belle Fair!' There were laughter and dangerous lights in his fascinating eyes. She felt she must take care in dealing with this bold young baron from the Welsh Marches. He bowed out of the royal presence and left the chamber to its occupants, but not, mused Isabella, in quite the same state as when he had first entered.

Isabella could glean scant information about Mortimer's activities over the next few weeks, but she caught herself thinking about the handsome young baron in moments of idleness. In the meantime she accepted the fact that Edward would never be as other men. A woman would not hold sway over his tastes. Pragmatically, Isabella turned her attention to matters of state, with special emphasis on foreign affairs. After all she was the daughter of Philip IV of France and had been weaned on political manoeuvrings. Even the Despencers could not completely steal her thunder in that field and she was determined to hold on to what little influence she had with her husband.

Matters in Scotland were beginning to boil again and much as Edward tried to avoid the issue, he was committed to continue with the war which his belligerent sire had started. He shrugged his broad shoulders at his lords and magnates when they tried to force him to a decision at the summer Parliament.

Orders were issued throughout the length and breadth of England for men to stand in readiness and practice armed drill for the coming confrontation with the Scots the following spring. It allowed time for all business at home to be settled before the forthcoming campaign.

However, one Jeanne de Bar, wife to John de Warenne, Earl of Surrey, had more than a Scottish war on her mind when she demanded an audience with her kinsman Edward Plantagenet. Tearfully she explained that although now old enough to be Warenne's wife he had refused to share a marriage bed with her, declaring that he had a wife already.

'Is that confounded earl still flouting my authority? A wife, you say!' He stood up and thundered the words again: 'A wife! What in God's name are you talking about, woman? How can the man take a wife when he already has one?'

Jeanne was startled at the effect she had created by her disclosure. She had half-feared that Edward would look on Warenne's default with indifferent eyes. Never for a moment had she thought to gain such an immediate response from her vacillating cousin.

In that moment Edward was his father's son. Courtiers witnessed the Plantagenet rage which exploded before the amazed group like a red-hot comet. Even the favourite Despencer looked on with alarm. He noted this new facet to the king's character with some concern, but instantly decided that this anger would have to be carefully managed in future.

It was Isabella who smoothed over the situation and spoke to Jeanne in private. 'We are all subject to the whims of our husbands, my dear Jeanne. I pray you do not press this matter further at this time. There is a rift betwixt the king and many of his nobles and Warenne is a respected earl who, since Gaveston's death, has sided with Edward. You have the power to sever their newborn allegiance and I beg you think carefully, bury your own pride, if not for Edward then...then for England.' She had spoken with such fervour that Jeanne had gone away promising to hold back, at least for a while longer, but the Countess of Surrey was far from happy with her lot.

The king had called on the Church to enforce his wishes on the recalcitrant Earl of Surrey, but it would seem that nothing would bring that man to court. However, moves for Warenne's excommunication were set in motion.

Circumstances arising at Stirling Castle suddenly brought the Scottish war to a head and the king could no longer avoid a confrontation with Robert Bruce. The governor of Stirling, one Philip Mowbray, finding himself besieged by Edward Bruce, brother to the Scottish King Robert, had promised to relinquish the English-held castle if no reinforcements arrived to relieve him by Midsummer's Day 1314. This single statement had committed both England and Scotland to open warfare.

Neither monarch wished to be brought face to face at this time, Edward because he was no lover of war, and Bruce because he felt that this was not the most propitious moment for a pitched battle with the English.

It was a fever of excitement that Roger Mortimer, accompanied as always by his sombre servant Meyrick, found on his return from his royal commission in Gascony. Having placed the heavily sealed despatches into Edward's own hands and receiving copious thanks on a successful trip and without finding out exactly what information he had so carefully carried across the Channel, Roger retired to pursue a personal matter.

Mortimer requested an audience with Queen Isabella. After being kept waiting for almost an hour he was finally ushered into the queen's own bower. She waved her attendants to a discreet distance before she turned to look at her visitor. She hadn't realised just how much she had wanted to see this man again. He had succeeded in making her feel like a desirable woman and not merely a figurehead of state. Was it such a sin? She was young, starved of affection and personal friendship.

He came towards her, bowed low, then dropped to one knee; the act was not one of submission but of respect.

'Arise, Sir Roger. We are glad to see you back safely from your travels.'

'I thank you for your concern, lady; it is kind of you to spare a moment of your precious time to see me.'

She did not dare to let him take her hand but indicated for him to accompany her to the window. As she passed him he could smell the delicate perfume which surrounded her lovely form.

'I…I saw something that I thought might please you and took the liberty of bringing it back.'

She hesitated. 'Have a care, my lord, we are watched.' Her eyes moved to where Eleanor Despencer, wife to the younger of that title, sat pretending to stitch a sampler, but making it quite obvious that she had them both under close scrutiny.

Mortimer threw back his head and laughed out loud but, as he did so, manoeuvred both Isabella and himself behind a pillar and away from the prying gaze. He continued softly, 'It is of little value, a mere trinket, but I hope it will find favour in your eyes, madam.' He fell silent, feeling for once in his life at a loss for words in the company of this beautiful queen.

She felt a flush creep up her throat and flood her cheeks. 'We do not expect such gifts, my lord of Wigmore. That you were able to serve my husband the king is enough. But…' Her tone was softer than before.

He took a tiny casket from his tunic and slipped it into her slim grasp. 'Say nothing, madam, and if it does not please you then give it where you will.' His golden eyes were eloquent in their sincerity. They heard a movement and became aware that the Despencer woman had altered her position so she could see them both clearly once more. But Mortimer had achieved his purpose and, bowing graciously, nodded towards the vigilant chaperone and removed himself from the company of women.

The tiny gem-studded casket clenched in Isabella's hand hurt her fingers but she kept her secret gift well hidden. She was burning with curiosity, but did nothing to arouse her 'watchdog's' suspicions.

An hour later she finally dismissed her ladies-in-waiting and drew aside to a private corner where she could be sure she would be unobserved. She opened her reddened palm. There the tiny casket winked and sparkled up at her. It was silver, worked in neat, tiny scrolls and studded with gems of every colour and hue, opals, amethysts, emeralds, pearls and diamonds. She opened the lid and there inside lay a necklace of pearls and sapphires, all so perfectly matched, and at the centre a large sapphire in the shape of a heart.

She clapped her hands in delight. Jewels she had in abundance, but nothing of such a personal manner. She would cherish it like some childish treasure. Her feeling of elation and excitement remained with her for the rest of the day.

That evening she wore her necklace. She had taken so much care with her appearance. The gown was of ivory silk with fleur-de-lis around the hem and sleeves which complemented the rope of tiny pearls and sapphires with its blue heart nestling in the hollow of her breast. Her hair she wore loose, a narrow band of gold on her brow.

No one could deny that England had a fair and elegant queen. She shone that night, brighter than any jewel. The crystal-blue eyes scanned the trestle tables to where she saw the proud dark head of Mortimer. He sat, unusually silent, the sumptuous fare of steaming joints of meat, savoury pies, haunches of venison with the rich appetising sauces and bowls of fruit, nuts and figs all unable to tempt his palate. The only thing he could think of was Isabella and he groaned at the implication of his discovery.

Here he was, Roger Mortimer, Baron of Wigmore and Ludlow, Lord of Trim and Leix, Constable of Builth and Brecknockshire, in love with Isabella of England! The fact hit him hard. Even in thought it smacked of treason, he who had thought himself immune from the power of women. When he caught sight of the necklace lying around her pale throat he had a strange intuition that someday, somewhere, she would be his, and the notion staggered him.

Isabella acted as though under the influence of a heady wine, but Edward was too deep in conversation with his minions to notice anything amiss with his wife. However, Eleanor Despencer noticed the queen's sparkling eyes and dewy loveliness. The narrow eyes scanned the hall to watch for anyone present who could account for the queen's demeanour. For an instant they rested on Mortimer, but that canny young man had not completely lost his wits and kept his eyes well averted from the royal dais, though it cost him dear to do so.

When at last he sank into his bed, sleep would not come to him and visions of the beauteous Isabella filled his head and heart. His body ached with its new yearnings. He laughed softly in the darkness – this was madness, utter and total madness. Just because she had accepted a gift from one of her subjects did not mean she would

ever think of the donor. After all, it was not out of place in that day
and age to give a sovereign a token of esteem. He remembered how
the gems had nestled against the delicate contours of her throat and
bosom and the thought drove him mad with desire.

He flung himself from his bed and poured out a large goblet of
wine, but even the flaming liquid did not quell his lusty desires.
He threw on a shirt and pulled on his hose, tugging on a pair of
soft kid boots. He shrugged on a leather tunic but left the thongs
unfastened and walked into the silence of the castle corridors,
and out into the night. The heady scents of rosemary and thyme,
lavender and coriander intoxicated his senses.

His steps automatically led him towards Isabella's apartments.
He stood in the shadow of an old yew tree and looked up at her
window. How long he kept his lonely vigil he never knew. Suddenly, he noticed a white figure framed in the casement and
without thinking he stepped into the moonlight. It was Isabella he
was certain of that.

They both stood motionless bathed in the moon's unearthly
light. He saw her hand move and he could have sworn that she
touched her lips before turning back into the darkened bower. He
stepped back into the shadows and remained until the morning
dew covered him in a moist mantle. As dawn's first light flickered
its pale rays amid the blue-blackness he returned to his own
chamber, threw himself onto the covers and slept.

Isabella had seen the dark figure standing in the pale moonlight
and knew it to be Mortimer. In the moment when the years of
loneliness and frustration swept over her, she touched her lips. It
was folly, the action of a silly girl and not a royal queen. She was
the daughter of a king and Mortimer a member of the subordinate
ranks of her court. It was a sobering fact. Like the final gesture of
one dreaming, she flung up her hand then turned back into the
silence of her chamber.

There was no place in her life for such dangerous thoughts. The
Despencer woman would soon sniff out any false move on her part
and she already walked a slippery path with Edward: he was so
influenced by his sycophants. She must let all feminine foolishness
vanish; she had the capability to become a strong queen. She
would not let emotions be her master.

When her women came to dress her the next day Isabella was in full control of herself once more. It proved an easier task than she dared hope.

Mortimer rode from the court two days after his moonlit vigil, leaving Isabella determined not to fall prey to the Despencer woman's gossip.

The season moved on apace and the warm summer days melted into sharp autumn splendour, with the rich reds and yellows painting the dying leaves, and the lingering purple of the heather which mingled with the russets of the fading bracken.

Edward with his court made for his favourite manor at Langley and he managed to forget, for a while at least, the growing hatred for his premier earl, whom he blamed for Gaveston's death. Isabella and her infant son accompanied the cheerful cavalcade; she had always liked the pleasant surroundings of the mellow manor house in Buckinghamshire. The tension of the last few months seemed less conspicuous in this more informal atmosphere.

On Christmas morning, Isabella sat swathed in a rich, ermine-lined cloak, listening to the voices of the choristers. Edward's not unpleasant tenor mingled with those of the choir. She listened to the Mass in a nostalgic mood remembering the Yuletides she had spent in France with her doting parents and brothers.

How she longed for those carefree days when she had been spoiled by her family and had shared hours of laughter and fun with them.

However, the shadow of war hung over the festivities. There appeared no way of avoiding the inevitable confrontation with Scotland now. Mowbray's ultimatum had made sure of that, and Edward had become reconciled to the idea, although Isabella had overheard a conversation with Hugh Despencer the elder which caused her to think that Edward hoped for Bruce's submission.

Elisabeth de Burgh, wife to Robert Bruce, and his daughter Marjorie, a child from his former marriage, still languished in English prisons. There was also a sister, Mary, and the Countess of Buchan, both in cages high on the walls of Roxburgh and Berwick Castles. Bruce's other sister, Christian, was also safely ensconced in a convent, and now only Edward Bruce remained from the large number of Bruce's brothers. All the others had been executed by the English. Maybe Bruce would stay his hand for fear of reprisals by his hated enemy, the English Plantagenet king. Nothing else would seem to curb the audacious usurper, whose tenacious courage appeared unconquerable.

'I had hoped 'the Bruce' would not be drawn into this damned battle,' hissed Edward to his aged advisor. 'He must be afraid of what we may do to his wife and child. God's blood, hasn't he lost enough of his family in this useless struggle. When will the man see the error of his ways and bend a knee...'

'Hm!' The elder of the two Despencers interrupted. He was a grey-haired, wrinkled-faced old man, with gnarled hands, but the eyes were still clear, as clear as his mind. He continued, having gained Edward's attention, 'My liege, I think that he is too committed to this cause by now. He will not let the blood of his brothers go unavenged, and I'm sure he does not think that Edward Plantagenet is a murderer of hostages. No, no, my lord, Robert Bruce will only give up now with his death, that alone will stop him. My agents tell me that he is uniting the unruly factions and is about to bring Highlanders and Lowlanders to the same conference table – no mean feat.'

Edward looked up at the old man. 'We shall see, we shall see, but I think that he will be forced into submission. His army is not strong enough to withstand our weight of numbers. But enough of matters serious, this is a time of goodwill, Sir Hugh, and I will not be diverted from my present state of enjoyment to dwell on matters of war.'

So Edward fell into his old ways, spending more time with the carpenters and workmen than with his councillors, and Isabella was left much in the company of her women. Her infant son was the source of the only comfort and love in her life, but she always endeavoured to be at her best in Edward's presence. She felt her duty lay towards her vacillating husband and the way to prove her worth as a true queen was in that direction alone.

Many miles away, Roger Mortimer was also celebrating the holy day of Christmas with his wife and family. Since his return to Ludlow he had thrown himself wholeheartedly into all and any activities around him, recruiting men and arms, hunting from dawn until dark, wrestling, swimming, all to no avail. Nothing it seemed could dull this new-found ache as familiar to him now as breathing. He had sought absolution from some travelling priest, but all in vain. He was desperately infatuated with Isabella and naught in heaven and earth could alter that.

He never became too intoxicated lest he should utter her name aloud and betray his secret, and maybe place her in danger. There was no cure for this emotional illness and much of his old bravado left him.

One day John his brother caught him looking intently into the waters of the Teme.

'Such deep thoughts on such a brisk morning? What notions lurk in that curl-strewn head now, may I ask?'

Roger did not look up as he replied, 'The future, the mystical future, my dear John.' He turned and threw his arm around the more slender frame of his brother and together they walked along the banks by the tumbling waters which sparkled and gurgled at their feet.

'I think this time we shall all be called upon to face the Scots.'

'Is it true that Warenne has refused Edward's call to arms, and that he will be excommunicated if, by the end of the year, he has not put Olympia aside?'

'So it is said,' reiterated Roger.

'There is one fact of which I'm sure, no woman would win you away from a course you had set your heart upon!' laughed John. He felt the muscles in his brother's arm tense at his words and all mirth slip from the familiar face.

'Do not gamble your life on that wager, dear brother,' and with that he ruffled the younger man's hair before running swiftly along the narrow path, followed by a rather perplexed John.

On many occasions after that day John tried to draw Roger into discussing the ways of love and women, but he never got any satisfaction, only jocular remarks and inane innuendos. He eventually gave up the thankless task but often wondered over his brother's words.

The holy festivities were soon at an end. The keynote now was war, and the coming Parliament. As Roger had feared there was much dissension at the spring session and the haughty Lancaster, chief of the Ordainers, a body of magnates, noblemen and prelates set up to oppose the king's ineffectual rule, refused to serve in Scotland, calling the venture folly, though he sent men and monies. The belligerent earl also failed to appear at Parliament. So it left most military matters in the capable hands of the Earls of Pembroke and Hereford.

Stores, horses and men were gathered from all parts of England. It left the land bereft of able-bodied men to till and sow the earth for the coming season.

As Mortimer's sergeant-at-arms gathered men in the square at Ludlow, the cracked voice of an old woman was heard to shout above the clamour, 'How does the son of Longshanks expect the womenfolk to manage without their men?'

There was a general outcry at her words but she would not be gainsaid. 'Mark well my words, the only harvest reaped this year will be of bloody corpses and starving mouths.' Her thin voice rose and fell and even after the veteran sergeant had had her removed, the mood of the onlookers changed. They remembered her last prophesies all too well. She had foretold the year of the old king's death and had 'seen' the bloody end of the proud peacock Gaveston.

Try as the sergeant might to carry on his business of recruitment in an orderly fashion, there were now deep rumblings of discontent amongst the assembled folks. He felt a certain sympathy towards them, for it was true they had to bear the brunt of war in heavier taxes and levies. Families would suffer without their menfolk, coupled with the loss of their precious livestock.

He scanned the crowd before him; there were many in tears at leaving their loved ones. Some he knew would never return again to their homes, but for others it was a means of breaking the bondage of the land and starting afresh. As in all wars, it was the beginning and end of many ways of life, ties of duty and loyalty exchanged for the king's service. There would be those who would prosper, for in battle there was always the chance of booty and ransom for the victors, and adventure and excitement for those bold enough to seize the opportunities. He realised many of the young man recruited that day saw this war as their chance of a better life.

CHAPTER XXI

Just a few miles from Stirling Castle
24 June 1314

Roger Mortimer sat his wearied charger with a look of grim tiredness etched across his handsome features. The golden eyes were clouded by his inner thoughts, thoughts that he would never voice aloud. His gaze studied the remains of what had once been the greatest army in Christendom.

The narrow strip of water, known as the Bannock Burn, with its muddy streams and surrounding bogs and marshes, now ran with the blood of the English dead and dying. Many had fallen into the boggy depths. Nothing remained of the pomp and splendour once displayed by the mightiest houses in England. The overwhelming confidence felt by many had quickly faded on the field of battle. The ragged, hard-faced men of the Highlands and Lowlands of Scotland gave no quarter. Their leader, 'the Bruce', had led them with the fire of conviction in his soul, the strength in his fighting arm, and cool logic in his head. His army was a mere third of the English strength, with no great number of heavy chivalry, and armour worn only by the few earls and knights who had rallied to the banner of Scotland. In the main, the fighting men were on foot, clothed only in kilts and tartans, naked to the waist, fiercesome warriors armed with claymores, sickles, staffs and scythes from the land.

Mortimer heard again the laughter that had run through the English mounted ranks of Edward's army at the sight of the enemy, but it was Bruce who could laugh now, for many of those smiles of the morning had been replaced by the sneer of death.

Edward and Despencer had already fled the field. Initially, Edward had fought like a true king, surprising not a few of his followers. However, his reckless act of bravery had placed him in mortal danger and after a heated argument had been forced to leave the conflict in high dudgeon.

The disgust felt by the young baron at the outcome of the battle only added to his present discomfort. His once shining armour, a gift from his bride Joan, was now tarnished and blood-spattered; so too were his face and hair. The blue-and-gold surcoat with the arms of Mortimer emblazoned on the fine material, torn and muddy. His limbs ached with the day's efforts; sweat had now turned to icy rivulets which ran down his weary body.

Meyrick sat in silence at his elbow sharing that terrible moment of defeat. Roger turned to him. 'It has a taste like no other, Meyrick.'

'Aye, m'lord, conjured from the kitchens of hell!'

For a minute more they sat and watched the straggling numbers that that had managed to escape from the fierce Scottish contingent. There were pitiful sights as some wounded tried to drag maimed colleagues from the field. An urgent call from his rear brought the young baron's attention from the horrendous scenes of death and carnage.

'Are you awaiting capture, nephew? Or did that Scottish heathen I saw you engaged with back there knock the wits completely from your head?' The cracked voice of the Lord of Chirk echoed in the younger man's ears.

Roger wheeled his tired mount around and slowly made his way to his uncle's side. Meyrick fell in behind them.

The older Mortimer continued, 'I do not think many of the Welsh archers remain, well, any that live that is.'

His normally harsh voice had grown husky from the day's shouted orders, and his narrow face, now free from the mighty helm, was sweat-stained and streaked with blood and grime.

'Then let us from this accursed Bannockburn, for more good men have died here this day…' Roger's voice broke but he went on, 'and…and for a sovereign that fled the field in ignominious defeat.' The bitterness in his tone did not escape either of the two men that rode close by.

They rode on in silence until they caught sight of a band of bowmen whose whole demeanour reeked of defeat. Some were being borne along on makeshift litters, and the groans and cries of the wounded could be heard even at that distance.

Roger turned to Meyrick. 'See how they fare, what numbers

there are, and in whose company they served. I would place as many miles 'twixt us and those Scottish devils who will be full of vain-glorious bloodlust. See, the scavengers of death have already moved in on the fallen over yonder, they pick the carcasses of better men than they for whatever they can find. Damn them! Damn them to the fires of hell!' His voice was full of pent-up wrath.

'This is the darker side of war, m'lord,' murmured Meyrick, 'the side that no balladeers do sing of.' His quiet words summed up the aftermath of battle. Plunderers moved over to the fallen, like gleaners over a bloody harvest, seeking whatever jewels, armour, clothes and anything they could sell, ransom or eat. Dead fingers which refused to give up their treasures were merely hacked off for the prize.

'So many,' whispered the younger Mortimer, 'so many slain that did laugh so scornfully at Bruce's ragged band.'

'He proved himself a man as well as a king this day, unlike the craven coward Edward Plantagenet. I say Bruce deserves his title as "King of Scots", he has earned that crown; would that England had such a monarch, then nothing would gainsay us.' Roger rattled the words off to his companions as if to soothe his own wounded spirit.

'Have a care, nephew, even the wind will betray you in such treasonable thoughts.' The black eyes of the Lord of Chirk looked hard at his young kinsman.

'God, I'm weary! Let us rest tonight and tomorrow...' The young baron urged his flagging mount away from his uncle's side. The sound of a galloping horse brought him to attention, and he hailed the rider. 'Where do you make for in such haste?'

'To take tidings of the deaths of the Earl of Gloucester and Henry, the Earl of Hereford's nephew, m'lord, by none other than Robert the Bruce himself. I have a list of many who have been captured and the conditions for their ransom.'

'Do you go by way of Wigmore or Ludlow? I'll see you are well rewarded. Tell the Lady Joan de Geneville, my wife, that I am safe, as is the Lord of Chirk.'

'Aye, m'lord. I'll take thy tidings right willingly.' The messenger spurred off into the gloom.

'He'll make his fortune if he completes his ride alive,' muttered the Lord of Chirk, having once more ridden to the side of his nephew.

'If any man can make an honest gain from this day's folly, then I for one do salute him.' Roger was annoyed; he wanted to be alone to gather his wits and emotions. His confidence had been badly shaken by the outcome of the day's events and he needed time to compose himself.

Meyrick found a place where a gnarled old tree with its bent branches curled round to make a natural shield from the light wind which had sprung up with the coming of darkness. He guided his master's faltering footsteps and gently stripped him of his armour. The rich gambeson was soaked with sweat and blood and as the chain shirt was removed a low groan escaped Mortimer. A small but deep wound had reopened and started to bleed copiously from his shoulder.

The faithful servant moved forward just in time to catch the fainting form of his master. As gently as any woman he laid down the unconscious Mortimer and quickly started to cleanse where the arrow-head had made its entry into the hollow of the shoulder, at the point where armour was at its most vulnerable.

When Roger regained his senses he was wrapped in a thick blanket, his shoulder bandaged, and a small fire crackled at his feet. He closed his eyes again, not wanting anyone to know that he was awake. The warmth from the busy little fire ran up his aching legs like a warm liquid. Slowly he felt the tension seep away and sleep took hold and let his tormented mind and body slip into oblivion.

Next day dawned chilly and damp. The wound was stiff, but through the diligent administration of Meyrick was quickly losing its intensity of pain. Roger had risen and was part dressed before Meyrick was completely awake.

'You are feeling better today, m'lord?' he said, yawning.

'Indeed, thanks to you. My mother knew what she was about all those years ago. You've nursed me through fights and tournaments and if I do not always show my gratitude, know that I am aware of your true worth, Meyrick.'

The normally straight face broke into a smile at the compliment, but he remained silent.

The journey back across the border to Berwick was a shambling, disunited affair. There were foot-soldiers, knights, squires and engineers, any, in fact, who had escaped the Scottish wrath and were able to make their way homewards. Some had been carried out of the field of the main battle, whilst others had been in individual skirmishes and were only now linking up with what remained of the English forces. The once bright pennons, gonfalons and standards now flapped soiled and besmirched and, like the dreams of victory, torn and rent asunder.

The straggling remnants of the English chivalry converged on Berwick and it was there that Roger Mortimer learned of Edward's movements after the ignominious flight from Bannockburn. But amid tragedy there was also joy, as John had survived the battle and was there at Berwick.

The two brothers fell on each other in their relief at meeting again when so many former family ties and friendships had been cut short in those few brief hours. There were unashamed tears in Roger's golden eyes.

'God be praised, I feared for your life, little brother.'

'It was a sorry affair and no denying. How fares our uncle?'

'Oh, he is hereabouts trying to find what is left of the Welsh bowmen.'

'Edward has ridden to England,' John said quietly.

'Then let us hope he conducts himself better round a council table than he did on the field of battle,' hissed Roger between gritted teeth.

John continued trying to avert his brother's rage. 'They say that Lancaster has been waiting to see the outcome.'

'Yes, and at this disaster will seize his opportunity to bring Edward to heel, methinks.' The two brothers looked at each other.

'Then I think it politic for me to attend future meetings. What say you?' Roger's eyes were almost cat-like as he spoke.

'Indeed, and if I'm not much mistaken, our uncle will not let you go alone.'

'Dear John, when you can, go and see that all is well at Ludlow and Wigmore. I have sent word, but it is not certain that it will reach them and it would set my mind at rest.'

'It's as good as done.' John hesitated a little, then said quietly, 'Were you afraid out there...on...the battlefield?'

'Afraid?' echoed Roger. 'God's teeth, I was too damned busy to be afraid.' But he had noticed John's hesitancy and dropped his arrogant tone. Then he said, 'Yes, I'll not deny there were moments I would not live again. I felt anger at the debacle. Many good, brave men died needlessly.' He slapped John on the shoulder and said more cheerfully: 'At least we live to fight another day, and I am thankful that I have nothing more to show for my pains than a small arrow hole.'

John looked concerned. 'Are you sure you are all right?'

'Yes, yes, of course I am now, don't start worrying like some whey-faced maid. Come! We have much to do before I ride for York.'

Roger would never confess his admiration for the warrior king, Robert Bruce. Even though his loyalty had been shaken, the Mortimers had been adherents of the English monarchy for many generations, and one reversal would not change their allegiance.

As soon as he could ascertain the numbers and whereabouts of survivors from his contingent, Roger made arrangements for their journey home, whilst he and his uncle prepared to join Edward at York. With the shoulder wound healing well Roger's mood changed from grim depression to determined optimism.

It was true that Bruce's army had despatched the hotheaded Henry de Bohun, nephew to the Earl of Hereford, in mortal combat. The young knight had thought to end the conflict by killing Bruce when he had come across the Scottish king and a small scouting party. But though outhorsed and with only a shirt of mail as protection Bruce had proved his prowess as a fearless fighter. The lance of Hereford had proved worthless against such a seasoned campaigner and, with only an axe, Bruce had split the rash young man's skull like the shell of an egg.

The victory at Bannockburn had not made Bruce complacent, far from it. He now sent his forces as foraying parties to harass his enemies from the Borders to the Northern Marches, learning from long experience not to allow an adversary time to regroup or reorganise. For once his coffers would be filled with ransom and booty and the weapons retrieved from the English fallen would enable his army to be better equipped in the future.

On the journey back to England Roger Mortimer's spirits rose again. Was he not alive, and did the sun not feel good upon his face? His body was fast recovering from its hurts and none of his immediate family had been slain or maimed. He chatted conversationally with his uncle and a number of other young lords on route.

The defeat had indeed chastened Edward Plantagenet who was now ready to accede to all the demands previously laid down by the Ordainers. Thomas Lancaster took this opportunity to air grievances long held in check. During those long days Edward sat miserably listening to charges brought against his close adherents, Despencer, Beaumont and the like. All were arraigned by the haughty Lancaster, and Edward was helpless to oppose him. Much as the king tried to prevaricate, on the issue of Despencer's banishment Lancaster was adamant. Edward eventually agreed and, much to the chagrin of the thin-lipped Despencer, had to bow to the wishes of the council.

When Edward returned from the Parliament at York, Isabella could not fail to notice the difference in his manner. He would sit brooding for hours and thoughts of Gaveston were once again at the forefront of his mind. He even had the body exhumed from its resting place at Oxford and transferred to his favourite manor at Langley where he could grieve in private.

Try as she might, Isabella could not win her husband from his dark depression as he felt that all hands were against him. It was difficult for she knew in her heart that Edward blamed her in part for Gaveston's death. She had, indeed, complained bitterly at her husband's indifference towards her and the matter of the dowry jewels had never been fully resolved. However, it was her displacement in Edward's affections that had been the core of her complaints. Surely this was not an unnatural requirement for a proud and beautiful young wife? Hard as she tried, and with much gentle patience, nothing would sway the moody king from his present frame of mind, not even the comfort of his baby son.

CHAPTER XXII

Olympia sat under the deep green boughs of an old apple tree in the garden of her lovely manor house. The warm summer sun dappled through the branches and touched the delicate face and hair. Her tiring-woman sat some distance away stitching a sampler. The book Olympia had been reading lay closed in her lap as she drank in the pleasant scene around her. The limestone walls of her home could be seen through the thick foliage, but the slanting roof was lost amidst the density of the leaves. A wide grass sward lay before her, edged by colourful borders of flowers and herbs. Birds sang sweetly overhead and the bees hummed busily amongst the bright blossoms. She felt truly at peace with her surroundings.

A butterfly alighted on her kirtle and she smiled down, noting the beauty of its fragile wings. She offered up a little prayer of thanks for these precious days and for the love shared with Warenne. Now to crown it all, she was to have his child. As yet she had not spoken of it, wanting to keep the knowledge to herself for just a few days more.

A commotion from the outer courtyard brought her back to the present and the butterfly flew nervously away. She saw the broad figure of Warenne striding across the lush grass towards her.

His face was serious. She stood up, and the forgotten book fell to the floor at her feet.

'My love, what's amiss?' She felt concerned by his stern expression.

'Defeat. The Bruce has routed the king's army. Many are captured, and Edward has run to Lancaster, that proud felon, for support. Bah! A sorry day for England, I fear.' He took her hands and pulled her to him and kissed her curving mouth. His face softened.

'My dismal news has spoiled your sanctuary. Forgive my thought-lessness.'

'No, my love, all things I would share with you, good and bad.' She took his dark, brown hand and laced her long, pale fingers in his and smiled tenderly up at him.

'You can never forgive Lancaster's part in Gaveston's execution, can you?' Her words were like tinder to a flame.

'Execution?' The word exploded onto the soft summer air. 'Bloody murder, cunning knavery, treachery beyond forgiveness.'

She squeezed his hand.

'You will not let your personal loathing cloud your vision, though, will you? There are stronger issues in England nowadays than old grievances and revenge.' Her great green eyes looked up at him through dark lashes.

'Me?' he spluttered. 'Think you that either Edward or Lancaster will want me near them in any event. To one I am a reminder of his traitorous deeds, and to the other a disobedient vassal. No, I say, the council tables will not be ready to listen to my excommunicated voice.'

Olympia sat down again in her former seat, but the mood of the afternoon had been shattered by his news. Warenne dropped to her feet and sat staring blindly as she stroked his dark, shining head. She bent and kissed his hair and he turned and smiled softly up at her.

'Your gentle touch soothes the grumpy bear. How fortunate I am to have such an understanding captor.'

'And I such a fearless bear.' She ruffled his hair as she spoke.

'Have you any news of the Mortimer family? Or John de Giffard?'

'The only reliable information I have at the present is that Gloucester is dead and Hereford prisoner, his nephew Henry slain by Bruce himself, but I shall make all efforts to find out more, sweetheart.'

A few evenings after Olympia told Warenne they were to have a child in the spring. The dark-blue eyes had been filled with such love and tenderness that she had wept in his arms. The feeling of fear that passed through him was lost on her. His sweet Olympia was so slender and childbearing such a precarious thing, he could not quell the anguish that gripped his heart at her disclosure.

They had been so happy here in the heart of Surrey, hunting over the Downs, exploring his old childhood haunts together, and he delighted in showing her the surrounding countryside. On market days there was so much hustle and bustle with traders and farmers alike selling and buying everything from a new plough to a thimble for a wife or mother. Now he could not completely conquer his new fear and caught himself watching his beloved Olympia for any untoward signs of distress. If she was aware of his watchfulness she did not speak of it.

Summer turned to autumn and then to snowy winter. The lack of men to harvest and tend the land was now beginning to tell. There were shortages throughout the land and it was still only the onset of winter. What would happen at the season's end? The question was on all lips, both rich and poor alike, bound together by this common calamity.

But somehow the urgency did not touch Warenne and Olympia. Their farms had been well tended, for Warenne had sent monies to the Scottish venture, and by sending only a minimal force to the wars, his lands had been well looked after, the barns were full and livestock hail and hearty. His concern lay not with his farms and estates but with his adored Olympia. After Yuletide it became obvious her pregnancy had started to take its toll on her. She did not complain, but the dark shadows under her green eyes advertised her lack of wellbeing.

In his anxiety Warenne sent for the best physicians in the land, but the answer was always the same: they could find no cause for this sudden decline. Daily Olympia became weaker. Even though Warenne ordered the very daintiest of morsels to tempt her palate, she would push the food away. He was close to despair.

'My love, you must eat, if not for yourself, then for the sake of the babe.'

'I know you are right but it causes me such sickness and pain I just cannot bring myself…' The sentence trailed off. She knew his concern and loved him for it. 'I'm sure this will pass, women are renowned for their fickle fancies at this time. Pray do not fret yourself, sweetheart.'

Her gentle reassurances did not allay his fears and in his desperation he sent for Adela de Giffard. On her arrival Adela was shocked by the change in her young friend. Olympia drew strength from the arrival of her friend and rallied a little, but the phase soon passed and she once more slipped from her short-lived bout of health.

One evening, long after Olympia had retired, Adela and Warenne discussed every morsel that the pale young mother-to-be had partaken of that day.

'I must admit this condition is beyond my comprehension,' she said as she studied the dark countenance of Warenne before speaking again. 'I've only once heard of such a case and am loath to even speak of it again for you may think me foolish.'

'Madam, I welcome any suggestion foolish or otherwise. If we do not act quickly then death will claim the only thing that truly means anything to me in this life. So, for pity's sake, speak and let me judge for myself the merits of your doubts.'

'Well...' Adela hesitated. 'I can remember hearing my aunt speak of a woman many years ago suddenly failing for no apparent reason. There was no disease or anything logical that could account for the woman's condition, that is, until her young son found...' Again Adela halted, her clear, grey eyes looking warily at her host.

'Go on, woman, what did the boy find?' Warenne was becoming agitated at her hesitancy. She continued slowly, watching his face to see the reaction her words would make on him.

'The boy found a doll-like creature stuffed in the cleft of a tree which appeared to be a model of his mother. In its stomach there were long pins.' Adela let out a long breath, glad to be free of her knowledge at last.

Warenne's eyebrows rose for an instant. 'Are you saying that Olympia is...is bewitched?'

'That is the only explanation I can think of if the physicians can find nothing untoward in her condition.'

'God's death! Witchcraft!' Warenne sat down heavily. 'But who could want my sweet lady's life?'

'My lord earl, you are in a better position to answer that question than anyone else.' Adela watched the swarthy-faced earl for a moment. Then he stood up abruptly and caught her hands.

'Madam, you may have it! By the Rood, we shall search this place and the grounds as soon as 'tis light and if your theory be correct, then you shall have my everlasting gratitude.'

It was good to see the light of hope once more fill those dark-blue eyes. From her arrival she had been watching the depth of feeling shown by this somewhat forbidding man towards her friend Olympia. Adela had heard the gossips around the halls and at court about Warenne's behaviour towards his wife and the dispute which his decision to live openly with Olympia had caused. But after seeing them together she brushed aside any reservations she once had about the union. They were deeply in love with each other and she had observed the tenderness in their eyes when they talked to each other. There was a more intimate conversation in a glance than any words could convey.

Adela sighed; it had taken more courage than she had realised to speak to Warenne about her witchcraft theory. 'If you will excuse me, my lord earl, I think I will retire. We can continue with our investigations on the morrow.' She walked to the door and with a graceful curtsey left her host to muse on her revelation.

Over the next few days the manor and its grounds were thoroughly searched. Adela made the excuse that she had mislaid her rosary so as not to arouse Olympia's suspicions, but the search was fruitless, and Warenne became more introverted than ever. He had masses said daily for Olympia's health, and his family priest did not falter in his duty to his benefactor, although the earl was still under the cloud of excommunication.

Soon it became clear as the winter progressed that death had marked the beautiful Olympia for itself. Her eyes seemed huge in the pale, pale face and her skin was like transparent gossamer over her bones. Adela watched Warenne carry his torment in silence in an effort not to show his true fears to his loved one. When Olympia finally collapsed and was carried to her chamber, Adela saw tears in Warenne's dark eyes and for once her own hold on her emotions threatened to betray her.

The chamber had a breathless hush over it. Candles flickered and softened the dark depths, leaving only the corners in blackness. Outside, the February blizzard had ceased, leaving all white-carpeted and fast in the snow's cruel grip.

Warenne held the almost transparent fingers of Olympia, who lay ashen-faced on the large canopied bed. The child had come too quickly. Born before its due span, it had struggled briefly for life but the spark had been too faint and the tiny girl had died within the hour. Now Olympia herself was slipping from life's grasp.

Warenne's gaze never left her face, and he kissed the cold hands and lips, trying to breathe some of his own warmth and strength back into her slim form. His heart was in his eyes and his swarthy features were set hard as granite in their own battle to remain composed. Adela stood in the shadows and watched this desperate parting, her own heart moved by the scene.

Stark fingers of dawn light pierced the shadows of the chamber and bathed the watchers in its cold rays. The reclining figure gasped and murmured. Warenne moved closer to gain her speech. Her eyes opened as she panted, 'My…love…you have made me…so… so very happy. I will…not cease…to love…you, our…love…is… all…death naught. I…shall wait…for…you…you…my…own… darling.' She tried to rise as he held and kissed her pale curving lips. On his kiss she left life with a sigh. For an hour or more he rocked her gently to and fro, refusing to accept that she had left him alone. Frequently he bent and kissed her pale hair and lips, and spoke softly the intimate endearments that they shared together. No one, not even Adela, dared to interrupt.

All that day he held her to his breast until late afternoon when the truth of her stiffening face and hands finally penetrated his tormented consciousness. Those that hovered outside the doorway heard a mighty cry that echoed around the silent house. A moment afterwards he came out, never looking to the right or left, but those who saw him never forgot the look of tortured agony that was etched across his features, nor the look of despair in his eyes. He pushed past them all, out into the snowy evening, and ran till he could run no further, finally falling to his knees with the cry of a wounded animal.

'Olympia! Olympia! Do not sentence me to live in this world without thee, for Christ's sake.' He sprawled full-length in the snow and wept, his great shoulders heaving under the racking sobs.

Hours later they found him still lying prone on the ground almost frozen and carried him back to where Adela and his servants tended and nursed him back to life.

For many weeks Adela would find him standing over the ground where they had buried the lovely Olympia. Silent, his face remained a mask of grief and despair, and the running of day-to-day affairs fell to Adela, who had stayed out of loyalty to a lost friend and a true concern for the grieving earl.

Eventually it was decided that the steward should send to the Lady Jeanne de Bar. After all she was his wife. Adela had tried to dissuade the man on his course of action, but had been overruled. She was merely a guest and friend to the late Olympia, his loyalties lay with the earl's wife. Warenne was too immersed in his own feelings to care what went on around him at that time and when Adela left abruptly he scarce missed her going.

It was only at the arrival of Jeanne de Bar that Warenne roused himself from black depression into a mood of even blacker rage. When Jeanne was ushered into his chamber she found him sitting stone-like before a roaring fire, his swarthy features grey and ill-looking. His powerful frame had lost much weight, the clothes which hung about him emphasising the fact.

Even Jeanne was shocked by his appearance. At her entrance he neither looked up nor acknowledged her, but Jeanne was not put off by his cold reception. She stood for a moment surveying the scene before her. She was well aware that the dark-blue travelling habit she wore complemented her glowing cheeks and pale-blue eyes. At almost twenty-one she had become a vibrant, tantalising woman whose Plantagenet determination had made itself known on many occasions at court.

'So…all that I have heard is true, my lord, they say you have been conquered by grief and 'twould seem they speak truth for once.' She pulled her hands from the fur-lined muff and discarded the heavy cloak. She came and stood before him. 'Come now, there is much that needs your attention; you have fallen lax in your duties. Maybe now we can call a truce to our petty wranglings. I could aid you in your bereavement.' She lingered over the word and he did not fail to notice the note of triumph in her voice.

The dark-blue eyes suddenly flickered. He looked straight at her and she almost faltered at the venom she saw in their depths.

'Get out, hell whore! Get out of my wife's house and don't you ever set foot on any of these lands under pain of death. Do you hear me, madam? When I am in the earth, then you may do as you will; but whilst I still live and breathe, until I request your presence, stay away from me, is that clearly understood?' He rose as he spoke and for an instant she thought he was about to strike her. He came and looked down into her widening eyes.

In faltering tones she managed to mutter, 'I came in good faith and this is my greeting, sirrah! I thought that we could…could… make a fresh beginning.'

'Beginning! A fresh beginning!' he thundered. 'We have never started, nor will we, madam, on that you have my oath. If I never set eyes on you again then it would still be the memory of you that plagues me. I would sooner die by my own hand than share anything with you. Now leave me and trouble me no more.' He had not spoken so many words since Olympia had died.

Jeanne still stood her ground. He was her husband – the challenge she had long ago decided to accept and win whatever the cost. She was not a Plantagenet for nothing.

'Sir! For mercy's sake, what have I done to deserve such hatred from you? I did not seek our marriage,' she faltered, 'nor have I ever raised a hand against you. I wish that we could come to an amicable understanding. I am not ill to look upon. Do you think I have no feelings? If I did not have the friendship of the queen, I would be scorned and ridiculed throughout the land. Think on't, my lord, I would be woman enough for your manhood, doubt it not!'

He turned his back on her. 'My ears are deaf to your pleas, madam.' He turned back and looked at her with such a haunted expression she winced under his gaze.

'You have no conception of loneliness and misery, nor could you ever hope to. It's not within your nature. You devil's spawn! Plantagenet seeds are corrupt and blighted, they devour all in their need for power and pleasure. That need being in your make-up, you sweep all aside to the calls of your own wants and desires.'

'Your accusations are unfair, sir, it is I who have been swept aside for *your* passions. A 'wife' you called your dead…whore. I will make sure you only ever have one wife on this earth, my lord earl, and that shall be *me*, come hell or high water.'

'Don't you ever speak so of a woman who would be more 'wife' to me than a thousand Plantagenets. I would willingly die for just an hour in her sweet company than be given everlasting life with you. It is only that you were not close at hand that stops me from accusing you of some devilish plot to kill my own true wife.'

His words caused her to pale. What had he learned? She regained her composure. Of course he knew nothing, how could he? She rallied. 'Then, if you are deaf to matters of a personal nature, maybe

England will find a better ambassador. I came to plead her cause, for she is in dire need and though the king be my kinsman, your banishment was on…on…' She did not finish the sentence but continued, 'There is no longer any need for you to continue your enmity towards your sovereign and anointed king. The realm is in urgent need of your counsel; put aside personal issues for once. I pray you, heed my words. Pembroke is no longer held in such high esteem since Bannockburn, and Lancaster, whom I know you despise, is gaining more and more power. He and Warwick will have the rule of the land if something is not done soon.' She walked to the window and looked out. The snows were gone and spring buds had started to appear; even the icy winds could not stay nature's routine.

'Plantagenets have been known to be loyal, my lord. Be assured I shall not forsake this marriage; you have lost your lady. Look to those that still live for comfort. The grave is our certain end, but life has many sweet facets that may not be to your taste as yet, but…your body will dictate the need for a woman 'ere long, I dare swear, and I will accept that need if not your…devotion.'

'I will say this for you, madam, you are nothing if not persistent, but I shall not look to you for anything, comfort or otherwise; surely I speak plain enough, even for you.' He slumped down in a chair as if the interview had wearied him beyond his endurance.

She stood looking at his hunched form and sighed. 'It's a pity, methinks we would make a formidable pair.'

'We shall never be in harness, madam, neither on this side nor the other side of hell.'

She pulled on her cloak and walked to the door, turned and said quietly, 'Don't forget my words about the needs of your king. Pray let my journey not be in total waste. If I've failed for myself, do not let me fail for my country.'

She waved her hand and swiftly left the sorrowing earl to his memories. It had not gone as she had hoped. No reconciliation, no closer to healing the bitter breach, but the powers of darkness had proved they could remove an adversary, even though the spirit had been pure. Jeanne had been accused of being a true Plantagenet and she smiled at the thought. There was truth in Warenne's accusations; now she must find a way to bring her erring husband into her orbit and on that issue she was adamant: failure was unthinkable. She would once again seek the aid of the daughters of darkness, not for death this time, but for a love potion. These thoughts comforted Jeanne de Bar as she journeyed back to Reigate Castle.

CHAPTER XXIII

Meanwhile, in the Welsh Marches in the County of Glamorgan, during the first weeks of 1315, one Llywellyn Bren rose up and took the castle of Caerphilly. Urgent action was called for on the part of the Marcher lords to quell this rebellion before it could spread throughout the length and breadth of Wales. England could not sustain a war with both Wales and Scotland, and Bruce was not sitting idly back after his victory at Bannockburn, sending two of his now famous lieutenants, James Douglas, styled the 'Black Douglas', and Thomas Randolph, Earl of Moray, on raids against the soft underbelly of England with so much success that they had reached as far as Richmond.

Roger Mortimer, glad of some positive action, had handled the Welsh uprising in such a decisive manner that he had brought about Llywellyn's surrender personally on the eighteenth of March. The weeks of vigorous fighting had dispelled much of Roger's erstwhile low spirits and he had regained much of his old bravado. On his return to Ludlow he was once again full of confidence, his self-esteem restored after the galling experience at Bannockburn.

However, the good humour quickly melted on hearing the news of Olympia's untimely death. Each of the Mortimer family mourned the passing of the lovely young woman who had filled their lives with her warmth and good humour. Forgotten the slur of adulteress and whore, in their hearts they knew she never deserved that title, being always a true and gentle lady whose only sin had been to love too well.

Roger knew that his brother John was hard hit by Olympia's death, and he tried to keep him as busy as possible to stave off the gnawing pangs of grief. This was no difficult task, for the whole land was now in turmoil. The weather did little to help. Torrential rains filled the rivers and streams to overflowing, and when the banks burst and the lands flooded, many feared for the spring crops.

To make matters worse the news from Ireland was a serious cause for alarm. Edward Bruce had landed in Larne with the Earl of Moray, Thomas Randolph, with some 6,000 mail-clad soldiers.

'The hounds of war are nipping at our heels on all sides, it would seem,' Roger said as he sat before a crackling fire. His uncle, brother and a number of knights from the Marches sat around.

John broke the gloomy silence. 'You will have to go to Ireland by the sound of it and this time I would like to accompany you.'

Roger looked up from the flames and studied his brother hard. His eyes looked yellow in the reflection from the fire. He missed nothing of the younger man's expression. He knew John was deep in a world of private misery at the loss of Olympia. Whilst she lived, there had always been the possibility that one day she would return to Ludlow or Wigmore, and John would have been there to comfort and cherish her, but in death there was no hope, only the desire to join her.

Roger cleared his throat. 'I need you here, John. I think the Welsh may try to rise again, and I must have someone I can trust, who is capable of dealing with any emergencies whilst I'm away.'

'Then let our good uncle stay.' John's face was full of pleading. The Lord of Chirk grunted at the mention of his name.

'I'm for Ireland, with the king's licence. Edward Bruce is as hotheaded as his brother is cool, and we owe our dead comrades a victory over that accursed family.' He ran his fingers along the blade of a deadly-looking dirk as he spoke and his lips curled back in a snarl.

'The fate of a younger brother is not always an easy one, I know, but, believe me, I must have someone here whom I can rely on in a crisis. Serve me in this, John. I will not always stand against your will.' Roger patted his brother affectionately on the shoulder as he spoke.

John shrugged half-heartedly. 'Have it as you will.' He rose and helped himself to another cup of ale.

The talk continued far into the night and to offset some of John's chagrin, Roger finally agreed that it should be his younger brother that applied to the court for leave to go to Ireland on his behalf, at least in some measure easing John's disappointment.

When all had sought their beds, Roger remained and sat gazing into the dying embers. In a few short weeks he would be eight and twenty, a father of nine children. He had tasted the pleasures and the defeats of life. He had gained a reputation as a man of action and astute in matters judicial, but he sometimes caught himself thinking of Isabella and grudgingly conceded that men were often weak-willed creatures.

Joan was his true and loving wife; they had grown up together. She was a good mother and had made Ludlow a warm and comfortable home. He loved Joan, of that there was no doubt...but... nevertheless how many times did Isabella come unbidden into his thoughts?

He had desperately tried to forget her, but always failed miserably. Even during his busiest days she would steal into his mind. How often had he pondered on her wellbeing? It was bitter irony that she had been matched to the weak half-man who, pleasant enough as a companion, lacked the metal of his sire. But Isabella had made even Edward man enough to sire a child. Roger could not suppress a smile. Below that ice-blue stare and aloof exterior he sensed the true woman beneath. Was it not a fact ice could burn?

Unable to still his racing thoughts he kicked the last embers into ashes and went to seek his own repose. There was much to be done in the coming months. Ireland would need all his acumen and courage. Much as he liked the Irish chieftains he knew it was not politic to place too much trust in their loyalties. That would only court disaster and he was not foolhardy enough to ignore the fact.

The de Lacys had fled to Bruce's court when Roger had routed them some years previously; he was certain they would be only too willing to return and try to regain what they had once possessed. To seize a chance to settle old scores and fulfil the threats they had poured onto his head would prove too great a temptation, of that he felt certain.

There were matters on the home front too which caused him deep concern since the fateful disaster at Bannockburn. The steadying hand of the Earl of Pembroke, Aymer de Valence, had lost much of its old standing with Edward. Thomas Lancaster and the 'Black Dog of Arden', the Earl of Warwick, were now the mainstay of Edward's advisors with the ever present Despencers. God! Poor Isabella, surrounded by the likes of that craven bunch;

at least the Church had taken her part and would be a powerful ally in times of crisis now that Pembroke had been virtually replaced.

Roger Mortimer slept little that night and the sound of the rain drumming on the window did nothing to aid his sleeplessness. He would be glad when he could leave for Ireland, at least then he would have something positive to do and little time to brood.

It was as Roger had predicted. The de Lacys had joined with Edward Bruce and through that wet and stormy summer Ireland had been in ferment. The Earl of Ulster, Richard de Burgh, father-in-law to Robert Bruce, had been defeated at Antrim. With the taste of success in his mouth, Edward Bruce had swept across Ireland and invaded Meath, where there had been a fierce battle between the Scots mercenaries and the Mortimer troops. Outnumbered, the Mortimers had been defeated, and the de Lacys were once more in control of Trim and Leix.

Roger returned to England in 1316 in a high state of dudgeon at his failure to beat his old adversaries. However, he had little time to dwell on his losses as he was summoned to help the Earl of Pembroke subdue a rebellion by the burgesses in Bristol. So incensed was that body of men that it took a siege engine to compel their surrender.

All was unrest! All was turmoil! All was failure! The harvest failed for the second year through the unseasonable weather; poverty, starvation and sickness ran through the land like a running sore. As Roger rode back to London he was deeply moved by all the scenes of privation he passed. Even the king's own keeper-of-horses had been assaulted and robbed, such was the mood of the people.

Grim-faced, his mind heavy, defeat and civil disturbances had set their mark upon him. The only light in his life was the thought that he would see Isabella once more. Isabella! Ma Belle! He spurred his horse at the memory of those clear, crystal-blue eyes, eager to catch just a glimpse of the woman who disturbed so many of his thoughts.

During his short sojourn in London Roger did in fact see Isabella, but only from afar. She looked as delightful and elegant as he had remembered and nothing of her personal life marred the loveliness of her face or clouded the brilliance of her eyes. She had not aged an hour since last he had seen her, and his heart beat so loudly at the sight of her he felt all could hear its thundering.

In the council chamber he encountered Warenne and was moved by the change in the earl. He had aged considerably, with a sprinkling of grey around his dark temples. His features were set granite-hard and the look in the dark-blue eyes, cold and distant. He had sat in the meeting of magnates saying hardly a word and it seemed to Roger that Warenne had almost to be accosted before he spoke. In a lull in the debate, Roger made his way to the side of his friend.

'Good day, my lord earl. This company looks as if it finds no favour in your eyes.' He hesitated, unsure whether he would get any response.

'God's death! Their preamble is little better than a load of haggling fishwives.' Warenne rose and beckoned Mortimer to follow.

They left the crowded hall and walked for some time in complete silence. Roger spoke first, fearing that Warenne would never make the effort and remain silent.

'I hear you have become the most prolific champion in the lists.'

They had reached a rough, rustic seat which nestled in the shadows of a yew arbour.

'I court death with the fervour of an ardent suitor...but...she plays the coquette and turns her face, leaving me with a vain title of "Champion of all England".' He laughed a dry, humourless sound. 'Nothing has any meaning for me these days without...without... Olympia.' He spoke the name in hushed tones. 'This chatter in the council chambers is trivia. What care I if Edward is content to lay the realm at Lancaster's feet and distributes the rest of his inheritance to such minions as that creepy little toad Despencer and his sniffling son.' Warenne turned his stern gaze on his handsome companion. 'Aye, a sorry state on all fronts, and you have not fared so well in Ireland by all accounts.'

'It is but a temporary setback. Edward Bruce is too rash, unlike his brother Robert. Did you know they have crowned Edward Bruce king of the Irish?' Warenne looked askance.

'Now there's a pretty state of affairs! What do you think Robert Bruce will make of that? I would like to be a fly on the wall when those two meet again.' The old grin suddenly flashed across the swarthy face.

Roger nodded in agreement. Silence fell as the two men sank into their own thoughts. They watched courtiers and servants walk past and acknowledged a wave or nod from acquaintances and friends. Had Roger been alone rather than with Warenne, he would probably have spent time in gossip and exchanging news. As it was, John de Warenne did not invite small talk, or uninvited companionship.

After a while Roger said slowly, 'We were all deeply distressed at Olympia's death. She meant a great deal to all of us, especially John and my mother.'

Warenne did not answer for a time, then slowly, as though the words cost him dear, said, 'She took all that was good in me with her. My only consolation is that I know we shall meet again on the other side of the grave. My life is so empty without her and the irony of it is I who loved her more than anything else on earth was the one who killed her.'

Roger looked up at the implication of those words. 'Childbearing is a natural business, you cannot take the blame upon yourself, it's God's will. Olympia herself would not countenance that verdict, I'll warrant. She who was so full of life and happiness would mourn to see you brought to such a low degree. Be true to her memory, but I beg you take up the threads of your life again and live.'

Warenne did not speak for some minutes. 'How can you comprehend such a loss as mine? How can anyone for that matter? Pray, let things be, Mortimer, I'm sure you speak only out of friendship.' The subject was closed and Roger knew better than pursue it further. Just then he espied a young maid looking towards them. She was a comely wench, with flaming hair and wide, dark-brown eyes, her mouth lifting in a smile. As she approached she dropped a deep curtsey to Warenne and then to Roger.

'Good morrow, my lord earl and my lord baron.' Roger studied her with the experienced eye of a soldier, noting the full breast, tapering waist and flaring hips. She was quite a striking wench and no mistake. But the dark-brown eyes were intent on Warenne.

'I do not think you remember me, my Lord of Surrey.' Her pale face was sprinkled with freckles, but there was a fresh vitality about her. This was no shrinking violet.

Warenne stared up at her then rose from his seat. 'I'm afraid you have me at a disadvantage, mistress.' Roger wanted to laugh for Warenne seemed almost boyish in his embarrassment.

'Maud, Maud de Nereford, from Norfolk.' The dark-brown eyes had never left Warenne's face.

'Ah, yes, of course, now I remember, but you were only a child then and…and…now quite full grown.'

'Handsomely so if I may say.' Roger smiled at the intruder, his golden eyes sparkling flirtatiously at the young girl.

'Why, thank you, sir,' she said and tore her gaze away from Warenne to look at the speaker. For a while they studied each other with unabashed appraisal. 'If I'm not mistaken, you must be Roger Mortimer, Baron of Wigmore.'

'At your service, Mistress Maud.' He bowed and took her neat little hand and kissed it. She blushed to the roots of her fiery hair.

'Yes, I have heard much of your exploits with the ladies.'

'Indeed! Do tell me more.' He twinkled at her, enjoying the exchange of banter. 'Methinks you mistake *this* Mortimer for my uncle!'

Suddenly Warenne interrupted. 'Come, Mortimer, do not tease Mistress Maud, she can be a formidable wit when the need arises and if she has not fallen prey to the shallow habits of court will speak as direct as any man.'

Maud went and stood by Warenne. 'I have not lost my forthright tongue, my lord. I am in constant hot water through my speech and am presently to be returned to my father's house because of upsetting some old dame.'

Roger laughed. Maybe this diverting young wench would be just what Warenne needed to brush the cobwebs of mourning away. There was no doubt that this girl found the swarthy earl to her taste for her eyes never strayed far from his face. Feeling the moment propitious, Roger excused himself from their company and made his way back towards the stuffy council hall.

As he rounded a neatly trimmed hedge he came face to face with the queen and her ladies. He immediately fell to one knee. Isabella came towards him and extended her hand for the kiss of salutation and homage.

'Why, it is the Lord Mortimer, is it not?' Her voice was as clear as her eyes.

'At your service, Highness.'

'We have not seen you at court of late.'

'I have been in Ireland.'

'Ah, yes. We fare as unsuccessfully there as in Scotland, 'twould seem.'

Her words cut into his pride and he raised his eyes; they flamed with the fires of anger that even the royal lady could not ignore. He rose and stood before her. 'Merely a reversal of fortune! We were ill-advised as to the accuracy of their numbers, but I will be avenged.'

'You...' she half-smiled at the vehemence of his words. She turned to her ladies as she said, 'Indeed, I'm sure we shall all feel safer in our beds now that we know you have the matter in hand.' Her cool speech wounded like tiny sword pricks.

'Edward Bruce is like a mad dog, and as such will be brought to bay, madam. I do not speak idle boasts.' His eyes challenged her, turning to a strange yellow in their anger. She had never seen such cat-like eyes in a man. Her skin tingled under his gaze as she realised she had hurt his pride. Immediately she was contrite. 'Pray excuse my hasty derision, my lord baron. For a moment I forgot your success against the Welsh. It was churlish of me to speak thus to the one man who, over the last year, has tasted victory.'

The look that passed between those two proud people was not lost on the ever-watchful Eleanor Despencer. The Mortimer men were virile, bold and ambitious. She must see that this forceful, handsome member did not gain any influence with the young queen. A word in her husband's ear would not come amiss.

Isabella took her leave and walked on through the pleasant gardens, her women still laughing and giggling at the interview, all that is except the Lady Despencer.

Roger remained where he was for a while longer. The scent of Isabella was still fresh, and he felt bemused by her fragrance. The touch of her hand had thrown him into a cauldron of conflicting emotions. That strange feeling that somehow, someday, he would win the love of this proud, beautiful ice queen was stronger than ever. The notion was inconceivable. She was the Queen of England, of the blood royal; and he, for all his self-assurance, was of a lowly, although powerful, order in the ranks of nobility. But the feeling would not be shaken and with its teasing presence he felt some consolation, though the sting of her taunts still rankled.

CHAPTER XXIV

In the February of 1317, Roger Mortimer raised a large army at Haverfordwest to oust the arrogant King of Ireland, Edward Bruce, who still ran rampant over the Irish countryside.

The English and Welsh forces landed at Youghal in southern Ireland during Easter week. Mortimer, who had been appointed Warden and Lieutenant of Ireland, knighted two of the thirty-eight squires in his company, one John de Bermingham, and Nicholas de Verdon.

Upon establishing contact with the remaining loyal Irish, Roger, in his new guise, called for a Parliament in April where plans were drawn up to overthrow the Scottish contingent.

In June he encountered his old adversaries, the de Lacys, and defeated them, even though they twice tried to rise against him. They finally fled from the onslaught of the fierce Marcher lord back to Scotland.

His success was as much due to his own charisma and decisive nature, and many of his old allies came to the aid of their new overlord. He was no mealy-mouthed prating Anglo-Norman but a strong leader and seasoned warrior.

The imprisoned Earl of Ulster, Richard de Burgh, was released as a consequence of one of Mortimer's many successful raids. That gruff and fiery man found much in Mortimer to his own liking, and they worked well together but with guarded respect.

So well did the new administration function that Mortimer left for England in late autumn, not wanting to be away from his family any longer than was absolutely necessary. He had achieved what he had set out to do and regained all his old lands and titles. Besides, he was yet to see his new offspring, another daughter whom his wife had christened Agnes. He had now sired no less than ten children, four sons and six daughters, and he still only in his thirtieth year.

The thought brought a smile to his handsome, weather-beaten face. Joan his tiny wife had proved a fruitful and dutiful partner. Already their second daughter Maud had been married in the previous year to the eldest son of John Charlton, Lord of Powys. It was a good match. He would endeavour to gain the best marriages for all his children.

However, his heart ached to see his beloved Ludlow and Wigmore once more. Much as he had relished the vigorous action and power that his new office in Ireland had afforded him, there was a strong bond of affection for his little wife and their energetic brood. However, even ties of family failed to quench the intense longing he felt for Isabella who always filled his body with such sweet, overwhelming yearnings. But there was another reason why Roger wished to be back in England with all speed. John his brother had sent a messenger with such a tale of wild improbabilities concerning his uncle and namesake, Roger Mortimer, Lord of Chirk, Only a personal assessment would sort out the rights and wrongs of the situation. There had been 'crime', a heinous crime, mentioned, and John feared the cause would ignite another uprising in Wales.

Roger rubbed his chin; his uncle was after all a Justiciar of Wales, what crime would a man in that position commit? His weakness was mainly women, but surely that was not cause enough for a rebellion. Or was it? Roger could not help worrying over this new situation. If after all his uncle had been indiscreet with the wrong man's wife or daughter, God knew what mischief could be let loose on the Borders in the name of injured pride and honour. The Welsh were very touchy on both counts; much in the same way as he himself might react. After all he had Welsh blood in his veins.

He had also heard earlier reports of acts of sadistic violence that the elder Mortimer had been guilty of in his earlier life; perhaps it was under that heading that the sudden outbreak of hostilities had erupted. John was not a scaremonger, he would not have sent a messenger hotfoot to Ireland for nothing.

So it was with mixed feelings that Roger boarded the vessel bound for England during the last days of October. At least he returned with the satisfaction of knowing he had staunched the tide of Scottish supremacy in Ireland – no mean feat. Now perhaps Isabella would regret her words of last summer.

After what seemed like an interminable journey home, Roger

resolved to enjoy the Yuletide festivities with his wife and family. The days were filled with the sounds of laughter and noisy revelry at his home-coming, to the delight of his wife Joan and their bonny children.

As yet, Maud was too young to become a wife in anything but name, and her equally young bridegroom was also among the numbers that visited Ludlow that year. Other familiar faces were Lord John de Giffard and his handsome wife Adela. Warenne and the pert Maud de Nereford too were guests. The haunted look of a year ago had softened a little with the passing of time, and Roger applauded the fact that the Norfolk wench had managed to snare her man. Of course the liaison had scandalised the court and Warenne was once more in disgrace, but still pursued the elusive divorce with his old persistence. How he had managed to persuade Joan to invite him for Yuletide, being as he was under the cloud of royal displeasure, Roger had yet to discover.

Roger did not miss the look of consternation in the young Maud de Nereford's face when Adela de Giffard sought out Warenne.

'My lord earl, it is good to see you again.' Adela's mellow voice was low and pleasing to the ear. Warenne smiled at the Lady de Giffard. He liked this self-possessed, handsome woman.

'Pray will you not call me Warenne? Surely we should not stand on ceremony in such informal circumstances.' Adela was cradling the newest Mortimer arrival in her arms. 'Why, madam, you look like a Madonna nursing her babe!'

Adela smiled. 'I accept your compliment for I know you would not cozen me... Warenne.'

'I have not heard the name said so well since...' he hesitated, and then softly, 'Olympia.'

'You still carry the image of that lovely lady in your heart and where'er you go, methinks!' Her clear, grey eyes looked at him; she leaned over and kissed his dark cheek. 'The world is a sadder place without her sweet presence. She was a true friend, as I would now be to you.' The baby began to cry. Adela smiled down at the bundle of life.

'I think she has had enough of our company and seeks her wet nurse.' So saying, Adela rose and handed the child back to the nurse who was hovering close by. Neither of them noticed the petulant looks Maud de Nereford was casting in their direction.

Warenne had expected Adela to admonish him about his new relationship with Maud. However, Adela was cognizant of a man's need for female companionship. The girl did not touch his heart, of that she was certain.

As for Roger, not even the season of revels was about to divert him from discovering the cause of this new threat from Wales. So, without further ado, he sought out the lords Charlton and de Giffard to find out the exact nature of his uncle's transgressions. But neither man would be drawn on the subject and Roger could not even get his own brother to say more than he had already written. Determined to get to the root of the matter he made plans to ride to Chirk and confront his kinsman at the earliest possible convenience.

However, the feast of Twelfth Night delayed any immediate action. It was a great feast which was held in the hall at Ludlow with such a vast gathering of lords and their ladies, burgesses, merchants and the like that the castle was filled to overflowing with all manner of merrymaking.

It had long been Roger's policy to encourage trade, being wise as to its importance for the growth of his demesne and the future prosperity of his people. He brought together many who would, under normal circumstances, not have come into contact with each other, and with the example of their host's informality towards one and all in the convivial atmosphere of the festivities many new ventures were born and new partnerships forged.

Mortimer was well pleased. He noted how the wine loosened stiff pride and reserve. Satisfied at his achievement he drank a silent toast to himself. The golden eyes were as mellow as ripened corn and he nodded and smiled at one and all, mingling amongst the throng, patting this back and sharing a jest with that burgher. Yes! Here he was at ease with his surroundings. Nor even the cloud of his uncle's indiscretions spoiled the festival. Nonetheless he was determined to settle the matter as soon as he was able.

Through most of his adult life the Lord of Chirk had been a mentor to the young Mortimer. Now as the latter studied the evidence before him he felt nothing but revulsion and loathing.

After many years of fighting in Wales there remained an undercurrent of tension between its people and the powerful Marcher lords. During much of Roger's jurisdiction the uneasy peace had held with the exception of the revolt by Llywelyn Bren, Now, through this single act of unprovoked madness by his uncle, all stood to be lost.

A certain Welsh knight, Sir Gryffiths, had seized the opportunity to move swiftly against the Lord of Chirk slaying many of his followers on his return from Builth. It left Roger facing a delicate situation as to his next all-important move. To bring about a solution acceptable to both proud men would test all his diplomacy and tact. He had somehow contrived a meeting between the two men which could prove more than a little touchy; both the Lord of Chirk and Sir Gryffiths were still in hot blood over the incident and Mortimer now called them to order so that each could state his own case.

The scene on that crisp January morning of 1318 was hushed and expectant. Whispers ran round the grim hall of justice. All had come to see how the Baron of Wigmore would handle this highly charged situation.

The two men stood before the bench. To one side sat a grey-clad clerk, holding a quill poised ready to write down their words verbatim. Mortimer nodded towards the clerk who rose and addressed the crowd to bring them to order. Then, bowing towards the younger Mortimer, he indicated to the two litigants to be seated.

Roger took a close look at each of the men before him and was thankful for his time with the volatile Irish; that experience would stand him in good stead during this session.

His uncle rose and burst forth with a tirade of abuse towards the still-seated, giant-like Welshman, whose hand flew to the lethal-looking blade at his waist.

Roger raised his hand. 'Gentlemen, I will not tolerate any violence in this courtroom. We are here to determine the facts which have brought Wales once more to the brink of war. 'Twould seem that many think I shall be biased in my judgement. Know you this, my only concern today is to ascertain the truth and then decide on an honest method of sentence.' His voice was steady, the handsome face stern as he spoke to all there gathered.

The disgruntled Lord of Chirk sat down again, obviously displeased by his nephew's statement, but it seemed to find favour with the red-headed Welshman.

'Now if you are ready, Master Clerk, we shall hear from Sir Gryffiths why he thought it necessary to slay the entourage of the Lord of Chirk.'

The Welshman rose, his bulk seeming to fill the courtroom. He spoke rapidly in Welsh until Mortimer raised his hand.

'I understand your language, Sir Gryffiths, but not at such a rate. I pray you, more slowly for my sake.' He indicated towards the clerk, 'And for our hard-pressed scribe.'

The big man nodded and began again in a deep baritone voice that rang around all the corners of the room. 'As you know, my lord baron, it is the duty of the Lord of Chirk to collect levies and taxes from these Marches at certain times of the year, and last September he came to the hamlet of Penkelly, some five miles from my own manor. All the able-bodied men of that place had gone with your good self to Ireland, leaving only a feeble-witted old man, a veteran of Evesham, who was so badly mutilated he was but half-man, and the womenfolk with their young ones.

'It left hardly anyone to harvest the corn and tend the sheep, some of which had strayed, been stolen, or died from lack of attention. The harvest, like the sheep, was of no consequence to speak of, and when that...' he turned his gaze to where the Lord of Chirk sat and spat out, 'devil's bait came to collect the dues and was told of their plight, he was totally unmoved by their pleas, gave them a day's span to collect the said dues and bring them to him on pain of death.

'That night Chirk and his men spent drinking and whoring in the neighbourhood, and when they arrived to collect the monies and hides, they were still well laced with their excesses. On finding the situation unchanged, that fiend of hell crucified the old man in his own doorwell. They then proceeded to rape and murder the womenfolk and butcher the children. All but for one girl, who managed to hide in a tree in the garden of her dwelling till the slaughter was over. She marked well the coat-of-arms on the tunics, which undoubtedly identifies the murderers.'

The Lord of Chirk rose, his black eyes glittered with hatred and rage. 'Will you believe this...this madman's rantings? I'm Justiciar of all Wales and only in deference to my namesake came hither to stand like some common felon before my inferiors.' He looked towards his nephew who did not fail to note the inflection on the last words.

'For God's sake, dismiss these farcical proceedings and let us be about our business.' The golden eyes of the younger man held those of his uncle for an instant, the expression causing the older man to drop his gaze.

'That, sir, is what I am doing. Do the allegations brought by Sir Gryffiths have any truth?'

'None!'

The Welshman broke in: 'My lord, the girl is willing to tell her tale, but wishes someone to stand by her side, for she truly fears the Lord of Chirk.'

The young Mortimer nodded and indicated for his ever-faithful servant Meyrick to go and guard the child. She came forward hesitantly and visibly shivered when her eyes rested on the dark figure of the elder Mortimer.

With difficulty and obvious terror, she related all the gory details that had been outlined by the giant Sir Gryffiths. Roger sat tight-lipped, horrified that his own uncle could act thus, even in drink. His whoring was common knowledge and no woman was safe when he rode abroad. That, however, was not the issue. It was the fact that men serving their liege lord should return to find their homes and loved ones abused and slain by a kinsman of the very lord they served.

After the child had finished, a silence fell over the assembly. Roger sat for some time deep in thought. Then slowly he said, 'The men would all have received the king's coin for their services, why did they not send some to their families so that the annual taxes could be paid?'

The Welshman answered, 'They did, my lord, but as fate would have it, the messenger was waylaid, robbed and murdered. The money never arrived.'

When Roger spoke again, he kept his eyes fixed on his uncle. 'How many men did you lose?'

'Eighteen dead, two wounded, and five horses.'

Roger looked across towards the Welshman. 'You agree those numbers.'

'Aye, my lord.'

'And how many were slain at the hamlet?'

'Two men, seven women, and nine children.'

'An equal number. Then here is what I suggest, and if it finds favour with you and your people, Sir Gryffiths, the matter will then be closed forever. No feuds, no further action on either side.'

The Welshman nodded. 'We await your lordship's verdict.'

'Then here is my judgement. That an infirmary be built on the site of the hamlet, at the expense of the Lord of Chirk. That it be maintained by him and his heirs in perpetuity. That a physician and priest be on hand to attend to the needs of the flesh and of the spirit for the people of that district, these also to be paid a yearly sum by the Lord of Chirk. That I will lay this evidence and recommendations before the Bishop of Hereford and whatever punishment he deems fit for such a crime, then the Lord of Chirk will submit himself, under my surety, to serve any penance prescribed.'

A gasp ran round the room. The big Welshman stared hard at the young man who had just finished speaking. 'The final word must be with the relatives of the deceased.'

Roger nodded, keeping his eyes on the wall at the back of the courtroom; he was aware of the suppressed rage of his uncle, who sat seething beneath his black, saturnine exterior. After Sir Gryffiths had made his consultations he returned to the bench.

'We find your sentence just and fair, but the men on their return will have neither land nor stock with which to restart their lives.'

'Then payment will be made. I will offer permanent tenancies on some of my demesnes, or service in either household or as soldiers. The choice will be theirs.'

Sir Gryffiths nodded his great red head. 'Then I say that is a sound course, your honour.' He stood, then said in a burst, 'We did not think you would find against your own kinsman, my Lord of Wigmore, but I applaud your good fairhandedness in this matter.'

Roger rose and swept from the court, relieved that things had turned out so well. He caught sight of Meyrick, the pale frightened child still clutching at his hand.

'Tell Sir Gryffiths, if he agrees, that I shall take the girl and raise her with my own family.'

His uncle had tried to speak with him, but Roger was so full of gall that he swept past him without a backward glance, giving instructions for his own men-at-arms to escort his uncle back to Chirk to await the Bishop of Hereford's findings.

Roger returned to Ludlow in a pensive mood. He had deplored the actions of his uncle, but felt certain that the Lord of Chirk would manage to sidestep any serious condemnation from the bishop, Adam Orleton, but the savage butchery of the villagers was to stay with him for many months.

As always the sight of his beloved Ludlow served as a balm to his troubled spirits, but not for long, for as he, Meyrick and the swift-riding company of guards trotted through the gateway, it was to a mournful-faced Hamo as Roger flung himself from the saddle and handed his reins to the wizened little groom.

'What ails you, man?'

'Master! 'Tis a sorry day for the Mortimers and no mistake. My old heart breaks to have to be the one to tell you.'

'Tell me what? Come, come, Hamo, it's not like you to chew on news like yesterday's meat. Out with it, man.'

''Tis Master John, he's dead. Slain at a tournament in Worcester.'

Roger felt those words like a physical blow. 'John? But surely John had taken a fever and was confined to his bed?'

'Aye, m'lord, though he could scarce stand, nothing would bend him from his purpose. I tried, on my soul! The baroness, God bless her, came and begged him not to go. Knelt on the ground and besought him in the name of the Virgin Mary, but…to no avail.'

Roger saw the sadness in the old man's face and gripped the bowed shoulder hard. There were many good memories attached to this old face and frame, and not a few with his brother.

'Master, he were so weak he could hardly hold the lance, nor sit straight in the saddle.' The old rheumy eyes were filled with unshed tears. 'The knight who struck the fatal blow was Sir John de Leyburne. I did diligently trace that man's history and think there was no malice; it was an unfortunate strike. It seems he thought that Master John was either drunk or feigning drunkenness and he merely wanted to floor him to teach him a lesson.'

Roger could not speak. He turned and walked through the outer bailey, his mood even darker than the shadows of night. His beloved John, so trusted an ally, gone. So he had had his wish in the end. Since Olympia's death the light had gone out of living for his brother.

No longer constrained by loyalty and duty, he had died to be near his love. Pray God he had not died in vain!

The golden eyes filled with scalding tears and he sought refuge in the round chapel where he sank to his knees and prayed. But his sorrow seared through him and he wept unashamedly. After a while he rose and lit a candle; there had been no truer friend nor dearer companion than John. Roger felt that a chapter of his life had closed with his death, the end of a good chapter, of the carefree boyish days of childhood. He struggled to regain his composure before facing the rest of his family and learning somehow to survive the loss of such a dear heart.

CHAPTER XXV

On 9 August 1318, Roger Mortimer and his uncle sat amidst the ranks of nobles, prelates and magnates, listening in on the council meeting that was to be known as the Treaty of Leake.

Isabella, who had recently given birth to her third child, a daughter, Eleanor of Woodstock, was also in attendance. To Roger, she looked as devastating as ever. Childbearing had not marred or thickened her graceful figure, nor detracted from her flawless beauty, unlike his wife Joan. He had not seen Isabella for many months and his eyes devoured her every move, but he took care that his intent scrutiny was unobserved.

She sat in the close atmosphere of the crowded hall, paying rapt attention to the wranglings, dissensions and resolutions with the same detached calm that he remembered. He knew those clear-blue eyes missed nothing of the details of the various speakers, nor what they said.

Over the past few years, since the defeat of the English at Bannockburn, Thomas Lancaster, premier earl of England, and hereditary Steward, had become the power behind the throne, Edward being only too happy to leave any major decisions of policy in the hands of his cousin. Now that Warwick was dead, Lancaster's supremacy went almost unchallenged.

As the younger Mortimer's gaze flicked round the table he noticed that Warenne had put in one of his rare public appearances. The feud between Lancaster and Warenne was by now a well-known fact. The wedge of hatred had been driven even deeper when Lancaster's wife, Alice de Lacy, had sought refuge with Warenne by being 'kidnapped' by one of his squires to ensure her safety as she sought a divorce from Lancaster.

During a break from the council chamber when many of the members sought a respite from the serious business of government on the hunting field, Roger, unencumbered by flying a hawk, remained free to ride amongst the party at will.

Whilst exploring a hillside a little way from the main field, he spied Isabella unattended and detached from the main group. She sat her palfrey with youthful elegance and grace, her head back as she watched the hawk sweep onto its quarry. He spurred his horse forward; this was an unlooked-for opportunity and he was not a man to pass such a chance. As he approached, she turned, suddenly aware of her vulnerability.

'Ah, it is the good Lord Mortimer.' She was instantly at ease again.

'La Belle Queen Isabella.' She laughed at his salutation.

'It has been a good day for the king's gyrfalcon, has it not?' she said.

'But I have the prize, methinks, madam,' he said, his eyes full of the burning emotion she always evoked in him.

'Take care, my lord, you tread on dangerous ground.'

'Would you betray me?' He looked deep into her eyes and saw the flush spread over her delicate pale face.

'Forgive me, Highness, if I appear too forthright; blame your beauty for making my tongue bold in your praise.' He grinned boyishly. The tension was broken. She was uncertain for a moment. The look in his eyes did not altogether match the bantering tones.

'You cozen me, my lord.'

'I would not stand accused of a crime I would never commit against *my* queen.' She noted the inflection.

'Really, my lord, I can never tell when you are serious and when you jest.'

'When I pay such a beautiful lady as yourself a compliment, know I am in deadly earnest.' He edged his horse closer to her. 'Will you accept my congratulations on your safe delivery. Your health is always close to the hearts of your subjects.'

She could not fail to note the seriousness of his tone nor the ardent look in those magnetic eyes. His nearness made her hands tremble and her heart race. 'Do you mean that truly, my lord baron?'

'More than you will ever know, my lady.' The last statement was said in such a rich, soft voice it caused her to catch her breath. The memory of a solitary figure standing in the moonlight and the gift of a necklace with a sapphire heart caused her usual self-composure to slip for a moment and the woman beneath to shine through. She felt stripped of her usual confidence and icy calm. The sound of approaching hooves broke the spell of the moment.

Edward came galloping up accompanied by his squires and the ever-present Despencer. 'Did you see? My falcon had first blood. Is he not a fine hawk?' He was so engrossed in his success that he had failed to notice that his queen sat alone, all that is but for the handsome knight, Roger Mortimer.

'It was a fine kill, sire!' Roger's voice had become cool and impersonal. He felt cheated of Isabella's attention. Nor could he entirely shake off disdain for his monarch's weakness towards his favourites. Isabella deserved more. Roger dropped his gaze, afraid that all his aroused emotions would be clearly read by the newcomers. Instead he bent forward and patted his horse's shining neck, but the queen did not fail to notice the change in the Lord Mortimer at her husband's arrival on the scene.

On their ride back Isabella looked under her lashes at the Baron of Wigmore. He was no longer a fanciful youth. Since their last meeting he had matured both physically and in reputation. Almost single-handed he had turned the tide of the Scottish invasion in Ireland and had used his wits to quash a certain rebellion in Wales. Their chance meeting had awakened fires within her she thought long conquered. Just the memory of the look from those magnificent eyes disturbed her more than she cared to admit. In just a few moments he had destroyed the years of rigid discipline she had imposed on herself.

But at the feast that evening Isabella once more captured her wayward emotions and no one guessed at the confusion that afternoon had caused the queen. The meeting with the handsome knight from the Welsh Marches had brought Isabella face to face with another side of her nature and the knowledge disturbed her greatly.

Edward was a good father, there was no denying that fact, and she had done all within her power to sway him from the taint in his character. They had three healthy children, the result of her efforts to be a good wife as well as a queen.

On that level she and Edward had found a measure of contentment and she had deluded herself that the love of her children was all the affection she needed. Now she knew otherwise. She caught herself watching couples: the secret signs, the unguarded caress, the stolen kiss. These things caused her as much pain and anguish as anything she had felt heretofore, and try as she might she could not still the nagging yearning that filled her every waking hour.

It was obvious that Edward could no longer hold his place at the head of the government. Nowadays he was too prone to the simpler pursuits of life and finding ways to please his favourites, a fact exploited by the Despencers who were gaining power and wealth daily.

Since the death at Bannockburn of Gilbert de Clare, Earl of Gloucester, a battle over inheritance had been raging through the courts of England for all the lands and estates that went with that title. At first the earl's widow had held up proceedings by declaring she was pregnant until it became obvious that there was to be no child. Therefore, all titles and estates pertaining to the dead earl now came under the jurisdiction of the Crown.

Gilbert's three sisters were co-heiresses: Eleanor, the eldest, was married to Hugh Despencer the younger. Margaret, widow to the late ill-fated Gaveston, had subsequently married Hugh Audley and Elizabeth was married to Roger Damory. The heart of the dispute hinged on the fact that Eleanor, being the eldest, claimed the title of Earl should now fall to her husband Hugh. The other two claimants did not agree with this reasoning and therefore wished to have a legal ruling on the matter.

The Despencers were nothing if not ambitious for land and titles. They meant power, position and wealth, and the younger of that name had already managed to alienate his wife from her sisters in his favour in their pursuit. This course of action would eventually bring about the downfall of both Despencers and the king, but not until they had brought England to the brink of civil war and gained most of the lands in Wales, to the ire of the Marcher lords and magnates.

During this time Aymer de Valence, Earl of Pembroke and one-time chief advisor to the Crown, seeing the shortcomings of the mighty Lancaster and the power-hungry Despencers, started to gather about him men of a more liberal disposition, who formed the 'Middle Party', together with John Salmon, Bishop of Norwich, John Hotham, Bishop of Ely, Humphrey de Bohun, Earl of Hereford, Walter Reynolds, Archbishop of Canterbury and

Bartholomew, Lord Badlesmere, a Kentish knight of great wealth. De Valence also sought out the Mortimers and other supporters of the 'Ordinances', which acted to restrict the power of the king by a baronial council.

But Roger had little time to play any significant part in that party of venerable nobles and prelates, being once again commissioned to attend the wars in Scotland.

England teetered ever closer to civil war. The Scottish situation had never been successfully brought to a conclusion, and every year men and equipment were sent against 'the Bruce'. It was a plague on the English nation and its treasury.

France too was making unfriendly noises, unhappy about Edward's lack of co-operation in paying homage for the lands and titles he held there, added to which the Welsh remained ever poised for some legitimate excuse to break the dominance of the Marcher lords.

So it was with a certain amount of relief that Roger Mortimer left the web of verbal intrigues and turned his head once more to his homelands. His only regret was that he must leave Isabella, but he was powerless to aid her in any way and realised that any open move on his part could bring down more trouble on her head, and that he would never do.

As he and Meyrick rode back into the hills and valleys of Shropshire, the majestic scenery served to quell his misgivings for the future. The bounding rivers and teasing waterfalls gurgled and chattered along and he felt the magic of the countryside. His spirits flew free once more. Through all the times of his life, the joys and sorrows, strife and anger, the permanency of these surroundings never failed to please him. For his life's span he was their guardian and protector, and along the rolling slopes and in the dark woods he could sometimes escape from his role as Marcher lord and be just like he was as a boy, carefree and at one with nature.

But times changed; and even in those rare precious moments when he was alone the inner ache he felt for Isabella was ever present. This was no mere lustful illusion. She was no boyish fancy, but his ideal, his knight's quest to cherish and love and share in life's wondrous pageant.

The name beat through his head in time with the rhythm of his horse's hooves. Isabella! Isabella! Isabella! God have mercy on us both, me for loving such a woman and she cast in the role of queen to a misbegotten man wholly unsuited to his part as England's king and ruler and husband to the 'Ice Queen'.

CHAPTER XXVI

Jeanne de Bar paced angrily along the corridors of the palace at Reigate. She marvelled at Warenne's dogged persistence in trying to gain a divorce and she frowned at the implications. He had obtained a Papal Bull upholding his claim that their marriage was invalid, and only her kinship with Edward Plantagenet stood in the way of the court's acknowledgement of the Pope's edict.

Now Warenne had sent a messenger to inform her that he was allowing her £700 per annum, together with lands and estates around Reigate, which included the castle itself, for the duration of her life.

It was a bitter blow, for this was a sure sign that Warenne would never be reconciled to their marriage. The pale-blue Plantagenet eyes were filled with tears of frustration and anger. The powers of the 'daughters of darkness' had failed. She had done everything that they had asked of her, gained a garment newly stained with his sweat; gathered hairs from his brush and stolen a pair of worn hose, but still he remained as aloof from her as when they had been first wed.

The strumpet that he had recently taken to his bed had already given him two illegitimate sons. Hellfire! What more could she do? At least here, in her own palace, she did not have to hide the feelings that were tightly mewed up whilst at court. All day she raged and ranted around her luxurious apartments, throwing clothes and vessels and even slapping some of her serving women in her fury.

She had faithfully administered the love-potion concocted by one of the evil-smelling witches. How sure she had been that Warenne would soon succumb to her desires, but instead the swarthy earl had merely fallen into a deep slumber, only to wake with a thundering headache and without as much as a glimmer of interest in his Plantagenet wife.

Jeanne returned once more to the crone with the one eye and after relating the failure of the potion the old woman cackled a dry eerie laugh. 'Your man is protected by a power stronger than mine, lady. Or he has the constitution of an ox. Mebbe both, heh! There was enough strength in the dose I gave ye to bring a thousand men to your will, but...' She twisted her long, bony fingers and then continued, 'If you want to win that one's heart and body you must look to the spells of a wizard. We witches have our limits, 'twould seem.'

Again the sound of that weird laugh. Jeanne shuddered even at the memory and she felt a chill run through her body causing gooseflesh. 'Then dame, tell me, where do I find a wizard? I tell you I have travelled too far along this path to give up now. Will you not help me? You were the one whose power took the life of his first paramour. Will you not see this thing through with me?'

The bright, bird-like eye seemed to penetrate into her mind. Then the rasping voice came again. 'It will take some of your pretty gold to find a wizard who is willing to work against the power that protects the one you would possess. Believe me, I have never known such a force and my magic has been successful against all forms of spells and incantations. But I knew before you came that my power was not strong enough this time.'

She threw some white powder into the flames in her hearth.

Then she muttered words in a language Jeanne had never heard before. The bright black eye looked up. 'A year and a day, then thrice you must pay, to visit the one with the power. Come again in a year, lady, on the eve of All Souls. The black art is at its strongest then. Bring a purse of pure gold and I will summon my master, he may come to your assistance.' She waved her thin, gnarled hand and dismissed Jeanne like some inconsequential serving wench. It had taken all of Jeanne's willpower to stay her hand from striking the insolent old hag, but she had too much at stake to let a trifling insult provoke her and besides she felt afraid.

It was useless to argue that a whole year must pass before she could try again to win Warenne. So she must be content meantime and only let her anger free in the confines of her own walls. When next she met Warenne in public she would try and be as courteous and as pleasant as she could, do her utmost to break through this impenetrable barrier which was between them.

Besides, there were other ways to win a man and she knew she was not without considerable charms. If only she could entice her elusive husband. Maybe feminine wiles could succeed where the black arts had failed.

As Jeanne mulled over her new strategy, Warenne, the cause of all her endeavours, rode across the Downs at Lewes. He had been hunting, but had outstripped his party on their return journey to the castle.

As Warenne sat surveying the familiar scene, memories rose up to greet him like old friends. His dark, swarthy face softened for an instant as he relived again his lost childhood. Tears filled the dark-blue depths as he saw again the girl, as pale as moonbeams, who had laughed and chatted her way into the heart of a grubby, surly youth. Silently his lips formed her name and like a whisper it escaped from deep within him. 'Olympia!'

Then to the gathering clouds of evening he called the beloved name aloud. 'Olympia!' It echoed down the green valleys and the valleys threw the sound back to the man whose heart still mourned for the loss of the only woman he had loved. She was burnt into his soul for all time and even the pretty, brown-eyed wench, Maud de Nereford, had not managed to quench the desire for his beloved Olympia.

Theirs had been a love complete. Nothing fey nor false; nothing hidden nor pretentious, a oneness, both giving and receiving in equal measure, one flesh, one passion, one undying love.

He felt the pain of his loss like a mortal wound which seared him through and through. The intense and utter loneliness she had left him to endure was almost unbearable. He spurred his horse as if to ride away from the hurt and stormed into the courtyard at Lewes in a spray of sparks from the iron-clad hooves.

'My lord, a messenger is awaiting your return.' The tall page ran to aid his master from the sweating horse.

'A messenger?'

'From the king, judging by his livery, my lord.'

'Damn! What does that weak-kneed monarch want with us this time, Will?'

The page grinned; he admired Warenne more than any other man he had ever met and had been delighted when his father had sent him into the household of the 'Champion Jouster of all

England'. Warenne was a man of action and few words. He was a hard taskmaster but a fair one and that was no mean reputation in those hard times.

'Perhaps we are called to serve against the Scots.' The man looked into the bright, eager face of the boy.

'And would that please you, Master Will?'

'Indeed, my lord.'

'Aye, 'tis the way of the young to look at war like a glorious crusade. Only the reality smashes that vision. Come, boy, we shall see what this messenger wants and put all our minds at rest.'

Warenne strode into the Great Hall. A squire brought the messenger before him. Bowing low the man handed a scroll of vellum to Warenne who, on recognising the seal, knew that his young page's supposition was correct.

Without looking up he nodded. 'We shall be ready to serve our king and country, tell your sovereign.' Warenne indicated to the steward, 'See that the king's messenger is well fed and rested for his return journey.'

A plague on this Scottish war, the heart had gone out of most of the English since Bannockburn, and it was only Plantagenet stubbornness that prolonged the inevitable outcome. Robert Bruce would prevail, for he was made of the true stuff of kings, strong, determined, with the ability to win men to his cause even when the odds seemed overwhelming. Still the venture would please his squire, no doubt, and Warenne shrugged off his displeasure. After all, this might be the excuse he needed to free himself from this life of loneliness and join his Olympia.

The words of Adela de Giffard often came back to him: 'Be patient, even a lifetime of many years is as a shadow and life passes swiftly before we've scarce grown accustomed to its pleasures and sorrows.'

As always, before he left his home at Lewes he rode the dozen miles to the neat graveside of Olympia and saw the flowers encircling the marble headstone that simply bore her name. He had made provision with the steward of the household to keep the grave well tended and adorned with fresh flowers. He knelt beside the green mound and murmured her name, talking as if she merely slept beneath the dark earth and harkened to his words. He touched the glittering talisman as he spoke and vowed again that he would never part with it whilst he still lived, and his instructions had already been given for it to be around his neck when he went to join her in the grave. Little did he realise that the fair hand of Olympia had stretched beyond the grave to protect him and that very talisman had averted the evil powers of the black arts which had been administered by his legal wife Jeanne de Bar.

After bidding his dead lover farewell he mounted and rode away, one of England's most powerful earls who would have gladly traded all for just a single day in the company of his beloved Olympia.

CHAPTER XXVII

1319

York hummed with excitement and activity. Parliament was again being held within its august walls and all the great lords and magnates of the day vied with each other for the best accommodation. The fresh May morning was filled with the wind which blew off the Yorkshire Dales and spring flowers danced and waved their colourful heads at its capricious whim.

Lancaster, haughty and indomitable as ever, made known in no uncertain manner the claim that he alone should be in charge of the king's household, as was his right as Steward of England. The position had been denied him at the previous Parliament and was held by the bluff Lord Badlesmere, a wealthy baron of the second order, who was firmly entrenched in Pembroke's Middle Party.

As the debate ran to and fro a weary messenger arrived to inform the gathering that Bruce had retaken Berwick, and all former discussion ran to ground with the enormity of the news. Berwick had been an English stronghold for many years.

Instantly orders were issued for all able-bodied men to muster at Newcastle in June, and so all there gathered sent urgent messengers throughout the length and breadth of England to inform the shires of this new call to arms.

A few weeks after, Mortimer and Warenne sat looking down a knoll over the heads of the milling throng of troops waiting below them that sunny June noon. The countryside was once again scorched by man-made fires and littered with rotting carcasses.

'Maybe one day we shall see this land standing knee-high in corn and fat beasts grazing across its skyline.' Mortimer spoke thoughtfully.

'There speaks the romantic. Idealism has no place in these fraught times. Blind greed and a well-trained army are more in keeping,' the dark-faced Warenne answered cynically.

'Ah, but one day, methinks, this Robert Bruce will achieve his objective and bring Scotland to a more peaceful age. His is a true military mind, God help us! Here we have the finest Welsh bowmen, the best-equipped heavy chivalry and the greater number of men-at-arms, whilst our spies tell us that the Scots have precious little of any of these commodities.' The golden eyes crinkled at the corners at his own words. 'What has happened to date has been more like a mummer's play than war manoeuvres.'

Warenne nodded. 'One has to concede the 'Bruce' is lacking nothing in courage or audacity. I for one will be keen to see how he handles this new move.'

Mortimer grinned. 'There's one thing for sure, he will not be left witless or in awe of such numbers, we have learnt that of the man if naught else. Come! Let us see what the imperious Lancaster has to say on the subject.'

For once a grin split Warenne's dark face and his crooked white teeth gleamed against the swarthiness of his skin, which had been tanned to an even darker hue than usual by the sun and wind.

They were a striking couple: one tall, broad of shoulder with unusual golden eyes burning from a tanned beardless face and neat curling black hair, who sat his courser with an easy grace; the other, broader, bearded and moustached, whose dark-blue eyes had a somewhat sad look to them. His straight-black hair shone like a raven's wing and his powerful thighs gripped his mettlesome mount which pranced and sidled along towards the bustling camp.

'A brace of dark knights,' called a saucy camp-follower as she grinned invitingly towards them. Mortimer bowed mockingly. Warenne ignored the remark. Lines of picketed horses nickered and watched the two ride through. The smells of the camp filled their nostrils and intermingled with the acrid smoke of the scorched land. Great cauldrons of stew bubbled and hissed. Blacksmiths, busy shoeing two queues of waiting horses, shouted for the lads to keep the fires hot, and the singeing hooves gave off that distinctive odour as the mighty hammers smote the heavy shoes onto waiting hooves. Leather tunics and human sweat all helped to make the smell unique. Armourers applied their own special skills as they sat amongst the gaggle of tents, many aware that in their hands lay the power of life and death. Men-at-arms ran hither and thither to their sergeant's bidding, and small pages carried pails of water and trays of victuals to their masters. Somewhere a tenor voice, as clear as a mountain stream, rose high above the clamour, and Mortimer laughed across at his companion.

'If it were merely a contest of voices and not of arms, then my Welsh troopers would annihilate allcomers with the first few bars.'

The notes from a lute somewhere over the other side of the lines rose and mingled with that glorious song, and the listeners wondered whether they would still be alive to sing such melodies after their next battle.

In July, when most of the English had mustered and were now formed into tight groups under their various gonfalons with the bright standards displaying the positions of the earls and their followers, bugles rang out to proclaim that the siege of Berwick was underway.

Mortimer had been ordered to take his bowmen to higher ground to enable them to pour arrows down over the lower defences on the outer limits of the grim castle. He did not doubt that many would find targets but whether soldiers or civilians was another matter. He shrugged such notions from him; war had no conscience or compassion.

As the days moved from warm July into humid August the English waited for Bruce's retaliation. News reached them that he had sent a fast-riding, heavily armed troop deep into the Yorkshire countryside and was even now making for York, where the queen and exchequer were ensconced.

The very audacity of the move left many overawed. Mortimer for one felt a cold grip at his heart. He did not doubt that Isabella would not by intention be physically harmed, but taken prisoner as Bruce's wife had been years before. The thought did not bear dwelling on and for once the irresponsible Edward appeared to be most put out by the import of this move by the Scots against his wife.

This canny ploy by Bruce had exactly the effect he wished for. Lancaster and many of the northern magnates insisted on withdrawing from Berwick to return with all speed to defend their own lands and estates both in Yorkshire and along the borders. The now famous 'Black Douglas' had earned his reputation in the cause of his beloved Robert Bruce and was now carrying out his monarch's orders to the letter by harrying, burning and looting any valuable plunder on his route.

After the devastation at York, Douglas rode swiftly on to Pontefract to Lancaster's own castle. These guerilla tactics enabled Bruce to negotiate a reluctant two-year truce with Edward.

Isabella managed to escape by water but had avoided capture only by a hair's breadth. Edward, after the immediate panic subsided, slipped deeper into his apathy which had him in its thrall. The torpor, cowardice and complete indifference to his realm were now so apparent that even the most loyal could not make any further valid excuses for Edward's incompetence.

All hope of reconciliation with Lancaster was shattered and when Parliament next sat in York in the January of 1320, he flatly refused even to attend, saying that the king was suspicious of his every move and all hands were turned against him.

Edward was completely unmoved by what went on at his Parliament and when he left for France in the summer, the Middle Party was still in control, with Lord Badlesmere Constable of Dover Castle and Warden of the Cinque Ports.

Mortimer was glad to turn his face once more towards his Welsh Marches away from the incessant arguments between the overbearing Lancaster and the king's favourite, Hugh Despencer the younger.

However, Joan de Geneville was not at Ludlow to greet his arrival. She had gone to Stanton Lacy to rest after the recent birth of Beatrice, their latest daughter.

Maud, his second daughter, had run across the bailey to meet him and the ever faithful Meyrick, as the younger children danced and chattered around his heels like a pack of excited hounds. The two elder boys, Edmund and Roger, were already in other households as squires, learning their new duties much as he had once done.

Roger Mortimer loved his children with a strong and protective passion. He knew all their strengths and weaknesses, but it did not diminish the plans he had to advance the Mortimer family on the ladder of his ambitions. One way was through marriage and he smiled and nodded and kissed each child in turn. It was a good thing for a man to have such a merry brood and, with some already linked to the most powerful houses in England. A good way to achieve his ambitions.

Only one of his offspring, Geoffrey, had inherited the dark, curling hair and golden eyes, but he would never match the beauty of his sire.

'Oh, father, are you home for long?' Maud's bright, dark eyes shone as she clung to his hand.

'Aye, for a while at least. Now what's this you tell me of your mother's stay at Stanton?'

Maud was full of importance as she was in charge of Ludlow in her mother's absence and was happy to fill the role of hostess to her beloved father. She had been married to John Charlton since her ninth year, but was now, at fourteen, a wife in more than name only and would soon have a household of her own to run.

Joan, the third daughter, was also married, to one James Audley, son and heir to Sir Nicholas Audley, a Welsh Marcher lord of some import. She had been well named for she had more than a passing resemblance to her mother, being both on the small side and with the same oval face and sloe-coloured eyes.

His fifth daughter Katherine, a tall, lissome girl with thick, black tresses and clear grey eyes which so reminded her father of his own dead brother John, was betrothed to none other than Thomas de Beauchamp who would one day be Earl of Warwick: an excellent match.

The absent Edmund, Roger's heir, was affianced to Elizabeth, daughter to Bartholomew Badlesmere, one of the staunchest members of the Middle Party and a very wealthy and powerful man to boot, though not of the first order of nobility, but wealth brought great advantages to a marriage contract.

Then came Roger's namesake, for whom he was negotiating a marriage with the daughter of Edmond le Bottiler of Ireland. As yet his other children were still to find matches, but their futures were ever in the thoughts of Roger who would do much to ally them to the greatest names in the realm.

He was glad to be back in the familiar surroundings of Ludlow and listen to the voices of his offspring.

The long miles of travel and months of tension, both in the field and at the council tables had made Mortimer appreciate the comparative calm and tranquillity of his home. The atmosphere acted like a buffer against the ills of the world.

'And will no one tell me of your granddam's wellbeing?'

His youngest son John piped up. 'She is full well, sire, and took me hawking not a se'nnight since.'

'And you could have no better tutor, she always had a good eye for a hawk.' Roger studied his youngest son, whose features were undoubtedly de Geneville. He was a sturdy boy, so unlike Edmund, who for all his mother's careful cosseting retained a hollow cough which plagued him more so in the months of winter.

Then there were Isabel and Agnes, the inseparable twosome, who stood back a little from the others, clasping hands and watching their sire with great, dark eyes.

'And what, pray, are you young maids up to lurking there in the background? Plotting mischief, I'll be bound.' Roger laughed at them.

'No...indeed, sir, we are not,' they chimed in childish unison, for as yet their handsome sire was a little overawing in his half-armour, spurs and stained riding cloak, with the grime of the roads still on his face.

'Come, babes, you have all grown since I last saw you and are eating me out of house and harbour, no doubt.' Even the two shyest members of the family could not remain aloof for long in the aura of their handsome father.

Life at Ludlow soon fell into a more normal pattern especially on Joan's return from Stanton Lacy, and she was quite spellbound at Roger's detailed account of the queen's narrow escape from York.

Little did Mortimer realise how precious these days would be for him in the peaceful lands surrounding Ludlow and Wigmore. He took delight in riding out with his family, hawking and hunting both the deer and wild boar. They all visited Wigmore frequently, and it was during one of those pleasant sojourns that a monk brought information at the behest of Adam Orleton, Bishop of Hereford, that was to cast a dark and ominous shadow across the lives of the Mortimer family, and would have far-reaching effects on them and many other notable families throughout the Welsh Marches.

It seemed the ever acquisitive Hugh Despencer the younger was now in open dispute with his two brothers-in-law Sir Nicholas Audley, father-in-law to Roger's own daughter Joan, and Roger Damory. Not content with the lands he had gained from Audley at Gwennllwyg Despencer had forced him to surrender the lordship of Newport in exchange for lands to the south-west.

In Carmarthen, Despencer had gained Cantrefmawr, and the old stronghold once held by the princes of Wales, Drussland; then in Glamorgan, he had been granted sovereignty as complete as any the Earl of Gloucester had ever possessed. Now with Lundy in his control there was no doubt that he would have mastery of the Bristol Channel. As to the territories in the west he only needed the lordship of Gower to round them off with the River Loughor acting as a boundary between his lands and those of the Earl of Lancaster's lordship of Kidwelly.

However, Gower was the property of one William de Braose, an impecunious Marcher lord who saw a way to make a fortune by selling his lands to the highest bidder. Unfortunately, the ill-fated Braose had died earlier that year leaving the ticklish situation in the hands of his son-in-law, John Mowbray, who promptly seized both the baronies of Swansea and Gower, much to the chagrin of the younger Despencer. This forced Despencer to show his hand, which he did by persuading Edward the king to declare that Gower had escheated to the Crown. This raised a vital question of privilege for the Marcher lords as to whether they became subject to English law.

Scarce had Roger and his mother been made aware of these new moves than messengers from throughout the Marches pounded the roads to Ludlow and Wigmore to bring first-hand news from the various houses who were at the heart of the dispute.

On Roger's hasty return to Ludlow he found John de Giffard already there, seething with indignation.

'I take it you have already heard of the new tactics by this syco-phant Despencer?' The grey, stern face of John de Giffard looked as if etched out of marble; only the keen eyes blazed with fierce fires of hatred.

'Is there word from either Damory or Audley?' Roger asked quietly, only too aware of the seriousness of the situation.

'God's blood! We all thought them well entrenched in Edward's favour,' Giffard exclaimed as he paced the stone-flagged floor in his ire, 'but 'twould seem that Despencer outruns us all in his quest for power and lands.'

'Aye!' Roger murmured. 'And by all accounts even presses Edward for the title of Earl of Gloucester.'

At that remark John de Giffard stopped dead in his tracks. 'Is there no stopping this man's avarice? I heard it rumoured, but thought it no more than idle chatter, but you say there is substance to the gossip.'

'So 'twould seem from my source, who is none other than Adam Orleton, Bishop of Hereford.'

'Then we Marchers must make a stand against this upstart or he will rule and rob us all. Even the mighty Lancaster is a little worried by these new moves and sees his own lands in Wales threatened.'

The two men stood and stared at each other for a moment.

'I think we should sound out all the lordships of the Marches and see how each stands in this matter, then we can act as a body, for a single voice would be brushed aside by Edward, of that there is no doubt,' Roger muttered grimly.

John de Giffard nodded his grizzled head in agreement. 'Then let us not delay, for we do not want to give the wily fox Despencer too great a start in this hunt, methinks.'

'I can speak for many of the Welshmen,' said Roger thoughtfully. 'They will take arms against Despencer right gladly for it was by his urging that Edward had Llywellyn Bren executed.'

'Good, good! That at least is something! Well, I must away, and we will keep each other informed of events. I have left Adela in charge in my absence and though I doubt neither her courage nor her wits it is not a woman's place to hold the responsibility in these difficult times.'

Roger half-smiled. 'You have nothing to fear! I'll warrant she's a match for any man!'

John de Giffard's face relaxed for an instant. 'There's truth in that, but I'll not be easy till I return…I have heard that this Despencer has held certain widows and ladies prisoner in their own castles until they have surrendered the deeds and titles to their lands for their freedom. It is beyond words, but of that scoundrel I find it easy to believe.'

In the ensuing months the Borders were in a ferment of activity, but it was not until Despencer made his final move against Humphrey de Bohun, Earl of Hereford, that matters were finally brought to a head. In a single stroke Despencer managed to arouse so much resentment throughout the confederation of Marchers they were now determined to resist the schemer at all cost.

Edward the king was all too well informed of the events on the

Borders and in January of 1321 ordered the Earl of Hereford and other barons 'to refrain' from discussing the affairs of the realm and in March even came to Gloucester in person to forbid the assembly of men in the Welsh Marches, but his instructions were ignored. The time for talk was past and the Confederation of Marchers was armed and ready for action.

Roger Mortimer, Baron of Wigmore, proved his mastery of guerilla tactics in warfare during those early months. Together with the Earl of Hereford, Humphrey de Bohun, John de Giffard and a number of other Marchers he overran Glamorgan, seized Newport and utterly defeated Despencer, forcing Edward to agree to produce his favourite for judgement at the next Parliament.

The king did not take these moves lightly and he showed his displeasure towards Mortimer by removing him from office as Lieutenant of Ireland. Though this was a blow, Mortimer had few regrets, as by his actions he had managed to staunch the flow of Despencer's greed, no mean feat when he considered that Edward still retained the loyalty of a few prestigious earls like Pembroke and Arundel.

In April, Edward summoned the Earl of Hereford and the Baron of Wigmore to appear before him, but both Humphrey de Bohun and Roger Mortimer refused to acquiesce in this royal command, knowing full well that their lives stood forfeit if Despencer had any say in it!

During May, Roger and his uncle were kept busy in Wales. They took Cardiff Castle and its governor, Sir Georges Gorges, was taken prisoner and held at Wigmore to await ransom.

Ludlow and Wigmore were both as busy as beehives that summer, with recruits constantly training for immediate service and the trail of wounded returning after each battle or skirmish.

Margaret Fiennes, dowager Baroness of Wigmore, put her previous experience to good use and her calm authority was invaluable during that period of crisis.

Towards the end of June the two Mortimers attended the barons' convocation at Sherburn-in-Elmet. Lancaster and many esteemed churchmen, together with knights, bannerets and magnates from both north and south came together united for once in a common cause.

Sir John Bek proclaimed the reason for the assembly which was to rid the king of his 'evil councillors', chiefly the Despencers, and to stop the practice of banishments and forfeiture decreed without judgement by the peers; last but not least, to bring a halt to imprudent foreign treaties and the inequities of the staple system in governing the wool trade.

After much debate the council retired to deliberate on these weighty issues.

The bishops agreed to aid Lancaster against the Scots but wished to discuss the other matters at the next Parliament. However, this was not so with the barons who for once were in complete agreement over the instant removal of the Despencers and their desire to bring about a more legal democratic system than of late. As the next Parliament was due to be held in July it was agreed that all should stay their hands until after that month.

When the time came many of the barons, Roger and his uncle included, rode into London all dressed in green with yellow gauntlets on their right hands as a sign of their unanimity.

It was a lively session that July. The Despencers were openly attacked for their sins and the younger Mortimer took a conspicuous part against them. Though Edward tried to deny the lords their hearing it was on the advice of the once highly esteemed Earl of Pembroke, who pointed out that the mood of the majority was such that homage would be withdrawn and Edward himself replaced as ruler if he did not acquiesce in the demands. This piece of news shook Edward to the core, especially as it was his old advisor who urged him to banish the Despencers for the safety of his throne.

In mid August, at the conclusion of that memorable sitting, the young Roger Mortimer was pardoned for his part against the 'favourites' and for ignoring a royal command.

As soon as it was possible, Roger left his quarters at St John's in Clerkenwell and turned his face from London. He had thought to rid himself of the dark foreboding which had been troubling him of late, but the feeling remained as persistent as ever. He wondered what Isabella thought of his actions; did she judge him disloyal? He hoped that she would see that his was the only course under the circumstances. By all the saints in heaven, could he never still that ever constant desire for another man's wife who also happened to be a royal queen?

CHAPTER XXVIII

October 1321

Maud de Nereford sat gazing into the fire, her neat hands folded before her in a moment of rare inactivity. She had heard the clatter of horses' hooves in the courtyard and knew it to be Warenne returned from a day's hunting. Her dark-brown eyes were troubled and a tiny frown played across her brow.

She had come to live with Warenne against all the laws of the Church and her family's displeasure because she loved her 'dark knight' to distraction, and nothing would turn her from her purpose. Even with the knowledge that he had loved another who was now dead, she had felt sure of her own charms and youth which, combined with her passionate nature, must surely win Warenne's love, but now she knew better.

It had been five years since she had entered these walls to share her life with her lover. Two baby boys played in the nursery, fruits of her love. Her love! Not Warenne's. Hers alone; she had filled a physical need in him but did not, nor never would, touch his heart, of that she was now certain, and the knowledge caused her great dismay.

A sigh escaped from her pursed lips and a tear rolled down her cheek. She had given everything, all of herself to him and he was as distant from her today as when she had first met him as a child. True, she knew his moods better, knew his tastes in food and the bedchamber but his heart was buried beneath the black earth with his dead mistress and Maud was faced with her own defeat, not an easy thing for one so spirited and proud.

She had made her decision days ago but could not bring herself to face the inevitable moment. She shook herself mentally. This was so unlike her true nature; was she not still a de Nereford and perfectly capable of facing the future alone? She was no longer able to live with the man who would never be free to return her own powerful feelings of love.

Again she sighed. Just then Warenne came into her solar and walked towards the welcoming fire, stretching his hands towards the flames.

'It grows cold, lass.'

She made no response, her heart heavy within her, but she was resolute in her intentions.

'My lord.' The words sounded hollow even to her. 'I can no longer remain here with you.' The sentence hummed in the air like a stray arrow. Warenne gazed down at her as if she had lost her senses.

'Why? What nonsense fills that fiery head of yours now?' He answered lightly, trying to avert the impending scene.

'No nonsense, sire,' she said softly, 'just plain good sense at last, that is all.'

He came and knelt before her, his look of utter disbelief almost turned her from her purpose.

'I can no longer live with you, my lord!' The words were full of tears.

She tried to rise, but his nearness unnerved her as he put an arm across her path. She sank back.

'Come, Maud, are you with child again? This is some foolish feminine fancy, I'll warrant.'

'Nay, 'tis no fancy and I'm not with child.' Her self-composure was fast slipping away.

'Then what in heaven's name ails ye, girl?'

'You! You! You!' The words battered the stone walls and echoed back to the couple. This time he remained silent sensing the rising hysteria in the seated figure.

She burst forth. 'Oh, sweet Jesus! I love you so...' tears were now rolling swiftly down her face, 'and...you...will...never...never... love me.' She sobbed as the flood let loose could not be stemmed, and she continued, 'I was vain and foolish to think that my love could eventually sway your heart but...but...' The tears won and she wept uncontrollably, covering her face with her hands.

He was always undone by women's tears and besides he had no answer for the weeping girl. He let her tears take their course for a while, then softly he said, 'I never promised you love, Maud.'

She raised her tear-stained face and, pathetically for one so proud, said, 'Yes, I thought I could live with that but I...I...cannot and my heart breaks within me. 'Tis such a waste...she can never comfort you or care for you now, why can't you let her go?' The cry came from her soul.

He paused for a moment, then said quietly, 'Because we do not rule our hearts as do we our heads, alas! Do you not think I suffer too? You cannot know what it feels like to love someone you know you will never see again in this life; to listen for a voice that will never call; to long for a touch, a kiss that is ever denied you!'

The room was silent all but for the fire's busy crackling. He came and knelt before her again. 'But we can comfort each other, Maud, you out of love, me out of need. We can find succour in each other, surely!' He took her hand which trembled in his strong grip.

'We have unburdened our souls this hour and I think the relationship will be stronger and better for it! And if not for ourselves, think of the boys. I have recognised them as my sons and will provide for them.' His voice dropped almost to a whisper, then, 'Would you deny me the joy of seeing them grow? Or the need I have, though it be not what you would have, but mine is a genuine need for you, Maud.'

She knew she was lost, her generosity of nature could not watch the man she adored on his knees before her asking so humbly for her to stay. 'You were ever a clever adversary, my lord,' she whispered. She could not leave him now, but they both knew the day would come when they would part, but not for a while yet.

For them the Yuletide of 1321 was a gentler festival than in former years. Warenne for the first time spent all of his nights with Maud and their love-making took on a more tender aspect than heretofore. As yet, the quarrels of the Despencers and the Marchers were mere rumblings, though Warenne did attend a number of meetings, but was loath to be drawn too deeply in the mesh of growing intrigue and friction. He still struggled to free himself from his marriage, but when official duties dictated that he should be seen publicly with his wife, he fulfilled his position with as much civility as he could muster, but remaining aloof from Plantagenet demands wherever possible.

Alas, the new-found harmony between Maud and Warenne did not have much time to blossom as the king sent for the earl to be

one of the mediators in his differences with the Confederation
of Marchers. As Earl of Surrey, Warenne was respected by most,
feared by many and his impartiality in the matter was well known.
With great reluctance he parted from Maud and his two baby
sons, John and Thomas.

On the king's orders, Warenne rode with all haste to Shrewsbury.
He was quite taken aback with what met him on his arrival there.
The king and his army were drawn up waiting to cross the River
Severn, at his side was the craven Hugh Despencer the younger,
returned from a period of banishment at the behest of Edward.

'Ah, well met, Surrey, you made excellent time, but then you
always are well mounted.' The pale-blue Plantagenet eyes roamed
over Warenne's mettlesome stallion with undisguised envy.
Warenne merely bowed, he was not about to offer Edward his best
mount. The wily Despencer sat smirking at the newcomer.

Edward continued, sensing that Warenne was not about to submit his horse to please the royal admirer. 'We are bent on crushing
Lancaster and his minions. Pembroke has written to the Mortimers
for their surrender, but, as yet, received no reply.'

'Then you think they might offer a fight?' Warenne's eyes
showed no emotion as he spoke.

'Our spies tell us that de Bohun, Mowbray and Giffard have all
fled to Lancaster's stronghold in the north but that the Mortimers
are in Shropshire. What their plans are remain to be seen for who
can say with that family. They will not shun a battle but...' The
royal hand waved in an almost feminine gesture.

'I cannot think they will risk their homes in a futile fight.'
Warenne spoke in clipped, concise tones.

Suddenly Despencer spoke for the first time. 'That is what we
are hoping, is it not, Sire?'

Warenne could feel his bile rising at the wheedling tones.

'Precisely, my dear Hugh!' Edward smiled blandly at his favourite.

'May I offer my services to negotiate with the Mortimers?'
Warenne's tones were emotionless as he spoke, but he wanted to
escape from this audience as soon as it was humanly possible. 'I
have some close acquaintanceship with the Baron of Wigmore.'

'Excellent, excellent! Then see if you can bring these arrogant
Mortimers to a clearer way of thinking, and show them it is futile to
resist.'

'You will of course give your royal seal to their safe conduct.' Warenne's eyes narrowed as he spoke.

'Of course, my dear Surrey, of course!' Edward smiled, but Warenne was uneasy as he rode away from the smiling pair. He missed the wink which Edward directed at his companion.

He decided that Newport would be a suitable site for the meeting.

'I like it not!' Roger Mortimer spoke between gritted teeth to his uncle, the Lord of Chirk. 'Damn Lancaster! Why in heaven's name has he not answered our letters? Surely he *must* have received one of our messages.'

The Lord of Chirk's black eyes narrowed as he answered, 'Lancaster was ever a tricky man. Maybe he wants us to try and stop Edward at Shrewsbury to give him time to assemble his own forces.'

The golden eyes of the younger man flickered. 'God's death! You surely do not think Lancaster wants us to sacrifice ourselves in his cause? We do not stand a chance!'

'Ah, yes, but Lancaster will not feel our loss.' The yellowing teeth of the older Mortimer showed as he snarled those last words.

'Despencer must now reign supreme. How he has galvanised Edward into action, the Lord knows!'

'The pity is Edward always moves at the wrong time for the wrong reasons.' The younger man paced up and down like a caged bear. 'We are caught between the devil and Hades.'

'I will abide by your decision, nephew! You have a family worth protecting, mine…are not worth a tinker's cuss.' He spat the last statement out with a mixture of hate and disappointment.

'Come now, uncle, your sons are learned and gentlemen of letters, not of the sword, there is no disgrace in that.'

'Pah! Three out of three all their mother's sons, none mine. You were ever generous, but it is not you who will lose all that you have striven for. You have sons who will not bring disgrace on the name of Mortimer.'

Roger would not pursue this new argument; he knew his uncle's views on his offspring all too well. The older man had been brought up in the time of war and strength of arms was all he wanted from his sons; none of the three showed any inclination to follow in their father's footsteps as knights and soldiers.

The next day the king's courier came to Ludlow bearing a number of letters. Among them Roger recognised the seal of Surrey. He hastened to his uncle's chamber to consult with the older man on the next move in their precarious predicament.

'Surrey's word is trustworthy enough and Pembroke is a man of honour. I think the time has come for us to treat.' That night Roger bade his family a sad farewell. He was unhappy at being betrayed by Lancaster, for that is what it amounted to. There was still no word from the north and none of the messengers had returned.

Tearfully Joan waved her husband adieu surrounded by the younger children, and they all knew that their father and uncle rode into an uncertain future. None realised it would be years before they would meet again. Edward would never forgive their father's part against Despencer, and Despencer himself would take his revenge, of that there was no doubt.

The two men rode in almost total silence with Meyrick at his accustomed place at Roger's knee. None relished riding meekly to an unknown fate, but there was a time to be politic and the younger man put his family's safety before his own pride.

Neither Roger nor his uncle were surprised when Edward had them sent in chains to London and the Tower, but Roger's golden eyes had burned with an unspoken challenge at Hugh Despencer, and that man had sat nervously as close to Edward as was seemly. For all Meyrick's insistence Roger had sent him back to Ludlow to take care of Joan and his family. It had been a sad parting, for the quiet, sober servant had been at Roger's side since boyhood.

'Dear Meyrick, this stark place of confinement is for the Lord of Chirk and myself. You are no longer in the first flush of youth and I can see no earthly purpose to have you serve a sentence that was for an act you did not commit.'

'But, sire, my place is with you. I promised your mother...'

'Then I absolve you from that oath. Besides, I shall feel happier in my mind if I know you are with my family. The wolves will bay at their gate and Despencer's voice will be the loudest, I'll be bound, but at least you would have wit and courage enough to defend them to the last, and that comforts me!'

In a rare moment of emotion the elderly servant bowed his head to hide the pained look in his eyes.

Roger gripped his shoulder. 'God go with you, faithful friend, and my heart goes with you back to Ludlow.' For an instant Meyrick's arms encircled his master, then he turned and left the chamber, not wanting Roger to see his unmanly tears.

As for Warenne's part in the negotiations, he now cursed Edward and his favourite for being 'men of straw'. Their word of honour was a mockery and he rode in the king's army in a black mood. Only the thought of defeating Lancaster spurred him on, for out of the two, Lancaster was his bitter enemy, Edward merely a weak and untrustworthy monarch.

The confrontation at Boroughbridge between Edward's forces and Lancaster's was a shambles. The Earl of Hereford was slain and after a short trial Thomas of Lancaster was executed. The king stood now unopposed and triumphant, at his side his favourite now with even more lands and power at Lancaster's death.

BOOK THREE

THE KING OF FOLLY

CHAPTER XXIX

Roger sat staring at the damp floor of his cell. He could scarcely credit the happenings of the past months. The trial, the days awaiting the verdict, and now a life's imprisonment stretching out before him like a living death. Some had said they were lucky not to have forfeited their lives. Lucky! The golden eyes moved over the lofty narrow cell, with its single window that was too high for any real daylight to penetrate the gratings, and even at noon it was still only half-light.

His uncle lay on a narrow truckle bed in one corner; his own was on the opposite side. Down at the other end stood a rough-hewn table and two stools, behind a wooden screen a pail served as a make-shift garderobe, and the jailers were none too swift in emptying the evil-smelling container. The walls of the cell ran with moisture and the whole place was dank and cold even on the hottest day.

At first they had been denied pen, paper and priest, but through constant badgering by the Church Edward had occasionally allowed these comforts to be given. Roger had written to Joan his wife, Margaret his mother and Adam Orleton but as yet had received no replies. It was a question whether any of the missives had got further than the Constable of the Tower.

It was through the little priest sent from Edward's court to hear the two prisoners' confessions that they learned of Lancaster's death at Pontefract after the battle at Boroughbridge, but though they pressed him for further news of friends and family, they could gain nothing else to ease the long hours of their confinement.

As the days dragged from month to month it was obvious that the Lord of Chirk's health was beginning to fail, but not the indomitable Mortimer spirit.

'Methinks this place will be the death of me!' he said one morning.

Roger was forever pacing. He did all manner of exercises to keep his hard body in shape though, because of the meagre rations, he had lost many pounds in weight. 'Don't give them the satisfaction of seeing you come low, uncle. I'll not let these accursed walls beat me, or Edward and his foxy-eyed playmate.' His eyes blazed with an animalistic fury. The demon that his parents had feared in him as a child was now loose, thanks to the long months of imprisonment. At times he would beat his fists against the running walls until they bled, then throw himself onto his mattress and remain silent for hours just glaring at the grim, grey granite.

The Lord of Chirk had aged greatly, his grizzled head now almost white and the once proud frame bent and racked with aches and pains. From time to time he coughed, a nagging reminder of a bout of fever he had suffered the previous winter, and he took great pains to hide the flecks of blood which sometimes stained his pillow.

One day after one of Roger's bouts of energetic frenzy, the elder man pulled himself up onto a bony elbow and hissed, 'Promise me you will avenge my downfall if ever you win free from this place, nephew!'

The golden eyes took in the ragged old man with the haggard face and soiled garments; only the black eyes were still recognisable as the erstwhile Justiciar of Wales, the Lord of Chirk. 'I *will* win free from this place, on that you have my oath if ever the opportunity presents itself. The Mortimers will take their revenge on all who have crossed their paths in treachery. This is the single thing which has prevented me from losing my sanity in this hell-hole.' He kicked over a stool in his frustration.

Not many days after this outburst another priest came to take mass. It was an Augustinian monk who entered the cell. The tall, bare-footed monk had strong features and an air of calm about him. For a few minutes the younger Mortimer stared, then suddenly went forward and took the bony hand in his. He did not speak but the look which passed between the two men spoke volumes.

This was none other than Brother Matthew, the self-same monk who had brought tidings to Wigmore of the Despencers' misdemeanours. To Roger the sight of that familiar face was like a sign from heaven, but he did not say anything to arouse the guards' suspicions.

Indeed, as Brother Matthew slowly and deliberately took their confessions, he managed to convey the first real news they had heard since their trial.

Joan de Geneville, Roger's wife, had been taken to Southampton with three of her daughters, Joan, Margaret and Isabel. His sons were in the Tower but not under such close confinement as their sire.

For the first time since his ignominious journey to London in chains, Roger's self-control almost broke on hearing how his family fared. The golden eyes filled with tears and he turned his head away from his kinsman and the tonsured monk. He would not let them see how close he came to weeping like a child.

Brother Matthew came and touched him on the shoulder. 'God will give you the strength to bear this trial, my son. Remember, there are many outside who work for your freedom and your family's welfare.'

'I thank you, Brother Matthew, but platitudes do not ease this torment of my mind and body. I am not used to feeling so helpless. However, thank the good bishop, Adam Orleton, he risks much to aid us, as do you!'

The monk nodded and said on a more even note, 'Now I must go. It will not do for me to linger too long on my first visit. The lines of communication have been opened and when they become established life will be easier for all of us.' He raised his fingers in benediction over the heads of the two Mortimers. 'May God be with you both in your hour of need.' He turned, banged on the door for the guard to let him out and with a click of wooden rosary beads and a swish of his rough woollen habit he was gone.

For a long while the two men just sat and looked at each other, then the younger man took his uncle's hands and drew him into a slow, clumsy dance around their dreary, dark cell. But the light of hope had been kindled in them both and a new strength of purpose was born in the Baron of Wigmore. He must endure this ordeal, he *would* survive this man-made hell and be stronger for it! He had great faith in Adam Orleton's astute brain and the capability of this messenger he had sent.

Brother Matthew's visits became the highlight of the Mortimers' world and during those first weeks he managed to smuggle in a purse of gold so they could purchase better food, warmer clothing and other creature comforts so long denied them.

The guards turned a blind eye as they also benefited from these visits and as for the constable, Stephen de Segrave, he was glad for the younger Mortimer as he had grown to like and respect his noble prisoner. Roger, being aware of this admiration, cultivated the friendship and shared many a cup of wine with his jailer.

Life became almost tolerable, but Roger did not cease to exercise or seek as much information from the outside world as he was able. He plagued Brother Matthew to find some means of escape and the monk caught something of the other man's desperation. Roger little realised that moves were already afoot to work out an escape plan for him. But Adam Orleton had given his courier strict instructions not to divulge anything of this to the prisoner as he feared Roger might become indiscreet.

The bishop had not seen the change as had the visiting monk. Gone was the youth of yore; in his place was a hardened man who had had to find untapped resources to sustain his imprisonment, for no one came close to comprehending his torment of spirit and physical distress this forced period of idleness placed upon him. He reminded Brother Matthew of a caged animal as he constantly paced to and fro and he caught the essence of underlying violence beneath the handsome surface.

Brother Matthew brought them the news of Roger Damory's execution at Tutbury; how Humphrey de Bohun, Earl of Hereford, had been slain at Boroughbridge; of the deaths of Clifford Mowbray and Dayville, both executed at York; how Lord Badlesmere had died at Canterbury, Sir Henry Tyres at London and fifteen others including their former friend John de Giffard, Lord of Brimpsfield, all victims of the executioner. Despencer vengeance knew no limits. However, Hugh Audley had escaped execution and was now confined to Berkhampstead Castle.

'The jackal has sharp teeth and Edward slays his one-time friends without compunction, it would seem, on the instigation of this... this devil's spawn Despencer. I would give much to meet that 'faggot' for one final showdown and he would taste my steel, by my oath he would.' Roger slapped his thigh in his fury.

Sometimes the monk knew not how he could comfort this man.

'I know it is not easy for you, my son, but pray for patience, gain as much intelligence of the lay-out of the keep and the routine of the guards as you can. It will be vital to those who work for your freedom.'

'Patience!' exploded Roger. 'I am so frustrated, Holy Father, I swear the following weeks will be like a century, but I will do as you bid. Fear not, I shall play the spy as well as I once played the role of Baron of Wigmore.'

The monk smiled; even in adversity there was a streak of humour in this magnetic person and he could well understand the king's displeasure at being crossed by one such as Roger Mortimer of Wigmore.

Over the next few weeks Roger gained all the necessary information and piece by piece the plans were laid for his escape until all that was left was the exact time. As the three men sat one afternoon talking softly, Roger suddenly smiled. 'I have the very day, Brother Matthew, one I think will amuse you and is very appropriate to our cause.'

The hawk-faced monk cocked an inquisitive eye at the speaker. 'Well?'

'The Feast of St Peter of Vincula, the patron saint of prisoners.'

Brother Matthew nodded. 'Very apt, the Saint of Chains.'

But already Roger was lost in his own thoughts and the golden eyes blazed with fires of enthusiasm. 'I know, I can invite the jailers to a fine supper and tell them it is in honour of my patron saint.' Brother Matthew frowned, but Roger continued undaunted, 'Do not think I tell a deliberate untruth, Brother Matthew, I promise he will forthwith be my patron and should I escape, I vow to build a chapel in his honour at Ludlow for all to witness my sincerity.'

The monk was won over. 'Then it needs only heavenly blessings on the venture and this,' he produced a small phial from his copious habit, 'the essence of the poppy.' He handed a small, innocent-looking flask to Roger who took it and promptly hid it under his rough mattress.

But a few days from the appointed time Brother Matthew came on his weekly visit with a troubled look about his normally calm features.

'My lords, it behoves me to be the bearer of ill-tidings which could, in truth, jeopardise our plans.'

The sentence pounded in the ears of the younger Mortimer like a death-knell. The sombre monk continued, 'I hope and pray you can swim, my Lord of Wigmore.'

'Indeed, like a fish.'

'Ah, thanks be to God, then all may not be lost. It seems the boatman we have hired cannot reach the lower walls of the Tower. He has tried several times and the guards have ordered him away. It means you will have to swim some four or five hundred yards.' The monk's deep-set eyes watched the baron's face to see the effect his words would have on the handsome captive.

'The waters of the Thames hold no threat for me!'

'But the tides and currents are dangerous.'

Suddenly the Lord of Chirk piped up. 'I'd wager my last piece of silver on my nephew's ability to outswim any man.' Roger's golden eyes appeared almost cat-like and to the onlookers they changed to an unearthly yellow; obviously some trick of the light, thought the monk.

'After long months cooped up like some broody chicken I welcome the challenge of the river of Thames. I would willingly face more fearsome odds than a dip in a chilly river to be free from this abominable place. I fear if I stay much longer tombed up in these walls I shall go insane.'

The monk nodded. 'Then all is settled and our plans can go ahead unhindered? You have had no opposition regarding the supper?'

'None! I think that our jailers lead as boring an existence as do their prisoners and anything is welcomed to relieve the monotony.'

'Good, good! We can only place our trust in God and Saint Peter. My own blessings on you both, my Lord of Wigmore and you, my Lord of Chirk.' Softly he said to Roger, 'I wish you success, my son, and hope we meet again one day.' He anointed the forehead of the younger man and then turned and made the sign of the cross over the Lord of Chirk's white head, 'And may God's beneficence be on you,' he said, touching the shoulder of the older Mortimer, 'for yours will be a hard burden to bear.'

The once fearsome Lord of Chirk, now a withered shell of a man, looked up. 'I thank you, good brother, but my days on this earth are numbered and if I am to suffer this sentence alone, death will be God's boon, but keep me in your prayers as I have, in the past, been a man with a large appetite for the pleasures of the flesh.' He paused wheezing, his lungs like a pair of worn-out bellows, but the dark satanic eyes flashed for an instant with the old fires. 'I think I serve my stint in hell here on earth, father.'

'It is God's will, my lord,' murmured the monk. Though himself devoutly religious, he was not blind to all that went on both at court and in the shires of the land and his sympathies lay, if not entirely with the older man, then wholeheartedly with the younger. 'I will leave you now. I shall make certain that all is in readiness for your swift departure, my Lord of Wigmore.' The monk and the noble embraced briefly, then Brother Matthew banged on the door for the warders to let him out into the world of free men.

The two Mortimers sat silent for a long while before either spoke. Finally the younger man broke the silence. 'The hours drag by on leaden feet; action is what I yearn for...'

'Aye, to be sure, but do not let your impatience show in your manner, nephew; we do not want to alert the guards at this late stage in the game.'

'I am being selfish as usual, uncle. I shall be loath to leave you here at the mercy of the Plantagenet rage and the spite of his jackal Despencer.'

'I know, I know, but do not trouble yourself about me. I have had my life and for the most part I cannot grumble.'

'France!' Roger breathed the word like a prayer. 'The very word spells freedom to mine ears.' Suddenly the golden eyes narrowed. 'Think you they will harm my children?' The two men looked hard into each other's faces.

'Edward will move heaven and hell to find you, but I do not think he would lay a hand on your family,' said the Lord of Chirk slowly. 'They offer no threat to him where they are. No, go and do not hesitate, it could be your undoing.'

'Mine will be the swiftest departure ever seen from this dismal place of suffering, I'll warrant.'

The two men talked long into the night. Roger was to offer his services to the king of France, Charles IV, Isabella's brother. Mercenaries could earn great rewards for feats of arms and Roger was well equipped for that role. Besides, France would be a rallying point for all who escaped Edward's wrath. Though the conversation hinged mainly on the younger man's plans for the future the two men were aware that this would be the last private talk they would have together, and the knowledge lay like a heavy hand on them both.

From far off they heard the watchman's cry of cock-crow which echoed up the vaulted walls and round the rafters, the only time the sound was audible.

'Well, the Feast of St Peter of Vincula is upon us, nephew.'

'Aye! Praise be – and let the morrow see me as far from this accursed place as horseflesh and water can put me...' Roger's golden eyes suddenly softened a little. 'You know my feelings on leaving you.'

'Bah!' The Lord of Chirk slapped his brother's son on the shoulder. 'Live for us both! You who have been more son to me than mine own. I begrudge you nothing, nothing, do you hear?' The men embraced, both struggling to hide their true emotions from the other.

'Enough of women's sentiments. We must look to the events of the day. You should rest now, nephew, it will be more tiring than you realise for all your confidence and youth. We have been closely confined for nigh on seventeen months and prison saps a man's strength quicker than a lusty wench,' he laughed, 'though my wenching days are over, but I have some rare memories. And you must pleasure a few of those French damosels in my absence.'

'That weakness very nearly cost you your life on more than one occasion as I remember,' Roger said, grinning roguishly.

'Your aunt never cared for the marriage bed and I found no one woman to please me more than fleetingly, though I will say the Welsh wenches take some satisfying.' He chortled at his memories, and for once the cough did not spoil his amusement.

Roger, however, remained silent on the subject; how could he tell this old roué that he truly desired one and only one woman, Isabella, whose very name made his heart beat faster. If he could but possess and gain that one woman's love, then he would be the happiest of mortals. She had remained locked in his mind and heart through every waking hour, and it was to her brother that he would go to seek sanctuary from the wrath of Edward and his minions. Maybe she would be sent to France as ambassador on Edward's behalf as she had been many times in the past.

The hollow footfall of the guards changing watch broke into his train of thoughts. 'Oh, blessed St Peter, do not fail me on this night, and I vow I will build a chapel in thy honour that will stand for a thousand years, but if my request goes unheeded, then let death be swift for I would not wish to live a day longer as a prisoner.'

That was the only time he had to pray that day for he had to rest for the adventure to come. Some hours later, when the August sun had passed its zenith, the Lord of Chirk looked down at his sleeping kinsman. The thick, dark curls had grown longer and the dark skin grown pale, starved of the sun and wind, but lying there with his strong arm thrown carelessly behind his head, the man had the look of the boy again.

'May you sleep in the arms of freedom, my son,' he whispered and as gentle as any woman touched the younger man's hand. The Lord of Chirk felt more love for this one human being than any other in his entire life. He was glad that this chance of freedom had come. Mortimers did not make good captives. Theirs was a spirit which thrived only when free. Even little Maud had died, but not as everyone thought in childbed. The girl's spirit had been dead from the first few weeks of her marriage to Theobold de Verdun, but that was history – he was rambling. He sighed, for memories would be all that he would have left after today. He turned and picked up a cup of wine. 'You and I shall become inseparable companions from now on, my little friend,' he wheezed.

The sleeper stirred and stretched. The strange, golden eyes flickered open. 'What hour is it, uncle?'

'Past four I think.'

'Then I shall wash and eat, for I do not wish to make my swim on a full stomach.'

The rest of the afternoon and evening seemed to drag by for Roger although he was busy preparing for the all-important supper. Outwardly he remained calm. At last the appointed hour drew nigh, and he heard the voices of Stephen de Segrave, Constable of the Tower, and the others who made up the regular guards.

How Roger stayed affable and at ease through that meal the Lord of Chirk never knew, but pleasant and jocular he was! Nothing was too much trouble and he poured the wine and served his guests with his own hands, hands which did not tremble or betray their master, hands which slapped backs, pressed food and wine until at last that moment when they slipped the drug which would steal their senses and enable the captive to flee.

Roger watched the last of the guards slump over the trestle. The poppy essence had done its work. Quickly he dragged the guard who was nearest to his stature onto the floor and stripped him of his tunic and hose. Roger's heart was beating fast and the blood tingled through his veins; action at long last!

Without any fuss he donned the rough leather tunic and woollen hose and with only a quick embrace from his uncle he ran to the thick door, fitted the heavy key and swung it open. The Lord of Chirk would die with the memory of that look which Roger flashed him as he left in triumph.

Stealthily he sped through the corridors to where one of his jailers, Gerard de Alspath, who had been well bribed to guide him, was waiting. Together they climbed staircases, hurried through dim corridors until at last Roger breathed the fresh August night air; to him it was more potent than some brew he had tasted in Ireland in his youth. But there was no time to stop and savour the summer night. He gulped another lungful as the nervous man indicated the part of the wall he should dive from and, without a backward glance, Roger leapt headlong into the forbidding waters of the Thames.

The shock of the icy waters all but knocked the precious wind from him and for one awful moment he thought he would never surface again, but it was only imagination. With strong, sure strokes he started to tackle the tricky currents. He strained his ears for any sounds of pursuit. For what seemed like an eternity he battled on, but there was no doubt he *was* making progress. As he swam round the edge of a jetty he saw a tiny craft bobbing innocently against the bank, the oarsman looking as though he were asleep or drunk.

By now Roger's arms were like lead and his legs felt useless and numb but he was too close to his goal now to fail. At last a pair of powerful arms hauled him into the boat and a blanket was thrown over him. Neither man spoke, Roger just lay gasping in the craft, while the brawny boatman plied his oars with a will. He had been promised much silver and would never again in the future have to rely on the fickle ferry trade of the river for a living.

How long that journey took Roger never knew, but when they finally reached the far shore he alighted with a new-found strength.

With every inch he gained from that dreadful prison the more certain he became of success.

Out of the shadows two heavily cloaked figures emerged, one holding a similar garment for Roger to cover the sodden uniform. Without a word they left the river, having handed a purse of silver to the oarsman.

Down alleyways and along deserted thoroughfares they sped until at last they came to an inn.

'Quick, sir! The horses are at the rear! This is as far as we go but our servant is trustworthy and will take you on the next leg of your journey. Godspeed and a swift passage.'

'I thank you, gentlemen, with all my heart. This Mortimer shall be forever in your debt. I shall find a way to put my thanks into a more tangible proof than mere words, on that you have my word. St Peter's blessings on you both.' With that the trio parted, the two Londoners John De Gisor and Richard de Bettoyne slipping back to their own homes, unaware of the repercussions their night's work would have on their lives in the coming months.

Roger, on the other hand, made his way swiftly to the rear of the inn, where, sure enough, sitting a mettlesome horse, the reins of another fine animal in his hand, was the servant.

'Quick, sir! These 'ere 'osses ain't used to standing. They're the fastest nags as ever I throwed me leg across.'

Roger grinned, taking the proffered reins. He leapt into the saddle and without any further preamble they clattered out of the inn yard and as soon as they had passed the last lit window let the fiery steeds have their heads and gallop into the night as fast as those horses were able.

For nigh on ten miles they raced before drawing rein. The wild-eyed horses were sweat-streaked but still full of running. Roger's arms and legs were trembling with fatigue but he felt so elated that he scarce noticed his weakness.

'We've another ten miles ahead of us, sir! Then a change of mounts; relays, ye see, all the ways to the coast.' Roger saw the gleam of teeth as his companion spoke but could distinguish little else. The fellow was no squire but a superb horseman for all that.

They rode for most of the way in darkness but neither of the fleet-footed steeds faltered in that headlong dash. As dawn's pale fingers stretched across the sky Roger was so weary he could scarce stay in his saddle. His companion drew rein. 'We can take a breather along this stretch of road. Don't want us to draw attention to ourselves, do we?'

'I'm at your disposal.' Roger slurred the words. Oh, how he longed to sleep, but his companion chatted on as though it were a regular outing they took.

'Reckon we've made good time. I've ridden this route a few times so's I'd know how to pace the 'osses. We'll make the ship by ten of the clock and as she ain't due to sail till eleven, well…'

How he survived that ride Roger never really knew. His guide was his salvation and it wasn't until the shore of England slipped out of view that he realised he had never asked the fellow's name. It was the last thought he remembered before blessed sleep came to still all consciousness.

CHAPTER XXX

1326

The golden eyes narrowed against the bright glare off the sea. All around him people cheered and clapped as they pressed forward to gain a better view of Isabella, daughter of France and Queen of England. But none in that colourful throng was more intent on that slender form than Roger Mortimer, Baron of Wigmore.

It had been almost five years since he had last set eyes on the woman whose face haunted his dreams and who had robbed him of his heart so long before. Now at last she was here in France, come as ambassador to intercede with her brother Charles on Edward's behalf. Mortimer had been in the pay of the French king ever since his arrival in France nearly two years since and as a mercenary he had gained much wealth and prestige and had won many victories for his patron.

Charles had paid little heed to Edward's pleas to return Mortimer to England. There was not such a dearth of seasoned commanders in France that he would lightly let his new champion go to certain death, when France had need of such talents as the warrior knight from the Marches possessed.

Mortimer had settled into his new role with gusto though never quite losing the taste of prison. He was energetic, fearless and had quickly won the respect of his troops. He tried to blot out the fears for his family with tireless campaigns, but nothing cured his feelings for Isabella, and even when he sought favours in another woman's bed they never really satisfied anything deep within. Only the body's lust was slaked in those encounters.

At last a louder cheer broke into his thoughts and Isabella herself descended from the gangplank onto the quayside. Mortimer let out a long, deep sigh; she was as slender as ever and he could see she smiled and waved at the crowds. Isabella! Isabella! His heart seemed to leap within him. She came slowly through the clamouring throng and just as she came level with where he stood, she looked up and for a single second those crystal-blue eyes met and held Mortimer's. It was like a moment stolen from the great clock of time. A sudden surge of people carried Isabella forward, however, and the moment was shattered. But all the bells in France could not have sounded louder than those echoing in Mortimer's heart.

Prydferth Isabella, she looked more ravishing than ever. Time had not cheated him. Her skin was as clear and unlined as when he had last seen her with no mark on her face to show her years of humiliation and frustration at Edward's hands.

Mortimer tried to ridicule his own emotions, to laugh at his feelings, for he was no longer a callow youth but almost thirty-eight years of age, but his love for Isabella was by now as much a part of him as was his own right hand.

During the next few weeks Mortimer constantly sought Isabella's presence, like a moth attracted to a flame.

He was powerless to resist the temptation of any chance word or glance she might cast in his direction and treasured those rare occasions like a miser.

Daily he sent her gifts, gloves, flowers, a girdle, anything he found that might please her and when his squire brought a phial of exotic perfume purchased from a merchant who had recently returned from the East, Mortimer was delighted. 'You have done exceeding well, Raoul. Methinks the lady will find this gift to her taste!'

'The merchant said it had magical powers for both the giver and the wearer.'

Mortimer laughed. 'He sounds a good trader and no mistake, but...' he smeared a little of the essence onto his wrist, 'it does have a most exquisite scent. You have surpassed yourself and I shall reward you anon.'

The young man was pleased; he had been in the service of King Charles until Mortimer's arrival on the scene and had been ordered to serve the Welsh Marcher baron for as long as he was needed.

By degrees Mortimer established a place in Isabella's entourage and soon found himself drawn into a more intimate circle of courtiers and attendants, for there were a number of English exiles now at the French court, the Earl of Richmond, the Earl of Kent, his brother Thomas Brotherton as well as the luckless ambassadors sent originally by Edward, and most found themselves in the royal party.

It was a hectic time with masques and feasts, hunting and hawking, or gliding along the rivers in low, richly decorated barges to the sound of melodic minstrels strumming lutes and harps. Sometimes the royal couple would play dice or chess, but it was when Charles suggested a tournament in honour of his sister's visit that Roger Mortimer found a way to become more to Isabella than just another member of the court.

It was agreed that a party of French knights should challenge the English, and Mortimer seized the opportunity to seek her favour, so on bended knee he made his request known. 'Highness, may I be the fortunate knight to wear your favour on the morrow?'

For a moment the crystal-blue eyes looked down into his as she said gently, 'Only if you promise me victory, my Lord Mortimer.'

'It is as good as done, *ma belle reine*.'

Isabella nodded. 'I believe you are serious, my lord, but had you not heard my brother's champion is unbeaten in the lists?'

'Then the morrow will see the invincible vanquished.' He caught her hand and kissed the scented fingers. 'The perfume found favour with you, madam.'

'So it would seem, my lord.' She smiled and her normal aloofness melted. 'Mortimer, if you win I shall dance with no other at the feasting, even though you have a price on your head. I shall choose to ignore your previous…adventures and show my gratitude and be your queen of the tournament.'

Mortimer was as good as his word; no man fought harder, or with more zeal and skill, than did the Marcher baron, and the erstwhile French champion was relegated into submission before Mortimer's deadly blade.

Isabella was overjoyed and kept her word and danced with no other at the festivities, wearing the floral crown with as much dignity as she did the crown of state. Those weeks in France had made such a difference to Isabella, she had lost that guarded look and felt at ease for the first time since her marriage, and being feted and flattered added to the flavour of her freedom.

As she whirled among the dancers Mortimer laughed down at her. '*Ma belle*, you look more dazzling than a May morning in the Marches.'

'You constantly surprise me, my Lord Mortimer. I would never have given you the title of poet but here you are waxing lyrical.'

'Ah, 'tis the Celtic blood which flows in my veins. My great-granddam Glwadus Ddu was a Princess of Wales, daughter of the Great Llywellyn.'

'Then I must beware for the Celts have magical powers, or so I have heard.'

'Indeed, madam, and I would use them all to win but one sweet kiss from those delicious lips.'

'Come now, Mortimer, you grow too bold, I fear,' Isabella chided, but she could feel his touch long after the dance had ended and the ardour in his eyes stirred something within her like a half-forgotten memory.

One evening a few weeks after the tournament at a more informal gathering, Mortimer came and sat at Isabella's feet, his back resting against her chair. A minstrel strummed an old French love song and his sweet, clear voice filled the chamber with music.

Conversation swelled and ebbed intermittently and requests were hurled at the singer unmercifully until Charles held up his hand. 'You would wear out my songbird with your demands, pray let us give him some respite.'

Thomas Brotherton, youngest son of Edward I's second marriage and noted for his quick temper, piped up, 'My Lord Mortimer has a charming voice, though he does not broadcast his talent as a balladeer.'

'Ah!' exclaimed Charles. 'I am curious as to why our Lord Mortimer is so backward as we have not usually found him so reticent.' There was a ripple of mirth amongst the listeners.

'My Lord Brotherton exaggerates, my liege. I do not sing.'

'Oh, come, come, Mortimer, why I heard you only a se'nnight ago serenade your horse most charmingly.'

'But my dear Thomas, he is tone-deaf.'

Isabella touched Mortimer lightly on the shoulder. 'I would like to hear you sing, my lord.'

There was no escaping a royal request and Thomas Brotherton grinned impishly at his brother Edmund of Kent. For once the normally confident Mortimer was somewhat put out by Isabella's request.

'Then I shall do as you command, lady, and hope that you do not regret your decision.'

Mortimer cleared his throat and started to sing. He had a deep baritone voice that was tuneful and melodic, but Isabella had never heard the song, nor the lilting language in which he sang. She sank back in her chair and closed her eyes and though she did not understand the lyrics there was a haunting theme that somehow echoed her own heart's yearnings, years of loneliness and humiliation, love denied, love turned to shame.

When the last notes died away, the whole company clapped including the erstwhile minstrel.

Charles leaned forward. 'In what language did you sing?'

'Welsh, my liege.'

Isabella's hand rested lightly on Mortimer's sleeve. 'And of whom did you sing, my lord?'

'Of a maid who was a prisoner in an ivory tower, guarded by a dragon, and she would sing to the wind to bring a lover who would slay the dragon and set her free.'

'Yes, I felt her loneliness,' she said softly. 'You must sing again.'

'Ah, madam, I am no balladeer. I beg you to release me, for when I sing of Wales my heart grows melancholy and I drown my sorrows in too much French wine.'

'Then you are released, my Lord Mortimer, for I would not wish to cause you pain.' He had turned to look at her as she spoke and her heart lurched within her at the look in those beautiful golden eyes; gone was the twinkling flirtatiousness she had come to expect, and she felt that just for an instant she had been allowed to see his true soul, all the hurt, all the pent-up emotions, all his desires. She dropped her eyes, not wanting to betray her confusion.

When Mortimer turned back he moved his position slightly so that his back rested against Isabella's leg, but she stayed mute. The physical contact was like an unspoken vow that somehow took their relationship to a more intimate level.

Young Thomas Brotherton, restless with all the singing, called for a fool to bring some merriment to their entertainment. Isabella felt Mortimer's laughter, which seemed to run through her own body like a chord. She must take care and not show any weakening of her resolve, for he was not a man to be lightly trifled with, of that she was certain. As yet he had flirted, played the gallant and that was quite seemly and accepted in her position, but she could not forget the look in those magnificent eyes. He was no weak-willed, vacillating knight, far from it, he oozed confidence and masculine vitality, and she was aware there was a new dimension to his personality: maybe it stemmed from his confinement in the Tower. He was ever restless like an animal captured from the wilds and held, and then, on returning to its natural habitat, guards the precious freedom.

The evening ended with everyone singing a French song remembered from Charles and Isabella's childhood. When Mortimer rose and kissed Isabella's hand she felt a sense of loss as he moved away from her to rejoin Tom Brotherton and the others.

Taking her brother's arm Isabella smiled and thanked the fool and the minstrel, then went to where Mortimer was standing. 'And we thank you, my Lord Mortimer, for being allowed to share your beautiful ballad of Wales.' He bowed low and bent his head so she could not see his eyes. She felt cheated but kept her disappointment well disguised from the rest of the gathering.

Charles, delighted with the evening's success, said lightly, 'I believe this sojourn in your native land is working on you, sister dear. Already you appear much more relaxed and we rejoice in your wellbeing.'

'It is gratifying to know that kingship has not detracted from any of the family love you feel for your sister.'

He kissed her hand affectionately. 'Adieu, sweeting, till the morrow.' She in her turn kissed his cheek and took her leave to seek her bed. But sleep would not come.

The June night was heavy and thunder rumbled ominously in the distance. Quietly so as not to wake her tiring-woman, Isabella rose, slipped on a soft, silk robe and stood looking out over the gardens. All the shrubs took on a whole new quality in the murky gloom.

A flash of lightning lit up the scene in an eerie, colourless light. The air was heady with perfume. She closed her eyes and breathed in the scent. Suddenly she stiffened; one of the bushes appeared to move – impossible, a trick of the night. But she strained her eyes, then, a man standing, illuminated in a flash of lightning, Mortimer, she knew him in an instant, a vague memory of years past when she was still little more than a girl.

The rain started and the thunder rolled closer, but she did not move. She saw him walk towards the foot of her casement and with the agility of a cat start to climb the thick, overhanging foliage. He clambered over the window ledge, droplets of rain running down his face, his thick curly hair shining with moisture.

'*Prydferth* Isabella!' he breathed.

She scarce knew whether this was some fanciful apparition conjured up out of her own imagination and stammered, 'Mortimer, is this really you? You could be killed for this folly.'

'But to hold you just once would be worth the dying.' He caught her to him and kissed her; at first she remained impassive but the fire of his passion kindled all her latent desires and she answered his mouth. Slowly her arms crept up around his neck, his sodden attire clinging to her, causing her own robes to become wet. How long they stood together lost in a world of delirious exaltation, she never knew, but when they finally broke apart she became aware of her surroundings once more. The storm was at its height, but Isabella cared nothing for the elements, only the storm that this man had caused in her own body.

'Mortimer!' she whispered. He did not answer but let his lips and hands speak more eloquently than any words. This was a woman of flesh and blood whose mouth moved under his, and the reality was far above dreams.

'*Cariad*,' he murmured thickly, his hands caressing her breasts, and he felt her tremble at his touch. Deftly he slipped off her robe and loosened the ties of her shift pushing the flimsy folds from her shoulders until she stood naked before him; the golden eyes lingered on the vision. Isabella could not read his expression, for he stood in the shadows.

'*Arglwyddes*, you are more beautiful...' A jagged fork of lightning followed by a terrifying crash of thunder made her seek the safety of his arms.

'Oh, Mortimer, what have you done to me?' The words were half-sobbed, but she did not try to move away. He swung her up into his arms and carried her to the bed.

'My woman...' she indicated the slumbering attendant; he nodded his comprehension and laid her gently onto the covers, quickly discarding his wet apparel. As yet he could not trust his voice but kissed her naked form from her brow to the soles of her feet.

At first she lay trembling beneath his caressing lips and hands, motionless, holding her breath. Mortimer knew that he must woo her and not let his own urgency destroy the spell that he was casting over the reclining figure. She quivered and he feared that she might push him away, but her hands had started to explore his hard, well-muscled body.

They lay swathed in their new-found intimacy. 'You are beautiful, my lord,' she said tremulously, his lips on her throat, then she moaned as he could no longer withstand his fleshly demands and plunged deep into her womb. For an instant she tried to escape but it was too late, marvellously, sensationally too late to break free from his passionate onslaught.

Then she cried out in her ecstasy, 'Mortimer, Mortimer,' and moaned under his mouth. When he looked down at her she knew she would always remember that look so full of love and emotion. 'Oh, my lord, I had no comprehension that the act of love could be so…so…' His fingers teased the thick tresses of her hair and she pulled his face close to her own. 'Do you always please your conquests so?'

In answer he kissed her shoulder and ran a strong hand down her spine so that she arched towards him. 'Is that what you think?' But he did not cease his actions.

'I…I know not what to think! Can scarce believe that this…this night has happened.' He chuckled sensually. 'Or this knight has won so great a conquest.'

The crystal-blue eyes studied him through half-closed lids. 'Then am I just another conquest?' She tried to disguise the doubt in her voice.

He took her hand and kissed each finger in turn. 'You are the conqueror, lady,' he said in a whisper. 'You will never know how long I have loved you! Watched you like some beggar over a hidden hoard of gold. Do you know how hard it has been for me to keep my feelings in check? Yours was the face that I kept before me when I was penned up in the Tower. And you will never understand how, with just one look from those generous blue orbs, you have made me king and pauper in turn.'

Gently she wound her fingers through his curls. 'And you are not disappointed. I am to your pleasure?' She smiled up at him.

'In every detail, lady. Tonight I have entered heaven,' he said, bending to kiss the contours of her firm, flat stomach. Even in the darkness Isabella, Queen of England, former Princess of France, blushed like a young bride.

'You have made mock of all my principles, opened the door to emotions I never knew existed within my being. But oh, I rejoice, my lord, that the woman is free at last to love and be loved.'

'And are we to waste the rest of this night on confessions?'

'Oh no, *mon amour*,' she stroked his broad chest with the palms of her hands. 'I have other plans for you, my wild Welsh seducer.'

Mortimer and Isabella were so deep in love with each other that they could not hide their feelings for long. At first Charles was amused and no one could deny the dark, talented mercenary made a perfect foil to his sister's fair and dazzling beauty, and she did dazzle. Everything about Isabella glowed with a new, devastating light. Her hair, eyes, skin and laughter were sung about by poets and minstrels alike.

But in Mortimer's eyes she outshone every verse and song, every summer moon, every hot ray of the sun. They were a perfect match, both in body and mind so well suited in all things. They delighted in each other's company, walking, talking, dancing, riding or just sitting playing chess together. The crystal-blue eyes of Isabella locked onto those magnificent golden ones of Mortimer lost in a kingdom of their own.

'I swear you are a mythical being from your beloved mountains. One day I shall awake and you will be gone!'

'Myths cannot satisfy lusty young women,' he countered. Her laughter was like a hand of bells tinkling quite deliciously on the ear of the listener.

'Hush! Would you shame me?' she said blushing.

'Never, *cariad*.'

Their newly discovered happiness was fleetingly overshadowed by the sudden departure of William Stapledon, Bishop of Exeter, who made it known before his leave-taking that he felt it his duty to inform Edward of this scandalous affair of Isabella with a branded traitor.

But between silken sheets at night the lovers lived only in each other's arms. Sometimes after passion's appetites had been appeased they lay confiding secret hopes and fears, each telling the other of the intimate details of their previous life and Mortimer would ofttimes become angry when he heard how Isabella had been subject to insult and humiliation at the hands of Edward and his succession of favourites.

'Gaveston was hated and feared by many,' Isabella said one night, 'but if he had not urged Edward to fulfil his duty to beget heirs, then I know I would have remained a virgin. I must admit I hated him at first but later…' she hesitated, 'later I was not completely excluded from their friendship and found under that sharp wit and gaudy exterior a shrewd brain and courageous spirit.'

'Maybe things would have been better if Gaveston had lived.'

'I think so, for he would not have let England slip into such a state that these accursed Despencers have, of that I am certain. True, Gaveston adored land, titles and riches, but he never pushed for power, that was all Edward's own doing, on that you have my word.'

'I think John de Warenne would agree with your sentiments.'

'Warenne, the Earl of Surrey!' she exclaimed.

'Aye! Under that somewhat forbidding facade there lives a brain as cool and as shrewd as any I've met and I think he understood Edward's nature and recognised Gaveston's assets, as well as his shortcomings.'

'But I thought Gaveston and Warenne fought a deadly duel at Wallingford when Edward awarded Gaveston the prize that was by right of conquest Warenne's, making the breach betwixt them irreconcilable.'

'Ah, but Warenne is one of those rare beings who is not completely blinded by his own passions and can see far more than he is often given credit for!'

'I never realised you and he were friends.'

'Not friends…exactly.' Mortimer lingered over his words. 'No, not friends, but as much akin to that as John de Warenne will ever allow, methinks.'

Slowly over the ensuing weeks Isabella and Mortimer grew to know each other's every mood and the powerful bond between them strengthened daily.

Not long after their conversation regarding John de Warenne, Edward sent urgent messages demanding Isabella's immediate return to England, but she ignored the commands, at first excusing herself by reminding Edward that the question of fealty for Gascony remained unresolved and she would stay in France until she had accomplished what she had set out to do on his behalf. A spate of couriers passed to and fro between the courts of England and France, but Isabella remained adamant; that is, until Charles, urged by the Pope to send Mortimer and Isabella from the French court for their unseemly behaviour, agreed to accept homage from the young Prince Edward instead of his sire.

Isabella was delighted, for when Edward agreed to this solution at the prompting of Hugh Despencer the younger, he little guessed that they had played right into the hands of Isabella and Mortimer, who were determined to stay together now at all costs.

'Don't you see, my love, when my son is here in France, we shall hold Edward in check? For I swear I shall never again return to England as long as that foxy-faced minion Despencer is still in office.' The crystal-blue eyes blazed with venom.

Mortimer watched her; he loved her every mood, she was proud and beautiful as well as passionate, ice and fire rolled into one tantalising female form, and she loved him, and only him. His premonition had not failed him. Isabella's voice broke in on his reverie.

'Mortimer, are you listening to me?'

'Sweetheart, I hang on your every word.'

'Bah!' she exclaimed, throwing a cushion at his head.

'You are irresistible when you are angry, *ma belle*,' he laughed.

'Our whole future demands your serious consideration, my Lord Mortimer.'

'See,' he said, frowning mockingly, 'as serious as a judge,' but she could see the mirth bubbling beneath his expression. 'Do not chide, my love, for I am only too well aware of the position you are in and I cannot bear the thought of you returning to a life of such unhappiness and shame, especially now I have seen you blossom into such a rare and wondrous woman. Besides, how would I survive without you? We have become as one, you and I, our fate is with each other, of that I am certain.'

She came and sat down beside him, her mood softened by his words. 'Only death will part me from your side, *mon amour*,' she said huskily as she stroked his face tenderly. 'If it were not for my son I would willingly forfeit my queenly role and be content to live in your wild Marches, but...' she frowned as she continued, 'I do not want my son to grow up in the shadow of a tainted crown. I have watched him carefully for any signs of his sire's weakness but, thank God, I have seen nothing which leads me to think that he is aught but a true king in the making and I will do nothing to jeopardise his inheritance.'

'Then, lady, why not crown your son and banish Edward, putting his cronies to the sword, for I have many scores to settle with those that turned their hand against us. I shall not rest until I see this debt paid in full.'

Isabella marvelled at how those golden eyes could grow pale-yellow and malevolent with anger. She leaned over and kissed his cheek. 'We make a formidable duo, do we not? Our enemies would quake in their beds if they did but know that Isabella and Mortimer were working to bring about their downfall.'

'From what my sources tell me the time is ripe for change. England is sickened by the Despencer greed and Edward's seeming indifference to what is happening throughout his kingdom. Aye, I say we should gather a well-trained force of seasoned mercenaries and raise your standard as soon as we land in England. I think we could overthrow Edward before he knew what we were about, so causing little bloodshed.'

'Mm, I think you have the right of the matter. Gain London before Edward can raise an army!' Mortimer nodded in agreement.

'Then I think, my dear, we can leave the court of France as soon as my son has performed the necessary knee-bending ceremonies, for my brother is making it perfectly plain that our presence here is too much of an embarrassment. So…I have given the matter my utmost consideration and think we should take our leave of France directly.'

'And where do you propose we should go to recruit our army?'

'To the Low Countries, to one William of Hainault, Count of Holland and Zeeland, whose brother John has recently come to the French court and knows of our delicate situation and has offered the hospitality of his brother's home for our convenience.'

'Then all is settled, things move apace but…'

Mortimer's arm encircled Isabella's slender waist. 'Let me show you something I purchased for you and, as it would appear from our discourse, is most appropriate.'

He took her hand, and like a child she followed obediently through the labyrinth of corridors and out to the stable block where Raoul paraded a pretty, dappled grey mare, with great flaring nostrils and huge, dark, gentle eyes.

'Oh!' Isabella exclaimed, unable to keep the wonderment out of her voice. 'She is so charming and sooo…pretty.' The mare nickered in greeting.

'Already she has fallen under your spell,' said Mortimer smiling, delighted that his gift had been such a success.

'I shall call her Athena.'

Raoul trotted the mare to and fro for closer inspection and said shyly, 'She's as gentle as a dove and as swift as an arrow.'

'Then tomorrow we shall all go riding and I shall find out for myself this lovely creature's paces.' She paused and turned to Mortimer. 'I applaud your good taste and obvious talent for choosing just the right gift at just the right moment.'

The two men grinned. Mortimer took Isabella's arm and thanked Raoul, who led the elegant little Barbary mare back to her stable.

'And what can I give my Welsh Marcher in return for his gift?'

Mortimer whispered in her ear and Isabella laughed. 'Why, how can I give what is already yours,' and the two smiled knowingly into each other's eyes.

CHAPTER XXXI

24 September 1326

Isabella held tightly onto Mortimer's hand; the coast of England was looming large before them. 'The great adventure begins,' she murmured and looked up at her companion. She could not read his thoughts and squeezed his hand for reassurance. He responded by drawing her into the harbour of his arms and raised her hand to his lips. She never lost the thrill his nearness caused within her. 'And where are your thoughts, my lord?'

'With my family. If we fail in our bid to win our way to London and overthrow Edward, I fear my children may suffer.'

Isabella nodded. 'Then we must be sure to take advantage of our surprise landing.'

'By the blessing of St Peter, we have, as yet, encountered no resistance, a good sign.' The golden eyes scanned the swift-approaching shoreline for any awaiting army. But all remained peaceful in the September sunshine. He relaxed a little. 'I think we should make for Walton-on-the-Naze tonight, then Bury St Edmunds. Send messengers with all haste throughout East Anglia and raise your standard so all those in sympathy with us can join the march on London without delay.'

Mortimer's confidence in the queen's cause proved accurate and the nobles and gentry of the country flocked to her standard, including Henry, Earl of Leicester, and Thomas of Norfolk, together with a number of bishops who all eagerly answered her call to arms. When Mortimer's spies returned from London with the news that none of the Londoners would stand with the king against the invaders, all boded well for their ambitions.

Only a handful of nobles fled with Edward and it was the name of one of their number that caused a frown to play across

Mortimer's handsome features: Warenne. What by all the wounds of Christ was Warenne doing with the king? But Mortimer had scant time to dwell on the matter, for now his prime objective was to gain the freedom of his family as soon as possible.

It was on the fifteenth day of October in the year 1326 that a mob forced the Constable of the Tower to surrender his keys, whereon John of Eltham, Isabella's youngest son, together with the Mortimer hostages, were all released to the hoots and cheers of the crowds.

Between smiles and tears both Mortimer and Isabella were united with their children and their happiness was there for all to see. Mortimer had already sent fast-riding soldiers to free his wife and daughters and also his mother, Margaret, whom Edward had banished to a nunnery for her part in trying to raise troops for her son's cause earlier that year.

But even in Edward's haste to flee from the forces of Isabella and Mortimer, he had still managed to offer a reward on Mortimer, dead or alive, but that reward was to remain unclaimed.

The ensuing weeks were a time of action, for Mortimer realised that the young prince must become head of state as soon as it could be arranged, but first Edward and his party must be captured. Once they had Edward in their grasp there would be little likelihood of any insurrection and the way would be clear for the young prince to be crowned and England brought under a more ordered regime than of late.

The first to be taken was Hugh Despencer the elder; on 27 October at Bristol without so much as a drawn sword the old man was captured, and there before Mortimer and the Earls of Norfolk, Kent and Leicester he was tried and convicted and put to death for his transgressions.

After the trial Mortimer and Isabella, together with their fast-growing army, made for Hereford. There they decided to remain, sending Henry of Leicester, with a Welsh clerk Rhys ap Howel as his guide, to track down Edward and the younger Despencer.

'If I were in their shoes I would make for Lundy, which is a Despencer stronghold, and then across to Ireland. Pray God Henry reaches them before they can escape, for I swear I shall not rest until that devil's spawn joins his sire in Hades.'

As luck would have it the weather, which had favoured Isabella, now again proved her ally and turned to storms which harried the shipping in the Channel, thwarting the plans of the royal fugitive and his companion who were now making for Glamorgan by all accounts, but on 16 November they were found at Neath Abbey with Robert Baldock, the Chancellor and Keeper of the Privy Seal.

Edward was placed in the custody of his cousin, Henry of Leicester, brother of the ill-fated Thomas of Lancaster, and on the following day the Earl of Arundel was seized by John Charlton and promptly executed without any formal trial.

Some days later Despencer was brought to Hereford for trial. Meantime, Adam Orleton, Bishop of Hereford, was sent to Edward to demand the Great Seal. Orleton was a more than adequate emissary and made Edward realise that he would only cause his son trouble if he did not relinquish the seal immediately, and within four days it was in the keeping of the Bishop of Norwich.

Mortimer was jubilant. 'See how easily our enemies fall into our hands!'

'And what of your Earl of Surrey?' Isabella remarked.

'Warenne is no enemy, he will see reason.'

'So will you have me pardon him?'

'He has not remained with the king and was not amongst those who drew sword against me and mine. No, my love, Warenne is not our enemy, merely misguided in his choice.'

She could not stand against her lover's arguments. He obviously valued Warenne and she would not gainsay his wishes. But on the subject of the hated Despencer they were in absolute agreement: he should die in a manner that was fitting for all the crimes he had committed.

Isabella never forgot the trial of her most hated enemy, Hugh Despencer. People flocked from far and wide to see the inevitable end of the notorious favourite. He stood, no longer proud, but a broken man whose only feature to remain alert was the fox-like eyes. At every opportunity the mob would jeer, but Mortimer wanted all to hear the crimes of which this man was accused.

Despencer at first tried to weedle his way out, but quickly realised that he was doomed, and the only thing he could do was to face his judges with as much dignity as he could muster under the circumstances. But even he shuddered visibly as the clerk read out the sentence.

'To be executed by the means of hanging, drawing, quartering and beheading, his bowels to be burned before his face, and may God have mercy on his soul.'

'And may the devil have you e'er nightfall,' hissed Mortimer under his breath.

As the tumbrel took the erstwhile favourite to his bloody end someone from the crowd ran forward and pinned a scrawled note to the rough wagon. On it ran the following rhyme:

The rope, because he is drawn with it;
The wood, because he is hanged thereon;
The sword, because he is beheaded therewith;
The fire, because his bowels will be burnt;
The horse, because he drew him;
The axe, because he is quartered thereof.

And so the once powerful and wealthy Lord Hugh Despencer the younger met his vicious and brutal end.

Amongst the crowd was Adela de Giffard, who did not turn those fine, grey eyes from the horrendous scene as she made the sign of the cross when she heard his screams. 'You have met the same end as my own lord who was a better man than you could have ever wished to be. Now let his spirit rest in your undoing and maybe the future will know a peace.' So saying she turned and left the jeering mob, to seek refuge on one of Warenne's many estates where he had given her shelter since her husband's execution.

After the trial Mortimer managed to slip away to Ludlow and Wigmore and to his delight found most of his scattered family gathered together after their enforced separation.

Joan his wife looked pale and thinner than he remembered her, and some of his daughters had grown out of all recognition. But all was forgotten when they fell into each other's arms to rejoice and savoured their new-found freedom.

Mortimer now had to face Joan's knowledge of his relationship with Isabella, for they had never tried to hide it from anyone. Joan's eyes were dark-rimmed and her neat chin thrust forward as she came to meet him.

'We are all glad to see you hail and well, my lord.' He heard the guarded note in her tones.

'As I am to see my family, safe and here where they belong, at Ludlow.'

He stepped forward to embrace her but she remained stiff and unforthcoming at his greeting, so he merely brushed her cheek with his lips.

'Come, Joan, I shall never let anything untoward harm you again and shall treat you with all the respect my wife deserves.'

She rounded on him, her eyes snapping sparks from her inner anger. 'How can that be, my lord, when all…know of your affair with the queen? Do you think these long years of confinement have broken my pride? I will not countenance this…this…'

He raised his hand. 'Do not say anything you may later regret, lady,' he countered, the golden eyes cloudy at this unexpected attack from his normally placid-tempered wife.

'Oh, my lord, what do you think me made of? To be paraded before all as the cuckolded wife so that the world can leer and laugh behind their hands. No, no!' She stamped her tiny foot.

'Joan, it is within your power to rent this family asunder and you would be within your right so to do.' He hesitated, then quietly continued. 'You hold a special place in my heart and will always have my loyalty. We grew up together, you and I, did we not? Learned the ways of a man and wife and parenthood. No one can take that take away. Believe me, Joan, I never played the unfaithful husband, not until we had been parted for many months, not until I met Isbella in France. Speak the truth now, you have not lost aught you really want back – the marriage bed?'

The couple faced each other, no longer the same people who had parted at Ludlow all those years before, but there was an unbreakable bond between them which went deeper than parenthood, deeper than marriage vows.

Joan stood for some moments considering his words.

'I have always been your dutiful wife.' Again she stopped. 'Mayhap I must now style myself "friend".'

'Our relationship is forged by loyalty and family, Joan.' Mortimer dropped to one knee. 'Our family…you…are as much a part of me as breathing. Do not turn away from me now, Joan, not when all is within my grasp.'

Suddenly Joan's expression changed, her moment of fire dispelled, and she came slowly to where he knelt.

'I have always been your obedient wife and shall continue to be so…but,' her voice broke, 'spare me any shame when I am in the queen's presence, I beg you.'

'My little Joan, trust me. Our time has come and the fortunes of the Mortimers are in the ascendant. You shall not be neglected by me, on that you have my oath.'

She was helpless against his argument and could only concede with as much grace as she could manage. The awkward moment was past between them and Mortimer was glad in his heart that he had won, if not her approval, then Joan's understanding of her situation.

'I must return to Hereford with all speed, there is much to be done, but know you have my undying loyalty. The only sorrow I have in all this is that my uncle did not live long enough to see Despencer's head paraded on London Bridge and know that I kept faith with him to avenge his downfall.'

Later it was agreed after the celebrations that the Mortimer sons should join their sire and take a hand in the realm's future.

'There is so much to be accomplished and I shall need those I can trust about me, for the carrion will gather, I've no doubt.'

On Mortimer's return to Hereford Isabella's joy knew no bounds for she could not bear to be parted from him longer than necessary.

'My life is nothing when you are away from my side and I cannot sleep without you.'

'*Cariad.*' He whirled her up into his arms and their love-making took on an even more ardent turn for power and passion are a potent aphrodisiac, and the festivities that Yuletide were the happiest Isabella had ever spent. Her enemies vanquished, her lover attentive, and the future laid out before them with such bright promise that she was confident and ready to meet any obstacles.

At constant urgings from the clergy Edward II finally agreed to his son's succession and in the cold, crisp month of January the young Prince Edward sat at the head of his first Parliament.

Mortimer had not forgotten his promise to the two burgesses of London who had risked much to aid his escape and had in October of the previous year made John de Gisors Constable of the Tower and Richard de Bettoyne the Lord Mayor of London. Adam Orleton, Bishop of Hereford, also featured, for he was both loyal and completely in sympathy with Isabella and his patron, Mortimer.

John de Warenne, Earl of Surrey, had also been persuaded to bend his proud knee to Isabella and her son and little realised that Olympia's memory, as well as her talisman, had once more stood between him and certain death. But Warenne did not like the change in Mortimer, who daily grew more arrogant and self-assured. The lands of his erstwhile enemy Despencer now came in the main into Mortimer hands and he lived in the style that his newly acquired wealth afforded.

'My father swaggers like a puffed-up cock,' echoed the dark-faced Roger one day to his brothers.

'Nay! More like the King of Folly, for he gains enemies like chaff after the harvest thrashing,' stated Geoffrey. Edmund remained silent and John nodded in agreement with his younger brother.

'But we must all follow where'er he leads us for we are bound by blood, loyalty and love, are we not?' None of the others replied, their silence obvious assent.

But if the head of the Mortimer house knew of his sons' feelings, he did nothing to alter a lifestyle he was fast finding to his taste and treated the other nobles with thinly veiled contempt. Only in Isabella's eyes did he remain perfect and the two lovers became more and more enthralled in each other. Their appetite for life together was insatiable.

Mortimer, though constantly pressed by Isabella to accept some office, persistently refused, that is, until she proposed an earldom, and Mortimer, conscious of his lowly rank, accepted with alacrity and from that time forward insisted on everyone using his title of earl. Even that had to be different and he chose to be known as the Earl of March, a title hitherto unknown.

However, all was not plain sailing, for Edward II, imprisoned though he was, could still prove an embarrassment, and Mortimer feared that, given time, he would be a rallying point for any who opposed the new order.

Isabella knew how much Mortimer advocated Edward's death, but something within her jibbed at the very idea. True, she had many grievances against Edward, but none to warrant the forfeiture of his life. He had been a good father to their children and now the shame of their conception lay in the past dimmed by the light of her new love. Besides, she loved Mortimer too much to see his hands stained with the blood of her husband, and she would not stand by and see her lover endanger his immortal soul with Edward's death and for once connived, in secret, to solve this delicate problem alone. Edward, after all, had merely been a weak pawn in the hands of manipulative men, and had he been born other than king would have lived out his life quite contentedly as a plebian.

It was Edward himself who forced Isabella's hand the second time he escaped, for she learned of Mortimer's intentions after eavesdropping on his plans for Edward's 'removal'. Swiftly, Isabella took action. Throughout her reign she had always held the respect of the clergy and maintained contacts in France. Now she moved to set her plans in motion for Edward's escape. Secretly Edward was taken from Berkeley Castle to Ireland, from where he eventually made his way to the Continent.

However, Isabella made a condition for his freedom. Edward must sign a pledge never to oppose his son by word, deed or action. The letter she had safely sealed within the vaults of a church, for Mortimer at times even overawed Isabella with his omnipotence and she was fearful, if he should ever discover the truth, what furies it might unleash.

Whatever faults Edward had, he was England's anointed king, a fact which Isabella never forgot.

But there were other issues to keep the two lovers busy; Scotland, the bleeding thorn in England's side, threatened to erupt anew and forced the two to take closer note of events across the border. There must be a truce, but it was a very nervous period between the two sides, which after all had been at war for nigh on thirty years.

It was over this single issue that Mortimer and Isabella suddenly came at odds with the young king. All the true Plantagenet steel was there in his youthful defiance and, much to the displeasure of his mother and Mortimer, he refused point-blank to treat with England's enemies and would not be gainsaid on the matter.

So England once more prepared for war with the Scots, but Mortimer made it known that this venture was against the best interests of the queen and that England needed a time of peace.

Robert the Bruce by now was undisputed king in Scotland, accepted by Lowlanders and Highlanders alike, something that had not really been achieved since the untimely death of Alexander.

Edward's adventure was to be a non-event, however. He sat before his armies at Berwick facing the Scottish forces, but neither side engaged and in a fury he rode from the scene, leaving the way clear for new negotiations to be opened and the longed-for peace obtained.

This, however, was not achieved without great cost to the English, for Robert the Bruce had campaigned too hard and long to let his adversaries off lightly. Though the treaty was dubbed 'the Shameful Peace', it gave both nations a long-awaited breathing space where life and trade could be rebuilt once more and both sides were able to fill their depleted coffers.

Mortimer, delighted with his success, rode at Isabella's side and his pomp and arrogance grew daily. He would answer to no one who had not addressed him with due deference and even his own sons grew uncomfortable at this new side to their sire's character.

The young Edward's resentment smouldered and slowly he gathered about him young men anxious to rise in the new reign, who were willing to help oust the now mighty and much feared Mortimer, for Isabella was completely under his influence and followed his wishes in all things. Safe in her own knowledge that her husband was safely abroad, to her inner relief she even had a large shrine built in his 'memory'.

Wherever they went in that year of 1328 Mortimer feted and heaped lavish entertainment on his beloved Isabella, reforming the Knights of the Round Table, and giving himself the title of Arthur, from whom he claimed descendancy.

At Bedford, on the occasion of the marriage of one of his daughters, there was feasting and merry-making on a scale rarely seen before in that county. However, it was at his precious Ludlow on a procession through the Welsh Marches that Mortimer excelled as host. Even Joan his wife joined in the festivities. During the day there were tilting, feats of arms, archery competitions, bear-baiting, cockfighting and wrestling, and at night fire-eaters and mummers would perform in the grounds of the castle, to the delight of all present.

When Isabella and Mortimer lay in each other's arms, she felt so full of love and tenderness for her handsome, virile lover that they seemed to touch paradise. 'My shining knight, so proud and strong in the lists, where all are brought low before your mighty blade, but whose touch can be so soft and gentle that it stirs my soul with so much sweetness, I swear I could melt with love.'

'*A annwyl, n cariad*, Isabella,' he whispered against her thick, shining hair as he caressed her curving breasts and hips. 'My true kingdom lies here in my arms.'

'Oh, beloved!' she whispered, but the urgency of the flesh was too great now for either to speak more and they answered each other's desires with only the dancing, singing waters of the Teme to serenade their love.

But even as Mortimer and Isabella revelled in their life together, the new peace had not been happily accepted by many of the English nobility. The rift was too deep. After six months, Henry of Leicester, brother of the ill-fated Thomas of Lancaster, refused to attend the Parliament at Salisbury in October of that year where the title of March was formally conferred on Mortimer. Even some of his supporters withdrew from the proceedings.

The storm clouds gathered once more over England as Henry mustered troops at Winchester, but Mortimer swiftly invaded the earldom of Leicester and occupied the town, forcing a grudging reconciliation with Henry in the January of 1329. Edmund of Kent's desertion was largely to blame for Henry's failure when he had sided with Mortimer, but his treachery was not really countenanced by the new Earl of March who, by means of a clever plot, managed to bring about Edmund's own downfall.

So in the March of 1330, Edmund was arrested and with many of his own arguments directed against himself at his trial was duly sentenced and executed outside the walls of Winchester city.

This very act hardened Henry of Leicester's resolve to once more take action against Mortimer, this time not in the field, but through more devious methods. Henry gained the ear of the young king who was by this time ready to break free of his mother and her lover and rule in his own right.

The small band of royal conspirators sent word to Pope John telling him of Edward's intentions to free himself of Mortimer and Isabella's influence and found the Holy Pontiff sympathetic to their cause.

Mortimer sensed the change in the young king's attitude and, when they reached Nottingham for the great council meeting in October of that year, immediately advised Isabella to accompany him to the safety of the castle.

Unbeknown to either Mortimer or Isabella there was a secret access by means of underground tunnels into the heart of the castle itself. Led by a constable of the castle, William Montagu, the king's chief ally, gained entrance to Mortimer's chamber.

Mortimer heard the commotion at the door, a cry rang out and he saw one of his squires fall dead from his wounds. With the agility of a cat Mortimer seized the dead man's sword and with a flick of his wrist slew the leading intruder. A fierce fight ensued but the odds were overwhelming and Mortimer was finally disarmed.

Isabella rushed into the chamber, her crystal eyes as wild as March winds.

'What in heaven's name is afoot?' She saw all at a glance; Mortimer, arms pinned by his sides, and her son standing triumphant in the doorway. Isabella ran towards Mortimer and threw herself in front of him, turning to face her son.

'Have pity on my gentle Mortimer.' She wept, but all her pleadings fell on deaf ears. Edward had achieved his aim and was unmoved by his mother's cries.

That very night Mortimer was escorted back to London and as he entered the Tower murmured under his breath, 'So you welcome me back like a jealous lover! This time only death will loose your hold, I fear!'

Two of Mortimer's sons were also taken at Nottingham, Edmund and Geoffrey.

'Our meteor has burned itself out!' Edmund said sadly, his pale, handsome face already with the look of death upon it.

'Our sire is indeed the "King of Folly"; my title suited better than that of March,' Geoffrey added wryly. He patted his elder brother's arm. 'Mortimers have fallen only to rise again and by God's good grace we shall not suffer for merely bearing the name of Mortimer, think you? This young king is not without honour.' But Edmund was too sad to answer, he was not a born optimist, and maybe he already felt the cold fingers of the grave clutch at his heart.

Warenne stood in the shadow of an archway. His dark-blue eyes missed nothing of the scene which lay before him. The gallows stood stark and still in the murky mists of that grey November morning. Only a few gathered to watch the end of the notorious Mortimer, the queen's paramour.

Overhead the rooks and ravens screamed and squawked and the chill of the damp air caused Warenne to draw his cloak closer around his broad shoulders. Glinting, even in the dismal light, was the brilliant ruby-and-diamond talisman which always hung at his neck. His fingers touched the hard gems and for an instant he felt Olympia's presence. He knew she was waiting there in the wreathing, swirling mist to guide her childhood companion into eternity. 'Olympia!' Warenne breathed her name like a prayer. 'Would to God it were I for whom you wait this morning.'

A distant drum roll announced Mortimer's arrival and the little congregation grew silent in anticipation. Mortimer came, walking proudly between his two guards, his dark head held high. He was completely naked. Warenne could see the clear golden eyes; there was no trace of fear in their depths.

Mortimer walked up to the scaffold and mounted lightly and gracefully. There stood an old, gaunt man who was plainly trying to hide his tears.

'Meyrick, do not grieve for I have had my share of heaven here on earth and can ask for nothing more than to die bravely.' Mortimer took the trembling hands of his former servant. 'Take care of my family and go back to Ludlow. I shall be there before you.' Without further ado Mortimer went and knelt before a brown-habited monk. 'And pray for my soul and for my Isabella, Brother Matthew, for this is one adventure I shall not be returning from!' He made the sign of the cross and kissed the crucifix held out by the monk, then without hesitation went to his death with a single word on his lips: 'Isabella.'

Warenne heard the snap of bone as Mortimer's neck broke, then watched the macabre dance for some moments. A tiny crack in the misty sky allowed the sun to break through for an instant, then all was gloom once more.

'So you have him now, Olympia, but remember, my love, to come for me when my time comes.' And with that Warenne turned and walked back to where Will stood holding his horse.

EPILOGUE

After Mortimer's execution Isabella retreated from public life for many months.

When she reappeared she was treated with great respect and consideration by her son Edward III and his wife Queen Philippa of Hainault. The question that remains is: would that have been the case if they had considered her guilty in any way of Edward II's death? They even named a daughter after her, another fact which emphasises their regard. Isabella formed a close relationship with her grandson, the Black Prince. Again, this must point to the fact that Edward held no doubts as to his mother's innocence. Sadly, the young prince did not live to inherit the throne.

Castle Rising became Isabella's favoured home where she received many visitors over the years, including her son and grandson, underlining the fact this castle was never a prison.

How Isabella truly felt about her son after he had executed Mortimer, we can only guess at! On her death, Isabella was buried in her wedding dress, clasping a silver casket containing the heart of Edward II. This fact I have always found strange given the years of abuse and humiliation she suffered throughout her marriage. However, most wealthy women made a will on learning they were pregnant, and this may hold the answer. Was the will that her son acted on the one Isabella made when she was carrying him? Logically this could explain the wedding dress and casket. At that time she was still a girl and lived in hope of bringing about her husband's affections.

Immediately after Mortimer's death his family were once again plunged into a state of disgrace and forfeited many lands, castles and much wealth to the Crown. However, Edward III bore no lasting grudge against the Mortimer family. Although Edmund,

Roger's heir, died only months after his father, his son (also Roger) eventually regained the title and became the second Earl of March.

The other children of Joan and Roger, with the exception of Isabel (who is thought to have died before Roger's return to England), had prestigious marriages. Three daughters became countesses: Katherine, Countess of Warwick, Agnes, Countess of Pembroke, and Beatrice, Countess of Norfolk.

Joan de Geneville outlived many of her children and died in 1356. Margaret Fiennes, Roger's mother, died in 1334.

John de Warenne never did have his divorce from Jeanne (Joan) de Bar recognised in this country. He and Maud de Nereford parted and he later took the high-born Isobel Holland as his mistress. Warenne was the last Earl of Surrey.

Robert the Bruce must be hailed as one of history's finest warrior kings. He possessed all the courage and military acumen that Edward II sadly lacked, which proves money and might of arms does not always win through. His band of loyal and seasoned commanders never lost faith in his abilities or his ambitions.

Edward III restored the 'Tainted Crown' and went on to be one of England's most successful and well-loved kings.

AUTHOR'S NOTE

Throughout history it has always been accepted that Edward II was brutally put to death in Berkeley Castle. However, I came across a number of 'clues' which may refute this scenario.

After Roger Mortimer's execution, Queen Isabella was sent to Castle Rising near the bleak coast of Norfolk and there she remained for a number of years, ostensibly as punishment.

Meantime, Edward III, during the first few years of his reign, sent emissaries throughout the length and breadth of Europe, their mission secret. These emissaries continued their search until one returned after interviewing a hermit in a remote mountain district in Italy. The hermit was reputed to be tall, fair of hair with startling blue eyes and not of Italian extraction. The details of this interview are forever a mystery. However, no further searches were ever sanctioned again on this mission and shortly afterwards Isabella returned to court and was treated most cordially by her son, his queen, and their children. She refused to stay permanently at court, being quite happy to appear on special occasions. She was visited regularly by friends and family throughout the rest of her life. The fact that her son allowed such visits is significant in itself!

Centuries later, in a remote monastery in Ireland, records were found relating to events just prior to the period of Edward II's death. It detailed a visit by a tall stranger from England, who stayed at the monastery for a few days until passage to France could be arranged. The stranger boarded the ship dressed as a monk of their order. The abbot was charged with secrecy in the matter—a secret he kept—as did the order for over five hundred years.

Could it be that Isabella had secretly rescued her estranged husband, Edward II? Religion, in medieval Europe, was strict in its teachings and the penalty for murder, eternal damnation. Maybe, Isabella had wished to avert such a sentence for both herself and the man she loved, Mortimer. Remember, Isabella was the daughter of Philip the Fair of France and sister to French kings; she commanded loyalty both here and on the Continent. It would not have been difficult to arrange.

I am not claiming this to be a historical fact – simply another possibility. But love can be a powerful motive for many things and Isabella undoubtedly loved Mortimer. Much wronged by Edward II, she had seen the brutal deaths of both Gaveston and Despencer, her 'rivals'. I like to believe she would not have wished to look eternity in the face knowing that murder would forever damn her and Mortimer to hell!

The epithet 'She-Wolf of France' was never used in her lifetime and chroniclers always paint the word picture in the light that pleased the person who was their patron – often decades after the actual events. I therefore, dear reader, leave you to make your own minds up about the mysterious facts regarding the death of Edward II. Were Mortimer and Isabella guilty or not?

Undisputed facts are that Mortimer's children married into the most powerful families in the land and his son Edmund regained the favour of Edward III. Joan de Geneville outlived many of her children and is buried at Much Marcle. John de Warenne was the last Earl of Surrey and had no legitimate heirs.

Edward III was one of the most powerful and respected kings to reign in England, whilst his gentle queen Phillipa of Hainault was beloved by all her subjects.

Fran Norton

Lightning Source UK Ltd.
Milton Keynes UK
13 October 2010

161227UK00002B/1/P